CW01184842

Bluebell Souls

Iain Mac Lachlainn

1 3 5 7 9 10 8 6 4 2

Copyright © 2011 Iain Mac Lachlainn
This edition 2020
Copyright © 2020 Iain Mac Lachlainn

Cover photography
Copyright © 2019 Cheryl McLachlan

ISBN 9798649566742

All rights reserved. This book is copyright material and must not be copied, reproduced, transferred, distributed, leased, licensed or publicly performed or used in any way except as specifically permitted in writing by the author, as allowed under the terms and conditions it was purchased or as strictly permitted by applicable copyright law. Any unauthorised distribution or use of this text may be a direct infringement of the author's rights, and those responsible may be liable in law accordingly.

This is a work of fiction. Names, characters, places and incidents either are the product of the author's imagination or are used fictitiously.

Please leave feedback
visit @iainmac.author on facebook
you can also rate/review this book on amazon

For Ciaran

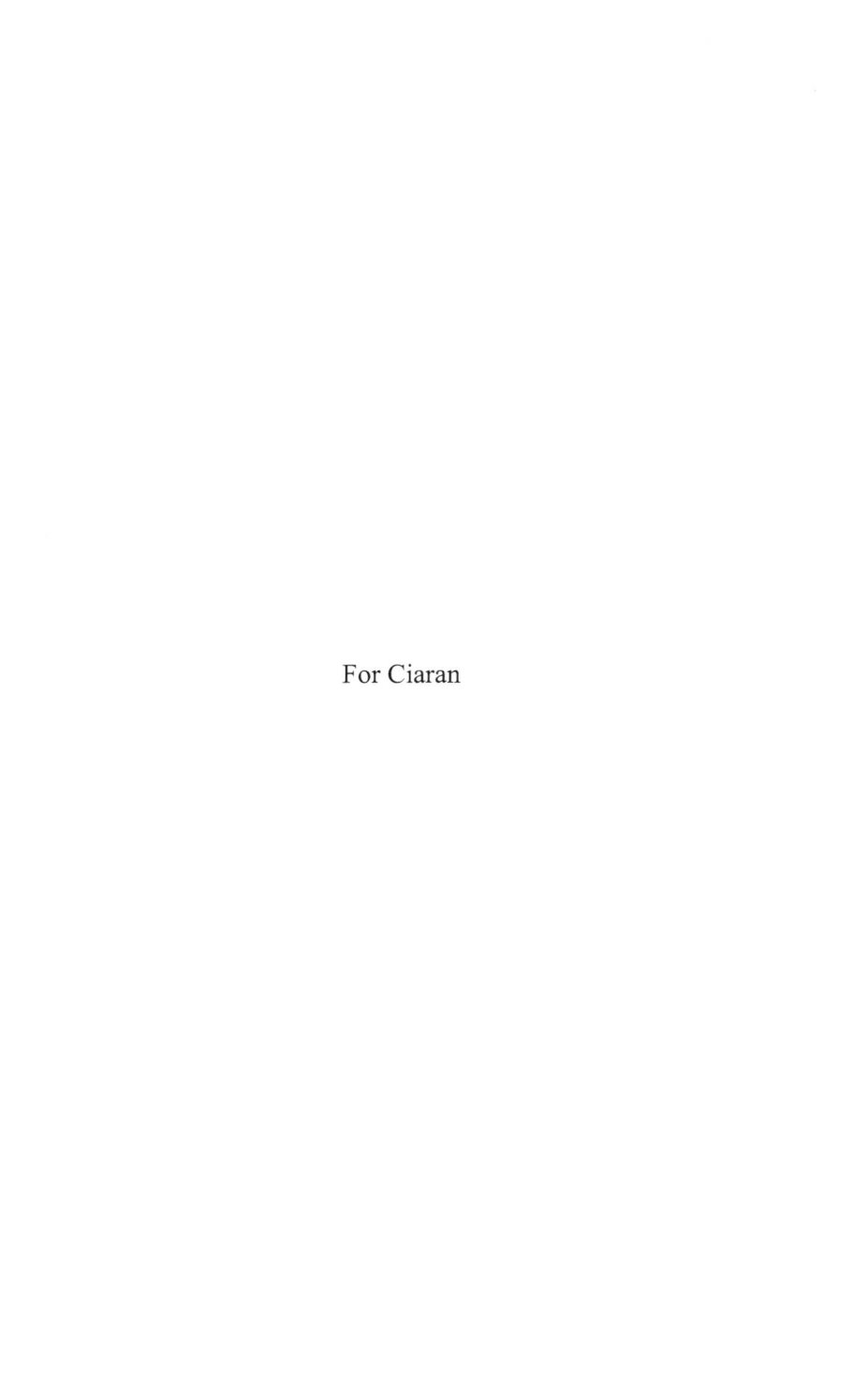

"The shadow over Culloden will rise and the sun will shine brighter."
Coinneach Odhar, The Brahan Seer

One

When the time came, they went to him.

They found him in a land far away in a time in which they could never have lived. They swept through the sky, approaching his country from the sea. A mile from the shoreline, great serpents writhed on the waves below and they flew over the serpents, shocked at the sight. They descended and they saw scores of great windmills that safeguarded his town, warding off intruders with their massive rotating blades. They slipped past these guardians of his hometown and found themselves beneath huge silver discs that were suspended high above the clouds. Afraid, they descended beneath the discs and down to the rooftops and amongst the homes and workplaces of the town's residents. They found his street and from the ink black darting eyes of a dozen ravens they looked upon their surroundings and saw the place in which he lived.

The clouds above them churned in masses of grey, brushed with sweeping strokes of red and gold as the late sun tried to penetrate the shield of cloud. A temperate wind ruffled the feathers of the birds and scattered the debris of the street through which they were sifting for nourishment.

The street was devoid of any character and was flanked by forlorn pavements and the bland facades of uniform four story buildings. Security doors with keypads were set at regular intervals along the street and mirrored windows reflected the twisted and contorted sky.

The street was almost deserted but now and then someone scurried along, keeping to the shadows of the high buildings. The faces of these fugitives were hidden behind facemasks and under hats pulled low over their eyes. They looked out from behind dark glasses and visors and despite the warmth of the evening they were dressed in long sleeved shirts and coats. With gloved hands they pulled their collars up around their masked faces. The shadows in which they sought refuge spread wider and darker as dusk approached.

Through the eyes of the ravens they saw a two-wheeled vehicle approach at speed. The birds dispersed in a flutter as it whistled by and then they resettled as it disappeared along the street.

One of the ravens separated and flew up higher than the others and alighted on a third story window ledge. The bird scraped around and found nothing of interest but remained there anyway. It became still and cocked its head so that one shining black eye could look into the window. The raven could see its own sable silhouette looking back, but they *could see through the reflective glass.*

They looked from the raven's eye and saw his white room, furnished with a large bed. In it they could make out two bodies. He was on the side closest to the window. He lay on his back and appeared to be sleeping peacefully, but as they continued to watch him he began to stir. They could not see into his dreams but they knew that something had disturbed him. They wondered if it was their presence and their immediate instinct was to leave him be. But they needed him, so they remained and continued to watch. They knew that he would not detect their presence unless they wanted him to.

The raven, unchecked by its guests returned to pecking and scratching around on the windowsill. As its head turned to and fro they caught sweeping images of him through the window.

They watched as his head began to turn wearily from side to side. They heard him mutter. His head movements became frantic and beads of sweat began to seep through the creased lines of his forehead, dampening his hair. He looked as if he was struggling to breathe, hitching in air in short rasping gasps. His head whipped from side to side and his lips were forming words that he could not force past his vocal chords.

Then his eyes snapped open and he regained control of his breathing. Slowly he sat up and he glanced at his partner, then eased his legs out from under the covers and sat on the edge of his bed. He lowered his face into his hands.

Their host continued to scrape and scratch, oblivious, and when it tapped the window with its beak, it attracted the attention of the man in the room. He lifted his head at the sound and got to his feet. As he stepped toward the window, they took control of the bird so that they could study him in greater detail. The raven stood like an ebony sentinel.

He looked straight back at the bird.
They were sure that he was the one.
Then they let the bird fly.
But they had not left him - they needed him.

Hampden, New Zealand, April 5th 2146

Sinclair Giacomo drifted up from sleep and felt sure that there was someone in the room. He tried to open his eyes but they remained firmly closed. He felt awake but his mind was disorientated.

The feeling that there was a presence in the room began to overwhelm him. Somehow, he could feel his mind closing down again, drifting back into unconsciousness. He fought to stay awake, to become awake. There was someone here, watching. He realised then that he was not breathing and he tried to inhale. But there was nothing. He had to wake up.

He could feel more eyes now, not just one pair. Scores of eyes watching intently. He tried to make his limbs work, to press his elbows into the mattress and prop himself up into a sitting position. An easy movement, one performed nearly every day. But he continued to lie, still as a corpse. Not breathing.

The eyes were boring into him, he could feel them. They studied and explored him.

His lungs began to hurt, to burn from lack of oxygen. His head began to spin and as he felt the strength seeping from him he tried frantically to push himself up off the bed. He tried desperately to suck air into his aching lungs. Blackness swirled around his head and the light behind his eyelids began to diminish into total darkness. And pale white ghosts began to emerge from the darkness.

Sinclair's eyes snapped open and he gulped in a lungful of air. He breathed in deeply and quickly until satisfied that he would not pass out. As his breathing slowed to a more regular rhythm and the spinning of the room abated, he became aware of the steadier breathing of the sleeping figure next to him.

He sat up slowly, not wanting to wake her; surprised that he had not already done so. He looked at her for a moment. She lay on her front, her long fair hair cascading over her face and pillow onto the mattress. Her pale, slender legs were uncovered and normally he would not have been able to restrain himself from reaching out and stroking her smooth warm skin. It seemed his usual desire had been reduced by the dream.

He realised now that it had been a dream. There was no one else in the room. Yet he had felt so awake . . . and still he could not shake the feeling of being watched. Gently, he swung his legs out from under the covers and sat on the edge of the bed. He put his head in his hands and waited for the content of the dream to drift from him as dreams should. His body was damp with perspiration.

A light tapping came from the window and he lifted his head. Through the polarised glass he could see a raven strutting about on the ledge. He rose to his feet and padded over to the window. To see a raven on his windowsill was odd. Pigeons were more usual. His heart jumped when it stopped what it was doing and watched his approach from the other side of the reflective glass. His green eyes remained locked with one jet-black eye of the raven for a moment. Then it opened its wings and took to the air.

He remained at the window with one hand on the glass and his eyes on street below. It was not quite dark yet and the street was still quiet. Although it looked like there had been good cloud cover during the day not many had been tempted out early. He could only see two or three people outside at the moment. Bakers or office cleaners probably. They had covered up well in spite of the clouds.

The air conditioning in his room was cool, as he liked it to be by day, but it had chilled his sweat-covered body. He shivered and remembered the eyes.

He wondered how early it was and thought about going back to bed before glancing at the time on the wall.

21:23.

Not worth it. It would be fully dark soon and he would have to get up and go to school. He turned and headed for the bathroom.

'Lights,' he said keeping his voice low. He squinted as the light bounced off the white room and the mirror on the far wall.

'Dim,' he said. The lights dimmed.

He stepped into the shower and a green light came on signifying that it had acknowledged his presence.

"Five."

Water fell from the rose above him, cascading over his body, but he still felt chilled.

"Six," he said.

Immediately he felt the water temperature rise. He stood with his face up to the warm water relishing the sensation before squeezing some gel into his hand and lathering it into his hair and body. He let the shower rinse the suds from him before instructing it to stop. Warm air blasted him from above and to the sides and he turned himself around until he was dry. He stepped out and stood in front of the sink, looking into the mirror. He rubbed his hand across his jaw line and thought about shaving and then decided against it, reasoning that he would get away with it for another night. He picked up his toothbrush and pumped tooth-gel onto it.

As he scrubbed his teeth he thought about the day ahead.

Teaching English to nonchalant teenagers was a pretty thankless task and he had given up trying to pass on his love of language and literature years ago. There were always some who were partially interested or now and then a pupil who seemed to show at least some passion for the subject, but he felt that he was failing with every student that passed through his class without taking anything in. He realised, of course that different people held different interests and that some subjects interested some kids more than others but it still hurt him as he came to terms with the fact that for the majority, English Language was a burden. Even students who aspired to embark on legal or scientific careers viewed it as a necessary evil. Some teachers even thought that there was no point in the subject at all beyond the basics, especially since Phonetic American had become the business and entertainment language of the world.

When he was training to become a teacher he had hoped that he would be able to captivate his pupils and convey his love of a dying language to them like some sort of messiah.

He had not succeeded.

If it wasn't for the security and the bills he had to pay he would seriously consider throwing in the towel. In fact, he *did* considered packing it in every time he was under the influence of alcohol.

He'd had some poems published when he was a student and he had the ambition to one day write a collection. This was something he thought about more and more lately. He had plenty of ideas but he never felt that he was in the right frame of mind to begin writing again. He could make the time but he didn't want to do it now and again as a hobby. If he was going to do it he wanted to devote himself to it. He needed to be at peace with himself.

As he looked at himself in the mirror he caught a movement from behind him. He hadn't heard Abbie getting up.

He froze as he realised that it wasn't her. His mouth popped open as he saw the head and shoulders of a young man standing behind him. The mixture of water, tooth gel and saliva ran down his chin and splattered into the sink.

The thought flew through his head that this was a crazed kid from the school and that his life was in danger. Instinctively, ignoring the fact that he was naked and of how ridiculous he must have looked with tooth gel residue dribbling from his mouth, he spun around to face the intruder and brandished his toothbrush like a knife.

He locked in that position as he tried to make sense of what he saw in front of him.

The intruder looked like a teenage boy of about fifteen or sixteen but something in his eyes, something that can only come from experience and maturity, made Sinclair think of him as a man. He could also make out objects that were behind him. He was translucent; like a projection. But there was something emanating from him that held Sinclair - that made it impossible for him to deny his presence. Something that made him *seem* there.

The boy returned Sinclair's gaze, his expression one of deep sorrow. He was soaked from head to foot as if he had just walked in out of heavy rain. His long hair was plastered to his head and laid against his shoulders in wet clumps and across his forehead in strands. The water ran into his eyes and down his nose from where it dripped off onto the floor. His skin and nipples were clearly visible through his drenched shirt. Draped over one shoulder and secured to his waist by a broad leather belt he wore heavy and sodden tartan plaid. Sinclair could see water falling steadily from it and heard it drip onto the visitor's bare feet and the bathroom carpet.

As they continued to stare at each other Sinclair noticed that the young man's face was dirty, scratched and scarred. Dirt ran down his arms, turned into muddy streaks by the water. He was sure that he could also see blood smeared into his skin, was sure that he could smell blood.

He tried to speak but the visitor spoke first.
'Thig agus cuidich sinn.'

Sinclair's brow creased, unsure if he had heard anything at all. It had sounded to him as if the stranger had sang the short phrase, or chanted some ancient spell in an antediluvian tongue.

'Thig agus cuidich sinn,' he repeated.

Sinclair saw condensation escape from the visitor's mouth as he spoke and even as he watched the water vapour become distinct he was only partly aware that the young man was receding and becoming less perceptible until, within a matter of seconds, he was gone. Sinclair wasn't sure if he had breathed throughout the whole bizarre spectacle but now he slowly exhaled. Rooted to the spot he stared at the patch of dampness on his carpet where the boy had stood.

He sank to his knees and reached out to touch the wet patch to ensure that it was real and not just a trick of the light, but quickly withdrew his hand in surprise. The dark piece of carpet was freezing, cold enough to make him put his fingers into his armpit to warm them. He withdrew his hand after a moment and looked at the stinging tips of his fingers. He saw the tiny sparkle of ice crystals upon them. When the cold receded from his fingers he looked at the carpet again and saw that the dark area had also gone. He began to shiver.

He got up and went into the bedroom. He found that the room had brightened from the light outside while he had been in the bathroom: the Daylights had come on. Although she had curled her legs up under the quilt into the foetal position, Abbie was still asleep. He thought about waking her and telling her what had happened. And then decided against it. What the hell would he tell her anyway?

He went to his side of the bed and pulled out his drawer and quickly dressed in T-shirt and jeans, and then as an afterthought, put on a warm shirt. As he sat on the bed pulling on his socks he glanced at the time.

21:41.

Not even twenty minutes had gone by since he'd last looked at it.

Thig agus cuidich sinn.

The words that the visitor had spoken ran through his head in that soft lilting voice. What did it mean? He knew that he hadn't dreamt it. He knew that he had witnessed something special but he had no idea what.

He surprised himself with how well he was coping with this. He had a feeling that right now the best thing that he could do would be to get an appointment with his doctor.

Abbie rolled over beside him and murmured.

'What time is it?'

'Nearly ten.'

She propped herself up on one elbow and looked at him with bewildered, sleepy eyes. 'You're dressed?'

'Just felt like getting up early, couldn't sleep,' he said giving her a smile. 'Want coffee?' He got up to go to the kitchen without waiting for an answer.

'Sinclair.'

'Yeah?'

'Are you . . . okay?' He never got up before her and he never made coffee in the morning, at least not in the three months that she had lived with him.

'I'm fine,' he said and left the room. He went to the kitchen and made coffee and stood with the cup in both hands and looked at a framed piece of paper on the wall. It was an old tattered recipe that had been handed down from his great grandfather, that his grandfather before him had brought from Italy. Although the paper was crinkled and worn and stained in places, Sinclair found it beautiful. He loved the handwriting and the shape of the Italian words. The ingredients and the listed method looked like poetry. He traced the loops and swirls of the old handwriting and sipped his hot coffee. Then he put his coffee down and left for work.

*

He ate nothing for lunch and hated more than ever the way that every mug of coffee from the vendor in the staff room always tasted exactly the same. There was nothing random about life anymore. Consumers demanded consistent quality and that was precisely what they got. Sinclair loved a good mug of coffee, but when there was absolutely no chance at all of getting bad, he felt that that somehow took the shine from the good.

He hated himself for being so cynical. He knew very well that he hadn't always been that way.

He thought about the incident in his bathroom that evening and now that some time and the normality of the early night had passed, he wondered about its solidity. After it had happened he had been in no doubt at all that what he had seen had been real. He didn't make the slightest attempt to question his mind or senses; he had been that sure. Now though, as he slouched in his staff room chair listening to his own cynicism of the world around him, he couldn't believe that he was being so self-righteous as to dismiss any doubts about himself.

Then he remembered hearing the water drip from the visitor's sodden clothing. Then he remembered his lilting voice, and the condensation that had escaped his mouth as he spoke. Then he remembered the ice crystals on his own fingertips.

Something *real* had happened, he thought.

The signal sounded for the end of lunch hour and he drained the last of his perfect coffee. It tasted good, and in spite of himself he wanted more.

*

After school he tried to plan for the next night's lessons, but he could not concentrate. He sat at his desk and closed his eyes. All he could see in front of him was the boy. He hadn't been able to get him out of his mind. He had decided to accept that what he had seen was real. It was either that or to book himself in for a full mental check-up. He didn't want to do that so he decided to look for a logical explanation for the appearance of the stranger in his bathroom.

Unsurprisingly he hadn't been able to think of any realistic reasons for a bedraggled young man to appear in his bathroom, say something in a foreign language, drip water all over his carpet and then disappear again. The most convincing explanation that he could think of was that he was some sort of guardian angel who had turned up to give him some important advice on where to go with his life now that he had decided that his original path no longer held any appeal for him. Only, his guardian angel had forgotten that he didn't speak his language.

'Thig agus cuidich sinn.'

The words didn't come from inside his head. He could hear water dripping onto the tiled floor.

'Thig agus cuidich sinn, Sinclair.'

The mention of his name made him open his eyes, even though he would rather have kept them shut. The visitor stood before him, looking exactly as he had done earlier. Soaked and shivering. Sinclair thought that he could hear the faint sound of his teeth chattering. He could see more clearly the blood that was smeared into the skin of his grief stricken face.

That tortured look upon his face, full of pleading, made Sinclair feel that he was the one in control here. He sensed that the visitor wanted something from him. He tried to talk but found that he couldn't. The things that he could say, the questions that he could ask span in his head for what seemed like a long time, but he couldn't select the opening line. They all seemed appropriate; nothing seemed appropriate.

While he sat there with his mouth open, the apparition began to fade again as he had that morning.

'Thig agus cuidich sinn.'

'Wait!' Sinclair shouted. He stood up knocking his chair to the floor, but the visitor faded to nothing. Sinclair craned over his desk and could see the brown and red tinted pool of mud and blood where he had stood. As he watched, the liquid evaporated.

Then something else caught his eye. It lay on a desk in the front row of the classroom. He walked to the desk and looked down at it.

He thought that it should be sodden, but it appeared to be dry. He reached out and poked it gingerly, remembering the freezing carpet in his bathroom. He felt only the soft cloth of the blue bonnet.

*

He was hungry and he wasn't ready but still he found himself hurrying to the Airbus station. He wondered if he was going to make the last bus to Dunedin. He knew that he should really wait for the first bus the next evening and get himself prepared. He had nothing with him, only the apparition's bonnet in a brown paper bag.

After he had found the bonnet he had gone to find John Sparling, the head of history at the school. He had asked him what he knew about Scottish history and John had replied honestly that he didn't know much at all. He only really knew about the modern history. The independence troubles, the occupation by the British, stuff from the first half of the previous century. He told him though, of Jason Lombard up at the University of Otago. He had known Jason for a long time and he was likely to know more about Scottish history than anyone else in New Zealand. Sinclair had thanked John and was glad that he hadn't asked him why he was suddenly so interested in Scottish history.

He continued down the street. His shadow cast by the Daylites, was lost amongst the crowd. He was almost running when he entered the foyer of the station and he came to a halt and looked up at the departures screen. He had time.

He quickly tapped a message for Abbie telling her that he had to go to the university urgently and he would explain why later. Even as he typed he wondered how the hell he could explain this to her when he couldn't even explain it to himself. After finishing the message he tapped a similar message for the Head of Language at the school. He realised that would take a bit more explaining but he would worry about it later. Then he turned his phone off and he made his way over to the bank of vendors and pressed his thumb onto the recognition pad of the machines and hastily purchased his ticket and something to eat and drink. He found his platform and was glad to find that there were plenty of seats on this late bus.

The air powered vehicle swept silently out of the station and entered the night and left the Daylites of Hampden behind them.

In the fields on the outskirts of the town Sinclair could make out the giant windmills that harnessed the wind and powered the town. The power of the wind, the waves and even the sun which now forced them to live at night, outwith its raw warmth, were providing man with the energy that he needed to survive.

Slowly, with man's help, the earth was healing the wounds that man himself had inflicted upon her.

Sinclair listened to the bus as it whooshed along the road, driven by an engine that was invented a long time ago, but was kept secret from the world due to politicians' fears for the economy. Until the choice had become simple: world economy or world survival.

In the secure interior of the bus, Sinclair removed his mask and ate his food.

Two

From everywhere they saw the cold, dark dawn.
From everywhere they saw dim light begin to filter into the sky over the mountains in the east. From everywhere they saw the thick, swirling mist over the dark rolling sea. From everywhere they saw the froth of the waves as they tumbled onto the shingle.

From the air, from the sea and from the land, they saw.

From the air they saw a funereal silhouette in the sea below them, moving steadily towards land. From the bitter tenebrous water they saw the rise and fall of the dark form as it carved its way inland through the waves. From the shore they saw the shape approaching.

From the eyes of the gull, of the seal and of the stag, they saw.

The boat cut its way through the sea towards shore and the seal dived through the icy water in its direction. Once it was below the boat they could see the oars cutting into the surface above them. They pushed against the sea creating bubbles which hung in the water after the blades were lifted back into the air. They saw that the keel of the boat was heavily scarred from where it had been dragged ashore many times before, but they also saw that the timber was solid. From the eyes of the seal they saw this in great detail.

As the boat grew closer to shore the herring gull swooped towards it and hovered on the draughts above it. Aboard the boat they saw eight men. Six rowed, and the seventh was the helmsman who sat at the rear with his hand on the tiller. The eighth man stood alone at the bow and looked towards land. In his hands he held a telescope and as they watched he raised it to his right eye. The gold bands which housed the lenses at either end glowed in the gloomy mist and they saw this in such detail through the eyes of the gull that they knew that if the sun's rays were to touch those bands they would ignite like dancing flames in the blackest night.

As the boat came near to land the lone figure at the bow turned and sat. The oarsmen rowed a little further before pulling their oars into the boat. Then they alighted and plunged thigh deep into the cold sea and began to haul the boat onto the shore. Their boots crunched on the shale as they struggled to pull the bulk of the vessel onto land. Once the boat was safely ashore they began to unload chests and carry them up onto the coarse grass a few meters above the shingle, stumbling occasionally on the unsteady surface.

While they did this the helmsman helped the man with the telescope out of the boat and onto the shore.

Through the eyes of the stag they could see that this man should not have needed help as he appeared much younger and more able than his assistant. The young man began to stride up the stony shoreline towards more stable land and his aide struggled along behind him with more items of baggage.

The stag held its ground and raised its nose to the air. As it took in the scent they too could sense the sharp freshness of the Atlantic, tainted by the sour sweat of the men working below. They could feel the pounding of the stag's heart quicken as it sensed that it should no longer be there. But it remained, so that they could see.

The young man reached the spot where the oarsmen had set the chests. He put his foot on one of the chests and began to survey the coastline on which they had landed.

As the light from the east strengthened they saw this man in great detail through the eyes of the stag.

He was dressed in fine clothes and carried about him a look of elegance that contrasted greatly with this dismally overcast morning and the men working around him. The young man looked like a bird of paradise amongst pecking crows. He cast his eye up the shore towards the glen and observed the stag as it stood watching him. He locked eyes with it for an instant before it broke away and went bounding up the slope toward the security of the high ground.

The young man spoke quietly to the retreating stag, but although his companions did not hear him, from the ears of a nearby hare, they *heard.*

'I am come home,' *said the prince.*

Strath Lachlainn, Scotland, July 28th 1745

Nature had carved out the glen with ice tens of thousands of years ago and had spent the intervening millennia crafting and perfecting a breathtaking landscape. A clear blue sky provided the perfect backdrop for this environmental masterpiece, illuminated by a lambent sun that warmed and bathed every detail of its natural brilliance.

A myriad greens were the forests, ferns, and grasses of the mountain side; swathes of purples, violets and blues lovingly sprinkled with vivid white, yellow and red were the heather and other flora of the glen. Glittering greys were the exposed rock faces, discarded boulders and moraine, draped in the folds of the slopes by glaciers which melted away long, long ago. Silver threads weaved their way down from the peaks and bound the land together. The mountain streams gave life to the glen and filled the loch below before the river could drain it from its western side and the still air caused no ripples upon its surface and the loch was a shimmering silver platter that reflected the magnificent sun in the cloudless sky above.

And the land, the water and the vegetation were by no means nature's only gifts to this wonderful place. High up on the mountain a herd of red deer grazed on the luxuriant slopes with majestic stags patrolling the outer reaches of the herd, watchful and protective. Grouse and pheasant also inhabited the mountainside while in the forest capercaillie called to their mates. Foxes, badgers, rabbits, hares and a whole host of others also shared the glen while the water teemed with otters, trout, salmon, pike and more. In the blue sky a golden eagle hunted for prey to feed its young, which were safe in their untouchable haven high up on a crag.

*

Seoras McLachlan woke from his dream and could see the eagle from where he lay in the heather. He watched as it soared slowly in ever descending circles before abruptly dropping out of the sky like a stone. He knew the fate of the unfortunate animal, a vole or a mouse maybe, would be so swift that it wouldn't even realise that its life had come to an end.

He sat up and rubbed his eyes. His head ached slightly from dozing in the hot sun so he put on his bonnet to protect his fair head from more abuse. He was unsure how long he had been there but the sun had shifted significantly enough in the sky to let him know that he should be getting back.

His grubby shirt was sleeveless and the fair skin of his arms and his legs had turned red. He gingerly touched those areas of his body, feeling the sting of his tight skin.

He recalled what he had been dreaming about while he slept, if he had been asleep at all, for he could remember neither falling asleep nor waking. That was always the case when he had his special dreams. The dreams that came to him to show him something.

This dream was different though, he thought, as he remembered its content. It hadn't really shown him anything at all. It had shown him some men landing on the seashore but unlike the dreams he usually had, there was no one in it that he knew. The landscape was one that he hadn't recognised.

Feeling bewildered he got to his feet and hooked his thumbs into the thick leather belt which secured his kilt around his waist and began to pick his way through the heather and down the slope.

Watching where he put his feet, he contemplated whether or not it had been a special dream at all. His previous dreams had all featured people that he knew or places that he had been to. More importantly, they had all been scenes that he himself had been involved in or at least would be witness to in the not too distant future.

The visions were so clear to him that when the event actually happened it was like an intense and prolonged version of *déjà vu*. He couldn't remember when they had begun but they had been going on long enough for him to tell the difference between a normal dream and a special dream.

A recent one, which was still lodged firmly in his memory, had been that of the death of his grandmother. In his dream he had seen her fall to the ground outside the door to her cottage. He and his elder brothers, Donchad and Seamas rushed to her aid and carried her gently inside to her bed where she lay still and breathless. Seoras had then rushed off to get his grandfather.

That had been it. Nothing more, nothing less.

Two days later, God took his grandmother quickly and painlessly in exactly the way that he had foreseen.

He had felt great sorrow at the loss of his grandmother but he also knew that there was nothing that he could have done to change things and nothing that he could have done to warn her. There was certainly no one he could have told about his vision.

Ever since he was very young he had learned through the stories that his grandfather had told him what the fate of a seer might be. To his people second sight was not a gift but a curse. If his secret was discovered at the very least he could be caged like an animal or driven from his home to wander the mountains as a beggar for the rest of his days. He had heard tell that there had been a seer in Sutherland that had foreseen a bleak future for his clan and that he had been boiled alive in a vat of tar.

It was a curse but one which he would not share. He could never tell anyone. All that he did was see. He could not help it, he could not control it: he just saw.

But his latest vision disturbed him all the same and he tried to put it out of his mind.

Instead he concentrated on his step as the slope became steeper. He was picking up speed as gravity took hold of him so he took his hands out of his belt to help keep his balance. He descended the slope quickly going down at an angle so that he could lean into it. When the incline began to shallow again he came to a dirt path that had been carved into the side of the slope by many years of footsteps. He began to trot along the path and the warmth and stillness of the air quickly drained the energy from him and made his legs feel heavy. He was glad when the path took him into some woodland that shielded him from the heat of the sun. Although the brightness of the sun still penetrated the wood in piercing shafts it was dark and he had to squint to see where he was going until his eyes adjusted to the difference in light.

As he trotted through the semi-gloom his mind returned to the vision.

He wondered how it could affect him if there was no one in it he knew and how it could have anything to do with him if he didn't even recognise where the events of the dream had taken place. How could it have any influence on his or his family's lives if they had nothing to do with it?

Although he was different Seoras was fourteen years old and still young enough to push his worries away with little effort. Gifted or cursed, he knew that he was different. He decided finally that the dream wasn't special and he reassured himself that he could dream about places that he had never seen and people that he had never met. After all, he had heard more than enough hearthside tales to fire his unconscious imagination. As he made that mental decision the dream was gone from his head in the same way that most dreams cannot be recalled shortly after waking.

He could see brightness a short distance in front of him and slowed his pace until he came to the edge of the woods. There, in the shade of the ancient Scots pine that towered above him, he came to a halt.

Now that he was lower down the slopes, and on the other side of the forest, he could see more clearly the floor of the glen below. He saw the river as it wound its way westward from the loch like a giant silver serpent. It travelled in wide, slow and quiet loops for the main part but in places with speed and fury as it fought its way through rocks and boulders and tumbled down falls. On either side of the river there were small copses of beech and oak and on the near side Seoras could see the collection of buildings and fields that made up the croft of his kin.

The nine buildings of the croft were made of rocks and clay, the roofs constructed from branches set up in a ridge and covered with thick turf. A vent in the roof let smoke escape from the peat-fuelled hearth. No smoke rose from them on a fine hot day like this though, but later as supper was cooked, thin tendrils would curl their way up into the evening sky.

Then Seoras remembered that no supper would be cooked in his croft tonight because tonight they would be eating at the croft of his elder brother's bride. This would not only be an important night for his brother though, because tonight would be the first time that Seoras would play his fiddle in front of an audience.

He was tutored by his grandfather and he could not have had a better-qualified tutor because his grandfather had been the Chief's own fiddler for many years until age had stolen the dexterity from his fingers. He had taught Seoras to play with great skill over the years but had never allowed him to play for others outside of his family until today. Seoras knew that although his grandfather had never said as much this was because he wanted him to be faultless when he played and to show that he himself was as good a teacher as he was a musician. Seoras didn't hold it against his grandfather because the old man never drove him towards this, but his ultimate ambition must have been for Seoras to regain his position as the Chief's fiddler. Passing things from the old to the young was the way of the clan. Tonight when he played his fiddle his grandfather would be on display as much as he was, playing every note with him without ever picking up an instrument.

As he looked down at the croft he knew that he should be there now instead of standing up here, but he could not resist admiring the glen for a few moments longer. He observed the fields, rich with the greenery of this years crops and he noticed the cattle, sheep, and hens milling around the buildings un-penned. He could see his own home and the home of his aunt, uncle and cousins, and he could also see the cottage that had once been his grandparent's and which, by tonight, would be the home of Donchad and his wife.

He recalled how he had stood at this very spot in the winter with his plaid wrapped around his head and shoulders to protect him from the biting cold and had looked down at a very different croft with the same profoundness as he did now. Then the glen had been buried under deep, soft snow and the glorious colours that he could now see were hidden by blinding white and the drover's road was lost under piling drifts. He had stopped at this point, exhausted after climbing through the swirling snow which had stung his face and had forced him to bury his head deeper into his plaid as he peered down at the croft. Smoke had poured from the vents in the roofs as the hearths were built up high to drive out the bitter cold. The only thing that remained unchanged was the river, which had flowed on, never slowing, never freezing, cutting like a polished silver blade through the blanket of white.

Still daydreaming, he began to trot along the dirt path heading for home and before long he had descended to the foot of the slope. There the path joined on to the wider drover's road that cut through the croft before fording the river. He passed through the outfields that had looked so different from his vantage point high up on the slope and soon saw his people as they bustled about preparing themselves for the night ahead. The familiar daily routine had been forgotten for the time being.

As he rounded the last of the infields he caught sight of his mother standing in the doorway. He could tell by the look on her face that she was anxious and he knew that he was the reason - or one of the reasons at least - for her anxiety. She caught sight of him and her look turned to one of relief.

She called out to him. 'Seoras, where have ye been?'

'I've-'

She cut him short before he could even begin to give her an unworthy excuse. 'Hurry up, ye have tae get ready.'

His mother was dressed in the clothes that she reserved for wearing to the Kirk. She wore a white blouse and a dark blue dress which flowed to her ankles and around her shoulders she wore a thin plaid shawl which was fastened by a silver brooch. Her dark brown hair was pulled to the back of her head in a tight bun and Seoras could see threads of silver glinting in the sun that he had never noticed before.

'And just look at the state o ye. Go and get washed and get yer good shirt and jacket on.' Without reply Seoras began to pass his mother and seeing her raise her hand to clout him he darted into the doorway. 'And brush yer hair!' she called after him.

In the dim light that the small windows would allow into the building Seoras could see that his elder brother Seamas was already brushing his hair, ready to go. Seamas paused long enough to smirk at his scalded younger brother.
*

The sun was still with them when the festivities got under way that evening.

A young girl had sung a ballad accompanied by a piper and Donchad and his bride began the dancing. When they had finished it was time for Seoras to get up and make his debut. He stood silent for a few moments with his fiddle held under his chin. Then slowly drew the bow across the strings and he began to walk his fingertips along the fingerboard. The rhythm began to increase and he could feel the notes snaking out into the air around him, coiling and twisting like rising smoke. The bow began to quicken, sea-sawing across the strings and his fingertips danced, faster and faster. The music stretched out and reached into the crowd, twisting around their feet and their feet began to tap and shuffle and their shoulders began to sway as the magic in the air began to seep into them. Seoras closed his eyes and his fingers became a blur and the feet in the crowd began to stamp out the beat on the ground. The music had wrapped around them now and seemed to twist and pull them and spin them in circles. Hearing only the music in his head, Seoras spun out the reel like a magical silken cloak, letting the rhythm rise and rise until he and the dancing crowd began to grow exhausted. Abruptly, he ended the reel, lifting his bow away and muting the strings. He stood for a moment in the silence, forgetting his surroundings.

The crowd began to clap and cheer, calling for more. He opened his eyes, startled and then he beamed. Once more, he lifted the fiddle to his chin and began to draw the bow.

In the crowd his grandfather stood with eyes closed and nodded his head and gently swayed in time to the music. The corners of his lips curled upwards in satisfaction.

The sky had begun to turn red in the east by the time Seoras finished his set and the piper took over the entertainment. He tucked his fiddle under his arm and made his way through the throng to where his family were gathered. As he approached them his father held out a mug.

'Here ye go son, ye deserve this.' Seoras took the mug and looked into it as his father clapped a spade-like hand on his shoulder. 'Ye really got the dancin goin wi yer music.'

'Thanks, Dad.' Seoras looked into the mug and strong whisky fumes nipped at his eyes. 'But I don't think the folk needed much encouragement tae get goin'.'

''Maybe so, but ye kept them goin son, and I'm proud o ye.'

'We're all proud o' ye.' His mother hugged him.

'Aye ye did well, ye wee shite,' Seamas said and punched his younger brother on the upper arm. Seoras looked down at his feet, his cheeks growing hot.

'Drink then, lad,' Tarlich prompted as he knocked his mug against his son's.

'Are ye sure?'

'On ye go, son. It's a special occasion.'

Seoras looked at the spirit in his mug and raised it to his lips and let about half of the liquor spill into his mouth. Immediately he felt the whisky searing his lips and mouth and he swallowed. He felt the fiery liquid burn down his gullet and into his belly and he began to cough and splutter.

'Aye, it's a fine dram aa right!' His father slapped his back while Seamas laughed. All his sons took their looks from him but Tarlich often thought that Seoras looked exactly as he had when he was his age. This wasn't so clear to others who had not known Tarlich as a boy. He had a thick beard and an ugly scar ran over the bridge of his nose and onto the cheekbone below his left eye.

In defiance of his brother's mockery Seoras regained control of himself and poured the remainder of the contents of the mug straight down his throat. It didn't burn so badly this time, his throat having been partially anaesthetised by the first swig, but it was still strong enough to make his face twist involuntarily. Already he began to feel his lips and tongue numbing.

'You go steady on that stuff,' his mother warned, 'Ye've still tae play that fiddle again the night.'

'I will,' said Seoras, looking into the crowd. 'Have ye seen Granda?' His father pointed through the crowd and Seoras followed his finger. Through the throng he could make out a group of old men that sat in a semicircle near the fire. His grandfather sat before them waving his arms spectacularly.

'You better go and make sure that the old man doesn't take all the credit for yer fine display,' his father said.

Seoras squeezed through the crowd to where the old men were gathered. They had chosen a spot near the fire and the drink was flowing freely among them. As he approached he could hear that his fiddle playing was indeed the current topic of conversation. His face grew red as he listened to his grandfather telling the others that Seoras would be the Chief's own fiddle player before very long.

He was about to turn away, planning to return when the discussion had moved onto another theme when he was spotted by one of the men.

'Seoras! Come and sit wi us a while, boy,' he called.

His grandfather turned to greet him and made space for him to sit. The heat from the fire was uncomfortably hot on his face and he hoped it hid his embarrassment. Once more he modestly accepted praise as the old men heaped it upon him. His grandfather received his praise more readily, Seoras noticed. He couldn't blame him for that - it was a proud time for him too.

He was handed another mug of whisky and he sipped at it. The fire in his belly from the previous drink had dimmed to a warm glow and he felt relaxed and at ease with the old crofters and fishermen around him. Occasionally the slight breeze would lift smoke from the fire in their direction carrying the pleasant odour of pine, much lighter than the heavy scent of peat that he was more used to.

Seoras listened to the men talk about old times for a while, something he would have normally enjoyed. Tonight though, he was restless. He rose to his feet, saying that he would go for a wander and see what his brothers were up to. He hadn't even congratulated Donchad yet, whose day it really was.

'Hold on a minute, Seoras,' his grandfather said getting up, 'I want tae talk tae ye.' He put his arm around his grandson's shoulders and led him away from the circle of old clansmen. Seoras noticed that he wasn't exactly steady on his feet.

'I just wanted tae ask ye Seoras, how did ye feel?' He pressed his open palm against his chest, 'What did ye feel . . . inside?' His eyes bored into Seoras' and the boy knew that he was looking for something specific from him.

'I felt as though I was givin them something that they needed, Granda.' He had no hesitation getting those words out, the drink within him giving him courage. 'I felt as though they were eating up my music and I was so happy.' He thought about what he had just said for a moment and then said, 'No, not happy, happy isn't the right word.'

'Contented.'

'Aye, that's the right word. I felt contented to be giving them what they needed. And when it was time for me to finish, I didn't want tae, I wanted tae keep goin - I wanted tae keep makin them dance. I still want to now. It's like the first time I dove off the big beech by the side of the river into the water. I really wanted tae do it, especially cause Seamas and Donchad had done it plenty of times before and I didn't want them to think I was scared. But I was scared. In fact I was absolutely shittin mysel Granda.' Seoras reddened again.

His grandfather laughed.

'Anyway,' he continued, 'I was really scared and my legs were shakin but I climbed along the high branch that reaches out over the water and I kept thinkin if I didn't jump as soon as I got to the point where I had to then Donchad and Seamas would start taunting me and I would lose my nerve and have to climb down again. I knew that I couldn't face that so as soon as I got to the place on the branch where it started to bend a wee bit, I dived . . . well . . . sort of.' He stopped to take a sip of whisky and grimaced. 'I fell through the air and into the water, plunged deep, and came to the surface feeling terrific. It was all over so fast. I was up the tree again without even thinkin about it, walkin along the branch like my brothers, so that I could dive properly.'

'And that's exactly how ye feel now isn't it?' His grandfather understood perfectly. 'Ye want tae climb back up the tree and do it again. Maybe even better this time and with more confidence now that ye know what tae expect.'

'Aye, that's exactly it.'

'Ye'll always feel that way though, Seoras, so be patient and take it as it comes. Ye'll hae plenty o' opportunities tae make folk happy wi yer music.'

The old man hugged his grandson and the boy hugged him back. 'Now, go and do some dancin o yer own,' he said pushin Seoras away.

He left his grandfather with the circle of clan elders and went to look for Donchad. He eventually found him, kissed his new sister-in-law and congratulated them and wished them all the best. This was followed of course by another toast of whisky. Then he found some friends and danced as the night grew fully dark, until they were illuminated only by the bonfire burning in the field.

When the time came for him to play again, he got up without hesitation and the feeling that he got was as strong as before. More whisky flowed after he had finished and the music and the singing and the dancing and the glow of the fire all became one entity from which he could not differentiate.

He began to feel giddy and staggered to a quiet spot away from the light of the fire and the noise. He made himself comfortable on the ground and looked up at the stars coruscating in the sky above him. Then they began to spin out of focus and he closed his eyes.

Later, people were again calling for Seoras to play but he was nowhere to be seen. When his father eventually found him in drunken slumber with his fiddle clutched to him, he put him over his shoulder and carried him home through the darkness.

*

Seoras was reluctant to be pulled from heavy slumber the next morning but his father's big hands roughly shaking his shoulders insisted otherwise.

'Get up boy, ye've got work to do.'

His head swam and it took him a few minutes to realise where he was. He forced himself up onto his elbows trying to remember how he had gotten home to his bed, but immediately flopped back onto his straw mattress when he found that his limbs were too weak to hold him.

'Get up boys, yer breakfast's ready,' his father said, louder.

Seoras' stomach turned over at the thought of eating and he had to make an effort not to throw up at his bedside. He rolled out of bed and got unsteadily up onto his feet. He stood and swayed and looked longingly at the warm and comfortable bed that he had just got out of and wished that he could collapse back into it. He became dimly aware through half shut eyes that Seamas was also rising out of his bed. His face was pasty and his jaw was slack and his eyes were dull and lifeless. He looked how Seoras felt. Neither felt that they could make a move to get dressed, never mind work.

'Just look at the state o the pair o ye,' said Tarlich as he shook his head in mock disgust at his sons. Without another word he stomped over to the boys and took hold of each of them by the arm and dragged them outside, naked. The brightness of the morning pierced into Seoras' head forcing him to squint but he suspected that his father had given them, and maybe himself, some extra time in bed.

'Slow down Da, I'm goin tae puke!' Seamas pleaded as Tarlich continued to pull them along the road.

Neither boy thought to ask him where they were being taken and just let themselves be hauled along. They reached the riverbank, the boys with their faces red and sweating. It was only at this point that Seoras' mind, dimmed and slowed by the heavy residue of alcohol, registered what his father meant to do. Already it was too late to struggle. Planting a hand firmly and squarely on their backs, Tarlich shoved his sons into the water.

The freezing river engulfed Seoras' body as he went under and instantly a new alertness hit his brain like an explosion. As he broke the surface he tried to yell out, shocked by the sudden coldness of the water, but no sound came out of his mouth. Instead he only hitched in air with lungs that spasmed as the icy temperature of the river seized his body. He splashed aimlessly at the surface of the water and for a few panicky moments could not keep himself afloat. It was as if his limbs could not understand the startled messages that his brain was sending them. He managed to scramble his way back to the bank and joined by Seamas he panted as he tried to control his shuddering body.

'Once ye've finished messin about in there ye can come and get yer breakfast,' their father called as he turned back toward the croft.

'Ye kn-know Seoras, that actually h-hit the fu-fuckin spot,' stuttered Seamas.

'Aye. I f-feel a whole l-lot be-better,' replied Seoras as cold refreshing water ran down his face. The brothers looked at each other with huge grins on their faces and then dived back into the water.

Afterwards, with their breakfast lying awkwardly in their bellies they headed out to the fields, walking behind their father's long strides. Seoras still felt quite weak and queasy but he was nowhere near the state that he had been in when he had awoken in the morning. He thought of Donchad with envy, who had been allowed to stay at home on his first day with

Catriona. Next year Donchad would have a rig of his own to attend to, but this year he would still be working with his father.

Seoras struggled with the weight of a large basket and he couldn't imagine how he was going to carry it once it was fully loaded. His father and brother carried shovels on their shoulders. In the field he could see the rows of dead stalks which had already been cut from the plants a couple of days ago. Taking a row each, Tarlich and Seamas began unearthing the potatoes. Seoras followed behind them between the rows, plucking the tubers from the ground and raking the loosened dirt with his hands to find more. Every single potato had to be lifted. They were a life saving asset to the crofters and made up the staple part of their diet to get them through the winter as well as paying the rent. He struggled behind his father and brother not wanting to fall too far behind them and appear weak, but was also careful not to leave any of the precious vegetables lying in the ground. When the basket was full, he heaved it up into his arms and swung it around onto his back. He steadied himself under the weight and began to stagger down to the bottom of the field where he gratefully emptied its contents. As he returned to the point where he had stopped filling the basket he noted with despair that his father and brother were now some way ahead and that he was never going to catch them up. Already his limbs ached and his morale sank when he realised that his next trip to the bottom of the field would be even longer. His only consolation was that on the next two rows it would be Seamas' turn to fill the basket and make the back breaking trip down the field.

The day turned out to be just as hot as the previous and he could feel the sun burning into the back of his neck. Seoras toiled throughout the morning, repeatedly wiping the sweat that poured from his crimson face. Swapping the basket for the spade offered no comfort to him and his back screamed in agony every time he bent to turn over the earth. He dreamed of collapsing onto the ground and falling into a deep, soothing sleep.

Around mid-day, Tarlich said that it was time for them to head home for a plate of broth. Seoras released an audible sigh. The hangover had been sweated out of him and now hunger was gnawing at his stomach. His mouth was furred up and in sore need of some cool water.

As they plodded down the field towards home Seoras could make out the figure of a man in the distance that hurried towards them and waved his arms in the air. It was his Uncle Ailen.

'Tarlich! Tarlich, have ye heard?'

'Slow down man, what's the matter wi ye?' Tarlich continued walking homeward as he called back to his younger brother, not slowing his stride, his sons trudging on behind him. They had seen their uncle in this state many times before and they were in no way curious as to what had excited him this time. He came to a halt in front of Tarlich panting heavily and from the look on his face Seoras thought that he was about to tell them that the world was going to come to an end. Tarlich continued to stride onward and forced Ailen to walk backwards in order to hold his attention.

'Have ye heard?' Ailen repeated.

'Heard what?'

'The Prince, Charles Stuart -' Ailen nearly stumbled and fell on his backside as he blurted out his news, '- he's landed in the Highlands.' At this point he grabbed Tarlich by the shoulders and forced him to stop so that he would have maximum effect for what he was about to say. It was as if he knew himself that he was guilty of going over the top and wanted to show that this piece of information really *was* important.

'He's raising an army to take back the crown!' Seoras could see his uncle's wide-eyed face less than an inch in front of his father's as he stressed the importance of what he was saying.

Tarlich removed Ailen's hands from his shoulders and continued to walk on.

'Well . . . Have ye nothing to say,' Ailen said to his back.

Tarlich turned and addressed his sons. 'Go in for yer broth lads, yer uncle and I have something to discuss. Tell yer mother I'll be in shortly,' and as an after thought he added, 'and don't mention this to her.'

Seoras and Seamas looked uncomprehendingly at each other for a moment and then went on their way.

'Ye know perfectly well what my feelings are on this subject, Ailen,' he said once they were gone, 'God knows we've spoken o it often enough.'

'I know what ye've said before Tarlich, but talkin about it and doin it are two entirely different things. There's a rebellion under way. It's actually upon us.'

'Everything that I've ever said in the past about what action I'd take if there was ever another rebellion, I meant.'

'Ye can't be serious. How can ye even consider it?'

'It's long overdue Ailen, and ye know it. We can't let things stay the way they are, not if we have a chance to change them, and ye know that I'm not just talkin about puttin a Stuart back on the throne. I'm talkin about our whole way of life - our very existence.'

'If we're foolish enough to stand up to the government we won't have a way of life, because we won't exist. Ailen sighed and tried to reason further with Tarlich. 'Look, ye know I hate the government as much as you and there's nothin' I would like to see more than the Stuarts back hame, but it's just not goin tae happen.

The Government are just too powerful for us now, we could never stand against them and if we try they'll crush us like they did in '15 . . . but this time they'll make sure that we never try again. They'll make sure we never have the capability tae try again. This time they'll hang everyone they even suspect o bein a Jacobite, whether they are or not, and those that are left will be driven off their land and shipped off to the New World to work as slaves. Imagine it Tarlich. Our land. Ours since time began, will be in the hands of people who hate everything we are. It'll all be gone . . . forever.'

When he had finished Tarlich thought for a few moments and then nodded.

'Aye, ye're right in what ye say brother.'

'At last . . . I'm gettin' throu-'

'Yer right when ye say that they'll hang us, they'll take our land and ship our folk off to God knows where. That much is true Ailen. What ye fail tae see is that they'll do that anyway. Whether we rise up or not they'll do it, only they'll do it more slowly if we don't rise. Bit by bit, glen by glen, family by family and clan by clan. Ye're right when ye say that they hate everything we are and they want to destroy us. Because they fear us. But ye're wrong when ye say that we'll be crushed. We were ill prepared in our father's time. King James has been plannin this over in France for years. We won't be on our own either. The French and the Irish will be with us too. And after it all Ailen, even if we do lose - which we won't - at least we'll have put up a fight instead of lyin down and lettin them slowly but surely snuff us out.'

Ailen shook his head in dismay when he realised that he was never going to get Tarlich to change his point of view. Then Tarlich had something to say that Ailen knew he had no argument against.

'And anyway, if the Chief calls us tae arms, which he surely will, then this debate is purely academic. Whether we want to or not . . . we fight.'

Ailen shook his head at the mountain peaks high above them. 'This is sheer fuckin madness,' he said before turning away from Tarlich and heading back in the direction from which he had come. 'And we're goin to have such a fine crop this year too,' he said without looking back.

Tarlich watched him go feeling a heaviness in his heart. His brother was going to have to do the most important thing that any of them would ever have to undertake. He knew that his brother was no coward but neither was he a fighting man. He wanted to tend to his croft and live in peace. Tarlich hoped that Ailen would see that if they didn't do this, if they didn't fight now, then they would never live in peace. Tarlich didn't relish the thought of leaving his home to go and fight, but he knew that it had to be done. It was the only way. It was overdue.

As he headed for home he found to his amazement that he still had an appetite and quickened his pace as he remembered the broth that awaited him. His mouth was bone dry from the whisky the night before and he badly needed a drink of water. He'd felt like shit all morning but had kept hard at it to set an example for his sons.

*

Before entering the cottage the boys took turns scooping water into their mouths from the pail by the door. It had been icy cold when their mother had taken it from the river earlier, but although it was now lukewarm, it still served its purpose in quenching their thirst. They went inside and slumped exhausted at the table.

'Where's yer father?', their mother enquired.

'Outside talkin tae Uncle Ailen,' replied Seamas.

'It's a fine day for workin,' she said as she stirred the broth.

'Oh aye Ma,' said Seamas. 'It's so fine that I think I'll forget my broth and get straight back to it.'

'Anymore o that oot o ye and that's exactly what ye'll be doin'. I don't hear Seoras complainin.'

'That's cause he's too knackered tae speak.'

'Did yer father say how long he would be?'

'He said to start without him,' said Seamas.

Mairi filled her sons' bowls with broth from the large pot that hung over the peat fire and placed them on the table in front of them before filling a bowl for herself and joining them. The boys bowed their heads while she gave thanks and when she was done they began to eat hungrily. The broth was filled with vegetables, barley and mutton. It was hot and Seoras blew on his spoon. As he ate he thought about what his uncle had said to his father.

The Prince, Charles Stuart - he's landed in the Highlands.

The dream of the previous morning returned. The sea, the coast, the boat, the men. The pounding heart of the stag.

Landed in the Highlands.

The spoon that had been shovelling broth into his mouth now moved slowly as it dawned on him that he had dreamed of the Prince. He had seen the Prince landing on the West Coast. Yesterday he hadn't understood. He hadn't understood why he didn't recognise anyone in the dream. He had no way of knowing how the vision was going to affect them directly, as all the others had. As he remembered what else his uncle had said before they had been sent home, the realisation of how it could affect them sent mixed feelings of excitement and dread down his spine. He lowered his spoon to his bowl.

He's raising an army to take back the crown.

His mother's voice pulled him out of his thoughts. 'Seoras, are ye all right?'

'Aye Ma, I'm just tired,' he said spooning broth into his mouth again.

'He's probably got heat stroke,' Seamas informed her with a smile.

Before she could enquire further they heard Tarlich drinking from the pail by the door. He came inside and filled his bowl before sitting at the table with his family. He bowed his head in short silent prayer and began to eat.

'The boys said ye were speakin tae Ailen.'

'Aye. This broth's good Mairi.'

The four of them continued to eat in silence.

As they waited for Tarlich to finish Seoras could feel his stomach soaking up the goodness of the broth and restoring some of the strength to his alcohol and work weakened body.

Tarlich finished eating and pushed the bowl away from him with a look of satisfaction on his face. He stood up from the table and kissed his wife on the forehead. 'Thanks Mairi, I could eat your broth and nothin' else 'til the day I die. Come on then lads, those tatties won't pick theirsel's,' he said heading out of the door.

Tarlich worked his sons well into the evening. He sensed that time was short and he didn't want to leave his crop rotting in the ground while he went away to fight.

Three

Dunedin, New Zealand, April 6th 2146

As he showered in the hotel room Sinclair thought about what he was going to say to the historian. His main concern was explaining how the bonnet had come into his possession.

He had called the university as soon as he had reached Dunedin and had made an appointment to see Jason Lombard before finding a room for the day. He dressed and picked up the bag containing the bonnet. As he made his way to check out of his accommodation, he looked inside the bag to make sure that it was still there and to remind himself of what it was that he had actually come here to do.

He made his way to the university on foot under the same light that illuminated virtually every other town and city in the world. The massive daylight simulating lights that were suspended in the sky. The Daylites. The human race had taken a severe dislike to becoming nocturnal.

The lights were not only powered by the sun's energy, they also stored and filtered it so that beneficial light was stored during the day and dangerous radiation was reduced to safe levels. This light was then released to shine down on the earth during hours of darkness so that the human inhabitants of the planet could go about their nocturnal activities while enjoying the advantages of diurnal light. The Daylites used solar energy and technology that had been developed in the first half of the twenty-first century to suspend them in the sky. Unlike almost all of man's technology that had been made up until that point, rather than pollute, The Daylites cleaned the atmosphere. The rays from the Daylites could tease a shoot up from the soil and open up the petals of a rose, just like the sun that fuelled them.

Sinclair knew the university well having studied there himself, so he needed no directions to find the office in which he had his appointment with Professor Lombard. He made his way directly there, not bothering to inform reception of his arrival. He walked along the familiar corridors past lecture rooms where he had spent many hours. He found the door to Lombard's office and knocked and poked his head in the door.

'Hi, I'm Sinclair Giacomo, I made an appointment to see you this evening', he said taking it for granted that the large red-faced man behind the desk was Lombard.

'Evening Mr Giacomo.' Lombard put aside the papers that he had been reading and rose to shake Sinclair's hand. He stood for a moment sizing Sinclair up and then indicated for him to take a seat.

'I must say that your message left me a bit mystified,' he began. 'I mean . . . If you want to talk about history you've come to the right place, and if you've come to talk about Scottish history then you've certainly come to the right place. What I cannot understand is why you've travelled here to see me so early in the evening and at such short notice.' Lombard sat back in his chair looking puzzled. 'What's the urgency?'

Sinclair suddenly felt that he should have known better. He had of course anticipated the question, not just from Lombard but from Sparling as well, and he still had to give Abbie some sort of explanation, but Lombard had a good point. Why was he here so early? What was he doing bursting into this man's office to pick his brains? He should have approached this rationally, he realised. People were going to think that he was mad. He should have messaged. He should have done some research of his own. Why hadn't he?

No time, he thought.

'I just . . .'

Why no time?

'I mean to say,' continued Lombard without waiting for an explanation, 'what's wrong with messaging? What's wrong with a search of the online knowledge fountain?'

The professor stood up from his desk and went over to a shelf on the wall where he took down a large volume. He returned to his desk and placed the book in front of Sinclair before retaking his seat. 'A Complete History of Scotland,' he said. 'I wrote it myself. In my own opinion I would say that it's easy to digest . . . I tried to write it that way at least. A number of hard copies were produced as a bit of vanity on my part so you can borrow that one. I hope you find time to read up on the chapter dedicated to the Jacobite rebellions before you return it Mr Giacomo.'

The professor's last sentence had a *that'll be all* ring to it and Sinclair could feel his face flush both with embarrassment and anger. He kept calm.

'I'm sorry if I appear to be rude professor and I don't want to take up much of your time, but my enquiry is more . . . specific. I don't think that your book will help me.' He'd been holding the brown paper bag in his lap and now he reached over the desk and placed it in front of Lombard. 'I'd like you to take a look at this, please, and if you could, tell me something about it.'

Lombard unrolled the top of the bag and looked inside. The lines on his forehead deepened when he saw the contents. He removed the bonnet and placed it on the desk in front of him. He looked at it thoughtfully for a few moments before picking it up and turning it over to examine the lining. He held it up to his nose, and his eyes closed as he inhaled. Sinclair thought that he looked like he was nosing a fine wine. After studying it he placed it back on the desk and sat back in his chair and looked straight into Sinclair's eyes.

'Where did you get this?'

'From a friend.'

'How did your friend come by it?'

'I don't have that information.'

'You mean you won't tell me.'

'Is it important?'

Lombard sighed. 'If you mean is the *question* important, then no, I don't suppose it is. If you mean is the *bonnet* important, then the answer is yes. At least it could be. Very important.'

'What can you tell me about it?'

'I'd like some time to think about this Mr Giacomo. I'd also like to let another of my colleagues see it . . . if I may? We could meet up later on tonight for something to eat and I'll tell you what I can then.'

'I have to get the bus back to Hampden tonight.'

'Okay then, earlier, say three hours time, two o'clock, at the station bar. I hear they serve okay food - and it'll be handy for you.'

Sinclair didn't like the idea of leaving the bonnet with this man that he knew so little about and who had shown so much interest in it, but he felt that he had no option but to trust him. He needed, for some unfathomable reason, to know what the old historian knew. He stood up from his chair and his eyes fell on Lombard's book. He picked it up and tucked it under his arm.

'Okay. Two o'clock at the station bar.'

*

He arrived at the bar about an hour early after killing time wandering around the shops and buying some new clothes. Thankfully it was quiet.

He ordered a beer and a sandwich and asked to borrow one of the notebooks they had behind the bar for customer use. He took the notebook and his beer over to a table in the corner away from the others who were dotted around the bar. After the barman had brought his food over he logged on to the notebook with his thumbprint and chose travel and tapped on the HydraSol logo.

While he ate and sipped at his beer he browsed through the timetables, connections, fares and standards of travel for ships to Europe.

There were two main routes he could take. East or west. East would take him across the Pacific to Panama. He would then have to go north again to New York before crossing the Atlantic to Glasgow. Seven days. West would take him round the south of Australia to Perth, before crossing the Indian Ocean to Cape Town. He would then travel up the west coast of Africa before reaching Lisbon. From there he would go on to Liverpool and Glasgow. Nine days. Ships left Dunedin to these destinations nightly. Mostly they were Cargo ships that also carried passengers. There were faster passenger only ships but when Sinclair clicked onto the fares for these routes he realised that he did not have the money to take this luxury. In fact, when he saw the prices for fares on the cargo ships he let out a low whistle.

This was a time when world travel was not entirely necessary. With the ability to hold virtual meetings and conferences across continents and oceans it was certainly unnecessary for business people to travel. Tourism was only a luxury for the wealthy. Tourism for the less well off happened in VR worlds. Without leaving home, people could stroll around foreign cities and landscapes in the warmth of the sun, or whatever other weather they chose.

Both cargo ship journeys were going to cost more than an English teacher's monthly salary. The eastern route was quicker but slightly more expensive. He had enough in savings.

He exited the Travel menu and he chose Personal Finance. He found his own bank's logo and tapped the on-screen prompts to transfer his savings into his credit account. He then returned to the travel menu where he entered his destination and preferred route. He pressed his thumb on the screen and reserved a cabin on the ship leaving in the morning.

After completing his transaction he returned the notebook and finished his sandwich. Wanting to distract his mind from what he had just done he opened Lombard's book to the first chapter. Sinclair liked the feel of a real book. He had some classic novels at home, including a leather bound edition of Stevenson's *Treasure Island* that he had been fortunate enough to inherit from a great uncle. He rarely read any non-fiction although he had often intended to read a history of his own Italian heritage. All that he knew of Italy was in the old framed recipe that hung on his kitchen wall.

After reading a couple of pages Sinclair looked up at the time screen on the wall behind the bar. Lombard was five minutes late. As the seconds ticked by his stomach began to tighten. His mind was racing with what action he should take if Lombard didn't turn up when the professor walked into the bar.

Sinclair watched him scan the bar and quickly spot him. He was carrying a brief case. Sinclair hoped that the bonnet was inside it.

I can't lose that bonnet, he thought.

Thig agus cuidich sinn.

Lombard strode over to him and placed the case down by the chair opposite Sinclair. Without sitting he removed his face-mask and asked Sinclair if he would like a drink. Sinclair asked for citrus water.

While Lombard was at the bar he considered picking up his briefcase and trying to open it just to make certain that the bonnet was in there. He decided instead to try and stay calm.

Lombard returned carrying Sinclair's drink and a beer for himself. Sinclair instantly wanted to ask him if he had the bonnet, but resisted.

'I'll tell you everything I know about the bonnet, Mr Giacomo, if you tell me how you came by it.' Like earlier, there was no small talk from the professor, which Sinclair was grateful for. He sat with his elbows on the table and his hands clasped around his glass. He had been in command in his own office and Sinclair had hoped that it would be different here on neutral territory. It seemed that he was wrong to hope.

'I can't tell you that professor, and there's a very good reason why I can't tell you. Please don't think that I'm ungrateful. I really want to tell you but . . . I can't. Maybe what you have to tell me will change that. Maybe when you tell me what you know about the bonnet, I'll be able to tell you something about how I acquired it.'

Sinclair felt like a fraud and broke the professor's gaze and instead looked at the back of his fidgeting hands. 'You see professor, and I'm being entirely sincere with you . . . I'm not sure *how* I got it.' Sinclair opened his palms out to Lombard.

Lombard looked carefully at Sinclair for a moment and then took a long draught of his beer. He held the glass in front of his face and watched the liquid swirl.

The professor reached down for his brief case and opened it up on the table. He withdrew Sinclair's brown paper bag, closed his case and returned it to the floor. He then returned the bag and its contents to Sinclair. As soon as he grasped the bag, Sinclair could feel the tension slide from his shoulders. He tried his best not to look like a spoilt child defending his sweets as he gripped it in both hands.

'As soon as I saw it,' said Lombard, 'I knew what it was - or at least what it was supposed to represent. The white ribbon stitched to the side in a kind of small rosette, it's called a cockade, was worn by the Jacobites of two rebellions in eighteenth century Scotland. The colour of the bonnet though, signifies that it would have been worn during the second of these rebellions. The Jacobite rebellion of 1745, or simply, The '45.

'The Jacobites were the followers of James, the man who they claimed should have been the rightful king of Great Britain, as opposed to George, the man who *was* king. It all boiled down to religion, really. And power. James' line was ended when the British government made it illegal for a Roman Catholic to sit on the throne. They had instead installed a new Protestant line from which George was descended. They, the new Royals, were Hanoverians. James was descended from the Stuarts, who were descended from Robert the Bruce and who had ruled over Scotland since the fourteenth century.

'The rebellions both started in Scotland because of the strong links that the Stuarts still had with the country and because of the predominantly Catholic Highlanders.

'Anyway, Sinclair, I don't want to confuse you with the politics, I'm here to talk to you about the bonnet.

'The colour of the bonnet and the white cockade was supposed to be the uniform of the Jacobite's and so worn by all, but the blue bonnet would only have been worn by senior clansmen, or officers. The clans that the Highlanders lived in, you see, were organised into fighting units for battle. A clan was in fact a regiment, or part of a regiment which was in turn broken down into companies and platoons, each with their own officers. I believe that the bonnet you have would have belonged to quite a high-ranking officer. It's lined with silk, and there wouldn't have been many clansmen, officers or not, with the money for that.

'When I first saw it, I didn't think for an instant that it was real. It couldn't have been - it's not old enough - even if it was skilfully preserved, the methods of preservation that they had in those times would not have been enough. Anyway, who would want to preserve a bonnet? Restoration would also be out of the question - you may as well make a copy of the bonnet for all that would be left of it. Also . . .' he added, 'the colour. If it were real, the blue would have turned to a kind of mouldy green over the last few hundred years.

'What intrigued me most about it though, was the way that it was made. The look of it, the feel of it, the stitching and the weave of the cloth. There's clear handmade craftmanship here that hasn't been seen for centuries. Even the odour that it gives off. Why would anyone make a Jacobite's bonnet that looks so authentic, even for a souvenir?

'I have to admit, Sinclair, that when you first brought it to me, I thought that this was some kind of joke dreamt up by John Sparling to wind me up. He knows how deep my love of Scottish history is, but the lengths that he would have had to go to to replicate it so well - not to mention the expense - would have certainly taken the humour out of it for him. I didn't think that he could have had this done. I wasn't sure that anyone could.' Lombard hadn't touched his drink since he had began talking, but now he paused to drain his glass.

'Can I get you another?' Sinclair asked.

'Could you make it a large scotch?'

Sinclair had earlier asked for citrus water because he wanted to have a clear head for what Lombard had to tell him, now he shared the old man's desire for something stronger. 'I think I'll join you,' he said.

While he stood at the bar waiting for their drinks, Sinclair looked back over at their table and gazed at the professor. He appeared deeply contemplative, as though he was wrestling with something in his mind. Sinclair was served and he returned to the table with two large whiskies. He gave Lombard his glass and motioned for him to continue.

'I had to find out exactly just how old it was, that's why I kept it, that's where I've been this evening. The colleague that I spoke of is an archaeologist. He's a bit like a forensic scientist and he has some pretty useful gadgets for identifying and dating material. His equipment told us that the bonnet was made no more than a few years ago.'

Sinclair's heart sank. Feelings of paranoia began to creep up on him. The bonnet was a fake, and, for no apparent reason, someone was out to make a fool of him. Or worse, the professor was lying about its authenticity so that he could take the bonnet for himself.

Mentally, Sinclair slapped himself in the face.

Lombard paused to take a drink of whisky at this point and Sinclair was sure that he could see a slight shake in his hand.

'Then though, it contradicted itself,' Lombard drained his whisky and grimaced. 'The test, I mean.' He set his glass down on the dark wood tabletop and stared directly into Sinclair's eyes. 'It seems that it was made of wool, *real* wool, nothing synthetic or cloned. That's hard enough to come by these days, even in New Zealand, but it is possible. What wasn't possible was what was used as a dye. We dated it again, to make sure that there was no mistake, and although it's a bit stressed and worn - it is definitely no more than a few years old.

'It was dyed in the same way that it was made, using old, traditional methods, and in the dyeing process the petals of a flower were used. The flower in question has been extinct since the latter part of the last century.

The plant was once found quite readily in Scotland during the time that they used these methods to make and dye a bonnet like this:

'The plant was *Hyacinchoids Scotia* . . . The Scottish Bluebell'.

Lombard opened his brief case and extracted a printout which he passed over to Sinclair. He looked down at the copy that he had been handed and saw a meadow, bordered by lush green trees, bathed in brilliant sunshine. The meadow was carpeted in brilliant blue. He wondered how it must have looked in reality if this was how it looked in a photograph. In the bottom right corner of the printout was a blow up of a single plant - it looked like a drawing from an old encyclopaedia. Its many heads nodded down to one side in the shape of bells, looking like a row of nuns kneeling in prayer. Long, glossy leaves grew from the base and fanned out around them, like a circle of holy light.

'How did such a plant become extinct?' Sinclair muttered the question, unable to understand how something so beautiful had been allowed to die.

'Simple really,' said the professor. 'The bluebell was a wild flower and grew in woodland and meadows like the picture in front of you. It was thought more of a weed than a flower. There was no skill in growing it; it did that itself - spread like wild fire in fact. In the 2040's when the environment became a stark truth that governments had to face instead of making promises and token gestures about, one of the policies they set about under-taking was re-forestation. Wood and wooden products were becoming vital to world economy and so they began to plant trees wherever land was available. While doing this they cut down existing forests, which were thought to be uneconomic because man could grow more trees per square kilometre than nature could in its random thoughtlessness. Governments all over the world who had shunned and denied environmental issues for over a century, hoping that the problem would go away, now realised that it wasn't just going to disappear. They were grabbing the bull by the horns. They were treating it like a dirty job. They were taking a deep breath, rolling up their sleeves and doing what needed to be done quickly, thoroughly and efficiently, in the way that you do an unsanitary job so that it won't need to be done again.

'Environmentalists, the same people who had for many years campaigned for governments to take heed, now had to plead with them to be moderate in what they were doing. They were repudiated in the same way that they had always been. When they were crusading for action they were told that they were over reacting, that they were obstructing progress. Then, when they lobbied for less drastic action they were told the same.

The habitats of many plant and animal species were obliterated. They tried to save some areas, and did so successfully, but the bluebell wasn't the only wild flower to be forgotten. Many others were lost forever. Man was missing the point. He was saving himself, not the planet.'

'Sadly, by the time they got the point, it was too late for the likes of the bluebell,' said Sinclair, summing up what Lombard had said.

'Right. So you see Sinclair, there's as much chance of your bonnet being only a few years old as there is of finding a bluebell growing in a Scottish meadow - absolutely none. It has to be at least a hundred years old, which according to my colleague's one hundred percent accurate dating technology, is impossible. We tried it a third time you know, at my insistence - he had every faith in his machine.' He sat back in his chair and sighed. 'Now Sinclair, I feel that I have told you more than enough to realise how important it is for me to find out from where you got the bonnet.

I'm going to get us another couple of drinks and then you can tell me all about it.'

Lombard got up and went to the bar and Sinclair realised that he was going to have to tell him the truth. He found that this was a relief. A part of him needed to recount his meetings with the apparition. He finished the last of his whisky before Lombard came back with another glass. The professor settled himself in his chair to listen to what Sinclair had to tell him. Sinclair could see no doubt in his expression that he was going to hear anything other than the truth. He wondered if that would still be the case once he had finished his story.

He told him exactly how it had happened, from the encounter in the bathroom to finding the bonnet on the classroom desk. The only part he omitted was what the visitor had said, because he didn't *know* what he had said. He simply told Lombard that the man had spoken to him in that strange lilting language.

'You can't think I'm mad Jason,' he said when he'd finished, 'I mean . . . you've seen the bonnet and the evidence of scientific technology for yourself.'

Lombard had listened in silence. He didn't speak or move and he didn't take his piercing eyes away from Sinclair's for a second. Now that he had actually spoken the words out loud to another person, Sinclair felt uncomfortable. But he had absolutely no doubt about what he had seen and heard in his bathroom and later in his classroom.

'I don't think you're mad, of course I don't. If you are mad then I am equally as insane. As you said, I've seen the evidence.' He sipped his drink and Sinclair marvelled at the way that the pair of them had managed to talk so calmly about the whole thing. There was a tense undercurrent that ran beneath their words and gestures, but outwardly both men had managed to stay collected. It was almost as if they were in a situation where to become over excited, or worse, to panic, would be bad news for them.

'One thing,' said Lombard. 'You told me that you don't know what he said because he spoke in a foreign language, one that you didn't recognise. Would it be possible for you tell me phonetically?'

'He said it four times,' said Sinclair, 'Twice each visit, and I can tell you exactly what it sounded like because it's been spinning around in my head ever since. . . Like a snatch of song. What he said was . . . *Hig ah-gus kood-yik shin.*'

'*Thig agus cuidich sinn,*' Lombard whispered to himself.

Sinclair sat bolt upright and pointed at him. 'That's it. That's exactly what he said!'

'It's Gaelic Sinclair, the ancient language of Scotland. *Thig agus cuidich sinn* means, "Come and help us."'

'Why is he asking me for help?'

'I don't know.'

'What does he want me to do?'

'I don't know. When are you going back to Hampden, Sinclair?'

'I'm not.'

'When are you going to Scotland?'

'The next boat leaves this morning.' It suddenly dawned on Sinclair that although he hadn't thought about it at all, he had known since meeting the Jacobite for the first time that he was going to Scotland. Not even the act of reserving the ticket had helped it to sink in. It had taken the translation from the old professor.

Come and help us.
Help us, Sinclair.

'Have you enough money?'

'Yes.'

'Do you want me to come with you? I can take leave.'

Sinclair could see in the professor's eyes that he was desperate to go. He looked like a child about to embark on an adventure. He felt bad turning him down. 'I think that I should go alone.'

Lombard's expression changed to one of resignation. 'Please tell me, Sinclair, if there's anything that you need.'

'Well there are a couple of things you could do for me.'

'Anything . . . within my ability,' the professor smiled.

'Contact Sparling at the school and arrange my time off.'

'Consider it done . . . and the other thing?'

'Stay here and drink with me please, Doctor Lombard, and tell me about the '45.'

For the remainder of the night Lombard told him of Charles Stuart, The Young Pretender, of the early victories, the retreat north, defeat, and the persecution of the Highlanders and the eventual break-up of the Highland way of life. Sinclair didn't know why he had to go to Scotland, and he had no idea what he was going to do once he got there, but he thought he now knew why the young soldier who had visited him wore such a look of grief on his face.

Lombard finished talking and Sinclair had to go back to his hotel to book in for another day. On unsteady legs they walked to the stop where Lombard would catch his bus home.

Sinclair held the history book he had borrowed out to Lombard, but Lombard pushed it gently back.

'You'll need something to read on the boat,' smiled the professor.

Sinclair thanked him and watched him climb aboard the airbus and take his seat. They looked at each other through the glass and the old man mouthed *good luck* as the bus pulled away.

*

The large cargo ship cruised out of Otago Harbour looking like a giant rugby ball half submerged in the water. It was as red-black as volcanic glass. The Daylites of the harbour glittered across its surface as it turned north and began the run along the east coast of South Island. It was driven by air and water turbines and fuelled by the sun via the thousands of solar panels which covered its surface.

By the time that the ship sailed parallel with Hampden, Sinclair had read about Scotland's earliest dwellers in the stone age and the bronze age, and was learning about the Roman General Agricola, who took his army to the Grampian Highlands in the north east to fight the Caledonian Picts.

When dawn broke the next morning the ship had left Auckland and Sinclair had gone to sleep for the day. He had marked his book at the chapter dedicated to St Columba who came to Scotland from Ireland in the year 563 to unite the peoples of Scotland in Christianity.

The ship slipped eastward through the South Pacific, glittering like a giant ruby as the sun glared on the solar panels. Below, Sinclair slept peacefully and dreamt that he was walking barefoot through the grass by the monastery that St Columba and his brethren had built on the island of Iona.

Four

<u>Strath Lachlainn, Scotland, September 14th 1745</u>

The night the tacksman came to collect the rent they were prepared.

He wouldn't be collecting his usual rent on this visit though. This time he would be collecting payment of a different kind. He would carry the fiery cross through the land cashing in on an ancient and unwritten pact made between chief and clan.

They had expected his imminent arrival. The glen had been full of talk about the impending uprising and they were in no doubt that Old MacLachlan would be rallying to the prince's standard with every clansman that he could muster. It had been the only topic of conversation between Seoras and his brothers and cousins.

Seoras felt sure that he too would be called upon to join The Prince's army. At least he hoped he would. He felt daunted by the prospect of going away, but he also felt honoured. He wanted to go away and fight for such a noble cause because he thought that it would make him respected and would make him a man. Seamas had told him that he would be left at home to feed the livestock and weave with the women but Seoras had already decided that he wouldn't let that happen. He would go whether he had to or not. If he had to run away to join the Jacobite Army, he would. The young men had filled each other's hearts with anticipation and each other's heads with dreams of glory and bravery, but

Seoras hadn't heard talk of it between his parents and the subject was never brought up with their sons.

Until the night that the tacksman came.

The preceding morning had been the first time that there had been any real outward signs that anything out of the usual was about to happen in the glen. They had felt the buzz of expectation in the air since the first rumours had reached the glen and there had also been the unspoken agreement to get the crops in as quickly as possible. Until then, there had been no tangible evidence that their daily lives were any different than usual. Not only had they managed to get the seasons crops in early but they had also cut most of the peat that would be needed for the winter and begun the process of preserving meat, fish and berries. They had cured furs and carried out maintenance and repairs to their homes to ensure that they were sound. A section of roof caving in under the weight of winter snow would be disastrous on a freezing late December night.

So far they had been preparing for the fight against winter, but on the day that the Tacksman came, they had begun to prepare for a fight of a different kind.

It was at the breakfast table that morning that Tarlich told his youngest sons that they wouldn't be working that day and that instead he had something else to occupy them. They went with him round to the byre end of the cottage and watched with interest as he began to remove some boulders from near the base of the wall. He revealed a hole partially dug into the ground and supported by strong timber. From this space he removed three bundles of various sizes, wrapped in oiled cloth and tied with strong hemp. He laid them on the ground side by side in front of Seamas and Seoras who tried to work out what the vague shapes were inside the cloth.

The first bundle was about four feet long, wide at one end and tapering to a point at the other. The second was over a foot long and was rolled up like a carpenter's tool kit. The third parcel was in the shape of a rectangular box.

Once he had laid these out Tarlich stood on one of the boulders and steadied himself against the wall with one hand. He reached up into the turf and heather of the roof with the other. He rummaged around for a couple of seconds before laying hold of something and he extracted it from the roof. This fourth bundle, also wrapped in oilcloth, was about three feet long. Tarlich stepped down from the boulder and sat on it, laying the bundle across his knees. Seoras could hear the faint clank of metal, dimmed by the material that it was wrapped in.

'Open the bundles lads,' said Tarlich.

The brothers knelt down and began to untie the bundles. Seamas went for the long one and Seoras took the box-shaped parcel. The strings were tied tight and he had difficulty loosening them. Seamas was having more success and Seoras could see from the corner of his eye that he had already unveiled the head of a large battle axe. The metal was dull from having been stored in the oil cloth that had been used to preserve it. Seamas stroked the axe with glittering eyes and ran his fingers along the edge of the blade and along the pike.

Seoras hadn't realised that he had stopped what he was doing to stare in awe at the lethal axe that his brother had unwrapped.

'Open the parcel, Seoras,' his father spoke gently to him.

His hands trembled as he loosened the knots. He could feel the greasiness of the oil on his fingers and he could sense the cold of the weapon beneath, almost as if it had an aura that pulsed with the coldness of the earth where it had been entombed. He had no idea how long these things had been in that hideaway but he had certainly never seen them in his lifetime.

At last the knots came away beneath his fumbling fingers and he peeled back the cloth to reveal a wooden box. He turned it around so that the small brass catch was facing him. He was vaguely aware that Seamas had now stopped his worship of the battle-axe to see what else would be unveiled. Seoras couldn't remember ever feeling so nervous. This surpassed diving into the river and playing his fiddle at Donchad's wedding.

Slowly he opened the lid. When he saw what was inside it suddenly dawned on him how close all this had been. Not just for the past few weeks but for longer than he had been alive - and probably longer than his father had been alive. He had grown up living in a croft in a beautiful glen. He was surrounded by his family and he was related in some way to nearly everyone on the croft. They were close knit and they had shared their lives, their work and their culture, not just in his lifetime, but longer than anyone knew. They passed on their culture from generation to generation through their craft, their music and song and through tales told by the old to the young. They had lived from the land around them which had provided them with building materials for shelter and clothes for warmth and fresh water. A variety of food came from the soil that was capable of yielding crops and sustaining livestock. They had fuel for heating and cooking and even the raw ingredients needed for distilling and brewing. And for as long as he could remember, apart from the odd land dispute or accusation of cattle theft, they had been at peace in the glen.

Their country hadn't always been peaceful though. Seoras and the other grandchildren had learned their history from their grandfather. He had handed it down to them on many long winter nights as they had sat huddled in the warm glow of the hearth.

Wrapped up in tales of mythological creatures and beings, of spirits and of magical happenings, were tales of full-scale battles between clans, of robbery, arson and murder. Seoras also knew from experience that life on the croft was not always easy. They had to work hard to take full advantage of the land and they rarely had the opportunity to rest. Nature could be cruel to them. Sometimes she would send winter along early, send it hard, and leave it there to stretch the endurance of the people to the extreme. A long bad winter would mean a shortage of food and fuel and its icy fingers would steal away the souls of the very young, the old and the sick.

In his own way he had come to understand that although life in the glen was hard this was where he belonged. He had no wish to change anything about his life. He was happy. He would work hard and relax and make music in the company of his kin. He would be taken care of by his family and he would look after them. One day he would find a wife and have children and grandchildren of his own and pass on everything that he knew to them, just as everything had been handed down to him, like invisible treasure. He hoped to live a long and happy life in this way as countless generations had done before. He would spend it soaking up the beauty of his home and of his people and their culture. That was life on the croft, in the glen and in the clan. Living it was the purpose of it.

That all changed when he saw the pistol in the box. That all changed when he saw the flask of gun powder. Realisation sank slowly into him when he saw the bag of lead shot.

They had never been crofters and he had never been a crofter's son. The crofting had only been there to keep them occupied until their true vocation came calling. They were, and they had always been, soldiers. Seoras and most of the others of his generation had gone through a large part of their lives blissfully ignorant to the fact that they were soldiers who had simply been stood down awaiting a change in circumstances and politics and for those with power to decide that the time to mobilise had come.

The time had come.

'Pick it up Seoras,' Tarlich urged gently.

He grasped the butt in his right hand and rested the barrel across the palm of his left. He felt its weight and felt the dead cold of its aura seeping into his hands and spreading up his fore arms as if they were conduits to his soul. He wanted to hurl it away.

'Your grandfather . . . acquired it at Sheriffmuir thirty years ago. We've had to be careful, the old man and I, because weapons are outlawed, but every summer we take it up into the forest and give it a go. It still works as if it was made yesterday. We've even stalked deer wi it. It's not brilliant 'cause ye have tae get quite close, but we've managed tae drop a couple over the years.'

'Can we have a go?' Seamas asked eagerly.

'Aye, I'll be showin ye how tae use it in case ye need tae.' He nodded towards the third bundle. 'Ye've still got one tae open.'

Seamas unrolled the carpenter's tool kit and inside were three long bladed dirks and two short *sgean dhus*, each stored in separate pouches. Tarlich unwrapped the bundle that rested across his knees, revealing two short bladed swords.

'Apart from the pistol, these weapons have been in the family for a long, long time. The axe especially. Your grandfather's grandfather told him that it was won in a battle against the Norsemen hundreds of years ago. They were made to last forever. There are others hidden over at Donchad's that the old man is showin him right now and there's more at yer Uncle Ailen's.'

Seamas stood up and hefted the axe, feeling the weight of it. 'Are ye goin tae train us Da?'

'This very afternoon lads, we'll all be goin tae a clearin in the wood to do a wee bit o trainin.'

The band of men that set off for the clearing consisted of Seoras' grandfather Donald, Tarlich and his three sons, his uncle Ailen and his two sons, Ailig and Euan. They made their way along the path and through the woods that Seoras had taken on the morning of Donchad's wedding and about halfway along it the three elder men left the track and began to make their way through the undergrowth. Seoras could see no sign of a trail but they all seemed to know where they were going. The five grandsons followed behind for about quarter of an hour before they came to a halt in a large clearing. There was a small shelter near to where they stood made from branches and packed with fern. It was barely visible in the shadows at the edge of the clearing and a fresh layer of foliage would have made it impossible to detect unless you were standing on top of it. Faint traces of camp fires could be made out a few feet in front of it. There in the clearing, under the watchful eye of Donald, his sons and grandsons trained.

Time was short for them so they concentrated on the basics. They were shown how to hold and wield the various weapons to gain the most effect. They were taught the classic parry with the shielded left arm and upward stab with the claymore or dirk in the right. They practised the fearful highland charge using saplings as the standing enemy which they slashed and stabbed and hacked. Finally they were taught how to load and discharge their grandfather's old flintlock pistol, each firing once into the trunk of a Douglas fir.

Donald decided that it was time to go back only when the clearing grew gloomy and visibility became poor. Seoras could hardly believe it when dusk had come upon them. The day had flown by. As they made their way back to the croft he realised that he was starving and that the air had turned chilly.

They all went back to Tarlich's where Mairi was waiting with Ailen's wife Anna and Donchad's wife

Catriona. They had prepared a stew which was brimming with meat and vegetables and had boiled some new potatoes and baked oat cakes. The smell made Seoras' stomach growl as he entered the cottage.

The men ate quickly and washed down their food with ale. When they had finished Seoras was bloated from the food and the drink and couldn't remember the last time that he had eaten so well. They sat around the peat hearth relaxing and digesting - warm, contented and happy.

His mother, aunt and sister-in-law were making jackets from a pile of rabbit furs. The rabbits had been snared by Donald in the spring and the skins had been cured and stretched and were now supple and strong. The women sang softly while they worked.

Donald got up to stretch his tired legs. The hike up to the clearing and back had been hard going for him and he could feel the pain burning in his hips and the small of his back. He reached up to a shelf and brought down his flask of whisky. He poured himself a decent sized dram before offering the others. Tarlich, Ailen and their wives each took one and the others stuck to ale.

As Seoras watched his grandfather settle back into his chair his mind drifted back to what he had been thinking about that morning as they had unveiled the weapons that were hidden at the base of the wall. He watched his grandfather as he looked around the room studying his sons and grandsons. He looked at the old mans eyes and felt more than ever that they were soldiers waiting to be called up.

Usually at a family get together like this the place would be alive with laughter and singing and bubbling over with conversation and debate and dancing in the enclosed space of the room. Tonight was a sombre occasion and they sat quietly sipping their drinks while they listened to the women sing.

'Do ye think he'll be here tonight?' Mairi asked the question to no one in particular.

The tacksman for the surrounding glens was David MacLachlan. He was a cousin of the chief who let his land to David and he in turn sub-let it to the clansmen. They paid for the rent with the crops that they produced, animals that they raised and hunted, fish they caught and anything else of value that they could get from the land. The tacksman would sell most of this at market and keep his own share and then pay the chief in cash and in kind. In peacetime he acted as landlord and local magistrate. He would resolve disputes between clan members and punish those who were seen to be in the wrong. For more serious crimes such as severe assault or murder he would seek the assistance of the chief. The clan lived by their own code of ethics and only answered to lowland law if they were captured in the lowlands and taken to court there.

In times of conflict the tacksman's tenants would become his fighting unit and he would be their captain. In the surrounding glens the tacksman could muster close to two hundred fighting men. Those who refused to fight had their homes burned, their possessions taken away and were driven off the land of the clan and left to fend for themselves in the mountains. No other clan would be willing to take in such refugees.

'They say he's riding through the glen today,' said Anna.

'Then he'll likely be here tonight,' Ailen said into his drink.

The room lapsed into silence as they all thought about the approach of the tacksman. The women had stopped singing and had put down their work. Everyone looked at nothing in particular, feeling awkward in the silence and not knowing what to say.

'Tell us about the last rebellion, Granda,' Seamas said at last.

'I don't think that your grandfather wants to talk about that right now, Seamas,' said Mairi.

'It's okay, I think that it's appropriate that I should speak about that for a wee while tonight. It'll maybe help in some way.' He looked around the room and saw that he had everyone's attention. 'In many ways it started in the same way as it has this time. It was the Earl of Mar who raised the standard then and he proclaimed James as King. That was in the August and there were well over ten thousand o us. We rallied in Aberdeenshire and within the month we had marched tae and taken Perth without much action. We stayed there for a while but I don't know why. It seemed tae us that we were wastin time and that, in the end, turned out to be the case. Part of our army marched soothwards tae make contact wi the Jacobites in the Borders - the rest o us waited.

'The Government had an army in Stirling under the Duke o Argyle and the news reached us that he had received reinforcements and was headin for us. We had no choice but to fight them. I remember the afternoon that we came in sight o them, at Sherrifmuir. A whole sea of *saighdearan dearg* is what I saw,' Donald said recalling the red coated soldiers, 'and I have tae admit that I was scared. The MacLachlans and the MacDonalds charged first towards their left hand side - we had our own quarrel tae settle wi the Campbells. We broke intae the enemy lines and we seemed tae be daein a lot o damage but then a thick mist came doon an it was difficult for us tae see anythin. Oot o that mist came the Government cavalry, chargin' straight for us. We held our ground for a wee while but men were fallin all around and we were forced tae fall back. It was then that I found the pistol that ye were practisin wi in the clearin. I found it on a craven Campbell bastard in a red-coat an' I decided that he had nae mair use for it.'

He raised his palm to Mairi and smiled apologetically.

'Sorry lass, but when I think o those traitors sidin wi the English it just makes my blood boil.' Donald continued his story without pausing or looking embarrassed, 'Anyway, by the time night came we knew that we had done a lot o damage tae them, but we were also in a bad way oursel's. Naebody knew if we had won the battle or no and our leaders decided that we should go back tae Perth.'

While he listened to his grandfather's account of the last rebellion, Seoras couldn't help thinking that it hadn't been well planned. He hoped things wouldn't go the same way this time.

'While we were there, we heard more bad news. The Jacobites who were in the Borders had invaded England but had been surrounded by armies of Government troops and had been forced tae surrender, and on top o that, Argyle had received even more reinforcements in Stirling. The only good news was that King James himsel had reached us fae France.'

'Did ye get tae see him, Granda?,' asked Seamas.

'Aye, he went among us, an he was a fine lookin man. A king and no mistake.' He then sighed and took a sip of whisky. 'But it was all too late. The government troops had become far too strong for us, so the King and Mar had tae escape back tae France and we were told tae make our own way hame. We had oor chance tae go for the jugular at Sherrifmuir, but we didna take it. I hope we dinna make the make a repeat o the mistake again if we're presented wi the wi a similar opportunity again.'

'What happened after that Granda?' Seamas had been on the edge of his seat, and now looked deflated at the anti-climax of it. He looked as if he was hoping for a last piece of action in the narrative.

'After that, the army arrested anyone they suspected of taking part in the uprisin. Some of the leaders were executed an the rest were sent tae America. The government passed a law sayin that we had tae give up oor weapons so we handed in our rubbish. As ye know, we hid the decent stuff for when we would need it again.' He finished his whisky and set down his glass. 'I just didnae think it would be so long.

'Now,' he said pointing to Seoras' fiddle on the shelf, 'that's enough talk. How about a wee tune tae cheer us up lad. I think that I'll join ye as well,' he said taking a penny whistle from his breast pocket.

Seoras took down his fiddle and stood with one foot on his chair, the fiddle under his chin and the bow resting on the strings ready to play.

'You start - gie us somethin tae get the feet tappin,' Donald cried out.

Seoras began to play one of his favourite tunes, one that always managed to cheer him up, and Donald joined in with the whistle. The rest of the family began to clap in time and then Tarlich leapt up and pulled Mairi from her chair and spun her around the room. The room became filled with laughter and for a moment they forgot about the tacksman.

Then Tarlich stopped and called for quiet.

They all listened. They could hear the thud of hooves approaching the cottage. Tarlich opened to the door and stood in the light that spilled out into the night.

'Good evenin, Tarlich,' called David MacLachlan as he pulled up with two of his men. One of them carried the fiery cross, now blackened and smouldering, orange flecks glowing and floating into the sky when the breeze lifted.

'Evenin, David. We've been expectin ye.'

The Tacksman swung off his horse and strode over to Tarlich. His men remained mounted.

'Ye'll know what I'm here for then.'

'Aye, I can see yer man there wi the blackened cross. Do ye want tae come into the warm for a while?'

'No, ye're okay. We have tae get on so I'll make it short. I don't know what rumours ye've heard, but this is the official version. Prince Charles Edward Stuart raised the standard of King James at Glenfinnan two days ago, and there was a big show of support from the clans. The MacDonalds and the Camerons are with him and that's given a lot of the smaller clans the courage tae join. The Chief has decided that we'll join the Prince's army as it marches south. Things are lookin good this time. We're promised two ship loads of men and arms from France that'll also be joinin us shortly. All fit men will be goin Tarlich and that includes your and Ailen's youngest.'

'Aye David, I thought that would be the case.'

'Ye have yer weapons ready?'

'They've always been ready.'

'Good. Stronachlachar by noon tomorrow. I don't think I need tae remind ye of the consequences of failin' tae appear.'

Tarlich's cheeks flushed. 'No, ye don't. There's no need for yer threats here. We'll be there - and willin.' Donald and Ailen then came to the door and stood on either side of Tarlich.

'Aye, there's no need for threats,' Ailen said, supporting his brother.

'Good,' the tacksman said while remounting his horse. 'I'll see ye there then. Not you though Donald, ye'll be sittin this one out. I hope ye're keepin well by the way.'

'Just fine thanks, David,' replied the old man.

The three horsemen then turned and rode away in the direction of the next croft.

'Cheeky wee shit,' Donald said into the night breeze.

The men went back inside where Mairi stood wringing her hands. A tear rolled down Catriona's cheek.

'Everyone get themselves a dram,' said Tarlich. They all stood around looking at each other, wondering what he meant. 'Quickly,' he commanded, 'get yoursel's a drink.' He then went out of the door and took in the bucket of water. He placed it on the floor and waited till everyone had a drink in hand.

'Now, what's happened has happened and there's no gettin away from it. This is somethin that we must do. Ye heard what the tacksman said - this time we've got help. We'll march tae Edinburgh and clear out whatever government troops are there in no time. Then James will be King of Scotland again and we can come home. There's no need for grief or tears, okay Catriona.'

Catriona nodded, trying to smile.

'Don't you worry aboot us,' Mairi put an arm around Catriona's shoulder and dabbed at her tears with a handkerchief. We'll look after the croft, nae bother. Just you make sure you all get back tae it in one piece.'

'Agreed,' Tarlich smile and continued. So instead of being down hearted let's drink a toast to success.' He raised his glass over the bucket of water.

'Cuidich 'n Righ.'

The others followed his toast, raising their drinks over the bucket, saluting King James over the water in France.

'And may God grant us a speedy return to our homes.' He sank his whisky and waited for the others. He then nodded to his father.

'Come on Seoras,' said Donald slapping his back and grinning. 'Let's get on wi' the entertainment.'

Seoras took a large draught of ale, put his fiddle under his chin and began to play. They sang and danced late into the night, trying to chase the morning away.
*

Seoras couldn't sleep. He lay on his back staring into the darkness wondering what lay ahead of them. Then from the darkness came a vision. At first he saw only thick smoke swirling in the night. It cleared slightly and he could see a man with his back to him but it was difficult for him to make out who it was. Someone else crouched beside him, cradling the head of a third person lying on the ground. The man who had been standing also crouched and then the smoke began to obscure his view again, hurting his throat and eyes. Tears welled in his eyes and he began to cough violently. He became aware of others all around him in the field. There was noise and then there was quiet. There was smoke and then there was blackness and he continued to stare into it for what seemed like an eternity.

He was not sure whether he had slept at all when he eventually heard his father rising. He got up and dressed quickly in the darkness not wanting to waste a moment of his last morning at home.

His mother had already made breakfast but he found it hard to force anything past the lump in his throat. The excitement and anticipation seemed to have deserted him.

As light began to show over the mountains it was time for them to leave. The three sons hugged their mother and grandfather in turn. Mairi's voice cracked and tears welled as she kissed them goodbye. Catriona wept as she embraced Donchad. Donald kept a smile on his face and wished them luck, adding that such fine looking young men would never need it. Then they turned and headed slowly up the drovers road while Tarlich said his goodbyes. He caught up with his sons and they were joined by Ailen and his sons. They waved till their homes were out of sight. At the ford they met with the other men from the croft and at the head of the glen, on the far side of Loch Shirra they rallied with the rest of the clan. Then they began the long hike to

Stronachlachar in earnest. Along the way they were joined by more and more clansmen headed in the same direction and before long they swelled into a large body of men marching east. When they marched into Stronachlachar an hour before noon they made up the numbers of the Clan MacLachlan to over two hundred.

Seoras couldn't believe that there were so many men in the clan to which he belonged. He stayed close by his father who talked with friends that he hadn't seen for a long time. He saw David MacLachlan going amongst his men making sure that they had all turned up and that no one had dared to stay away. Talk was aflame with the rebellion. There was a rumour that there had already been some action in the Coriarick Pass. A battalion of red-coats had been sent from Edinburgh to slow down their advance but a section of the Prince's army had ambushed them and defeated them in minutes.

Noon passed and they waited for stragglers to turn up before the Chief and his officers rode to their head. After taking what little rest they could they began the march to join up with rest of the Jacobite army.

On the evening of the first days march they caught up with the main body of the army on the banks of the River Forth, west of Stirling. There, as part of the Jacobite army, they camped for the night. While there they were briefed by their tacksman who had now become their captain. David MacLachlan informed them that the Government troops in Scotland, commanded by Sir John Cope, had headed north to Inverness. The route to Edinburgh was clear and the Jacobites would begin the march there in the morning.

Five

They sent the seer to her again.

She slept, but as he approached she opened her eyes and sat up. She was not alarmed by his presence. In fact she seemed happy to see him. She asked him his name but he only beckoned for her to follow. She swung her long legs from the bed and stood. She wore only a white cotton nightshirt with the hem riding high on her thigh and she did not pause to dress before following him.

He stepped from her bedroom door onto the moor and barefoot she traced his steps. He strode towards the place that he had to take her to and she trailed along behind him, asking him where they were, where they were going. He remained silent. She should know this place because it was where she had first seen him. He reached the spot and then turned to face her.

They could see that she was confused standing there in the middle of the moor but they had no better way of communicating with her. They had waited a long time to convey any information to her at all. They were grateful that, for now, she was not afraid. The sun was shining on her face and a slight breeze tugged at her dark hair. They had never seen features such as hers while they were on earth. She was so alien to them, but so beautiful. Her face was full of warmth and her oval eyes concerned and caring. Her honey-golden skin was smooth and glowing in the rays of the sun.

They looked through his eyes to the ground by his feet. She followed his gaze and watched as a small patch of turf began to vibrate. They saw her bare feet take a step backwards and he looked up at her.

'Tha e ceart gu leor,' *the seer reassured her, sensing her alarm.*

He looked at the ground and the turf began to churn, slowly at first and then furiously. Soil was thrown up as if something was tunnelling up from below. They could see the shape of the pistol emerging through the loosened soil. The movement stopped and the seer knelt on one knee to pick it up. It was rusted and rotten with age but as he gently knocked the last of the dirt from it, blue light began to crackle around his hands. The rust began to dematerialise and the rotten parts of the pistol began to strengthen and rebuild.

He held the pistol across the palms of both hands, showing it to her.

'He needs this,' *he told her.*

Before she could answer he put his finger to his lips and cocked his head.

They felt the presence of another and became afraid - more for her safety than their own. They could not escape - but she must. They had waited so long for her.

'There's more, but you must go now. He knows you are here.' *They could hear the growling and the snarling in the distance and their fear accelerated. Far away they could hear the tortured screaming begin. Pain emerged to rake through them.*

'YOU MUST GO NOW!' *Through him they screamed the words at her. They saw the startled terror in her face and she stumbled back a few paces before falling. Then they lost her as they disseminated and exploded in all directions looking for escape and shelter, undaunted by the futility of their action,*

Then came the torture.
Then came the pain.
Then came the demon.

Inverness, Scotland, April 13th 2146

As Namah lay thinking about getting up she became aware that he was in close proximity. She sat up to see him standing at the foot of her bed. She was slightly surprised, but completely unafraid. He had never been this close before. The previous times she had seen him he had been at a distance and he had been on the moor.

The first time had been fleeting and she wasn't sure whether she had seen him at all. She had glimpsed him through the tall birch trees that bordered most of the eastern side of the moor and had ran to the view-point to get a better look. She had leant on the rail scouring the expanse of the open land searching for him but he was nowhere to be seen.

The next time, two days ago, he had been closer. It was early morning and she was locking up the visitor centre to go home when she saw him by the twenty foot memorial cairn. She ran down the path to the cairn and got there in time to see him moving up along the path towards the Jacobite frontline. He did not glide along like a ghost as she had expected him to but had appeared as real as any man touring the battle site. He turned right along the Jacobite line and became hidden from view again behind trees and bushes. She sprinted to catch up with him but on turning the corner he had vanished again. She had searched the undergrowth for a short while but could find no trace of him.

The next time that she had seen him had been last morning. Exactly the same thing happened as had occurred the previous morning except this time when she rounded the corner he was standing facing her about twenty yards down the path. She was not afraid. She had sensed goodness coming from him as well as something else. As she stood there and faced him her heart had pounded with excitement. She did not need to feel the sadness that filled him because it was imprinted on his face. She did feel it though and it reached out and seized her heart. She felt foolish at having momentarily forgotten what had happened in this place.

She was about to ask him his name when he turned and walked off the path down the battlefield towards the Government lines. He became once more obscured behind the undergrowth. She went to the point where he had left the path and saw the familiar plaque telling visitors that this was the point where the MacLachlans and MacLeans had formed up for battle. Again she left the path for the moor and trailed his steps and looked for a clue that he existed. Again she had been unable to find him.

Now, it seemed, it was he who had found her, having come from the moor to her home in Inverness. She sat in her bed examining him and saw that he was soaking wet. Water dripped from his plaid onto the floor at the foot of her bed. He was shivering and she could hear his teeth chattering.

'What's yer name?'

The Highlander didn't answer her but gestured with his hand for her to follow him. Obeying, she swung her legs out from under the covers and stood by her bed. He began to turn and walk out of her bedroom. She thought about putting some clothes on over her night shirt but the Highlander departed into the hall and she hurried after him and she stepped through the door into the hall and the texture beneath her feet changed from the softness of the carpet to the roughness of heather. Her breath caught in her throat as she realised that she was walking on an open moor. She glanced behind her looking for the security of her bedroom but saw only the expanse of the moor. It stretched to the horizon on all sides like a vast North American prairie. There were no mountains or forests in the distance, only moorland and sky. She stood and felt the warm sun shining down on her and she raised her hands to the clear blue sky. The Highlander was walking away from her. She called out to him.

'Where are we? Where are we going?'

This time she spoke in Gaelic but he still didn't answer and kept striding ahead. She hurried after him and winced as the coarse heather scratched at her feet. She picked her way along placing her feet on soft patches of turf and hearing the ground squelch in places where it was boggy and feeling the cold wetness on her bare soles. She followed him, trying to keep up with him while selecting a less grievous path through the heather and gorse. He came to a halt and turned to face her. She saw that he was no longer wet and that the sorrowful expression had been replaced by one of urgency.

He looked down at his feet and she followed his gaze, puzzled. She stepped back in shock when she saw a patch of turf begin to shake between them.

'It's okay,' he said to her in Gaelic.

She felt calmed by his voice, as if his words were a narcotic and they both continued to watch the ground. Soil began to be thrown up and the green turf disappeared as the ground churned more quickly, as if an animal was frantically burrowing its way towards daylight. The earth became finer the more it was agitated and she could see a shape beginning to emerge. As it pushed its way up she could see the outline of a pistol. Finally the earth became still and she could see an old flintlock lying on the surface. She recognised it as a late seventeenth century weapon although it was badly rusted and rotted with age. There were many similar on show in the visitor centre, but in far better condition. This one looked as if it would disintegrate if it were touched.

The Highlander went down on one knee and gently picked it up, tapping the remaining soil from it.

As he did so she was amazed to see electric blue light swim around his hands. After a moment the light subsided and she could see that instead of a corroded, fragile weapon, he was holding a pistol that looked as if it had been made yesterday. He rested it across the palms of both hands and held it out, offering it to her.

'He needs this,' he said without looking up.

She thought about taking the pistol from him but instead waited for him to tell her who *he* was.

He kept his eyes on the pistol. 'There's more but you must go now.'

She became aware that dark clouds were racing across the sky. The sun was sinking quickly towards the horizon as if time had accelerated. Thunder grumbled across the open moor and the Highlander looked up at her in the overcast light. Where his eyes had been there were now two empty sockets swirling with black and grey smoke. He spoke, but it wasn't his voice.

'YOU MUST GO NOW!'

It was the enunciation of many souls screaming at her. It was a sound that she had heard on the wind many times before but now it was blasted into her face like a detonation. Terror seized her by the throat and she stumbled backwards and fell to the ground gagging for breath. The sun had nearly vanished and the slight breeze had grown into a gale laden with rain which whipped into her face and body and soaked her in seconds.

As she sat there stunned the Highlander vanished into the wind and rain like vapour. The sun sank below the horizon and she was plunged into darkness. In the distance she could hear the sound of screaming carried by the freezing wind which beat against her in gusts. She could also make out the barking and howling of large dogs.

She got to her feet and began to run in the opposite direction and the wind at her back propelled the awful sounds past her ears. The Highlander had instructed her to go but she had no idea where he had in mind for her to go. There was nowhere *to* go. He had taken her to this place and she had no concept of how to get back home. She kept running through the darkness, her feet being scratched by the heather and her unprotected legs torn by the gorse bushes that she stumbled into. She floundered on managing to remain upright and oblivious to the damage being done to the skin of her legs by the scrub. She could hear the snapping and snarling of the dogs growing louder and the growling was deep and threatening and somehow intelligent. She ran blindly into the darkness and although her lungs felt as though they would burst and a stitch was burning in her side like a ball of phosphorous she succeeded in increasing her speed.

Then, as she began to hear the thud of running hooves growing close, her left foot twisted on a clump of turf. She kept her balance and then went over her right foot as she advanced into a hollow. She yelped in surprised agony as the ligaments in her foot tore. She tumbled, splashing face first into the marshy wetness of the rain-drenched moor. She took a mouthful of peaty water as her head went completely under. She managed to flip onto her back, propping herself up on her elbows to keep her upper body out of the numbing water. She had expected the beasts, whatever they were, to be upon her ripping her to pieces in an instant. Nothing came charging out of the darkness.

She could hear blood pounding in her ears, she could hear her own breath rasping in the cold air, she could hear rain splattering in the pool in which she lay. But she could hear no dogs, no wolves, no monsters.

She lay on her back in the pool listening to the darkness around her. Her knees were apart and sticking out of the water and her upper torso from the middle of her rib cage was also above the surface. Her long, black hair hung heavily around her face and shoulders. Her nightshirt, which had hiked up around her waist, clung to her skin and showed her breasts and nipples, erect from the cold. She shivered and her teeth clattered involuntarily. The gale had abated and the rain was also subsiding. Then she sensed movement.

She held her breath and beyond the hammering of her own heart she could hear panting. Not the panting of a dog, but heavy lecherous panting. An appalling stench filled her nostrils and she began to gag. Then, against the purple-blackness of the sky she could make out the vague outline of a large man standing over her at the edge of the pool. Her stomach turned and she could feel vomit rising up her gullet as she realised that he was masturbating.

He began to laugh. Louder and louder. A laugh that she had never dreamt could exist on earth. An inhuman laugh that sent ice coursing through her veins.

Namah sat up and leaned over to the side and spewed onto her bedroom floor. The bile burned her throat and the back of her nostrils. When she regained her breath she wiped her mouth on the back of her hand and collapsed back against her pillows. Her head felt numb and cold and she began to shiver. The sheet knotted around her was soaking. She lay shivering in her sweat but unable to move through exhaustion. She tried to summon the strength to get out of bed but the nightmare had taken everything out of her. Her limbs were pinned down under their own weight.

'What the fuck was that?' She whispered to the ceiling. The nightmare was still vivid in the safety of her bedroom and the smell of the moor was still in her nostrils. She didn't even have to remember the dream, the sequence of events within it or the roles played by those who were in it, because it was as real to her as if the whole event had just actually occurred.

Eventually she found the energy to roll out of bed, yeuching under her breath as she stepped over the patch of vomit. When she tried to put weight on her right foot she yelped in agony and collapsed onto her knees by the side of her bed. She raised up her leg to examine her injury. She saw that her ankle was swollen and beginning to discolour and more alarmingly that her leg was covered in scratches. She lowered her foot cautiously back to the carpet and let out a long sigh.

How do you injure yourself in a dream?

She steadied herself on the corner of her bed being careful not to put any weight on her twisted foot. It was then that she noticed the dark wet patch on the carpet at the end of her bed where the Highlander had been standing in her dream. She remembered how he had been soaking at that point. Dripping wet.

It wasn't a dream. He was here.

She reached out to touch the carpet to confirm that the wet area existed and wasn't a trick of the light.

'Yeowch!' She pulled her hand back from the freezing carpet. She stuck her fingers in her mouth, running her tongue rapidly back and forth along their tips to warm them. The feeling began returned to the tips of her fingers but she hardly noticed. Instead she watched wide-eyed as the dark patch began to evaporate. A thick mist like freezing carbon dioxide rose from the carpet and disappeared into the air about six inches from the floor. The dark area was now gone and she confidently put her hand where it had been and was not at all surprised to find that it was completely dry.

'This is too fuckin much.'

She hoisted herself onto her left foot and hopped to the door where she steadied herself against the wall. She turned around and yanked the sheet and covers off her bed and balled them up and stuck them under one arm. Then, using the wall for support, she made her way to the kitchen where she stuffed her bedding into the washer. She stripped off her nightshirt and crammed it in as well. She closed the door and stood back to watch as the machine analysed the contents, the types of stains and dirt - *I'm surprised it doesn't call me a dirty bitch*, she thought - and selected the most appropriate cycle. While the machine began to wash she made her way along the walls to the shower room. She spoke some more instructions and began to shower.

She studied herself washing in a full-length mirror across from the shower. She felt tired and shaken. She soaped her jet-black hair and the honey skin she had inherited from her Chinese grandmother.

She rinsed the soap bubbles from her body and dried. The warm, blowing air seemed to ease the throbbing in her foot and she stepped carefully out of the shower. She winced as she put too much pressure on her injury and limped back to her bedroom to dress. She decided that she would have to give her father a call to let him know that she would be late opening the visitor centre.

She thought about what to wear and tried to remember what kind of remedies there were for sprained ankles in her books (her shelves were full of books on herbal remedies and homeopathic medicine), and all the while she endeavoured to forget the events of the early evening. She picked out a battered old notebook her grandmother had given her before she had died and selected a simple recipe for a compress for sprains. She peeled a leaf from a fresh cabbage in her vegetable basket and sprinkled it with mustard powder. She ran a rolling pin over this to bruise and soften the leaf and then placed it on a bandage and wrapped it around her foot. She knew people who would scoff at this, but she had faith. Her grandmother's remedies always worked.

*

Sinclair lay on his bunk with Lombard's book trying to get to grips with the Scottish Reformation. He found himself having to read and re-read sections so that it would sink in. If this book was concise, he dreaded to think what a more in depth book would be like. His head was spinning with Catholics and Protestants, Episcopalians and Presbyterians, Covenanters and Independents, Royalists and Parliamentarians. He could barely believe that a country could be so split and torn.

His phone rang and he jumped. He had forgotten that he had turned it back on to look up a definition. It was Abbie.

'Hello,' he said cautiously.

'Where the fuck are you?' Abbie's voice boomed at him.

Shit, he thought sitting up straight and clearing his throat. The sound of her voice had startled him, as though he'd put something in the oven and forgotten about it until he smelt the smoke coming from the kitchen. Not one thought of her had entered his head since he'd left the message for her at the Hampden Airbus station on the way to Dunedin. He tried to sound unruffled. 'Well, you obviously know where I am.'

'Yeah, I know you're on a fucking ship headed for Europe, but that's no thanks to you. So tell me, what work do you have to do so urgently?' Sinclair could hear her voice quivering with rage and he was glad that there were several hundred miles between them.

'You've spoken to Lombard.'

'The guy from the Uni, eventually, yeah. After I'd phoned the school to find out where the fuck you were. They couldn't believe that you hadn't told me that you'd left the country. I felt so small. They gave me Lombard's number and all that he would tell me was that you'd gone to Scotland to do some work. What the fuck are you playing at Sinclair?'

'I'm sorry, I had to leave straight away. I have to go and help a friend. I-'

'What friend!?' Abbie snarled.

'Look Abbie, I know that this sounds unfair, but I can't really tell you anything else just now-'

'And how are you paying for this trip of yours?'

'With my savings,' he sighed.

'So,' she said adopting a patronising tone that Sinclair didn't care for a great deal, 'Let me get this right . . . something happens out of the blue that requires you to piss off to Europe at the drop of a hat, spending your savings on a ticket, and not only can you not tell me *why* your going, but you can't even tell me that you're going in the first fucking place!'

He could understand why she was upset and he knew that she didn't deserve the treatment that he had given her, but all the same he wanted this conversation to end. 'I'm sorry, I was going to call you when-'

'When you were on the other side of the world!' Sinclair could hear her sobbing. 'Well you don't need to bother now. As far as I'm concerned you can fucking stay in Scotland with your fucking friend.' Her sharp, hate-filled voice was then cut off.

He sat on the edge of his bed with his face in his hands feeling guilty and retched. He couldn't believe that he hadn't at least called her but the truth was that she had never even entered his head. He decided to go to the bar. He picked up his book and left the cabin.

When he got there he found that the bar was in the process of closing down for the day but the barman allowed him to take three cartons of beer. He wedged his book under his arm and carried them up onto the main deck.

An immense ceiling of polarised glass and solar panelling covered the main deck. It was around fifty feet high in the centre and sloped down to deck level. It was still dark outside so looking upward he could only see his own head and shoulders reflected back at him from the deck of the ship. Over to the starboard side of the ship he could see the slight glow of red as the sun began to rise in the east.

He sat at one of the tables scattered around the expansive deck and tore the top from one of his beers and sank half of it in one go, enjoying the feel of the cool liquid spilling into him. He watched as the dim redness on the starboard side grew a little brighter as the sun tried to penetrate the protective dome of the ship and he thought of Abbie. He thought of her beautiful looks and pale skin. He thought of her sharp tongue.

He opened his second beer and he opened his book where he had marked it and continued to read about the Reformation under James V.

By the time he had completed that chapter and Mary Queen of Scots had taken over the burden of sovereignty he had forgotten about Abbie's call. By the time that he had read about Queen Mary's unfortunate life and execution he had forgotten about Abbie's beauty and by the time that his eye-lids grew heavy and the red glare of the sun had moved half way up the solar panelled dome of the ship - he had forgotten Abbie altogether. As Sinclair shuffled below decks to his cabin to get some sleep the ship slipped quietly north propelled by engines which drew their power from the hot, burning sun that glowered down on the world.

When he reached New York he had to change vessels. The new ship was smaller than the previous but retained the same rugby ball shape. As he began his eastward journey across the Atlantic, Sinclair was onto the third from last chapter of Lombard's book - The Nineteenth Century. Every now and then he would put the book down and think about it, sorting everything out in his mind. He didn't know why but it seemed important to him to have it all in the correct context. He had paid particular attention to the chapter on the Jacobite Rebellion of 1745, trying hard to commit the events and the consequences to memory. Reading about the aftermath and the following clearances had shocked him.

As he lay there he thought about his meetings with the Highlander. They now seemed so long ago - if they had ever happened at all. And Abbie's words came back to him: *What the fuck are you playing at Sinclair?*

He couldn't answer the question.

Six

<u>Prestonpans, Scotland, September 21st 1745</u>

Seoras was near the rear of the Jacobite columns that made their way through the bog in the hour before dawn. He followed the men to his front as they quickly and quietly wound their way through the marshy ground. They kept silent and used hand signals to communicate and they were careful to keep blades and weapons from clanking together. They had been filing through for some time when he heard a shout go up from the front. Then there was yelling and screaming, the explosion of pistols being discharged and the clash of steel. The men around him began to break into a run and stumbled into each other on the rough terrain, eager to get forward but packed together on the path through the marsh. Seoras ran with them with his targe up in front of him and his sword held tightly in his right hand.

The Jacobites reached the edge of the marsh where they fanned out and attacked everything in sight. The scenes of carnage that had been caused so quickly and violently halted Seoras. All around men in red coats littered the ground - maimed, disembowelled and dismembered. Then the rush of the charge carried him onward. Around him men hacked at enemy soldiers who had, by some miracle, been missed by the initial charge. Seoras ran forward with the group and witnessed the annihilation of the government troops around him.

He rounded an artillery gun which was rendered impotent in the close quarter charge of the Highlanders and there he came face to face with a red-coat. His musket was held out in front of him with the bayonet fixed and his terrified eyes locked with Seoras'. He jabbed at Seoras but Seoras knocked the musket away with his targe and raised his sword high above his head. The redcoat let out a high shriek that drilled into Seoras' ears before dropping to his knees and uselessly shielding his head with his arms. Seoras stood before him with his sword still raised but unable to bring it down on the frightened soldier. Then there was movement to his right and from the corner of his eye he caught sight of a large axe beginning its arc of decent. It embedded itself deep in the redcoat's skull and forced his tri-corn into the mess of his broken head. The axe man placed his foot on the redcoat's shoulder and retrieved his weapon with a satisfied grunt before he ran on and left the redcoat to spray blood at Seoras.

Seoras remained there with his sword still held above his head and gaped at the wrecked body of the redcoat at his feet until he felt himself being tugged along by the arm.

'Come on boy,' his uncle shouted. They moved forward with the throng and in the distance they could see some cavalry penned in against a wall. The *saighdearan dearg* were being pulled from their horses as they tried in vain to find an escape route. Strung out along the coast they could make out the remnants of the government army retreating at speed.

The battle had lasted for less than fifteen minutes and in that time hundreds of redcoats had been felled and lay strewn around the battlefield.

The Jacobite army began to regroup as the leaders took stock of the victory and around the field the standards of the clans were raised. Seoras searched for the MacLachlan standard, his head spinning with the skirl of pipes as they played out the victory anthems of a dozen clans. He stumbled over the corpses and horribly maimed bodies of government troops, unable to pull his eyes from the mess. In patches of boggy ground, so much blood had drained from the dead and injured that it splashed up his shins and calves. Seoras began to panic that he would never be able to find his way off the field and that he would stumble through these corpses forever. His heart pounded in his chest and his wide eyes scoured the standards, frantically hunting for that of his clan, where he knew his father would be waiting for him, where he knew he would be secure. He quickened his pace and stood on tiptoe and jumped to see over the crowds of cheering men. He thought that he had searched the length of the field and turned back. Taking a different route, he began to run, becoming desperate, until he tripped and landed in his knees, his flailing hands landing and slipping in spilled entrails. He sat back on his haunches and looked at his upturned hands and began to weep. Then a pair of hands raised him to his feet.

'Ye're a'right, son. Ye're a'right,' His father pulled him into a strong embrace.

Seoras held his father tight while around them the clan cheered and sang.

The Jacobite Army ran most of the way back to Edinburgh, and once there they dispersed into the alehouses where their victory celebrations began in earnest.

They continued to carouse for the five weeks that they stayed in Edinburgh. The people of the city made their visitors welcome and comfortable, although this was chiefly because failure to accommodate them would result in compromising the safety of their homes and businesses rather than any feeling of loyalty or patriotism. To the lowland occupants, having their city full of barbarous Highlanders was not a situation that they relished. Edinburgh Castle, sitting high on the rock, remained in Government hands, and various attempts to capture it were unsuccessful.

The days were filled with collecting supplies from the surrounding country and preparing for the invasion of England.

Seoras and Seamas spent their free time exploring the streets of the city together. The inhabitants went about their daily routines as well as they could and so the bustle of everyday life continued. The brothers wandered around gaping at the sight of the buildings and the markets and found it hard to take everything in. The traders continued to sell their wares even though supplies were running low - no ships from London or Europe ventured into Leith Docks after the Jacobites had entered Edinburgh.

Apart from becoming aquatinted with the alien ways of lowland life they also got to know many of their fellow clansmen and men from all over the Highlands. There were a number of Irish and French who were also fighting for the Jacobite cause. The majority of these meetings took place in the alehouses dotted around the city.

Often the boys sat outside an alehouse and watched the men eagerly make their way in and eventually stagger their way out again. They watched the transformation from sober to inebriated, the change in character from quiet to loud to boisterous to melancholy. The public houses opened their doors and inhaled sober men from the street and exhaled drunks on breath that smelled of hops and spirit and they belched out music and singing and shouting from within their bellies. Their father had warned them against going into the alehouses. He had said that they were nothing but trouble and that they were to stay away but they held a strong attraction to the brothers.

Three weeks into their stay, the lure of the pubs became too much and they searched for a suitable bar that they could enter where they might not be recognised. Seoras carried his fiddle wrapped in a sack and slung over his back and hoped for the chance to play in front of a crowd. They selected a bar away from the markets and the High Street and waited outside and built up the courage together to enter. They stood side by side on the street and listened to the racket coming through the doors.

'We're as much part of the army as they are,' said Seamas again.

Seoras nodded.

'If we're old enough to fight, we're old enough to go into a bar and hae a rink like all the rest.'

'Aye.'

'Come on then.'

'Okay.'

Seamas shouldered Seoras. 'You first.'

Seoras elbowed him back. 'You're oldest.'

In front of them the doors burst open and a highland soldier lurched out, blinking in the daylight. He swayed there for a moment, trying to focus on the brothers.

'The fuck you pair o fannies standin there for?' Without waiting for an answer he swivelled awkwardly on one foot and began to stagger down the street.

The boys looked at one another and then walked through the doors.

Seamas led and once inside he did not pause - not wanting to attract attention - and made his way through the crowd. They reached the bar where the grim faced landlord was constantly filling jugs of ale and setting them down. There was no question of Charles' army having to pay for their drink. The landlords of Edinburgh had been promised compensation once he had achieved his objective.

Seamas took two jugs from the bar and handed one to Seoras. They both gulped down their ale quickly. They wanted the confidence that they knew was in their drink. They looked over their tankards and took in their surroundings.

Men were crowded at the bar, the tables were fully occupied and the spaces between them were crammed with drinkers. The air was close and musty and difficult to breathe. A fiddler stood on one of the tables and played a jig and on another a Highlander danced with a local woman. As the boys watched the drunken dancers fell into the rowdy crowd amid laughter and shouts of anger. The room was full of noise as the patrons sang and shouted to each other over the clamour.

'I haven't seen you boys in here afore.' The boy making himself heard over the racket was probably about the same age as Seoras. The brothers eyed him with suspicion.

'That's cause we've nae been in here afore,' Seamas shouted back.

'What's yer names?'

'Seamas and Seoras McLachlan. We're brothers.' He squared his shoulders. 'Who're you?'

'We're all brothers,' he said smiling broadly, 'Lachlan MacLachlan, Shores of Loch Fyne. Pleased tae meet ye.' He extended his hand and shook with the brothers. 'So, what brings ye in here?'

'We were lookin for somewhere new . . . bored o the other places.' So far Seamas had done all the talking while Seoras stood at the side. He swigged the last of his ale and then asked the other two if they wanted more.

'Of course we want more, especially as it's from the Prince's own pocket,' bawled Lachlan, slapping him on the back. Seoras noted that his cheeks were flushed and guessed that he'd been in here a while.

Seoras went and grabbed three jugs from the bar.

'Is that a fiddle ye have on yer back?' Lachlan said when Seoras handed him his ale. 'Are ye any good?'

'Nae bad. What do you do?' Seoras changed the subject.

'Well, at the moment I play a very important role in the success of this campaign.' Lachlan raised his nose in the air, and looked down it at the brothers. 'I convey highly classified information from one strategic location to another.'

'Ye mean yer a messenger boy,' Seamas said.

'Aye,' he said smiling. 'That's about the size o it. Usually - back home that is - I'm a fisherman.'

Lachlan went on to tell them, without being prompted, all about the leaders of the rebellion that he had met. Bonnie Prince Charlie himself of course, and his generals: Cameron of Lochiel, Lord George Murray, Alasdair MacDonell Chief of the MacDonalds of Keppoch, John Sullivan the Irishman and nearly all of the clan chiefs. He told them of the finery up in Holyrood Palace. The gold from which they drank and silver from which they ate. The furniture upon which they sat and the beautiful carpets upon which they walked from room to splendid room and the beautifully detailed portraits and landscapes that hung on every wall. The boys asked him what they ate and he told them the finest delicacies, and they asked what they drank and he told them the finest wine and cognac, and what they wore and he told them that their clothes were stitched together with thread made from gold and silver and buttoned with pearls and ivory.

Then the brothers asked him what they talked about and he had to answer truthfully that he didn't know. They almost always spoke in the English.

Seoras listened to the story fascinated, hardly able to believe that Lachlan had been in the same room as the Prince, but also feeling a bit disappointed that the men that they were fighting for couldn't even speak their language.

While they had been standing talking to each other one of the drinkers at a nearby table had been watching them with interest.

'Hey lads!' He called over.

'What's the matter wi him,' Lachlan said out of the side of his mouth.

The man beckoned them. 'Come over here!'

They went over to him and had to squeeze past others to stand around him at his table. As Seoras looked down at him he could see that he was dishevelled, his hair was matted and his face had the slack look of a man who had done a lot of hard drinking and not much else for quite a while. But as he looked up at them, his bright eyes glittered like shards of glass and pierced into each of them in turn.

'Well lads, what are ye up tae.'

'Just havin a drink, the same as yersel.'

He laughed at Lachlan's answer. 'Good, good, I'm glad tae hear it. So yer enjoyin oor fair capital city then.' He paused and scratched at his dirty beard. 'Are ye no goin tae introduce yersel's?'

The boys told him who they were and where they were from. When they had finished he introduced himself as Gillies McGilchrist, Soldier of Fortune. 'I've fought in many a battle, and many have been slain by my sword,' he said toeing the weapon at his feet. 'If ye stick with me boys ye'll learn everythin' that ye ever needed tae aboot soldiery.'

'How many men have ye killed?' said Seamas at last.

'The count of those that've fallen at my sword would fill this bar twice over - if not more.'

Lachlan bent towards Seoras' ear. 'Aye, right. Let's make a move.' Seoras agreed with him, he couldn't understand why he had called them over just to brag.

Lachlan turned to Gillies. 'Aye, well, it was nice meetin ye. We'll be gettin' back tae the bar now.'

Seoras saw a flicker of annoyance on Gillies' face.

'Hold on lads, ye canna be goin back tae the bar tae stand and natter like women. Surely no young lads like you. Ye should be in for some mair action.'

'What kind o action?' Seamas asked.

'Well for starters,' he said nodding to Seoras, 'ye can get that fiddle off yer back and gie us a tune.'

'There's someone already playin.' Seoras answered immediately.

'That's no a problem.' Gillies got to his feet and used Lachlan's shoulder to steady himself as he stepped from his seat up onto the table. Once there he shouted over the heads of the crowd to the fiddler on a table across the room. 'Hey!' The fiddler kept playing. Gillies cupped his hands around his mouth and took a deep breath, swaying awkwardly on the table. 'FUCKIN' HEY!' This time quite a few heads turned in his direction but still the fiddler continued to play, oblivious to his shouts.

'Tell that cunt I want tae speak tae him!' He called over to one of the men at the fiddler's table. He in turn then tapped the fiddler on the calf, who, without pausing bent to look down at him over his instrument. The go between pointed at Gillies who was making cutting motions over his neck with his hand. The fiddler stopped playing. Seoras squirmed at the thought that this bother had been caused on his account and wished that he had left his fiddle back at camp.

'Would ye mind takin a rest for a wee while. I've got a young lad here who would like tae entertain us.'

'Aye, no problem, ye just needed tae say.'

'Well I'm sayin now okay!'

'I was fancyin a dram anyway,' the fiddler called back as he stepped down from the table.

'Come on then son,' Gillies said inviting Seoras up onto the table. 'Ye'd better be good, by the way.'

Seoras unwrapped his fiddle, handed the sack to Seamas and Gillies pulled him up onto the table. He felt the eyes of everyone in the bar upon him as he tucked his fiddle under his chin. He raised his bow to his strings and began to play. The crowd around him stood and watched for a few moments and once they had ascertained that he was a good musician they began to pick up the beat with claps of the hand and stamps of the feet.

Once he was into the swing Lachlan said to Seamas: 'He's good, yer brother.'

'Aye, our Granda taught him.' Seamas turned to Gillies. 'So, what kind o action were ye on about.'

A large grin split his beard showing black, rotten teeth. 'Well lad, its one thing standin about gettin pished. But what about a bit o fanny?'

'Fanny?'

'Aye, fanny son. Have ye never had a woman afore?'

'Of course I have,' he lied.

'Well,' he said getting to his feet. 'Come wi me lads and we'll find a decent tart for ye.'

He took them around the room to a table where a woman was drinking with a table full of men. She had one leg slung over the lap of the man next to her and Seamas took a lingering look at the bare inside of her thigh, before averting his eyes.

'How dae ye fancy a bit o that boys?'

'Fuckin right,' said Lachlan. Seamas stood and gawked, and wondered just what he was going to do with his bit. He also wondered how they were going to get a bit and as he did so he watched Gillies round the table to where she sat. He spoke into her ear for a moment or two and then pointed in their direction. She looked them over, then laughed and waved. Lachlan waved back and Seamus felt his face go hot and red, but he hoped that she would put that down to the drink and the heat of the bar. His veins began to pound with adrenaline.

Gillies continued to talk to her and he saw her first shake her head and then as Gillies pulled out a small drawstring bag and give her some coins she nodded and stood up. She gave Gillies a kiss on the lips and then headed for a door at the back of the bar.

'Come on lads,' he shouted across the table at them. 'We're in!'

He turned and followed the woman and the two young men quickly pushed their way through the crowd to catch them.

To Seamas it happened quickly and in a blur.

She led the three of them into a corridor and then up a narrow staircase and into a small dark room. There was a straw mattress in one corner and a small table in another with a dirty mirror above it. The three men stood at the end of the mattress.

Smiling broadly, she unbuttoned her dress down to her waist and pulled it open, letting them see her exposed breasts. Then she lay on top of the blankets of the roughly made bed and pulled up her skirts above her waist. In the grey light of the room, Seamas could see the dark patch of hair between her legs as she raised her knees.

'On ye go Seamas,' said Gillies pushing him in the small of the back. His heart was pounding in his chest and he was frozen to the spot.

'I'll go first,' said Lachlan dropping his bonnet to the floor and pulling his kilt up. He knelt on the bed and manoeuvred himself between her open legs and lay on top of her. Seamas watched, his jaw dropping as her hand slid down between them. Suddenly he wished that he was back in the bar with Seoras.

Lachlan was now thrusting his hips into her and she panted with his rhythm while gripping the cheeks of his buttocks in her hands. From the corner of his eye Seamas could see Gillies moving his hand up his own kilt.

Lachlan's thrusting didn't last long before his hips lunged forward and he let out a groan as his body jerked. With a mixture of dread and exhilaration Seamas realised that he would be next. Lachlan lay slumped on top of the bar girl while he regained his breath and Seamas couldn't believe that she was gently kissing his ear.

'Well done boy, ye can get off now.' Gillies grabbed a handful of jacket from Lachlan's shoulder and pulled him off the girl. He retrieved his bonnet from the floor before going over to slouch on the dresser.

'Son, she's all yours,' said Gillies clapping Seamas on the shoulder. Seamas remained rooted to the spot.

'I canna - no wi you's watchin,' he stammered.

'Go on,' said Gillies. 'Or would ye rather shag a sheep!' Seamas could detect anger in his voice. He then shoved him hard towards the bed. He landed on top of the girl.

The woman smiled up at him. He looked down at her and saw that her red fringe was clinging to her sweaty brow. She slipped her hand up between his legs and he felt himself grow in her gentle grip. She pulled him towards her.

*

While playing the fiddle, Seoras had observed his brother at the woman's table with Lachlan and Gillies and had watched them as they disappeared through the door at the back of the bar. He played a couple of tunes and then the previous fiddler resumed. He got down from the table and sat on Gillies vacated seat. He sipped at his ale and watched the door for their return. To his left a man had his face in the crook of his arm murmuring some drunken song that made no sense to Seoras.

It seemed a long time before he saw Gillies come back through the door followed by Seamas and Lachlan. Gillies was grinning and laughing but although the other two were smiling along with him, they didn't seem nearly as buoyant. When they got back to the table Seoras said to Seamas: 'Did ye?'

'Shag her,' said Gillies. 'Aye, but Lachlan greased her for him first, eh boy.' He dug an elbow into Lachlan's side.

'Aye.' Lachlan's voice was flat.

'Oh come on ye ungrateful cunts. I got ye a ride didn't I?' he said opening his arms. 'And dinnae worry aboot her, she's just a fuckin hoor. She'll be okay.'

'There was blood,' mumbled Seamas.

'It's all in a days work for a dirty slapper like that. I paid her an she wisnae tellin me what I could and couldnae do . . . and,' he began to laugh uncontrollably, 'I certainly wisnae goin up the same hole as you pair o fuckers!'

'Aye,' said Lachlan pretending to share the joke, 'anyway we'll hae tae be off now.'

'Off where?' Gillies had taken a long draught of ale and was wiping the spillage from his beard with his fore arm.

'We've got chores to do back at camp,' said Seamas.

'And I've tae get tae my post at Holyrood.'

'Aye, fuck off then.' Gillies pulled Seoras from his seat and slumped into it. The boys began to move away and Gillies called after them: 'Don't forget that you boys owe me - all o ye's!' Seamas and Lachlan slinked out onto the street with Seoras coming after them, still trying to work out what had happened.

'That guy's a fuckin heed case.' Lachlan was striding down the road towards the Palace end of The Royal Mile.

*

During the rest of their time in Edinburgh, Seoras and Seamas met up with Lachlan whenever they could get away from their duties. They stayed away from the alehouse where they had encountered Gillies, and others like it.

They didn't meet as often as they'd liked to have though, because they were kept busy with their various tasks, but whenever they did the prostitute was never mentioned.

In the following weeks the weather turned cold and the icy wind carried flurries of snow over the city from the Firth of Forth. The hot late summer day of Donchad's wedding now seemed like a lifetime ago.

On the first of November the Jacobite Army began the march south.

Seven

<u>Culloden, Scotland, April 13th 2146</u>

The airbus dropped Namah off at the top of the road and she hobbled down the mile and a half through the dark countryside. She was late but unable to hurry. When she arrived she found that her father had already gone through the routine of opening up the visitor centre.

'What happened to your foot?'

'I twisted it in the shower, that's why I'm late. I'm okay though . . . it's easing up already.'

'Well you could have taken your time you know. Everything's up and running, I managed okay. The exhibition rooms are open, so is the souvenir shop. The ticket and refreshment machines are all on.'

'Thanks Dad.'

'I quite enjoyed it actually. I think it did me some good. In fact I think I'll stay around for a while. You won't be walking the site today will you - not with that foot.'

'Aye, I'll walk the site. If I don't exercise it'll only stiffen up.'

'I'll come with you then.'

'No, it's okay. I'll be fine.' She said sharply. She wanted to walk the battle site alone. She gave her father a quick hug, hoping she hadn't hurt him. 'You stay here and look after the centre.'

She went through the visitor centre to the battlefield, switched on the floodlights and started down the path. Every evening after opening up she would walk the paths that ran around the boundary and crossed it along the lines where the armies had formed up for battle. It was a habit she'd gotten into when she had started running the centre for her father. It helped to relax her. She would feel the sadness that cloaked the place like a graveyard. But there was an underlying intensity. Those who had died here had done so suddenly and violently and their bodies had stayed on the moor. She sometimes felt that their souls had also stayed.

She had learned about the history of the place while still young, working here with her father in the holidays. He had bought it over when there was a danger of it closing down and had done most of the work himself in the early days to keep it going. It was a hobby to him really and took his mind off the sudden death of her mother. He sold all his other businesses and bought a house nearby. When he became old and unfit and running it was too much, Namah had been able to take over from him. He still came down to help her most days and assist with the accounts.

There wasn't much in the way of visitors. Foreign travel was expensive and restricted to the wealthy - and these tended to be people with little interest in walking around an ancient battle site.

What money they did make was enough to pay the wages. Apart from herself the only other full-timer was Cammie Stewart, who had been there when her father took over. He tended the grounds and mowed the grassed areas and carried out other general maintenance. In the summer he had two part-time assistants and a Government trust also paid for guides and assistants for the visitor centre. Her father regularly applied to various bodies for subsidies.

Through the winter there wasn't much work to be done but there was never any question of laying Cammie off. He was as much a part of the place as the heather on the moor.

Namah had felt a presence on the moor from the very first time that her father had brought her here as a little girl, but rather than frighten her, it had done the opposite. It had attracted her, as if it had a secret to tell, as long as you were patient enough and listened closely.

Soon after that first visit she began to hear them. Faint sounds as if far away and brought to her on the wind. The clash of metal against metal, the yelling of orders. The thump of guns displacing air and the screams of agony. Other times she could hear the lament of a ghostly piper, the wailing of the bereaved or the whispered words of children that she couldn't quite make out.

Tonight, as she began her walk she felt nervous and afraid. The night before, she had looked for the Highlander during her walk. She was eager to catch a glimpse of him again, but since the nightmare she was dreading his re-appearance.

Why did he show me the pistol? And what was it that he had said?

He needs this,
and:
There's more but you must go now.

Who was *he*? What else did *he* need?

She had a feeling that the Highlander would be back. Her confusion only heightened her fear.

She tried to quicken her step as she moved along the path that ran along the southern edge of the field, but the pain in her foot kept her hobbling along at a slow pace. She inspected the simple headstones marking the mass graves, thinking that they needed the moss scraped from them, when she walked into someone. She looked around her and saw that there was no one there to walk into. She was standing in front of the grave marked MacLachlan.

'Who's there?' She spoke into the wind and stretched her shaking hand out into the space where she thought she had walked into someone. She knew that it had been a person because she had felt the softness of clothing, the slight yield as she collided and the expulsion of breath onto her cheek as she knocked the air out of someone's chest. She repeated her question, this time in Gaelic.

She held her breath, waiting for some kind of reply, wishing that she could decide when to use her ability to see spirits instead of having images coming to her out of nowhere. She stood motionless for a while, but no reply came. She began to breathe again and limped on.

She had calmed down when she felt the hand upon her shoulder. She spun round, sending an explosion of pain into her foot, to see Cammie standing there.

'I'm sorry, I didn't mean to startle ye.'

Namah went down on her good knee and gently massaged her injured ankle, as if trying to absorb the pain into her hands. 'It's okay, I just feel a bit jumpy tonight.'

Cammie's eyes narrowed. 'Oh,' he said absently. 'What happened tae yer foot?'

'I twisted it getting out of the shower this mornin.' She wondered how many more times she would have to tell this lie before she could walk properly again.

'I see,' Cammie nodded. 'Are ye okay, Namah?'

'Aye, it's just a sprain.'

'Apart from yer foot I mean.'

She looked up into his concerned eyes. His hair was spiked with a thin line shaved down the middle, the hair to the left of it was pine needle green and to the right it was jet black. His right eyebrow was pierced and a gold hoop hung there and four more were in each ear. He wore olive green coveralls and sturdy walking boots. Various tools hung from a leather utility belt strapped around his waist. She had known Cammie nearly all her life, and despite the age gap, she always regarded him as an elder brother. She always felt that she could connect with him. When she was little Namah had always thought of him as some sort of super hero. Part of her still did. He lived in a room at her father's house, but spent nearly all his time here or in the surrounding hills, sleeping either in the work shed or in his tent. She had no idea how old he was and never asked. She guessed from his appearance that he was in his late seventies but he was very fit and active so she couldn't be sure. She hinted at him about retirement a few times but he had laughed at that. He told her that he was still a young thing and had plenty years of work left in him. She was glad about that because he did an excellent job and she had no idea how she would ever replace him. That aside, he was part of the family.

Her father knew a lot more about him than she did, but he never let her in on anything. She always got the feeling that they were keeping some sort of secret from her, maybe something hidden in his past. All that he would say was that Cammie was a marvellous man, highly committed and deeply loyal.

She knew that he was very intelligent and had no idea why he was working as a groundsman. When she asked him he told her that he loved the job and wouldn't swap it for anything. He was also a mine of information, especially where Scottish history was concerned.

Namah had studied history at the University of the Highlands and Islands, a love that both Cammie and her father had passed on to her, but she always felt that Cammie had everything in his head - on tap.

Apart from that he had a love of nature and the environment and was a member of the Scottish Greens. He worked for them, helping with leaflet distribution and the like in his spare time. When he could, he also got Namah involved. She was deeply fond of him and rarely saw him unhappy, if ever at all.

He had a serious look about him now though as he gazed down at her while she massaged her tender ankle.

'Come on, I'll walk wi ye for a bit.'

He helped her to her feet and she leant on his arm while they continued up the path. They walked in silence until the path came to the corner that Namah had followed the young highlander round on the previous two mornings. There they stopped.

'The place isn't gettin to ye is it?'

'No.'

'I don't have to tell ye that a lot o bad things happened here, a lot o death - a lot o sufferin. There's a strange energy about the place. The spirits are still here. I know you must have encountered them Namah, you more than anyone else. Ye've always had that ability. In ancient times they would have said that you had *taibhsearachd,* the gift of prophecy. They'd have called you a seer.'

'It's not like that though Cammie. It's not a skill that I have, it's just something that happens to me from time to time. A flash, a glimpse, as if a door is opened in front of me for a moment and I see inside and then it's closed again. Usually it shows me something of no importance at all. Sometimes I bump into a pregnant woman in the street and I see a picture of her holding a baby and instead of sayin "sorry" I feel like telling her that she's going to have a boy and that everything will be okay this time. Other times I pass by a section of road on the bus and I can see wrecked cars by the side of the road. I try to pretend I haven't but then I read about the anniversary of the crash in the news. She stood looking at Cammie with water in her eyes. He squeezed her shoulders.

'Aye, You're our very own Brahan Seer', Cammie said.

'Aye, but the thing is that he predicted major events. He predicted the Highland Clearances and the building of the Caledonian Canal. Some say he foresaw the Second World War and the Piper Alpha Disaster. And before that there's no denying that he predicted the Battle of Culloden. I'm not seein anythin like that . . . only wee things.'

'Maybe they're wee pieces o a bigger picture,' Cammie held her at arm's length. 'And don't forget that Coinneach Odhar also said "The Shadow over Culloden will rise and the sun will shine brighter".'

'What does that mean though, Cammie?'

'Maybe it means that the spirits here will be given peace. Maybe the sadness that blankets this place will be lifted. I always feel,' he said, 'that the energy is stronger at this time of year.' He was talking about the upcoming anniversary of the battle. 'Don't you?'

She thought about that for a few moments. 'Maybe, I don't know, but something is definitely happening this year,' she said with a dry laugh. 'Can we talk later, Cammie? I've somethin to tell you. God knows I've got to tell someone.'

'Sure, no problem. Why don't you drop in by the work-shed at about three o'clock. We can have dinner - I've enough to share.'

'Thanks, Cammie,' she said and kissed him lightly on the cheek.

'I'm off to tidy up Charlie's place,' he said. He meant the area from where Charles Edward Stuart had unsuccessfully commanded his army. He strode off in that direction and Namah continued along the path running across the Jacobite front line.

'Ye'll be okay in the mean time?' he called over his shoulder.

'Aye.'

She was glad that she had spoken to Cammie and knew that it would feel better to get the events of the last couple of nights off her chest. She felt soothed and reassured by him in the same way that the Highlander's voice had calmed her on the moor before things had started to go bad.

She walked north along the path before coming to an intersection. The path to the right continued along the front line and the other turned left towards the second and third lines. She followed this path past the Irish Wild Geese and French memorials before it joined again with the front line path. There it turned eastwards and wound its way through the rough moorland along the northern boundary for about six hundred yards, passing the Keppoch Stone about half way. She stooped to pluck a buttercup from the many that grew beside the narrow water filled ditch that ran alongside the trail. She held her palm to it so that the light from the floodlights reflected the flower's colour onto her skin. She wondered how it would reflect its radiance under the sun and was envious of the children in her father's stories who had held the flowers under their chins to see whether they liked butter.

The battlefield undulated over mounds and dips and the vegetation ranged from soft grass and wild flowers in the shallows to coarse turf, gorse and whin on the hillocks. There were also exposed patches of gravel and rock and a scattering of birch and spruce. This landscape continued to the north of the path but was interrupted about twenty yards away, out-with the domain of the floodlights, by the road that ran parallel. It cut through the land leaving a long, wide scar, as if a ruptured appendix had been removed from the belly of the land. Every now and then traffic whooshed along it, breaching the peace. About a hundred yards northwest she could see the huge boulder, from where the Duke of Cumberland had overseen the battle.

She followed the route southwards along the front-line of the Government troops and after a hundred yards she came to a viewpoint. She walked up to it and looked out over the field towards the Jacobite positions. To her left she could see the life-sized figures of twenty Highlanders charging into forty musket bearing redcoats. Her father had paid for the project depicting a scene from the battle and he had intended it to be much bigger, perhaps even portraying all the major incidents of the battle and showing the men formed up instead of only having plaques where the clans and fighting units had stood. They were able to add to it slowly when the money became available from grants and gifts or their small profits.

As she stood resting her foot, a dark wave suddenly washed over her. She felt slightly faint and nauseous and steadied herself on the large wooden plaque showing a plan of the battlefield. She felt like she was being drawn away from her immediate surroundings and increased her grip on the wood. Her sight dimmed and then swam into blackness. She began seeing mentally rather than optically.

When the darkness cleared, she was seeing the battlefield from the same position in which she stood now, except that it was broad daylight. She could tell from the sun hanging high in western sky that it was mid-evening. She looked over to the other viewpoint, which jutted out onto the field from half way along the southern path. There was a copse of tall silver birch behind it blocking out the visitor centre and in the undergrowth behind and to the left of the viewpoint she could make out two men peering from under a low canopy. They had camouflaged it well and they passed a pair of binoculars between them. She shouldn't have been able to see them, but somehow the area around them had been highlighted like they did on the crime watch programmes to show you more clearly the face of a thief caught on closed circuit cameras. She felt a jolt as her vision zoomed in on them and she could see now that

Cammie was one of the men - the other she had never seen before.

They were looking in her direction but they weren't looking at her. They were looking beyond the viewpoint - and they looked nervous.

Then she could smell the stench that she had smelt in her nightmare. Then she could hear the heavy, salacious breathing. Then her vision began to jerk back and forth. Quickly, slowly. The moorland rushed at her and away from her. Once more she felt as if she was going to vomit. She caught sight of the large bulk of a man. Then the vision was gone. She still felt like throwing up but held tightly to the plaque and breathed deeply and until the feeling subsided. She felt pain in her fingers and realised that she was gripping the plaque so hard that her nails were digging into the wood.

The visions of Coinneach Odhar, The Brahan Seer, had ended when he was executed by being plunged into a barrel of boiling tar. Namah had no wish for such a fate for herself, but she wished the visions would end just the same.

*

Her father hung around all night so that around three a.m. she was able to go down to Cammie's work shed.

The building was more of a barn than a shed. The ten-foot high walls were built two thirds of the way up with brick and completed with corrugated iron. It was plain that the building was very old (the solar panelling on the roof was added rather than built in), but it remained strong through Cammie's skilled handy work. Against the wall and the near side was parked a ride on power mower.

The door stood ajar and she gently knocked and went inside to find it deserted. There was an old strip light hanging from the ceiling which did it's best to reproduce daylight.

Along the wall to her right were arranged a large selection of agricultural tools and equipment. Smaller items such as secateurs and hand trowels hung from nails in the upper timber support and spades and shovels and an old scythe hung from a lower joist. Nearer the door a heavy roller leaned against the wall next to an old fashioned hand propelled rotary mower, the blades on which looked razor sharp.

A workbench ran three quarters of the way along the opposite wall, beginning at the door. She could see a solar battery charger sat on top of it at this end filled with the two standard sizes of batteries which blinked green signifying that they were fully charged. She could also see the cable running up the wall that linked the unit to the panels on the roof. A kettle stood on the other end of the bench and was kept company by three tins containing tea, coffee and sugar.

In the far left corner sat a very worn but very comfortable looking armchair, beside two old kitchen chairs. Above them were shelves holding a couple of dozen books. She realised with a tinge of sadness that this corner of the shed was where Cammie spent a lot of his time - he probably regarded it as home.

She went over to the corner and looked at the titles on the spines of the books that sat on the shelves. About half of them were horticultural books about the care of trees and shrubs. There was also a great deal of Scottish history books. Some of these she had read herself, including one that had more or less been her 'bible' at university written by Jason Lombard. There were a few old novels and the rest seemed to be about spiritual guidance and karma. She made sure that the kettle was filled and switched it on and then plucked one of the yoga books off its shelf and sat down in the armchair. She sighed with relief as the weight was taken from her foot and began to browse through the book. She felt relaxed in the chair, as relaxed as she would have in her own chair at home, and didn't feel that she was invading Cammie's privacy. She knew that he wouldn't mind.

Cammie entered the shed a few minutes later unbuckling his tool belt and observed what she was reading.

'My eternal quest for inner peace,' he said with a smile.

'I thought you'd already found that.'

'What makes you think that?' He asked hanging his belt on a hook.

'Well, I have to say Cammie, out of all the people I have ever met you have got to be the most at peace with ones self.'

'It's just a face. I'm still very much searching for the path to tranquillity.'

She laughed. 'But you're happy with your life.'

'Aye, of course I am . . . more than happy. I have a good life, and when I look back on everything that's passed, I've had a good life. Wouldn't change very much of it.'

'So what's with the quest?'

'We all need goals . . . even an old guys like me need to keep the mind supple as well as the body. Anyway, it's break-time. Glad tae see ye've put the kettle on.' He opened one of the filing cabinets and took out two mugs. 'Ordinary or tayberry?'

She thought for a moment. 'I think I like the sound of tayberry.'

'And you'll like the taste too . . . completely natural. So -,' he said as he prepared the mugs and withdrew a box from his bag, '- what was the problem tonight? Truthfully. I must have been on the right lines or you wouldn't be here now. At least I hope that you didn't come here to tell me that I talk bollocks.'

'I'd never think that you talk . . . bollocks.'

'So, have you had another vision?' Cammie handed her a steaming cup and opened the box, which contained wrapped sandwiches and fruit.

'Aye, but that's not all of it.' She took a deep breath and a sip of her tea and began to tell him her story, beginning with her first sighting of the Highlander and ending with tonight's episode on the battlefield.

'Wow,' he said putting down his half eaten sandwich, 'I didn't expect all that.'

'Do you believe me?'

'I believe you,' he reassured her. 'What are you going to do?'

'Ask me one on quantum mechanics; I might have an answer for that.'

'It's out there, ye know . . . the pistol. He showed ye where it is. And the guy . . . the one ye saw with me . . . ye're sure ye've never seen him afore?'

'Fairly sure. If I have, he must have been a visitor whose face I've forgotten.'

'What did he look like?'

'Early thirties, light brown hair cut fairly short. Eye colour I wasn't close enough to see, height I've no idea - he was lying down. He looked like he was wearing one of your coveralls. He was good looking I suppose and his face was smeared with dirt . . . you both were.'

'Which?'

'Eh?'

'Both good looking or both dirty?'

She smiled again. 'Both, both.'

'Well I certainly can't wait to see him if he's as handsome as me.' He laughed and put down his tea and looked at Namah carefully. 'Do ye think that we should go and look for the pistol?'

'I wouldn't know where to start. The moor was . . . different,'

'Show me where he led you off the path. That seems like a good place to start.' Cammie grabbed two shovels and headed out of the door.

*

The ship changed course and began the final leg of its journey north through the Irish Sea to the Firth of Clyde. The tail end of the Atlantic whipped around the southern coast of Ireland and in alliance with the skies it threw up a fierce storm. The gale force winds sent waves smashing into the vessel in a last attempt to halt her crossing of nature's inhospitable water which had claimed the lives of so many. It was the afternoon and by nightfall she would be safe in the sheltered waters of the Clyde.

Alone on the main deck of the ship, sheltered from the howling wind, the thrashing sea, the driving rain and the bitter, bitter cold, Sinclair could hardly feel the pitch and roll of the ship. She ploughed onwards oblivious to the insatiable sea's attempts to disorientate her and send her into an almighty impact with the waiting rocks. There she would be ripped and torn apart and sent back shattered to the sea to be devoured - but she remained innocent of these things and sailed steadily on course to her destination. Her ignorance of danger and lack of fear seemed to enrage the sea further and the storm stepped up, rising in its ferocity.

Sinclair looked about him as the weather worsened, marvelling at the engineering which had created this craft which not only kept its cargo safe from harm but produced a haven in which they were virtually unaware of the inhospitable world around them. He thought of the sleeping passengers below decks, warm and comfortable in their bunks and tried to imagine what it must have been like for the thousands of Highlanders who were deported westwards across these very seas towards lands that many of them would never reach. He thought of them crammed below in conditions worse than cattle, starving in their own filth, riddled with disease, having paid for their passage with everything they had and having nothing left - only the hope that they could maybe start anew in North America.

He had been worrying about his own circumstances. He had little money and would have to find bed and board when he got to Scotland. He was unsure about where he was going or what he was going to do when he got there (he definitely wouldn't be returning to New Zealand unless he found work and earned the money for a return trip). Although he felt exhilarated and free at having broken away on this quest for . . . for whatever, part of him felt foolish and lost. But then he imagined himself sitting in the Hampden High School staff room drinking coffee and dreading the afternoon. Then his misgivings abated.

Something had drawn him and he had let it seize and carry him and he was gratified to be taken. He thought of the Highlanders leaving their beloved homes, having their families ripped apart and scolded himself for his self-pity.

He picked up his book and tried to continue reading the penultimate chapter but his gaze was drawn to the storm and he was once more hypnotised by its energy. Through the redness of the panelling he could imagine that they were sailing through a vat of boiling mulled wine. He watched the huge waves crashing against the side of the ship in cascades of crimson, mere feet away from their murderous power, and then he made his way below to his bunk to get some sleep before they reached Glasgow.

*

The sun was still up and Cammie lay awake beneath the protective weathertex of his tent. He'd been drifting in and out of sleep and had been awake more than half of the day.

A lot of the time he had been thinking about the previous night, about the things that Namah had told him and where it was all leading - because he had no doubt that it was leading to something - and the fruitless search for the pistol. Now though, he thought about the old days. The *real* days when you got up in the morning and it was daylight and you walked in the warmth of the sun and went to bed when it was dark. Lying in the tent, he thought most of all about his time in the service of the Liberation Force.

He had been in Intelligence and had spent years living in the wilds, watching, gathering and relaying information to be used in the planning of sabotage, harassment and disruption of the occupiers. It was a way of life that he had never been quite able to let go of. He had a comfortable and well-furnished room but he spent much of his time outdoors. The occupiers were gone now so instead he watched the wildlife. There were people who wanted this information and he gave it to them. Sightings, numbers, dates, times, changes in habits, unusual characteristics. He drew them and photographed them and passed the information on just as he had done when he served the Intelligence. Now though, the intelligence that he gathered was used for the protection and development of the animals and birds living in the Highlands.

When he had been in the Intelligence he had spent most of his time alone moving around under cover, marking roadblocks, noting the movement of troops and equipment, but he had never been quite at peace. There had always been the threat of discovery that had hung over him if he was careless or unlucky (the occupiers had highly sophisticated counter-surveillance equipment) and although there had been occasions where he had come close to discovery, he had never been detected.

Ever since the withdrawal of troops he had continued his life in the hills and mountains, working voluntarily for various nature trusts. There was no threat, only the occasional disruption from poachers. Now there was only relaxation, peace and solitude.

Until today. He had been drifting in and out of sleep as he had in his Intelligence days, listening, watching with his high power binoculars and feeling that heaviness in his guts that warned him of approaching danger. The threat of detection had returned somehow.

The sun had begun to sink behind the mountains in the west and he rolled over and threw his portable solar panel out into the last of its rays. It was attached to his burner and would power it up enough for him to make tea in a few minute's time.

Then, with the sun safely over the horizon, he would wash in the nearby stream, and walk the five miles back to Culloden in time to begin work.

*

The airbus turned north into the Highlands and away from the Daylites of Perth. The motorway between Glasgow and Stirling had been well lit but now the only light came from the headlights of the bus and the other traffic using the road. On the journey, the place names that he had read about in Lombard's book flashed past his window on the road signs: Falkirk, Edinburgh, Dunfermline. He had seen the new Glasgow that Lombard had written about and could only imagine the old and dirty Glasgow. The shipbuilding had returned to the city after a long absence, like an ex lover who has returned after finding that they had made a terrible mistake. After realising that they should never have left, and begging for one more chance. One last chance to make everything right and never to leave again.

Shipbuilding had returned to Clydeside thanks to new technology and the end of fossil fuel and the people on the Clyde could not help but embrace its return as they still had the shipbuilding blood of their ancestors running through their veins.

He had disembarked early at around midnight and had made his purchases and gotten something to eat in the waiting lounge of the airbus station. He had been reading about Scotland's latest struggle for independence in the first half of the twenty-first century. He read how Westminster had allowed Scotland its own parliament. One of the Scottish Parliament's powers was the environment, including water, so when climate change brought severe drought to England and Scotland's fresh water was still abundant, the UK Government arbitrarily removed all powers from Scotland.

After their powers had been withdrawn the Scottish Parliament had decided to hold a referendum asking the people if they wanted to become an independent nation. A referendum earlier in the century had been unsuccessful, the campaign for independence had not been able to defeat the British media machine and propaganda and scaremongering had tipped the vote in the UK's favour.

The second referendum was likely to be a huge landslide in favour of independence and fearing that Scotland would have complete control over the water supply, the British Prime Minister had declared the vote illegal and sent in the troops.

For a time Scotland was left at the mercy of the British Forces and had to accept occupation. There was bloodshed as she struggled in her manacles. Demonstrations, guerrilla strikes and sabotage were all met with forceful reprisals. The British were well prepared for this having had centuries of experience in Ireland and India and the rest of the commonwealth. The United Nations looked on as they deliberated whether they had any right to interfere.

The British government demanded that the Scottish Parliament (now underground) be dissolved. To encourage the Scots along this path to 'peace' they bombed Glasgow, Edinburgh, Aberdeen and piped Scotland's fresh water south of the border.

In January 2086 a United Nations peace keeping fleet sailed into the Firth of Forth and demanded talks. London was told that Scotland's Parliament was legal and democratic and therefore the legislation that it passed was also legitimate. The troops were pulled out only after the UK Government made claims for compensation for loss of revenue due to the boycott. They also claimed that they had funded the original Scots Parliament and demanded recompense for this also.

The world courts threw out the British claims and the few remaining Commonwealth countries cut their ties with London. Scotland now traded her water and renewable energy, which had turned out to be a far more valuable natural resource than the oil had ever been.

Sinclair looked out of the window and beyond his own reflection he could see the moon hanging brightly in the sky. He pressed his face against the glass and cupped his hands to kill the reflections on its surface so that he could see into the night. As he peered out he became oblivious to the fact that he was on the vehicle and imagined that he was floating along through the darkness. He was flying along into the glens now and the moon shone from between illuminated ribbons of cloud and picked out the ridges and contours of the mountains in pale blue and coloured the dark shadows of the dips and folds in a deep night blue. Then he could see that they were not mountains at all but vast guardians watching in the night. Watching and protecting. He knew that he was safe here.

'They're beautiful, aren't they.'

He turned to look at the old woman who sat across from him at the opposite window, feeling slightly disorientated as he pulled away from the outside world.

'Yes. Very.'

'But you can't even see them properly.'

'No.'

'I've walked up them in the daytime, when the sun was shining in the summer It was hot and still down here but up there, there was a cold breeze. It is a coldness that you welcome after a long climb. It refreshes and cleanses you. Makes you feel new.'

Sinclair watched her eyes as she remembered and saw the smile at the corners of her mouth. He wanted to say something, say that he knew what she meant. But he didn't know and he remained silent.

'You could see so very far . . . in the summer. Even if I was young enough to climb I will never see that view or feel that breeze again, and that is sad. But not half as sad as watching you look out of that window. At least I've seen and the picture will stay in my head.'

'They say that the world is recovering. Maybe . . .'

'Maybe,' she said smiling. 'Maybe.' She lifted a magazine from her lap and began to read.

Sinclair looked at her for a moment and then looked at his watch. In an hour they would arrive in Inverness. He returned his attention to the window but the moon had disappeared behind thick clouds and he could now only see a vague silhouette of the mountains against the dark sky.

By the side of the road he saw the Highlander flash by. For a split second their eyes locked.

You will see the mountains and the glens.

Eight

Carlisle, England, November 16th 1745

She stood in the corner as the invaders rushed down the alleyway and passed her window in a frenzy. She waited for them to come to her home but she had little to give. Her husband had died three days ago when they had begun their siege - now his clothes and boots lay on the kitchen table ready for them to take.

She stood in the corner, waiting.

Her lips trembled as more soldiers made their way down the alleyway, shouting and calling to one another in a strange language. She slid down onto her haunches in the corner, praying that they had missed her, praying that she would be by-passed and that they would leave. She began to weep. She wept for herself and for her dead husband and then she looked up to see an invader smiling through the window at her and a squeal escaped her throat.

He moved towards the door and it burst open. He rounded the table and stood in front of her, breathing heavily. Slowly she got to her feet and raised a shaking finger towards the clothes on the table. He laughed and swept her offering onto the floor. Then he lunged forward and grabbed her forearm and threw her into the opposite corner. Her head buzzed as it connected with the wall and she sprawled on the floor. He took hold of an ankle and pulled her towards him. Looking up she saw that he had a knife and she held her shaking hands out in front of her, pathetically trying to shield herself. Then he was on his knees between her legs, slicing at her dress and underwear. Cold steel sliced the inside of her thighs. She closed her eyes tightly and began to wail, trying to block him out, trying to prevent herself from hearing his grunting. His fist smashed into her nose, turning her head into a surging world of shape and colour as the pain bloomed. He crushed her with his weight and his face was against her, his hot breath on her neck. She was dimly aware of him between her legs, poking and fumbling and then her bladder let go and she felt the warm flow of urine. With horror she realised that this had excited him even more and his movements and the awful animal sounds that he emitted became jerky and more desperate. Fresh pain was sent through her head as he butted her in the face. She screamed and knew that she was going to die. She felt the sharp line of the blade against her neck as he pressed his knife against her - and then he was gone. Up and away from her in an instant.

Gillies yelped in surprised pain as a large hand grabbed him by the hair and pulled him off the woman. Then he crashed to the ground as a foot came up and kicked him hard in the groin. He felt only a cold numbness at first and his hands instinctively cradled his rapidly shrinking genitals, and then, as he was dragged out into the alley by the hair a fire began to rage in his groin and abdomen.

Through the mist of his pain he tried to see who had brought such a violent end to his pleasure. The silhouette of a highlander stood over him and although he could not bring himself to speak, his eyes implored: *why?*

The silhouette drew back his foot and kicked Gillies full in the face then knelt down beside him and tilted up his head. A high-pitched whine was whistling out from between Gillie's split lips creating bubbles in the free flowing blood.

'You're a fuckin disgrace. Ye've no part in this army so if I was you I'd fuck off back to whichever hole ye came fae - because I promise ye this - if I ever see ye again I'll cut yer balls off. And here's yer dirk back.' He tore one of Gillies' hands away from his crotch and drove his dirk through it, pinning his hand to the hard packed dirt on the lane.

Gillies screamed, his free hand going to the handle of dirk. He had didn't have the strength to pull it from the earth and his hand went back to his groin. He curled up, pinned to the ground, his whimpers broken by screams as the pain pulsed through him.

As his assailant rose to his feet the woman came out of the doorway, one hand holding her torn clothes together and the other holding a cloth to her bloody face. She looked at Tarlich and he lowered his eyes.

Then she ran.

*

The Jacobites remained in Carlisle for less than a day before continuing their march southward and a week later they entered Manchester unopposed. They had hoped for reinforcements from the English Jacobites there but only about three hundred men joined them. The Army camped and rested after some hard marching through Lancashire and their superiors gave them the news that was returning from their scouts and spies. The Government troops, they were told, were extremely weak. A large number were committed to the war with France and were away on the continent. A force had been assembled under the Duke of Cumberland though, and was sailing to London with orders to quell the rebellion.

On the 28th of November the weather worsened. They were now on the doorstep of winter. In the Jacobite campsite, amidst his clan, Seoras sat close by the warmth of a fire tending to his feet. The backs of his heels burned with pain where his boots had rubbed. He had begun to limp during the march and every step had felt like walking barefoot through fire. He'd used every ounce of mental effort within him to keep on the move and to keep putting one foot in front of the other. He'd thought of home and the glen and had played tunes over and over in his mind so that the pain would be blocked out. When the march had halted there was still no relief as he'd been sent to collect wood and perform other chores before there was an opportunity to rest. Now rest had come and he just wanted to lie down and take the weight off his feet and fall into blissful, painless sleep. But he knew that he could not do that either. Specific orders had come down from Lord George Murray that the men were to take care of their feet, as they were their most important weapon. He had even made sure that thick socks and decent footwear was supplied to the men.

Seoras loosened his laces and carefully removed his boots and sighed as cool air circulated around his burning feet. Under his light touch he felt the encrusted heels of his socks. Blood and liquid had oozed from beneath the worn skin of his feet and had dried, binding the wool to his flesh. He gulped, knowing that the socks would have to come off so that he could clean his feet. He'd become well practised at this routine over the course of the march but he never got used to the pain. He rolled down his socks to the point where they became bonded to his flesh and then tore them off his feet in one sharp movement. He lay on his back with his teeth gritted and his eyes squeezed shut waiting for the pain to ease. When it did, he dipped a cloth in the bucket of warm salt water by the fire and began to clean his aching feet. At his side, Seamas had been trying to burst a blister with his *sgian dhu*. Donchad had seen his predicament and placed his younger brother's foot on his lap. He took the knife and pinched the skin of the blister between the pad of his thumb and the tip of the blade.

'There ye go . . . ye can squeeze it yersel.'

Seamas pushed at the bag of liquid until the watery fluid had all seeped through the puncture that Donchad had made, leaving only the loose skin covering the caustic flesh beneath. He then gingerly began dabbing on the salt-water.

The burning had now gone from Seoras' heels and was replaced by a pleasant cooling sensation as the salt cleansed his torn feet. He carefully pulled on his spare pair of socks that he had washed and dried the previous evening. Then he collected up his family's socks and took them over to a water barrel that was set aside for washing purposes. Chunks of soap lay on a slab by the barrel and he soaked the socks and lathered them with soap before rinsing and wringing them out. All around the encampment fires blazed and men milled about taking care of tasks such as this.

He returned to the fire and laid the socks out on a hot stone to dry before plonking himself down to stare at the skinned rabbit which his father was roasting on a stick for their supper.

This rabbit was given to them along with some biscuits when they had lined up for their rations. Sometimes they got pieces of ham or mutton or if they were lucky, beef. Mostly the meat was boiled and salted but sometimes, as tonight, it was given to them raw to cook themselves. Quite often they were given soup, which was made when supplies of meat were low. Along with this they were given either boiled potatoes, a hunk of bread or hard oatmeal biscuits.

While the rabbit sizzled on the spit Tarlich handed them each three biscuits. They would get porridge in the morning but the biscuits would have to last them until the same time the following evening. When the rabbit was cooked he ripped its carcass into quarters and dished out the pieces. They ate hungrily, sucking and gnawing every last piece of edible gristle from the bones.

As they finished the meal it began to drizzle so they each took their pair of steaming socks from the stone by the fire and shoved them up their shirts next to their skin. Their body heat would finish the job of drying them while they slept.

Seoras pulled his plaid over his head and curled as much of his body as he could underneath it. He was exhausted and his mind was empty of thought. Although he was lying on an uncomfortable surface, he immediately fell into a deep sleep.

When he woke he had no idea how long he had been asleep. He felt as though it had been hours, but he stuck his head out from under his plaid and saw that the fires around the camp still burned brightly. The rain had stopped but tiny beads covered his plaid and created a thin gauze that sparkled in the light of the fire. He heard snoring around him and the crackle and pop of the fires but save for that there was little movement around the camp. His right hip ached from where it had been pressing into the hard ground so he rolled over and tried to make himself comfortable.

He dozed into a light sleep.

He saw men lying in a field - hundreds of them - under a dark grey sky. The rain fell steadily on them in sheets and washed blood from their wounds onto the ground in crimson rivulets. Limbs twitched and phantom voices moaned in the bleakness.

He came up to a kind of dim wakefulness, his brow creased and then he drifted down into darkness again.

He saw pairs of feet swinging and kicking in mid-air, desperately seeking a foothold and finding nothing . . . again he felt himself drifting upwards to full consciousness and tried to swim upwards with it, wanting to awaken, but again he slipped downwards.

He saw women and children running, looking over their shoulders at an unseen pursuer, terrified. He saw his mother; grandfather; aunt; sister-in-law and others fleeing. Then he saw their spirits rise out of their mortal bodies and they were beautiful and ecstatic at having escaped but then their faces melted into masks of terror as they realised that something far worse awaited them, something from which there would be no evasion.

The screaming filled his head and Seoras sat up choking back a howl. He stared into the dying embers of the fire and tried to chase away the memory of the vision. He shuddered and a membrane of cold sweat seemed to cover his body. He moved closer to the warmth of the embers and hugged his knees, feeling some heat on his face. He looked around him at the sleeping figures of his father and brothers and wished for their peaceful dormancy.

He looked to the east and greyness was beginning to encroach on the night sky. It would be dawn soon and it would be pointless trying to get more sleep. The grey light continued to filter over his head and after what seemed like an age the pipers began to sound reveille. The encampment stirred into life.

Seoras' stomach growled but he did not feel like eating.

He did eat though and knew that he would need the food for the day's march which would begin as soon as they had broken camp and formed up in their regiments.

As the Jacobite Army continued southward towards Macclesfield the rain began to fall on them again, heavier than the night before.
*

On the evening of the fourth of December the Jacobite Army reached Derby. The Jacobites were one hundred and twenty-seven miles north of London and the city was in panic with King George preparing to flee.

General Wade had an army in Newcastle and the Duke of Cumberland had arrived back in England with another army and was marching through the Midlands to engage with The Jacobites.

But London had been left at the mercy of The Jacobites. Charles Edward and the Jacobite leaders held council to discuss their next move.

*

Seoras woke, cold and stiff and stretched and warmed himself at the fire while he waited for breakfast. When it was dished out he ate hungrily and then they were formed up to take their orders for the day. They were assigned general duties for the morning, making sure that they were in readiness for battle. In the afternoon they were stood down. Seoras was given the task of drawing water from the nearby river for drinking and washing.

The weather was cold but remained dry and he and Seamas told their father that they were going to look for a friend. They found Lachlan by the tents that had been set up as the Jacobite headquarters.

'What are ye up tae?' Seamas asked him.

'Just hangin around as usual.' He looked bored.

'Are ye comin wi us?'

'What for?'

'I don't know. We'll find somethin to do . . . go guddelin for fish maybe.'

'Aye, I saw a good spot this mornin when I was fetchin water,' Seoras said.

Lachlan took a quick look around and saw that no one was paying any attention to him. 'Okay,' he said. 'Let's go.'

They set off towards the river, winding their way through the encamped Highlanders and came to the outskirts of the camp.

'Hey, lads. Hold up!' They turned to see Gillies McGillchrist sitting nearby. 'Where are ye off tae in such a hurry? Ye're no desertin are ye?'

'Of course not,' Seamas said.

'Where are ye going then?' They noticed that for some reason his voice sounded strange and muffled. Then Gillies got to his feet and made his way towards them with a slight gait and now the boys could see him more clearly. His nose was swollen and appeared to be crooked. Beneath his eyes, dark purple bruises were yellowing at the edges. His left hand was wrapped in a bandage.

After their last meeting with him they were reluctant to tell Gillies where they were going. They looked at each other for inspiration but after a few moments of awkward silence Lachlan finally sighed and said: 'We were just goin tae see if we could catch some fish.'

'Without rods?'

'We're going tae guddle,' said Seoras.

'Well then, why didn't ye say,' said Gillies. 'I just happen to be the best fish tickler in the whole o the Highlands,' he said wearing the same broad smile that Seoras instantly remembered and mistrusted.

They began the walk to the river, Seoras leading the way.

Seamas took a closer look at Gillies as they walked. 'What happened tae yer face and hand?' he asked.

'Injured when we were takin Carlisle,' he said. 'Unless ye hadn't noticed we're involved in an uprising . . . do ye go around asking everyone stupid fuckin questions?'

'No, of course not.'

'Well then.' He walked along a few more paces then added, 'Actually, I was one o the first over the wall. On the other side I fell among at least a dozen o the cunts so I'm no ashamed tae say that they got the better o me for a bit . . . but I still managed tae fight my way through them.' He sounded as though he was going to go into a lengthy harangue about his personal experiences of the siege of Carlisle, but Seoras notified them that they had reached the spot on the river that he had picked out that morning.

They were on the inside of a wide sweeping bend in the river where the bank was flat and only about a foot above the water. The water was more likely to yield a catch here, as the flow ran slack inside the bend and was further sheltered from the main current by a small natural jetty that jutted out into the river upstream.

Gillies nodded in appreciation. 'The perfect place for fish tae lie, Seoras. Well done lad.' Gillies picked his spot and rolled up his shirtsleeve. 'One handed for me I'm afraid lads,' he said beaming. He rolled up the sleeve of hid good arm and got down onto his belly and sank his arm into the water. The boys followed his lead.

Seoras held his hands close together under the water and turned them upwards and within a few minutes he could feel his fingers already going numb. He kept them where they were and gently stroked the water among the grasses close to the bank. His mind began to wander as he lay there and he recalled how a few months ago he had been doing this very activity at home in the carse of the river which ran by his own croft. A few short months that now seemed like years.

In his mind he saw the glen. Not as he had left it still in glorious summer but as it would look now, in late autumn. The birch and oak beginning to reveal their bones beneath a red and gold crown and the fields bare of crops and thick peat smoke rising from the croft houses to become lost against the blanket of grey draped over the shoulders of the mountains. And perhaps in the evening, the cold northern wind bringing the first flakes of snow like pilgrims of winter.

The smooth touch of fish scales sliding along his fingertips pulled Seoras from his thoughts and he was cheered to find that the thrill of an impending catch was just the same so far away from home. He continued the slow motion of his fingers and held himself back from the impulse to grab for the fish and scare it away. He held his breath and waited for it to come closer, hopefully to nestle right across the palms of his hands so that he could scoop it up out of the water. Even though his fingers were throbbing with the cold he could still feel the current in the water that the fish was creating. He wanted to look down into the water and see it, but there was grass in front of his face, and he couldn't adjust his position now for fear of frightening the fish.

He felt the tail of the fish against the heel of his hand and knew the time was almost right. The fish felt big but he waited . . . a couple of seconds more . . . and then there was a splash and a shout from Gillies and the fish was gone in an instant. Seamus made a futile grab at the water and caught nothing but a handful of weeds.

Gillies called out in triumph as he scooped a brown trout out of the water downstream from Seoras. It flopped about on the grass as it began drowning in the open air. It flipped and writhed and looked as though it might have eventually made it back into the river if it hadn't been for Gilles picking up a stone and killing it with one swift blow to the head.

'What a fuckin beaut, eh boys!' Gillies beamed down proudly at his catch and Seoras saw with a pang of jealousy that it was in fact a decent two pound fish. Gillies picked it up and placed it further up the bank and then turned around to see that they were all watching him. 'Come on then boys, keep at it, I know it's a decent fish but it's no enough tae feed the four o us!'

Seoras turned back onto his stomach and bitterly plunged his arms back into the water. He had missed his catch by split seconds only to have to listen to Gillies boasting. Again the four of them began feeling the water and this time it seemed like an age before Gillies again threw a fish out of the water.

'It's a good thing I came along wi ye eh, boys, otherwise ye'd be lying there all day with fuck all to show for it but numb hands! Seoras, Lachlan, why don't the two o ye go and see if ye can get some wood for a fire tae cook these beauties on. Me and Seamas here'll try and catch a couple more.'

Seoras felt like protesting and telling Gillies that he had as much chance of catching fish as anyone else, that he had done it plenty of times at home. Instead he shook the water off his arms and dried them on his plaid and went off with Lachlan to a nearby copse to gather the driest dead wood that they could find.

'Gillies wasn't lying when he said that he was good at tickling for fish, eh?' Lachlan said once they were out of earshot.

'It was luck.' Seoras replied.

They returned to the riverbank with their fuel and cut out a patch of turf to build the fire on. They began to shave thin strands from the sticks to use as kindling. While they went about this Seoras was glad to see his brother catch a fish and then as they finished preparing the fire Gillies caught another. None were as big as the first, but they were all a good size.

Seoras was getting the fire going with a flint box, first sending sparks into the kindling mixed with dry moss and grass, and then blowing gently on it once it had began to smoulder. Small flames began to lick around the kindling and he and Lachlan began to slowly add some small twigs and as the flames grew they fed in larger twigs. The fire began to burn healthily once they had nurtured it through its early stages and it began to crackle and pop. They finally added the dead wood that they had collected and sat back to watch it as if it was an infant that they had raised and were now able to trust it to get along without full supervision.

Meanwhile, Gillies and Seamas had cleaned the fish and they were shared out between the four of them. They each took a sharpened stick, pushed it up through the open belly of the fish and pierced it into the back of the head. Once they were secured like this they held them close to the heat of the flames.

The trout did not take long to cook and soon they were picking off chunks of fish meat, blowing on their fingers and picking stray bones from their mouths until all that was left of their catch was head, tail, skin and bones. These were thrown on the fire where they sizzled and spat.

'That was a damn fine wee snack even if I do say so mysel,' Gillies said leaning back against a tree trunk and patting his stomach. Seoras licked every last bit of juice from his fingers and had to agree with him. He began to think that maybe they had been a bit hasty in judging Gillies.

Gillies reached into the folds of his plaid and produced a shining silver hip flask and unscrewed the lid and took a drink from it. He let out a contented sigh and passed it to Seamas. 'Dram?'

Seamas took a swig before passing it to Lachlan who did likewise and passed it to Seoras. The smooth curve of the flask felt pleasant in his hand and he saw that there was an inscription on the convex side. He couldn't read what it said as it was written in English.

'What does it say?' He asked Gillies.

'How the fuck should I know, I took it from some cunt in Carlisle . . . as compensation for my injuries ye understand,' he said with a laugh. Then he turned his attention to Lachlan. 'Do you know any

English, messenger boy? Ye spend plenty o time wi the Big Wigs.'

'I only know a few words,' he said thinking about it, 'but I do know that there's plenty o cross words being exchanged - especially between Lord Murray and Sullivan the Irishman.'

'What do ye mean?'

'Well . . . the two o them are nearly always arguing, sometimes face-to-face and they have tae be pulled apart. And the Prince, he seems tae be taking Sullivan's side.'

'Is that so,' Gillies said. Seoras had returned his flask and he stuck it back in his plaid. 'Well that shouldn't be the case - George Murray is an experienced leader and he knows us inside out. He's one o us for God's sake, the Prince should be listening tae him afore the Irishman.'

'What do ye think'll happen?' Seamas asked him.

'We'll march on tae London of course and we'll have these bastards on their knees.' He stood up and began kicking sand into the fire to extinguish it and the others helped him.

'Well boys,' he said putting his arm around Seamas, 'I think we'd better head back tae camp now. And remember,' he said, 'you lot owe me double now.'
*

The following day the decision to fall back was taken by the leaders of the Rebellion. They had come within a hundred and twenty-seven miles of London without facing a single set back and had caused great panic. Charles Edward had been at the head of his army on the march south but now as they sped northwards, he rode in the rear.

Ten days later they crossed the River Esk and were back on Scottish soil and the Highlanders struck up the bagpipes and danced in celebration.

They were now deep in the hold of winter and were in dire need of more supplies, for which they headed northwards to Glasgow. They would begin a new campaign, Lord George Murray told the troops, in the spring.

*

Cold and damp, Jack Easton stood in the ranks of '2' Company.

Pultney's Battalion had spent the last couple of hours waiting around in a copse near the roadside, huddling around hastily built fires and drinking hot water spiked with rum or gin in an attempt to warm themselves.

The infantry unit had halted unexpectedly near the town of Banbury while hurrying south with the Duke of Cumberland's Army to cut off the rebels as they approached London.

They waited for the arrival of Colonel Pultney to give them the reason for the halt in person. Jack thought that it must be highly important - any news that they received was usually passed down through the ranks.

'What's going on?' The whispered voice came from behind him.

''Ow the 'ell should I know,' came a gruff reply.

'I bet those fucking 'eathens 'ave chickened out.' Jack recognised the voice as belonging to Davey Roberts. *There* was a man who couldn't keep his trap shut for two minutes.

'I 'ope not though, 'cause I was looking forward to giving 'em a right good seeing to.'

'Quiet in the ranks! I'll cut the fucking tongue out of the next man I hear talking.' Sergeant Pullman screamed the order and the following threat over his shoulder from where he stood at the front of the parading soldiers.

'All right, calm down,' Roberts said under his breath. It was barely audible to Jack who was a file in front of him, but Sergeant Pullman heard him.

'Right, Roberts, I'm going to have you after this parade, you stinking pile of shit!'

Roberts was in for another hiding then. Jack hoped that it would maybe knock some sense into him this time. He doubted it though, he still had a broken finger from the last time, and that hadn't reminded him not to get on the wrong side of Pullman.

He wondered himself, though, what the reason for their halt was. He didn't believe that the rebels had turned back. Not because he was looking forward to meeting them in battle. He was dreading it.

He had seen plenty of action during his year and a half with the company since joining up and had fought under the Duke in Flanders against the French. They would have still been there if they hadn't been called back to England to put down this bloody rebellion. The faces in the company had changed a great deal since they had gone across the channel. He had joined up with a band of men from his home town in Somerset, hopeful of money, travel, adventure, and of course the uniform. He found it hard to believe as he stood here in the drizzle that the damp red overcoat that he wore now was one of his reasons for joining up. How quickly his goals had changed.

Most of the men he had left the town with, men he had known most of his life, had lost their lives on the continent. There would be no going back on leave in smart army red for them. No impressing the women with their tales of valour. They didn't even have decent graves for their mutilated and dismembered bodies.

Before joining up he had seen soldiers home on leave and he had coveted that red. Those days had seemed like a lifetime ago - in a different life. Eighteen months ago he had been a wide-eyed teenager but now he was a changed man. Like the other soldiers around him he had experienced too much to remain unaffected.

War changed men in different ways. Most were more than willing to follow in the footsteps of those who had already died, out of honour and duty for their country and the battalion and the uniform that they wore. Jack wanted to be out of the uniform and back home, working on the farm and close to Jane who he dreamt of every night. He wanted to be out of the overcoat before it turned a darker shade of red - stained by the crimson of his own spilt blood. Yet he would still rather go back and face the French than face the heathens from the mountains that he had heard so much about.

At least with the French you knew where the enemy were and how to fight them. The savages had already defeated a British army, by all accounts coming out of the marshes to hack them to pieces. They had also laid siege to other garrisons and ambushed and captured more troops. He had heard tales of how they came out of the mist and the darkness, screaming obscenities in ancient devil tongues.

The red coat tails of the soldiers flapped in an icy wind that had began to get up and Jack shivered from the cold and the thought of facing the rebels. Although he hated the misery of fighting and was sickened by the waste and destruction of human life that he had seen in Flanders, he was not afraid to stand with the other men in his battalion. In spite of the fact that he felt no pride in being part of this battalion, this army, he was not a coward. But he would still rather fight the French than the heathen rebels.

He heard the sound of hooves clattering along the road and turned his head in that direction. Between the heads and musket barrels of the men in the front rank he could see the colonel riding beside his adjutant and various other officers. Even from this distance he could hear their guffawing. They looked in high spirits, no doubt after a fine meal with plenty of sherry and port to wash it down. He had noticed that the majority of officers often seemed jolly and rosy cheeked.

The sergeant major bellowed the order that brought the battalion to attention and spun around on his heel to salute the colonel. He informed him, in a voice that rumbled through the dank afternoon air like thunder, that the battalion was present and correct and awaiting his command. Colonel Pultney thanked him with a broad smile that greatly contradicted the diligence with which the sergeant major was conducting the parade. As usual he seemed to be slightly amused by the spectacle. He seemed to look upon the sergeant major and the battalion not as men but as his very own toy or lovable pet that was capable of interesting tricks.

He remained on horseback and cantered over to the front rank between the company sergeants. He looked out over his four hundred strong battalion. Raising his voice, he began to address them.

'I have come this morning to give you the news that we have received from our scouts. I have come in person as I believe this is a great turning point in this, ah, what shall we call it-' he pushed his plumed hat back on his head slightly and scratched at his forehead. 'Campaign.

'It seems that our treasonous enemy have decided that they are in no way capable of confronting His Majesty's Forces. It seems, in fact, that their eyes have been bigger than their rebellious bellies.' The colonel adjusted his seating on his mount so that he was sitting up higher. 'In short men, The Young Pretender's band of marauders have turned tail and headed back north.'

A cheer went up from the men. Jack felt a great wave of tension flow out of him and the tight muscles across the back of his shoulders slackened. He hadn't dared to let himself hope, or even consider, that the rebels would simply turn around.

The prospect of the rebels marching into London had been a grave one. He had heard that businesses there had been boarded up and that civilians had fled from the capital. There had even been rumours that the King himself was preparing to leave the country. And then what would have happened.

The soldiers had worried over the safety of their own families - this after all was not a foreign field. This was home. On their course south the rebel army had already passed through a great deal of English country. The majority of the men in Pultney's Battalion were from the West Country but there were plenty of men from the North West and the Midlands. How must they have felt at the thought of a dangerous hoard of barbarians passing through or near the homes of their families? Jack didn't want to think about that.

'But still though,' the colonel continued once he had let the cheering die down, 'we must not become complacent. They are still a dangerous threat to the security of the Kingdom. We will make camp here for the rest of the day. At dawn we will begin the pursuit of our enemy. We will not rest until we have crushed this rebellion and brought its vile hierarchy to justice. I hope that it is the privilege of this proud battalion to escort Charles Stuart himself to London for execution.'

There was more cheering from the ranks.

'Tonight though, make merry, and I will ensure that there is plenty of rum at your disposal.'

Jack watched as the Colonel turned his mount and returned to his applauding entourage amid loud lively cheering and hat throwing. Jack clapped his hands and thought: Bollocks. All he wants is for us to fight and for him so that he can be praised and promoted and probably given more land to add to his considerable personal wealth.

The officers rode away to their comfortable quarters while the men were given the order to fall out and make camp. The quiet, cold men from the morning were totally rejuvenated, and went to their tasks with a new energy.

As Jack helped to unload the canvassing for his platoon he saw Pullman grab a handful of Roberts' hair and pull him to the side of a cart. The cat o' nine tails dangled from his hand. A brutal and unofficial flogging commenced as Roberts gripped the wheel. Without the complication of charges, officers and paper work.

Like Roberts, Jack would be not be celebrating tonight. He would be keeping his morale firmly on the floor until the day that he was out of this uniform and at home with Lucy in his arms.

Nine

Through an infinity of eyes they watched him wake up in the shade of the bushes.

They smelled his foul stench through the searching antennae of the insects. A mouse foraged nearby and stopped to sniff the air, whiskers twitching. Sensing him waking, the rodent scurried away.

He scratched himself and they *watched him as he heaved his corpulent body into a sitting position with his legs crossed like a disgraced Buddha that has been exiled from his monastery to exist among the rhododendron. His round head wobbled on the folds of his neck like a blood blister. His face and bald head were burned from the sun and the top of his head and his cheeks shone red through the peeling skin. By his side lay a cracked leather holdall. Through the sensors of the insects they felt his laboured breathing reverberate through the air. His chest sounded as if it contained the vortex winds at the centre of a tornado. Ants bustled to and fro about his feet. Flies swooped around his sweaty body and alighted on the leaves of the shrubbery around. Through their many eyes his image was constructed in the form of a grotesque kaleidoscope.*

He moved and the insects scattered into tunnels and deeper into the foliage or into the air. A fly soared into a web and began to struggle. Its efforts to free itself only succeeded in binding it even tighter to the trap - and alerting the predator to its presence.

The obese red faced-man uncrossed his legs and rolled onto his knees. He planted a foot onto the ground below him and used his knee for support as he heaved himself up onto both feet and his red head looked like it might burst from the effort. He wiped sweat from his forehead with the back of a fleshy hand.

Waist deep in the shrubbery he surveyed the park around him. It was deserted in the daylight. He unbuckled his belt, pushed his trousers down over his buttocks and thighs and produced his penis from beneath the rolling fat of his stomach. He urinated in a long arc and it puddled for a few moments in the impression that his sleeping body had left, before soaking into the soft earth. To the insects in the vicinity, the acidic, cloying stench was not offensive. Once he had finished urinating, he masturbated and after a few moments his semen was mingling with his urine. He broke wind noisily before pulling up his soiled underwear and trousers. He bent awkwardly for the holdall and walked out of the shrubbery buckling his belt and leaving a trail of devastated bedding plants in the border that skirted the bushes.

Now they viewed him from the eyes of a pigeon that was perched on the railings of the park and followed his route as he waddled towards the gate with the brown holdall banging against his leg.

The fat red man exited the park through the gate and turned left along the pavement at its northern boundary. He drew level with the bird and looked up at where it sat on the railings. The bird blinked back at him, its head cocked. They looked through the eyes of the bird and directly into the fleshy sockets of the obese man. Unlike the others that populated this strange world his face was unmasked and his features were clearly visible. His small cold eyes looked like the heads of lizards peering out of sandy burrows and his mouth a sidewinder snaking across the swollen dune of his face. They could not stand to look directly at the evil that lurked there and switched from the bird to a raven that was perched high up on the ledge of a window on the other side of the deserted street.

They watched him as he continued along the road and across an intersection and over a large stone bridge. The raven took wing and swooped down low over the bridge and the wide, dark river that it crossed, then up and up to alight on a ledge that jutted out below a giant clock face on a tower.

They watched as the fat man gradually made his way across the bridge and slithered like a slug along the pavement at the foot of the tower. He turned left and followed the road around the base of the tower and was lost from the raven's sight. They *left the first raven and entered three more ravens that sat on the northern side of the tower below a clock face identical to the one on the eastern side and watched him cross the road. There he followed the railings along the grounds of a large abbey.*

A gate opened up in front of him.

Beneath the clock face the ravens hopped from foot to foot, agitated and cawing as they sensed the alien energy within them compelling them to watch the fat man, coercing them to fly down from the ledge towards him in the grounds of the abbey. Like bats out of the moon, the ravens dropped down from the high clock face and plunged earthward like stones. They beat their shining wings and made towards the man. They landed on headstones and watched as he wound his way through the cemetary towards a small doorway set in the side of the great building. Above them the arched stained glass windows of the abbey looked down like huge eyes, glinting in the sun as it peered between passing clouds. The door opened silently as he approached it and they watched him enter.

Fear of the evil that lurked within the once holy walls prevented them from following further.

The door clicked smoothly shut behind him and a green light blinked silently on a metal panel by the door. The bells in the tower behind them rang out and shattered the silence. The bells chimed nine times and then they were gone from this place.

London, England, April 14th 2146

As he made his way through the nave his shuffling feet whispered to the empty rows of pews on either side of him. High above, the vaulting reached across the roof like skeletal fingers, touching in the centre as if in prayer, as if the ancient building knew that he was here and was closing its eyes tightly until he had finished what he had come to do - and was gone. From the nave he made his way through the choir and into the chapel of Henry VII. He knew exactly where he was going.

He had waited a long time for this.

From where he stood he could see the Coronation Chair. It was supported at the base by four lions with human faces that were frozen in menacing grins. He moved further into the chapel around the various tombs that were elegantly decorated and covered in precious stones and metals. Many had figures of the dead lying on their backs with their hands pressed palm to palm above their stomachs and their fingers pointing heavenward.

He passed by all of these and went directly to his master's tomb. Although his should have been the grandest of all, the tomb of his master was not ornate.

He lowered himself onto his knees and laid his hands on the cold stone. The floor level lid was simply carved with his name. No baroque carvings or pillars and canopy. No mention of his great heroic acts. No mention of how he had preserved the monarchy and saved the nation from destruction.

The fat red man felt anger rise within him as it had done so many times before and he tried to push it aside so as not to spoil this moment of elation that had been so long in coming. His master had been treated with a level of disgraceful low regard that he could scarcely come to terms with. Yet his master was greater and more powerful than they. Even in death.

Especially in death.

Here lay they in their majestic tombs all around him, yet they were no more than dust - empty husks. They were nothing. Even as he rested his hands on the stone of his master's resting place he could feel his heat and his power throbbing and pulsing beneath.

They were a nonentity, but *he* was here. *He* was a force.

His master who had watched over him and seen him through the long lonely years of confinement since he was a young boy and since he had dealt with his own parents for their betrayal . . . for their lack of gratitude. His master who had nurtured him and educated him and led him towards freedom.

'Master. I am here.' His voice carried across the chapel and slid off the walls.

Beneath his hands the great stone slab began to vibrate and he stood back to watch it slowly rise into the air, pushed up by crackling red electricity. The slab revealed the sarcophagus beneath and the hinges and lock of the sarcophagus exploded in neon red flashes and the hefty lid rose into the air to come to a halt and levitate below the slab.

He could now see down into the coffin and his eyes lit up as they gulped in the sight of his master's earthly remains. Sweat poured over his plump cheeks and seeped from between the folds of his chin and neck and soaked into his t-shirt. The fat man's putrid stench and the metallic electricity in the air mingled with the musty dryness of ancient decay rising from the coffin.

The Duke lay as he had been buried, in full military dress. The uniform still looked glorious even though it had sunk and crumpled with the decaying of the enormous body.

The red man reached down into the coffin so that he could lay a hand lightly on the chest of his decayed remains. His hand shifted down to the Duke's side where his sword rested and he ran a finger along the cracked leather of the sheath and up to gilded hilt. He then moved his hand towards the head and gently pushed the wig away from the top of the skull. On either side of the Duke's head, about two inches above where his hairline would have been, he could see the two small horns.

The red man then got up and stepped carefully into the coffin and planted a foot on either side of the Duke's waist. Slowly he lowered himself down onto his knees and the chapel was filled with the rustling and tearing of aged material and the dry cracking of three hundred year old bones as he sat astride the corpse.

He leant forward and cupped the skull gently below the jaw and lovingly kissed the brown-white of the cheekbone before running his tongue along the remaining teeth. He looked directly into the eye sockets and a deep swirling magenta glared back at him.

He sat up again and there was the soft sound of an autumn leaf being crushed in the palm of a hand as he lifted the skull away from the rest of the body, tearing the brittle remains of tendons and skin.

He held the skull high above him, below the crackling red light that was still holding the massive slab and the coffin lid aloft. He turned the skull from left to right, showing it the interior of the chapel that had been the final resting place of the Duke's family for centuries.

'You shall walk on this earth again, Your Grace.'

He then placed the skull gently on the floor by the side of the pit in which the coffin was interred. He climbed out, almost effortlessly. He was not labouring under his enormous weight now - he had taken on a new energy.

He opened his bag and removed a brown towel and in it he meticulously wrapped the skull and placed his precious package back in the bag. He zipped it up and began to walk out of the chapel back towards the nave. As he did so the electric red light dissipated and the stone slab and the coffin lid both came crashing down into the pit. The chapel was filled with the thunderous roar of shattering stone and splintering wood.

The obese red-faced man did not look back at the dust and debris clouding the air above The Duke's tomb.

Instead he concentrated on the journey ahead of him.

He felt The Duke's power within him and he felt his evil force flowing through his veins. He would put the energy that had been endowed upon him to good use before he reached his destination and the fulfilment of his purpose.

He had been locked away for so long, suppressing his needs and hunger and controlling his urges and hiding them from the probing doctors so that he might eventually be released. Now he needed to feed.

The red man exited the abbey through the security door by which he had entered. Still undetected and still under the protection of his master he made his way out of the grounds.

*

From the west side of Inverness the bus made its way through the quiet early evening streets towards the town centre and terminated at the main Airbus station. Namah got off the bus here as she did every morning and went to wait at the platform where she would take the Aberdeen bus the five or so miles eastward to Culloden. She would ask the driver, as always, to drop her off at the end of the road that led to the visitor centre.

When she got to the platform the bus was already there but the driver wasn't behind the wheel and the passenger door was still closed. It wasn't too cold this evening though so she didn't mind waiting. She leaned against the glass shelter and let her eyes drift around the station. She was trying not to think about the Highlander and trying not to think about whether she and Cammie should have another go at looking for the pistol. If it existed at all.

She became aware of people coming to queue alongside her but took no notice of them. When it was this early she preferred to remain in her own world rather than make small talk about the weather with strangers. Not that she disliked strangers. In fact she was very good with people. She had to be in the job that she did. She thought that it was something along the same lines as chefs only wanting to make beans on toast when they got home. She spent a lot of time on her own - an unnatural amount of time she sometimes thought.

She supposed that it was this weirdness about her, *knew* it was, that had led to her not having had many boyfriends. She told herself, with a rueful smile, that she would have to make more of an effort to be more outgoing where her social life was concerned. She knew full well that she had made this decision before and that she wasn't going to change but thinking about it was a step in the right direction. Anyway, she thought, I don't have a problem with the way I am - not for the time being at least.

She was trying to put a halt to this mental debate before it escalated into a full-scale argument when the driver came striding along to save her the bother. He climbed into his seat, started the engine, and opened the passenger door. Namah could hear the hissing of the engine compressing air as she stepped up in front of the driver.

'Culloden please,' she said. 'Could you let me off at the b-'

'Battlefield, aye, no problem,' he finished for her with a grin.

He punched some buttons and she pressed her thumb against the small payment window and as she went to take her seat near the back of the bus the ticket pinged onto her wristfone.

Once inside the clean air of the bus she loosened her facemask and let it hang around her neck. She could smell the slightly tangy bouquet of whatever they used to clean the upholstery.

She sat watching the people who had been queuing behind her get onto the bus without really seeing them or taking them in. They were just there in front of her tired eyes. She was wishing that the journey would get under way when some signal of recognition shook her out of her inertia. Her eyes focused on the latest passenger to climb aboard the bus.

He was tall and dark haired and carried a booklet or brochure of some sort in his right hand. She watched him as he spoke to the driver for a minute or so and from the drivers hand signals she could see that he had asked for directions. He nodded and smiled and she was sure that she had never seen him before. But something in her stomach told her that she *had* seen him before and that he was more than just someone she had met but couldn't recall. He took his ticket and turned to walk up the aisle to his seat. She hadn't realised that she had been staring at him intently but he must have noticed because he lifted his head to look her straight in the eyes. Her heart froze. She saw the corners of his mouth turn up in a polite smile then she turned her head quickly away from him to look out of the window. She could feel her face reddening. He had caught her unawares, whoever he was. But she knew now where she had seen him before.

The vision. The one she had last night at the viewpoint. He was the man she had seen lying in the undergrowth with Cammie.

She looked forward again and tried to look relaxed. He had taken his seat now but he was behind her. She pretended to look out of the opposite window and used the reflection to see where he had sat. From the corner of her eye she could see him a few seats behind her on the other side looking down at his brochure. Even though his face was clean, not covered in mud as it had been in the vision, she had no doubt that it was him.

The engine whooshed fully into life and the bus carried them out of the station. She faced forward, her mind in turmoil.

The familiar outskirts of Inverness passed by and they were travelling eastwards on the main S4 carriageway. The short journey dragged and it seemed to take an age before the bus turned off the main Aberdeen road to detour through the couple of villages that lay near to Culloden on its southern side. She desperately wanted to get off the bus and away from the man in her vision. She hoped that she was mistaken and that he would stay on-board when she got off and that she would never see him again. He had to be going somewhere else. If not, if he really was the man in her vision then he had come with some purpose in mind . . . and she had an idea, especially with what had been going on lately, that it wouldn't be something pleasant.

What had the Highlander said to her about the pistol?

He needs this.

Was this man the *he* that the highlander had referred to?

She looked out of the window and saw the dark wall of uniform pines through her own tired reflection. There were no Daylites out here and only a few areas were lit up by floodlights for farm or forestry workers but every so often the road outside was illuminated by the headlights of an oncoming vehicle. At last the bus neared the point where the driver had said he would drop her off. She got up and made her way down the aisle to the front where she steadied herself with the pole. The bus slowed and stopped and the door opened.

'There ye go,' the driver said as she descended the couple of steps. She hardly heard him as she was straining out of the corner of her eye. With relief, she saw that he was still in his seat.

Her ankle had recovered greatly since the previous night and she had awoken this evening with only slight bruising to show for her injury but as she stepped onto the road and heard the driver telling someone else on the bus that this was where they were to get off she felt it twist slightly. Fresh bolts of pain shot up her leg and a bolt of panic shot into her heart. As she limped away from the junction and down the road she glanced back over her shoulder in the direction of the bus.

He was getting off.

She quickened her pace. She was hardly limping now and the thought of the man behind her forced her to forget the pain and walk on. Her senses were at their peak and she could make out his footfall, maybe twenty paces behind her. She hurried on and blocked out the throbbing of her injured foot as it hit the ground. She turned into the visitor centre car park and a hundred yards ahead was the entrance to the visitor centre itself. Sweat broke out on her brow and a nest of snakes began to writhe in her stomach. She prayed that Cammie was around because she did not want to be alone with this man. She felt dizzy and was reminded more strongly of the vision on the battlefield.

He's not here to harm you.

'Then why is he here?' She hadn't realised that she had said it out loud.

She was about five yards away from the entrance now and had dug her laser key from her pocket. Behind her she heard his pace quicken. Her hand shook as she pointed the key at the lock and then, when she was unable to stand it anymore, she spun around to confront him.

'Why the fuck've you come here?'

*

He sat with his back to a tree and revelled in the afterglow of gratification. For the moment he was at peace and breathed deeply through smiling, blood smeared lips. He heard a low moan from the crumpled naked body a few feet away and was mildly surprised that it was still alive. That was an unexpected bonus.

Once he had realised that the tramp was his for the taking he had gone at him in a fit of furious excitement and everything had come out of him in an instant. There was no question of control. All that pressure had built up in him for so long and he was like an aerosol can on a bonfire, exploding viciously from every pore in his body.

During his long years of confinement he had planned long and hard about what he was going to do with his first victim. How he would trap it, how he would restrain it, what he would do first to begin the slow process of torture and abuse, how he would build up to a wonderful and massive crescendo, gulping in the pain and terror of the victim.

He had fantasised about the event many times, running through the imagined scenarios in his head over and over again. Sometimes he felt guilty that he did this almost as often as dreaming about taking his master north to the stone and becoming one with him. But he knew deep inside that his master would not disapprove. He had chosen him for his desires - for his complete harmony with his master's needs.

In the end it hadn't unfolded as he had seen it in the scenarios that he had pictured in his mind. There had been no cunning capture and no slow build-up of pleasure. But he wasn't disappointed. The immediate and total release of his load had been ecstasy like he had never known before.

It had all happened so quickly - the way he had stumbled across the derelict in the bushes while looking for somewhere to sleep for the night and realising that he was so very vulnerable. Instinct had simply taken over.

Fifteen years ago had been the first time, as an eleven year old boy. He had been too young to appreciate what he had done and too immature to revel in the joy. Too much lacking in self-confidence to sit back and eat up the vibrations that his actions had caused.

He had never been discovered. He was never suspected of the brutal rape and murder of that girl who lived nearby - the one that he hated so much. Like the monarchs of the past who were buried around the Duke, she had thought herself special. Like them, she had become nothing.

Somehow though, his parents had had suspicions. They had asked questions of him and had begun to snoop around his personal things.

His mother found his journal so he had killed her. Before his father returned home from work he destroyed his journal and decapitated his mother so that he could leave her for his father to see when he came home. He had sat there eating chocolate fudge ice cream with his mother's head in front of him on the kitchen table.

A bubbling moan came from the torn lips of the wino.

He remembered the look on his father's face and how he had collapsed to his knees and wailed on the blood splattered kitchen floor while he had sat and smiled and eaten his ice cream.

Eventually he had been taken away and then followed the doctors and the councillors. The isolation. The drugs that slowed and interrupted his mind. But his master had helped him through it all. His master had shown him how to survive.

The wino moaned again, louder than before and interrupted his thoughts.

He smiled at its resilience. He had beaten and broken it, bit and chewed it, torn and raped it in a fit of pure gluttony, but still it wasn't used up. That was good because he could feel his fulfilment abating.

Now the obese red-faced man was ready again.

He opened his bag and rummaged around inside. He lovingly caressed his master's skull before extracting a steak knife. He zipped up the bag and returned to the wino. The wino was semiconscious so the red man tried to coax him back to full awareness. He held the tip of the knife underneath the derelict's belly, and leaned close to his face.

'Hello,' he said softly. 'Can you hear me? I'm here, look at me.' The wino's pupils swam around and tried to focus on the face above him. 'Here I am, here, look at me, come on,' the red man continued.

The old wino coughed out blood from the back of his throat and finally focused on the red man. He tried to talk but his torn and bloody lips only flapped against each other like a dying fish. Then his eyes widened and he became fully aware as he felt the burning fire of the knife sliding into his guts. He shook his head feebly.

The red man withdrew the knife and gently fingered the wound. Hot blood seeped onto his hand.

'Oh that's wonderful . . . so good,' said the fat man.

He would rape this fresh new wound before his victim's heart stopped pumping.

Ten

<u>Perthshire, Scotland, January 17th 1746</u>

The day had been dismal and full of echoes from the night before. What daylight there had been now faded from grey to swirling darkness. The Jacobite army snaked its way northward into the dusk. It had become as one, not an army of thousands of fighting men, but one great animal. One mind driving it, one heart pulsing emotion and heat throughout its immense body. As the darkness came down on the great beast it did not pause for rest or shelter but instead continued to wind its way northward into the night.

A few hours earlier Seoras, Seamas and their father had caught up with the main body of the Jacobite Army and now made their way among their fellow clansmen. Their heads were bent into the driving sleet that seemed to have been pounding them ever since they had left Stirling three days earlier. But the weather, however atrocious, could not drive their spirits any lower than the depth to which they had been buried the night before.

Vague shadows hurried alongside Seoras in the darkness that pumped breath out of their lungs and transformed them into a single steaming beast. Few words were spoken in the darkness. The shouts of encouragement were given to men who had tired or carried an injury and yells from those up ahead that warned of an obstacle which those behind might stumble into. Above the whip of the wind and the infrequent cries of the men Seoras could also make out the thud of hooves and the protesting squeal of the wagons that carried their provisions. These sounds all played their part in the rhythm of the beast and were the only thing that kept his drained body moving forward. He followed his father, never letting him get away from him, never losing him in the crowd. He recognised him in the darkness only by the comforting shape of his head and shoulders and the hilt of his broadsword slung over his back. Every so often Seoras glanced up and checked that his father was still there and was reassured by the hilt of his sword. He had become so accustomed to following it, south then north again over hundreds of arduous miles, that it had become a symbol of security to him. As long as he followed the hilt of the sword, his father would be there.

On into the dark glens they marched and covered the terrain of their homelands in less than half the time that the Government troops could follow them. The men were oblivious to the cold and their minds were distracted by the rhythm of the march and by their own waking dreams. Their bodies were warmed by the energy that burned inside and around them as they huddled together like cattle. The vapour that rose from their damp skin and plaid mingled with the mist that sank into the floor of the glen.

Seoras' mind was hypnotised by the steady tempo of the march and he was transported to the previous night. A heartbreaking memory now and not a vision. A remembrance of the awful past and not a mind's glimpse of some dreaded future.

*

It was over six weeks since they had crossed the border back into Scotland where they found the people were unwilling to receive them. They had marched on and arrived in a Glasgow that was shrouded in deep snow on Christmas Day. The inhabitants of the city were as unenthusiastic about their arrival as the Borderers had been and it was only the intervention of the Highland chiefs that stopped the army running riot. Before moving on they had managed to muster supplies, mainly of clothes and footwear, which they were in desperate need of.

From Glasgow they went on to Stirling, where they laid siege to the castle. The clansmen could see little point in expending their energies in this way and went about it half-heartedly. When the news reached them that General Hawley's army was approaching them from Edinburgh, Stirling castle had still not surrendered. They left Stirling in Government hands and went to fight the enemy in a manner that they much preferred.

When they came in sight of the larger force near Falkirk it was still mid-January and the snow had retreated to the mountains only to be replaced by freezing sleet and stinging hail. Seoras was in his usual position near the rear of the clan, behind his father and Donchad. That was the way of the clans: Sons behind fathers, sub-tenants behind tenants. The elder men and those higher up the clan structure leading by experience and example. He could see little through the ranks of men in front of him and the mist that had come down with the dusk. He could hear less over the skirl of the pipes and the shouts of the men as they taunted the enemy.

As he swayed from foot to foot he managed to get a glimpse of the straight rows of *saighdearan dearg*. Their red coats stood out in the night like a deep slash on a dirty forearm. He was not aware that he swayed on his feet. It was not any message from his brain that moved his body but the pulse of fear and courage, love and hate, rushing through his veins. He wanted to charge and he wanted to run away. He wanted to push through the men in front of him and sprint at the enemy where he would hack down as many as possible before oblivion - he wanted to stand in front of them and tell them all to stop this and go home to their warm hearths and families. He wanted anything but to stand there waiting. But there he stood, blinded by the night and the mist and deafened by the pipes and the yells, weight shifting from foot to foot. Waiting.

Tarlich turned and knelt with his sons as the priest passed through the clan and blessed them.

And then the order had come down through the ranks, through colonels to captains to sergeants and pipers. To the clansmen.

'Caber Feidh!'

The Highlanders howled the ancient battle cry into the night air as they began the sprint towards the enemy lines. As soon as he saw his father and brothers move Seoras followed instinctively. He raced forward and the emotions that had assailed his body now exploded in his head.

Rippling thunder reached his ears as the men up front came into musket range. Clansmen fell to the ground, writhing and clutching themselves. Seoras had to hurdle the bodies.

The next volley that he heard was sporadic and the first of the charging clansmen were upon the enemy and the redcoats were firing at will. Balls of lethal lead cut the air about Seoras and he heard a muffled thump as a man to his left took a shot in the face and the back of his head came away in red clumps and his legs kicked out beneath him.

Acrid smoke joined the mist now and seared the back of Seoras' throat and his eyes streamed. He bounded forward over the broken ranks of the front-line and stumbled to a halt behind his father and brothers. Through the smoke he saw them hacking at the jabbing bayonets of the second line, and he rushed to join them. In front of him he saw the blurred faces of *saighdearan dearg* under black hats. A bayonet shot out towards his chest and he lifted his targe to block the strike and push the blade to one side. He simultaneously lifted his claymore and the red-coat was now defenceless. Seoras watched the look of terror in his eyes as he brought down his sword like a mallet. The ease with which the soldier's arm was severed shocked Seoras and he was rooted to the spot. The soldier crashed to his knees clutching his stump and black blood spouted between his fingers. His eyes were fixed on Seoras, screaming at him and bulging from their sockets. Seoras brought his sword down again and again, making him stop screaming, making him stop looking at him with those terrible eyes. The soldier was reduced to a sodden, bloody mess under Seoras' angry blade.

    He looked up and he was a machine now and saw that his father and brothers had gone. His clan had broken through the second line in places and the *saighdearan dearg* were in disarray and defended themselves on all sides. Cavalry came to the aid of the infantry and fired their pistols into groups of Highlanders and hacked with their swords before being swamped and pulled from their mounts. Seoras saw them come and go and he went forward slashing at everything in red. He was possessed and killing without thought, hefting a sword that he'd previously found heavy as if it was a dead branch. He had no idea how long this went on or how many had fallen under his claymore but finally the beast inside him had quietened. He sank to his knees and sucked in lungfuls of polluted air. He had become aware then that the battle was reaching a conclusion. His hands still clutched his targe and claymore that hung on the end of aching arms and he slid back into a sitting position. The beast had left his veins now and he listened as the explosions of pistol and musket became less frequent. The clash of steel moved away and the screams turned to the wails and moans of the maimed. He thought then about his father and about Donchad and Seamas. He tried to remember where he had last seen them. He let go of his sword, mesmerised by the blood that covered his right hand and was splattered up his forearm and chest.

He looked up and saw that there were still pockets of men fighting in the distance. He picked up his sword and got to his feet and went in that direction to look for his family. He stumbled over the bodies of the dead and dying and peered through the mist. The battlefield had become quiet now and it seemed to Seoras that the *saighdearan dearg* were in retreat. The Highlanders were chasing them off to the east, back to where they had come from. Most of the clansmen were looking for their kin and were forming back into their regiments. They sat or lay on the cold damp ground, or looked to upgrade their weapons from those who would not need theirs anymore.

There was still fighting though and it was towards this that he went, and it was there that he found Donchad as he faced up to a red soldier. As Seoras quickened his step to go to his brother's aid he saw Donchad lunge forward and saw his blade bite deep into the redcoat. He reached Donchad as he stepped away from the man to watch him die. Side by side they stood and watched the soldier, his face in the dirt.

Donchad said, 'Are ye all right, Seoras?'

There was a long, wet sucking sound from the red soldier's mouth.

'Aye, fine.'

And then he was quiet.

'We'd better get back to the others,' Donchad said as he turned.

The musket explosion rang in Seoras' ears and Donchad's arms went up and his legs went out from underneath him and he was on his back spitting blood. Seoras dropped to his stomach beside him and looked for where the shot had come from, keeping his face close to Donchad's, talking into his ear.

'It's okay, he's gone. The battle's over now, let's go back.'

'I can't feel anythin, Seoras.'

'Well, he must have missed ye then.' Seoras could sense a wall of brittle ice holding back the fear. 'C'm on, let's go, Donchad.'

'Aye, but ye'll have tae help, my legs are tired.' Thick liquid that looked like treacle in the darkness spilled from the corners of Donchad's mouth as he spoke.

Seoras struggled to lift him as his eyes closed. 'Home, Donchad, we're goin' home.' The mess of Donchad's open chest was against his own and he held him tightly and tried to drag him back until he could carry him no more. Donchad's mouth was by his ear and he could feel the shallow breaths. Gently he laid him down. 'Wait here, I'm gettin Da.'

Drenched in his brother's blood he sprinted back to where the clans were re-forming. He darted along the lines and looked for the MacLachlans and then looked for his father. An arm shot out from the crowd and halted him. His father had found him again.

'Where have ye been? The enemy are re-grouping . . . we've got to get going.'

Seoras stood, his eyes wide.

'Where's Donchad?' Seamas was by his father's side now.

Seoras stood.

His father saw clearly now. 'Oh God, no.'

Seoras took them to where Donchad lay but he had gone.

The Jacobite army was beginning to move out as they carried his body to a copse where Tarlich used his broadsword to cut and lift the turf. He placed the squares of turf to the side and still using his sword he loosened the earth underneath. His sons stood silent and looked down at their elder brother's body.

He paused and looked up from his work. 'Help me.'

The boys got to their knees and with their hands they shovelled out the earth and stones that Tarlich had loosened. When the hole was deep enough, Tarlich stuck his sword in the ground and stepped out.

'That's enough,' he said.

They wrapped Donchad's body tightly in his plaid then gently lifted him into the grave.

They stood at his feet and Tarlich searched his memory for the words of a priest. Instead he said: 'Father, look after my son. We'll be back for him soon and we will take him home to lay at rest in his own glen.' He paused to rub his eyes with the heels of his hands.

Seoras watched his chest fill with air, then, slowly, he exhaled. 'Goodbye, son

. . . Amen,' he said.

Seamas and Seoras held their bonnets in their hands and looked at each other with red eyes. 'Amen,' they echoed.

Tarlich got to his knees and began shoving the earth back in with his hands and his sons got down and helped. Carefully they replaced the turf so that it fitted neatly back into place. By the time that they had finished the Highland army had gone but they stayed with Donchad a while longer. They stood and watched heavy raindrops fall from the great beech sheltering the grave and explode against the rocks with which they had marked it. Then they left and hurried through the dark to catch up with the Jacobite Army.

*

The blackness faded to greyness and in the dawn Seoras couldn't even begin to guess how much distance they had covered. The night had passed him by as he relived the memory of the past months, the battle at Falkirk, and his brother's death.

The morning sky brought some blue with it but no warmth and at last, after they had seemed to have been marching forever, they stopped to make camp. Seamas was picked to go into the surrounding hills as a lookout and Seoras busied himself with camp duties. Later, his young body switched off and he collapsed into a deep, exhausted sleep. He did not dream and he did not remember.

*

A month later, Seoras sat in another camp beside his father and some men from their croft. They had skirted the Grampian Highlands, through Tayside, Aberdeenshire and Moray and they were now in Inverness. The Jacobite leaders had discovered too late that General Hawley's army had been heavily defeated at Falkirk and had not re-grouped to pursue them as expected but had instead ran all the way back to Edinburgh. The Jacobites had failed to take advantage of the situation.

Seoras looked into the flames of the campfire, and listened to the men talk.

'They say that Hawley built scaffolds in Edinburgh tae hang us on.'

'Aye,' said Tarlich, 'But instead he had tae hang his own deserters.'

'We should have followed them tae Edinburgh . . . they were running like rabbits. The capital would have been ours.'

'Maybe, but we didn't know that they were running and we had no idea what awaited us in Edinburgh . . . I've heard word there's a stronger army on the move north.'

'We could have hanged Hawley on his own fuckin gallows.'

'I think he would have ran that fast that we would have had to chase him all the way back to London.' It was Graeme McGilchrist who spoke now.

'What are we doin' here, Tarlich, skulkin in Inverness when Scotland should be ours?'

'Scotland would still be ours if we had never left it in the first place.'

'Is that so, Tarlich?' The men around Tarlich got to their feet at the appearance of the tacksman.

'That's my opinion, aye.'

'I see,' said David MacLachlan. 'And is it also yer opinion that ye shouldn't get tae yer feet and show an officer proper respect when he's addressin ye?'

Tarlich got slowly to his feet and looked down at David. 'An officer or a jumped up rent collector?'

'I'm yer tacksman and therefore yer captain in battle, Tarlich. Ye'd better remember that if ye want tae keep a roof over yer family's heads.'

Tarlich clenched his fists but remained still and silent, like a bear in chains.

'And where's that brother o yours? I haven't seen him for a while.'

Since coming back to the Highlands the Jacobite army had been plagued by desertion. Morale was low and the pull of their homes when they were so close to their native glens was too strong for some. A few days earlier Ailen had approached Tarlich to tell him that he would be taking his sons home, but that they would be back. Tarlich knew his brother wouldn't lie to him. Ailen had asked Tarlich if he would come too, but Tarlich told him he thought it was pointless going home only to have to come away again. Not fair on the women, he had said, especially with Donchad gone. He had also asked Ailen not to break the news to them yet. He would do that himself once they were home for good. Once it was all over.

'He's away on a foray doon the Great Glen.'

'So why don't I know about that?' demanded the tacksman.

'Because he was hand picked by someone who didn't think that they'd have to go through a jumped up rent collector first.'

The tacksman flushed. 'That'd better be the truth, Tarlich.' He looked around at the men. 'And from what ye were sayin, ye'd better not be plannin on sneakin off yerself.'

In a blur of movement Tarlich had David's arm up his back and his dirk at his throat. David's eyes darted around the group for support. 'Get him off me.'

Only Seoras moved. 'Let him go, Father,' he said placing his hand on his father's forearm.

Tarlich ignored his son and spoke into David's ear. 'I lost my eldest son in a battle which, in my *opinion*, should never have been fought. Still I stay, and my sons stay until the Chief bids otherwise.' Tarlich spun David around and held him by the throat so that he could look into his face. 'Donchad's blood and our allegiance is our rent. It's been collected and until it's due again we have no more business with you.' He shoved David away and he was caught by two of the men to keep him from sprawling in the dirt. 'Now, fuck off.'

David shrugged off the two men who held him and stormed off. Rubbing his throat and pointing back at Tarlich. 'Ye've not heard the last o this,' he said.

Tarlich sat down and the others sat around him. There was a strained silence until Graeme spoke: 'The tacksman could make things difficult for ye.'

'David MacLachlan's got ideas above his station, that's all. He'll see sense.' Tarlich looked around the men. 'He just wants tae go home, same as the rest o us.'

Seoras took in his father's words, glad that he had calmed down. He had seen a change in his father and in Seamas too. He had seen Donchad die. He wasn't sure whether they were full-filling their honour or standing by

their beliefs, but he was sure that this rebellion was destroying them.
*

The weeks passed and any hope of going home became thin. Rumour and speculation continued. Whenever they saw Lachlan he told them of the continued bickering between the Prince and his generals. He told them that The Duke of Cumberland's army was in Aberdeen waiting for better weather before he came for them with his powerful army.

Tarlich and his sons were sent with the rest of the clan to Dornach where they forced a Government out-post to surrender. They returned to the encampment to find Ailen waiting for them.

'I wouldn't have blamed ye if ye never came back,' Tarlich told him. 'Our over-zealous tacksman'll be happy tae see ye, though. He's been worried about ye.'

'I'll bet he has. It was a hell o an expedition doon the Great Glen.'

'How's everyone back home?' Tarlich asked, lowering his voice.

'Worried . . . and upset that ye didn't come hame wi the boys.'

'But they're okay?'

'Aye, they're fine. In fact, I've got some good news for ye. Catriona's goin tae have a bairn.'

Tarlich was silent for a few moments. 'That's great news,' he said turning to Seoras and Seamas. Ye hear that, boys . . . ye're goin tae be uncles.'

'Aye,' Ailen said. 'And Donchad'll live on in the bairn.'

'It's magic,' said Seamas. 'It's a pity we can't have a drink tae celebrate. The public hooses in Inverness've all been drunk dry.'

'But ye can have yer dram, lad,' Ailen said. 'Granda sent us back wi' a wee present . . . the good water from the glen.'

The men of Seoras' family stood together and one after the other put the flask to their lips.

*

'You'd better pay attention 'cause this is going to save your mate's life, you fucking excuse for a soldier.'

The morning was cold but still and dry and Pullman's words rattled around them like pebbles in a tin. A Platoon of 2 Company had been paraded early to begin training at their new camp on the outskirts of Aberdeen. The sergeant had begun to tell them about the new drill that they would be learning when he had noticed Roberts fiddling with his musket.

Roberts had joined the battalion along with other new recruits after they had returned from France. Jack thought that he talked too much and his mind wandered. He had tried to explain to him that if he was going to be a soldier he had to keep his trap shut and not do anything until he was ordered to by an officer or NCO. He didn't listen though and Jack had begun to think that he must like the feel of the cat; he'd already had more lashes, official and unofficial, than half the men in the company.

'Get back into line!' Pullman screamed into his face. Jack was amazed that Pullman hadn't put Roberts on another charge. He regularly dished out strokes, even to the best soldiers in the company. Jack had the scars on his own back for the usual offences: dirt on his uniform, kit missing from his backpack, being a few seconds late for parade. But he'd learned. Roberts wasn't learning. The only men now who had a higher total than Roberts were those who had committed serious offences such as drinking on duty.

Sergeant Pullman regained control of his temper and continued to explain the new drill to his platoon. 'All you men that think you're the big heroes an' don't need to listen can think again. This ain't Flanders and we ain't fighting the French. We're not fighting an organised army but a band of marauding savages. The new drill which I am about to demonstrate will mean that you will be able to defend yourselves effectively against the charge of the 'eathens.' He turned to a wagon behind him and pulled off the sacking to reveal piles of crude wooden swords and shields. 'Roberts,' he said smiling. 'Come out here.'

Roberts went out and stood at attention in front of the sergeant. The Sergeant took his musket from him and thrust a wooden sword and shield into his arms. 'You are now a savage, go and stand over by that rock,' he said pointing to a spot about twenty yards away.

He looked around the platoon for another volunteer and his eyes rested on Jack. He instructed Jack to stand facing Roberts with his musket thrust forward as if defending a charge with bayonets fixed. He then turned his attention back to Roberts. 'Take your boots off Roberts, savages don't wear boots. Did you know that Easton?'

'No, Sergeant.'

'Did any of you know that?'

'No, Sergeant,' the platoon chanted.

Roberts now stood on the mud in his bare feet. 'Take your breeches off Roberts, savages don't wear breeches.'

Roberts stood where he was and gaped back at Pullman.

'Take your fucking breeches off!' He roared at Roberts, sending crows flapping from nearby trees. When he turned back to Jack his voice was calm. 'Did you know that savages don't wear breeches, Easton?'

He knew that they wore skirts. 'No, Sergeant.'

'Did any of you know that?'

The platoon chanted: 'No, Sergeant.'

Roberts now stood before them, naked below his red coat. Muffled laughter came from the ranks and Pullman let them have their laugh. 'He looks silly, doesn't he?'

'Yes, Sergeant.' Some of the men were laughing out loud now, a rare occurrence in the ranks of the platoon that was usually reserved for the poor jokes of officers.

'And that's how the 'eathens look.' He was laughing along with the men himself now. 'Except they wear skirts, but we have a lack of those round 'ere so I won't be making Roberts wear one. That's a pity, though. I think 'e'd suit one. Don't you?'

'Yes, Sergeant.' All the men were laughing now, except Roberts.

'Except when they come at you, they lift up their skirts so that they can run faster.' Pullman held on to his stomach as he laughed along with the men. 'Can you imagine that, them coming at you with their tackle swinging to and fro?' There were spluttered "no, sergeants" and "yes, sergeants" from the ranks.

'And then, when they get near you they raise their swords in arms that are strong from 'olding onto sheep so that they can fuck 'em,' Pullman went on

The men doubled over or held onto each other, helpless with laughter, and in a second Pullman's expression changed from hilarity to rage.

'And then 'is arm, strong from fucking sheep, brings 'is sword down and cuts your 'ead in half like a turnip so that 'e can stick his arm down your throat and steal the biscuits from your fucking bellies!'

The laughter stopped.

'They may look funny, but when they come at you they'll be howling like wild dogs and you'll be shitting yourselves.' He looked over his shoulder. 'Howl like a wild dog, Roberts.'

Roberts howled.

'Like a wild dog, Roberts, not a pig what's being fucked by an 'orse.'

Roberts howled with increased ferocity and Pullman went to stand at the left of Jack, still carrying Roberts' musket.

'Right, Roberts, when I say now, I want you to charge at Easton. When you get to 'im I want you to knock 'is musket out of the way with your shield and bring your sword down on 'is 'ead.'

'Yes, Sergeant!'

'Now!'

Roberts charged forward howling and slipping in the mud. He reached Jack and knocked his musket away and as he raised his wooden sword, Pullman drove the muzzle of his musket into Roberts' exposed ribs and sent him sprawling to the ground, howling in pain.

Pullman turned to the platoon. 'Unfortunately, I didn't 'ave my bayonet fixed, but what 'appened there was that I defended the man to my right, instead of attacking the man in front of me. That's what you'll be practising today and with discipline and faith you'll be able to repel any charge from the 'eathens.' Without turning he said, 'Get up and get dressed, Roberts.'

Roberts began to crawl back over to where his boots and breeches lay with a hand clamped to his ribs. Pullman kicked his bare backside and continued to address the platoon.

'You'll be split into two halves, the first half practising the new drill and the second half being the savages - so expertly demonstrated by Private Roberts - to provide an enemy. Whether you like it or not you'll be binding your muzzles in rags - I don't want you damaging them on each others ribs - and -' He added with a wry smile, 'When taking the part of a savage you'll be keeping your breeches and boots on.'

The sergeant divided the platoon in two and the first half padded their musket muzzles in cleaning rags while the other half armed themselves with wooden swords and shields from the back of the cart. For the rest of the morning and well into the afternoon they practised the drill under the watchful eye of Pullman. To begin with, plenty of them were taking blows to the top of the head with wooden swords when the man to their left had failed to protect them and had instead jabbed instinctively at the man who had charged straight at him. Jack could see that it was going to take guts and a great deal of discipline to leave your own defence to someone else while you defended another. But the frequent whacks to the head and the bellowed threats of Pullman helped them gain that discipline.

They began again in the afternoon after a quick meal of biscuits and water and there was a marked improvement. The blows to the head were less frequent and Pullman had now given those on the receiving end permission to turn around and whack the man who was supposed to provide defence.

Pullman called an end to the training early but the good mood of the men did not last. It wasn't because he thought that they had done well that he had ended their training but because 2 Company were on guard duty that evening. They were given time to go and get something to eat before parading for duty. They were warned to be spotless. Jack knew that he would be spending more time brushing mud from his redcoat, boots and gaiters than he would be eating. He'd rather go hungry than be given a half dozen lashes in the morning. Besides, he had none of his weeks shilling left and could not buy any beef or mutton. He would keep his rationed cheese and loaf till later.

*

Jack pulled the collar of his jacket up around his neck in an attempt to block out the bitter wind that cut through him. He stamped his frozen feet on the ground and looked out into the blackness. He could see nothing from his post a quarter a mile out from the camp. One numbed hand held his musket by his side, while he breathed on the other to bring feeling back into it. He wished that he could put his weapon down and shove both hands under his jacket and into the warmth of his armpits but he had already passed through the guard inspection without picking up lashes and he wasn't going to risk being caught neglecting his duty.

He looked longingly over his shoulder at the fires dotted around the camp. The rows and rows of tents housing ten thousand soldiers and officers. The regiments were divided by roads that gave the encampment the look of a small shanty town. He imagined men wrapped in their blankets, asleep and oblivious to the cold or sipping ale by the heat of the fires. Surely Pullman wouldn't be out prowling on a night like this? He reached into his pocket for his cheese and began to nibble it as he reasoned with himself. Of course he would, the sadistic bastard. He'd love to find someone skiving so that he could personally give him the cat at muster parade in the morning, or better still, find someone asleep so that he could hang him from a tree.

The whipping wind brought the wailing of bagpipes to his ears from where the Argyll Militia were tented way over to the north. He had seen them in their skirts but they were also wearing the King's redcoats the same as his own and wearing tri-corns the same as his own. He had heard them talking in their strange language and wondered what made them different from the heathens that were their enemy. He knew that they had sworn allegiance to the King but couldn't understand what made them fight against their own kind.

The officers had told them that the enemy were not proper soldiers. That they were shepherds, farmers, fishermen and thieves, but from what he'd heard they had always been belligerent. Their rivalries stretched back hundreds of years. If that was the case then fighting was in their blood whether they were trained or not. He did not know why they had sided against their own but he was glad that they had. For all their talk and jokes about heathens who wore skirts, shagged sheep and couldn't speak English, no one ever went near the Highland men camped to the north of Cumberland's Army.

Jack continued to chew his cheese slowly and hoped that the energy that it gave him would warm him a little. His thoughts turned to home and Lucy. He had known her all his life but had only begun to court her when he'd gone home after basic training, before he'd gone to France. That seemed like a lifetime ago and he wondered if she would still be waiting for him like she had promised. He'd met her again in the tavern on his first night of leave and his head was swirling with the gin and ale that all the locals had been filling him with. She had never paid much attention to him before but she was ecstatic when she'd seen him in his uniform. They'd danced and kissed all night and later in the dark she had let him cup and kiss her breasts and let him rub between her legs and then she'd felt him in her hand. But that was all. She'd said she didn't want to get into trouble because then he would go away and forget her. He'd told her that he'd never forget her and he'd meant it. The next day they'd walked and talked and he knew that he loved her and at night they lay in each others' arms and then in the morning she'd cried as he left her.

So many times he had dreamt of her. So many times he had wanted to desert and go back to her. He wanted her now and dreamed of lying with her and in his mind he could feel her in the darkness and he could see the glint of her eyes and he felt himself grow and forgot about the cold.

'Easton.'

Jack's heart jumped and he spun around, Lucy forgotten instantly. 'Higgins,' he smiled. 'I nearly shat myself.'

'Sleeping on your feet, was you?'

Higgins was an old soldier and he had seen plenty in his time. Jack often thought that he would be a sergeant by now if he had been able to read and write. 'Well you can go 'n' get some proper kip now. I've come to take over. Good job I got 'ere before Pullman, eh.'

''ope the fire's still going when I get back.'

'It is that, you lucky bastard. It's fucking freezing out 'ere.' Jack turned back towards camp when Higgins said: 'Listen, Jack.'

'Yeah?'

'Pullman was talking to some of the lads tonight . . . about Roberts. Said that the cat wasn't working on 'im and that maybe they should sort 'im out themselves. "It's you what 'as to fight alongside 'im after all," 'e says, "I'd turn a blind eye of course," 'e says.' Higgins looked at Jack. They both knew that Pullman had insinuated that Roberts should meet with a disabling or fatal accident. They'd seen it happen in France.

''E's just a young lad, 'e'll learn.'

'I know, that's why I'm telling you. I know you like 'im.'

''E's just not a natural soldier, but 'e'll learn. Everyone does sooner or later.

'You tell 'im then, Jack, that it'd better be sooner, 'cos you know what the lads'll do.'

'I'll tell 'im, and I'll speak to the lads.'

'Night, Jack.' Higgins turned to face the hills, a bitter four hours ahead of him.

Jack began the walk back to the warmth of his blankets and the fire. As he walked he decided that he'd talk the lads into only giving Roberts a warning, to scare him. He took the last of his stale loaf out of his pocket and his thoughts returned to Lucy as he chewed.

*

Seoras had been with his father in Inverness when the pipes had struck up and the drums had beat to gather the Highland army together. Once assembled, they had begun the march to Drumossie Moor, south-east of the Highland capital.

The usual rumours and the little hard fact that they had been presented with told the men that although the Prince and his Irish aide were in high spirits, other members of the leadership were not so happy with the way that things were going. Lord George Murray was not happy with the choice of battlefield and the men had to agree that the flat and open Drumossie Moor did not suit their style of warfare and that it was perfect for the guns and cavalry of the Government troops.

Seoras marched with his clansmen to Drumossie not knowing what to expect. When they arrived there was no sign of an enemy. They sat around and grumbled.

'This is no place for men o the glens tae be fightin,' his father had said.

Hungry, they waited for their food, only to be told that the supply wagons had not yet arrived from Inverness. Some said that they had not even left. There was still no sign of food when the pipes rallied them into their regiments. The tacksmen went among them, telling them that Cumberland was camped at Nairn, celebrating his birthday and getting his men drunk. They set off to surprise the enemy in the night., They were promised that by morning it would all be over.

They had marched off into the dusk, watched by local women and children who had come to see the battle. The sleet and hail came down on them once more as they snaked away into the east, towards the enemy.

Through the night they marched, some of the men getting lost in the dark, having never seen this part of the country before. They were weary, cold and hungry and they were making slow progress. Seoras squelched through the bogs and stumbled over the thick heather and waited for the same momentum that had swept him along at Preston Pans. His tired eyes peered into the night and prayed that the same would happen here. That the destruction of the enemy would be swift and that what was left of them would run away back to England and that he and his father and brother and the rest of his clan could go home and forget. He prayed that they could pick up where they left off, never again complaining about the long, harsh winters and getting down on their knees and thanking God for the fresh spring, the warm summer and the bountiful autumn.

But the swift attack that Seoras prayed for never came.

In front of them, over the Grampians, the first grey streaks of dawn penetrated the darkness. The enemy were nowhere in sight and it was clear that they were never going to reach them and surprise them before dawn. The dispirited Highlanders turned around and retraced their steps. They stumbled back the way they had come, over the dead, matted heather and through the bogs. They made their way back to Drumossie Moor where they would once more assemble to face Cumberland's army.

*

Gillies had seen the croft on the way to Nairn and now on the return march he decided that he wasn't going to starve any longer. He was going to help himself to some food and hopefully some drink. He badly needed a drink. As he stumbled through the grey dawn he rubbed subconsciously at the itching wound in his hand.

'What a heap o bollocks,' he muttered to himself. 'I'm supposed tae be servin a Prince's army but instead I'm wanderin about half starvin like a beggar.'

The croft house that he had seen earlier came into view and he was glad to see that there was no light from the windows and no smoke whipping up from the roof.

'Well fuck them. I'm goin tae help mysel tae some breakfast.' He strode on, his shoulders hunched against the sleet that was hitting the back of his neck. 'And for their sakes they'd better have some drink in . . .'

He halted.

In the gloom he could make out the figure of a small boy huddled by the side of the road. He was wrapped in his plaid, asleep. Gillies poked him with his foot and he stirred. When he looked up at Gillies his eyes widened and he jumped to his feet, making to run off. Gillies held him firmly by an arm.

'Be still boy, I'm not goin tae hurt ye.' The boy stopped struggling. 'Are ye from the croft?'

'No, from Inverness,' he squeaked. 'I followed the army out . . . are you a warrior?'

'Aye, lad. That I am.'

The boy smiled in awe. 'Did ye win?'

'Eh, no. It's not over yet . . . a change o plan.' Gillies went down on his haunches and spoke softly to the boy. 'Listen, how would ye like tae be my apprentice?'

'What?'

'My helper. I can teach ye everything that ye need tae know about bein a great warrior like me. Would ye like that?' Gillies licked his lips.

'Aye, aye.' The boy's eyes were alight, his cold and hunger forgotten.

'First though we need tae get oursel's somethin tae eat . . . ye must be starvin.

Quietly, with the boy by his side Gillies approached the door of the croft house. There was no sign of life and he motioned for the boy to remain where he was. Then he stepped back and kicked the door in.

The boy stood where he had been told and waited. He could hear muffled cries from inside the building and decided to abandon his post and go and hide in the nearby whin bushes. He heard someone rummaging around and then the warrior appeared at the door with a sack in one hand and a bottle in the other and a black-toothed smile on his face. When he saw the boy was gone the smile vanished from his face and he snarled intae the night.

'Where the fuck are ye, ye wee bastard?'

The boy in the bushes held his breath.

Then the highlander pulled the cork from the top of the bottle with his black teeth and took a long drink. 'Fuck it,' he said and stomped off up the road into the dark.

*

A field mouse, tiny, unseen, crept through the camp and through the trampled grass, pausing to sniff at horse droppings. It came to a canvas wall that disappeared into the night above them *and looked like the end of the universe. It crept along the sides of the canvas and stopped to nibble at some discarded food. They could hear the singing of the men as they celebrated the birthday of William Augustus Cumberland. The rodent nibbled at the remains of a discarded pork rib and* they *urged it on.*

The mouse crept under the canvas and sat on its haunches in the undisturbed grass in one corner. It sniffed the air and looked up and they *saw Cumberland before them.*

He sat alone with his back to them, writing at his desk, and then he stopped abruptly and looked about him. They *forced the mouse to sit still.*

Cumberland pushed his heavy frame up from the stool and poked his head out of the flap of the large tent.

'Sergeant, under no circumstances am I to be disturbed.'
His voice fell from his mouth like dirty roadside mud and they recoiled at the sound of it.

'Yes, Your Grace.' *A muffled voice replied through the canvas.*

'Under no circumstances.'

'Under no circumstances, Your Grace.'

The Duke closed the tent flaps tightly and picked up his stool and placed it in front of a large wooden chest. He opened the lid and then prised open the underneath of it with the tip of his letter opener. A wooden shelf swung down that fitting neatly on top of the chest and converted it into a small table. On top of it there was an inverted pentangle, painted white and framed by a circle. From inside the lid he took five candles and placed them at each of the points. He lit them and as he did so he mumbled to himself.

In the corner the mouse began to quiver and thick, yellow urine leaked from its bladder. They could not hear his words, but they knew who he spoke to.

He reached inside the recess of the lid again and withdrew a black cross on a thick gold chain. He held it up so that the inverted cross dangled in front of his face. He kissed it and hung it around his neck.

'Nema, reverof, yrolg eht dna rewop eht, modgnik . . .' *he began to chant, his awful voice filling them with terror.*

Then the mouse darted back under the canvas and scuttled away. They did not try to restrain it. They wanted to be gone too.

They left the field mouse and they also fled.

*

The buglers marched down the roads between the regiments sounding the reveille. Jack got himself dressed and was already buttoning his coat as the other men in A Platoon were still fumbling around and moaning about hangovers. The Duke had sent brandy and rum to every company to celebrate his birthday but Jack had drunk little. He saw no reason to celebrate. From the corner of his eye he saw Pullman making his way down the road from the sergeants' mess and quickly stood to attention.

Pullman eyed him with distaste. 'Start getting the fucking tents packed onto the wagons, you idle cunt,' he spat at Jack.

'Yes, Sergeant.' He'd had to endure this harsh treatment from Pullman ever since the night that Roberts had died. The night that he had been murdered. Jack had arrived back from his sentry post that night, too late to talk to the lads. Too late to give Roberts a chance. He was trampled by a horse, they'd said, his head smashed. He was already wrapped in a blanket with the red blood seeping through the grey cloth. Jack had gone to see Pullman straight away.

He was just a boy.
So?
They killed 'im, Sergeant.
The 'orse killed 'im, Easton.
You practically ordered them to do it.

Pullman had gripped Jack by the throat and hissed into his ear, his spittle hitting the side of his face. *You're forgetting yourself, Private. I run this fucking platoon, and if you don't keep your mouth shut you'll be the next to be sorted out. Understand?*

Yes, Sergeant.

I'll be watching every move you fucking well make.

Jack should have known better. Talking to Pullman hadn't brought Roberts back and he had only succeeded in making life hell for himself.

The platoon quickly packed up and the company's wagons rolled off to join the supply train on the right hand column of the army. Pultney's Battalion were with the other infantry in the centre three columns while the cavalry and the artillery took the left.

As the Government troops set off for Drumossie Moor, The Duke sat to their right among his senior officers, taking the salute. All eyes turned in his direction to acknowledge him. He waved his hat for them and they cheered and Jack was reminded of victories in Europe. *Flanders, Billy. Flanders, Billy.*

A single blood cell amongst a flowing vein of crimson, Jack could not see the obese frame of the King's second son, William Augustus, Duke of Cumberland.

*

The butt of a musket rattled his jaw and brought Gillies out of his drunken slumber. Redcoats were all around him and he leapt to his feet and reached for his sword. It was gone. They had taken it while he slept. He reached for the pistol in his belt and the dirk in his sock but they too were gone. Then more blows rained down and he was knocked to the ground. He saw a rope looped over a branch on the tree above him and a noose swung at its end. He struggled violently but they held him and brought the noose down over his head.

'No, no. Stop. Ye can't do this.' He began to cry as they tightened the noose. *'No. NO! NO-O-O-O!'* He screamed and kicked and then he was up into the air and swinging and looking down at the upturned faces of the redcoats. He felt hot liquid stream down the inside of his thighs and even as the rope set fire to his throat and his vision began to dull he tried to spit in the redcoats' faces.

But soon the blackness came.

And the demon.

Come to me, dog, you are mine now.

And then he saw no more soldiers and felt no more hempen rope.

*

After they had passed the swinging Highlander the men whispered excitedly around Jack. 'The scouts caught 'im and 'anged 'im . . . it's an omen . . . fortune is with us today . . . there'll be one swinging from every tree for miles before the day's out.'

Jack didn't believe in good fortune, not any more. He would be keeping his head about him and surviving this battle. Whatever happened he would be deserting as soon as they got back south of the border. He would be going home to find Lucy and together they would flee to some other town where they would never bother to track down a worthless private. He would get a job and somewhere for them to live and they would have a family and be happy.

He just had to get through today. One last battle.

He'd seen enough action in France and no one could say that he hadn't done his bit. He was a good soldier. Pullman was a murderer and if he stayed here he would surely die as Roberts had.

His ankles and calves ached from twisting and stumbling over the heather and his feet were frozen from being soaked in the bogs and streams but finally he heard the buglers telling them that the enemy had been sighted. The Duke's army marched onto the moor at the regulation seventy-five paces a minute and began the manoeuvres that brought them from marching columns to ranks ready for battle.

After ten minutes they halted and the drums were quiet.

About two miles away over the moor and through the driving sleet Jack could just make out the dark clumps of the rebel army.

Remember the drill, he told himself, remember the drill.

Even though the wind was blowing away from him, Jack could make out the sound of the pipes playing defiantly.

*

His father's hand shook him out of his sleep and he dragged himself to his feet. Instantly the hunger began to chew at his belly and he wished that he could lie down again. Sleep. He could forget the hunger if he was asleep.

'They're comin, Seoras.'

He looked from his father's face to Seamas'. Their eyes were heavy and hollow. The skin hung from their faces and they looked as old as each other. 'It's nearly over then?'

His father managed a smile. 'Aye, son. Soon be home.'

They moved to their positions among the clan and the pipes struck up the ancient reels and they sang. The sky darkened and the wind drove the unrelenting sleet into their eyes with added fury while the priests went among them and blessed them. It was the afternoon now and they had managed about two hours sleep since returning from their aborted attack on Nairn.

The singing intensified as they watched the massive red columns march across the moor. Above them their standards flapped vividly against the grey sky. Gold. Green. Buff. Red, white and blue.

Eleven

<u>Culloden Battlefield Visitor Centre, Scotland,
April 14th 2146</u>

Sinclair blinked, startled. 'I . . . the visitor centre, I came to see it . . . and the battlefield. I'm sorry if I scared you.'

The anger disappeared from her face. 'I wasn't . . . ye didn't . . . scare me. The visitor centre. Of course.' Namah turned and opened the main door, hiding the redness that had crept up her face. 'We're not quite ready to open yet,' she said nodding at the sign on the wall. It told Sinclair that the centre would not be open for another half an hour.

'That's okay,' he said pointing out a nearby bench. She nodded vaguely, seeming not to have heard, her eyes far away. 'Are you okay?', he asked her.

'Aye.' Her eyes locked with his again. 'I just get the feeling that I've seen you before. Look, I'm sorry that I was rude. God knows I don't want to scare visitors away. Why don't you wait inside 'til we're ready? It's a cold night.'

'Thanks, that'd be great,' Sinclair said following her in. 'Though I doubt if you've seen me before . . . I've never-'

'In a dream, it was in a dream.' She made the remark in a casual way, as if it was an everyday occurrence for her. She moved around the foyer switching on the food and drink machines. 'Ye can get yerself something, and,' she said pointing to a rack on the wall filled with historical magazines and leaflets,

'There's plenty of stuff to read. Everthing's available on the app as well, of course.' She opened the door to a glass fronted souvenir shop. 'And ye can have a look around the shop if ye like.' She came to stand in front of him and her bright blue eyes looked at him intently.

'Thanks,' Sinclair stepped towards the magazine rack.

She smiled warmly, 'And if ye like I'll come and get ye, and give ye the guided tour.'

'Yeah, that'd be great.'

She turned away. 'Right, see ye in a wee while.' She went behind the reception desk and disappeared through the door behind leaving Sinclair with the sight of her silken black hair trailing behind her.

He picked up a few tourist leaflets and sat down to look blankly at them, thinking only about the girl he had just met. After a while he got himself a coffee and wandered over to the souvenir shop. It was small and reminded him of an old photograph he had seen of a train station newsagents. The shelves in the middle were full of mugs, soft toys, address books, hats, t-shirts, flags. They all had the same theme: lots of tartan and Loch Ness monsters. He only glanced at this and went over to the bookshelves on the other side.

He had never seen so many books in one place outside of the university library. He sipped his coffee and looked along the titles. There were dozens on Scottish history and among which he noticed Lombard's and remembered his own copy lying in his bag. There were many on Culloden, The Forty Five and The Jacobites, and others focusing on specific periods and lives: The Wars of Independence, Robert the Bruce, The Stuart Dynasty, Mary Queen of Scots. He by-passed these and went on his haunches to look at the books on the bottom shelf. They were all various types of English-Gaelic dictionaries.

He picked up a pocket sized one and looked up the word Cuidich. It said: *assist, aid, help, succour*.

Thig agus cuidich sinn.

Come and help.

He took another from the shelf, *Gaelic for Beginners*, and stood up with both the books. He went over to the till to wait for the girl to come back. His eyes fell upon the stand beside the till that was filled with key rings with various clan names on them. He took one of the key rings from its hook and looked at it lying in the palm of his hand. It showed a clansman on a background of tartan with his shield held high covering the lower half of his face and his long dark hair flowing out from beneath his bonnet. His claymore was held out in front of him pointing downwards as if to parry a blow. Underneath on a banner it said: MacLachlan.

'B' aill leibh. 'S mise Namah.'

'Sorry?' said Sinclair looking at her extended hand.

'I said, I'm sorry for keeping you waiting, and I'm called Namah. I didn't introduce myself earlier. *De 'n t-ainm a tha orra?'*

'Oh.' He looked down again at her hand and guessed that she had just asked him his name. He still clutched his coffee in one hand and had the key-ring in the other and the Gaelic books under his arm. He shrugged awkwardly and smiled.

'Here, let me,' she said setting his coffee down by the till.

She returned his smile as she shook his hand and Sinclair felt at ease with her for the first time. 'Thanks . . . I'm Sinclair Giacomo.'

'Mas e bhur toil e chon thu.'

'I have no reply to that, I'm afraid,' he said feeling slightly foolish.

'I'm pleased to meet you,' she said nodding at the books under his arm. You want to learn?'

Sinclair flushed. He'd taken them almost without thinking about it. Because of the Highlander, in case he came back, in case he spoke to him again. 'I . . . Yeah, I thought I'd try and pick some of it up.'

'You must be staying for a while, unless they've started speaking Gaelic in Australia.'

'New Zealand.' he corrected her. 'Yeah, I thought I'd make it an educational trip,' he said vaguely wondering how he was going to get the money together for the return fare. 'Get some of the language, some of the culture. I have a good friend and colleague who is an expert in Scottish History at the University back home.

He inspired me to come and visit Scotland.'

'That's great,' Namah said. 'And Culloden is the first stop on your trip?'

'Yeah,' Sinclair tapped some of the keyrings on the stand and shuffled his feet.

'Well, I'd like to help you as much as I can, so feel free to ask me anything at all . . . it doesn't have to be about the battlefield.'

'Thanks, I will.'

'Shall we begin the tour then?'

'Whenever you're ready. You can leave your bag in my office.'

Namah held the office door open and Sinclair opened his holdall and tucked the paper bag containing the bonnet under his shirt before setting down the holdall. Namah watched with interest but didn't comment.

She began by showing him around the small museum which illustrated the history of the Seventeen Forty-Five Rebellion through chronological displays. There was also a room dedicated to how the Highlanders lived during the eighteenth century and another room lined with glass cabinets displaying weapons, clothing and other exhibits, many recovered from the battlefield. She took her time showing him around and explained everything as she went and answered his questions. She left him alone in the small forty-seat cinema while he watched a half hour documentary on the Battle of Culloden.

Having passed through the centre, they exited it at he other side, and for the first time Sinclair saw the battlefield.

In the light of the powerful floodlights, it was nothing like he had imagined. He could not see the colours of the moor as he had imagined them while reading Lombard's book. To the north there was only darkness. No Moray Firth cutting into the land, no ghostly shoreline of The Black Isle beyond, and to the south there were no looming giants of the Highlands propping up the vast swirling sky. He couldn't help feeling disappointed.

'What's the matter?' she asked, sensing something was wrong.

'Nothing . . . I just-'

'Wish you could see it during the day.'

'Yeah, something like that.'

'You can,' she said, 'But only from inside the protection of the centre. Not the same I know, but that's the curse we all have to bear.' She began following a path leading down a slight incline toward a small wood of birch and fir. Beyond that, bathed in the floodlights, the moor rose into the darkness, like a landscape hanging in a colossal black gallery.

She took him first to the Leanach Cottage, a farmhouse which, she told him, had survived the battle and had been preserved the way it had been then. There had been a barn among the outbuildings, she said, where over thirty men were deliberately burned to death.

From there they made their way down the path and through the graves of the clans. Namah pointed things out to him and supplied him with information.

As he walked, Sinclair became increasingly aware of the atmosphere creeping up from the ground around him. The place was silent, but not restful like any normal cemetery. In fact it was the opposite.

She pointed out to him how no heather grew over the green mounds of the clansmen's graves, and he felt a chill as he read the name MacLachlan carved plainly into a rough headstone.

From the graves she led him along the path that passed by the Memorial Cairn before ending at the main viewpoint. This one was virtually dead centre of the battlefield, as it had been, but now looked out from the trees.

As Sinclair studied the layout of the field, Namah looked across at the viewpoint on the government side, where she'd had her vision the other night. She glanced down to her right and remembered how she had seen Cammie concealed in the bushes, with the man who stood next to her now.

She studied him as he studied the plaque.

'What?' he said without looking up.

'I . . . nothing.'

Sinclair looked up from the plaque. 'Are you thinking about the dream again?'

Namah looked at her feet and turned to walk back up the path.

'Was it a bad dream?'

'Just weird.' She beckoned him to follow her up the path. 'C'm on.'

'I know the feeling,' he said. 'I've had my share of those lately. In fact, that's partly why I'm here.'

Namah became aware of her heart thudding in her chest, as if it hadn't been beating previously. She remained silent and continued up the path.

Sinclair followed, unaware of the apprehension that had crept into her eyes. 'I'm not even sure they *were* dreams. I -' Sinclair cut himself short, feeling that his mouth was running away from him. He had no idea why he was telling this to a woman he had only just met.

Namah carried on walking by his side, only glancing at him as she spoke. 'Did he come to see you too?'

Sinclair stopped in his tracks. Now it was his turn to feel the beat of his heart quickening in his chest.

Namah turned to him. The blazing sapphires mounted in her honey-golden face locked with his green eyes. She looked as if she belonged here, a fairy princess gracing a mythical landscape. She looked beautiful - and afraid. He wanted to go to her and hold her.

'Did he come to see you too?' she asked again, her light voice floating away on the breeze.

Sinclair looked skyward. Beyond the floodlights he could see only blackness. If there were stars up there, then his eyes could not adjust to pick them out. 'Yes. He came.' He looked at her to see what her reaction would be. 'And they weren't dreams . . . He was really there.'

'We need to talk,' she said.

But Sinclair seemed not to hear her. 'He dripped water on my carpet and it froze and burnt my fingers.'

'I think that we should go back to my office and talk this over properly. There are things I think ye need to know,' she said taking a pace towards him.

'I could see his breath even though the room was warm.'

She reached out for his forearm and he clasped her hand making her jump. 'He spoke to me, and he left me something.'

Under his jersey she could feel his arm trembling.

For the first time since meeting the Highlander Sinclair felt that he had gained a grip of his mind. The Highlander wanted something from Sinclair and that was real. As real as the ground that he stood upon and the cold breeze that brought water to his eyes. The reality scared Sinclair.

Gently, Namah tugged at his arm. 'Let's go back.'

*

They returned to the visitor centre and Namah showed him into the small administration office while she got them hot drinks. They sat in silence for a while on either side of the desk and sipped their coffee.

'That's what the *Gaelic* books are for,' Namah said finally.

'Yeah.'

'So that ye can look up what he says.'

The corner of his mouth twitched. 'Yeah. Stupid. But I don't need them now . . . I've got you.'

She lowered her eyes. 'How did ye know he wanted ye to come here?'

'A couple of weeks ago he came to see me, and I tried to tell myself that I was hallucinating.' Sinclair put his coffee on the table, not letting go of it, still cupping it in his hands.

For the second time, he told his story to someone he barely knew. He told Namah about how real the highlander was, how he had spoken in that strange language so that Sinclair was not sure if he had spoken at all, how he could see and smell the blood and dirt on him and how he dripped water on his floor that had been so cold that he had burnt his fingertips when he bent to examine it. He told her how he could not erase the voice or the look of torment on the boy's face from his mind. And then again when he had appeared a second time in his classroom, except that time he had left the bonnet. He told her how he had dropped everything and that very night he had gone to Dunedin to see Jason Lombard.

'You know Jason Lombard?,' she raised her eyebrows. She thought about her battered copy of his book at home and the many hours she had spent with it at university. She remembered seeing it on Cammie's bookshelf as well - and of course they sold it in the shop.

Sinclair nodded. 'I was told that he could tell me anything that I needed to know about Scottish history. He wasn't very helpful at first, but that was before I showed him the bonnet.' He watched her eyes over the rim of her coffee cup as she steadily sipped and wished that she would throw in some information about her own experiences with the Highlander instead of letting him go it alone. 'The tests showed that the bonnet was only a few years old,' he continued, 'And they also showed that that was impossible.'

'Why?' Namah put down her cup and he paused to look at her.

He found himself wanting to talk about anything rather than what had taken place back in New Zealand. Instead of asking her if she ever tied her hair back so that people could see more clearly the beautiful shape of her face, he explained about the bonnet. How it had been dyed using a plant that had become extinct about a hundred years before and how it could not have been preserved so well or retained its colour if it was an original.

'He's right. Did ye see the bonnet in our museum?'

Sinclair admitted that he hadn't. His attention had been taken up by the array of menacing claymores and axes and how the cold steel had seemed to emit violence and death through the glass.

'It was dug up from a peat bog in the nineteen-fifties. The bog had preserved it pretty well and even though we know that it was originally blue, it's now the blue-green colour of deep water. Is it a bonnet that you have under your shirt?'

'Yes,' he said and patted the bonnet.

Sinclair stared at the desk and he felt like a dry leaf on a windy night. Nothing had been solid since the

Highlander had come into his life and he found himself wanting answers. Although Namah had whipped up the storm within him a little more he felt that she was also the key to the calm. She would have answers. She could help him put his feet back on the ground.

'Can I see it?'

'Sure.' He took the paper bag out from under his shirt and pushed it across the desk.

Namah removed the bonnet from the bag and examined it in much the same way as Lombard had, but without the doubtful look that he had had in his eye.

'It's real.'

'How do you know?'

'I just do. I can feel something coming from it . . . it's like the battlefield. I can't explain it. I know that it's been here before. I know that someone wore it at the battle.'

'How do you know?' he repeated.

'After what you've just told me, I think that you'll believe - understand - what I'm going to say.' Namah put the bonnet down in front of her and gently stroked it with the backs of her fingers. She looked at Sinclair differently now, as if she was really noticing him for the first time.

'I can see things,' she said.

Sinclair watched her hand go back and forth over the bonnet, gliding slowly over it, barely touching it, then lifting slightly and returning. The motion of her hand was strangely hypnotic and he found himself wanting to reach out and stroke her long black hair in the same way. 'You mean that it wasn't a dream that you saw me in before. You knew that I was coming.'

'Well, no. I didn't know that you were coming . . . but I did see you . . . in a sort of dream.'

'A vision?'

'You could call it that I suppose.' She let out a long sigh. 'Look, for any of this to make sense, I have to tell you everything.'

'Good,' Sinclair smiled. 'I was beginning to feel like it was only me doing the telling.'

Namah returned his smile.

'I'm sorry,' she said. 'I suppose this is even more confusing for you than it is for me. I've been around this place a long time and I've grown used to it.'

The rhythm of her hand stroking the bonnet soothed Sinclair as he listened. She told him how after her mother died her father had become custodian of the moor. She told him of how she had always felt a presence in the place, even when she was little, and about the voices on the wind that she had often heard. She believed her mother had passed on the gift. She told him that she still loved it here in spite of this, and that even though it wasn't at peace, the moor still deserved to be cared for. A lot of people died brutally here, she said, for causes that were not their own.

She stopped stroking the bonnet and laid both hands lightly on top of it and told him about her more recent experiences with the Highlander. She told him how she had glimpsed him a couple of times, face to face, and she said that she had also seen the look of anguish that Sinclair had seen. And then she told him about the Highlander coming to her flat in Inverness and taking her onto the moor. How the pistol had come up from the ground - the pistol that was *for someone*. Her grip on the bonnet tightened slightly as she told Sinclair that the Highlander had then told her to go, screamed at her to go, and that he had vanished and she had ran across the darkened and stormy moor, being chased by something.

'I found myself back in my bed then,' she said. 'And when I got up I found that I had sprained my ankle. In fact, it's still a bit painful to walk on.'

Sinclair let out a low whistle. 'Well I'm glad he didn't take me on such an eventful tour. Otherwise I think that I would have resisted the urge to come here and got myself some serious professional help instead.'

'You think that we're mad?'

'No, I don't. Not now that I'm sitting here talking about it with you. But if I was back in New Zealand on my own-'

'You would have serious doubts.' she smiled.

'Yeah.' He felt himself relax for the first time in weeks at the sight of her smile.

Then she said: 'There's more.'

Some of the tension came back to Sinclair's shoulders.

'Shit. More.' He drained the last of his coffee.

'The following night, last night in fact, was when I had the vision in which I saw you,' she said, beginning to stroke the bonnet again. She told him how it had happened, how she had seen him and Cammie - quickly explaining who Cammie was - concealed in the bushes.

'But there was someone else there too. Someone that I didn't see, but could sense. I could feel his evil . . . and of course there was the smell.' Her face twisted in disgust at the memory. 'I'm sure it was the man from the moor. The other moor. The moor that the Highlander took me to.'

'Do you think that he's coming here too?'

'*You're* here, aren't you?'

They both looked around when they heard footsteps coming across the foyer and around the reception and both jumped when the door opened.

'Hello, Namah,' said her father as he entered the office. He seemed to sense that he had interrupted something and looked suspiciously at Sinclair.

'Hi, Dad,' she replied. 'This is Sinclair Giacomo. He's visiting us from New Zealand.' She stood up and hugged her father. 'Sinclair, this is my father, Alex Robertson.'

Sinclair stood to take his hand and noticed that his eyes were the same startling blue as Namah's. 'Pleased to meet you, Mr Robertson.'

'Pleased to meet you Mr Giacomo. That's a good Italian name. It means Jacob. A real Jocobite has come back to Culloden,' Mr Robertson smiled.

'Yes, although the only Italian heritage that has been passed down is an old Florentine pasta recipe,' Sinclair smiled in return. 'I hadn't thought of the Jacob connection.'

Mr Robertson nodded. 'New Zealand, eh. That's a long way to come for a visit.'

'Well I'm not here just for the sight seeing. I was hoping to get some work here. I'm a teacher.' Sinclair wasn't exactly lying, he would have to find work if he was going to get back to New Zealand.

'Well, I hope you enjoy your stay.'

As they spoke, Namah put the bonnet back in its bag. She didn't want to worry her father with anything that was going on.

'I'm sure I will.'

'I was just giving Sinclair some background information on the battle before we went out onto the moor,' she said handing the paper bag to Sinclair.

'Aye, that's fine. I just came down early in case you were running late again, but I'll do some work while I'm here,' Alex said nodding at the desk. 'How's the foot by the way?'

'Much better, thanks Dad,' Namah said pushing Sinclair out of the door.

Alex laid a hand on his daughter's arm. 'Is everything okay?' he asked lowering his voice.

'Everything's fine.'

'He's a fine looking man, a teacher too.'

'See ye later, Dad.' Namah smiled as she closed the door behind her.

Namah led Sinclair back onto the battlefield, but this time they headed down towards Cammie's workshed. 'My father's been ill lately,' she said as they walked. 'I'd rather he didn't know about any of this.'

'What's there to know?' Sinclair said. 'We hardly know anything ourselves.'

'I think that we're going to find out a lot more, and soon. I don't know about you, but I have a few ideas of my own about why you're here.'

'I don't know what to think,' Sinclair admitted. 'But I wouldn't mind you sharing some of your theories with me.'

'Later,' she said as they approached the workshed. 'First I want you to meet Cammie, and then we're going to look for your pistol.'

They found Cammie buckling on his tool-belt. When Namah introduced Sinclair he didn't seem in the slightest bit surprised and when she told him that they were going to look for the pistol again he was already stepping over to his tools.

'You think we'll be able to find it this time?' Cammie said lifting his shovel off the wall.

Namah shrugged and although she didn't think that they'd need it, she didn't bother to tell Cammie to leave the shovel behind.

The shadows around the three of them stretched and shrank in the light of the floodlights as they made their way along the southern side of the battlefield and towards the Jacobite lines. This time they by-passed the graves of the clans, the memorial cairn and the viewpoint. Namah strode on ahead of the two men. She was eager to get to where ever it was that she was taking them, and Sinclair wished that he could share her enthusiasm.

As she walked, she talked. 'I would see him from about here, and he'd be standing up there, at the corner of the path,' she said pointing to the spot about a hundred or so yards up ahead of her where the path turned north-west along the Highland lines.

As they looked in the direction that she pointed, most of the floodlights went out across the battlefield. The section that they stood in was plunged into blackness.

*

The day had been bright as he had followed the route that his master had taken three hundred and fifty years earlier, but now the dark hand of night was casting a grey shadow over the country. Soon there would be traffic on the roads and he wanted to remain unseen. He slowed the airbike and pulled in at the side of the road. The suspension groaned and squealed as he eased his immense weight off the bike. He pushed the bike well away from the road and he concealed it in some bushes before carefully placing his bag beside him and making himself comfortable for the night. Through the branches above him he watched the sky turn from grey to black. As he listened to the sounds of the forest preparing for darkness he picked at the peeling skin on the top of his bald head and the backs of his hands. The sun had been hard on him, and he knew it would eventually kill him, but he had no fear of the sun and no fear of death. Soon he would be a part of death itself.

He reached into the bag by his side and withdrew the bundled up towel and carefully opened it up on his lap. The boughs of the tree above creaked as a stealthy wind began to sigh through the woods. Swirling carmine illuminated his face as the skull of his master glared up at him.

He had been hungry but now the gnawing in his belly was forgotten. He had been exhausted from a full day on the road but now his weariness was soothed and he became relaxed. He had been anxious that he would not reach his destination in time to do what his master required, but as he gazed hypnotically into the crimson eyes of the skull his worries were washed away.

You will receive what has been promised, the voice told him. *An eternity devouring the souls of the weak. An undead existance, creating terror and slaking your thirst upon it. My faithful servant. The waiting is nearly over, and then you will join us.*

The corners of his mouth turned up in a drunken smile as the detached voice swam around his head. A dribble of saliva spilled over his lip.

'Thank you, Master.'

First though, you have work to do.

His eyes widened. He knew about the work and he was eager for it. Both for his own satisfaction and to prove his worth to his master. 'Yes.'

The branches above him, bearing only a hint of the first buds of spring began to wave like skeletal arms as the wind strengthened.

First you must fight for me.

'Yes.'

There will be a battle and we will be victorious.

The wind skimmed the dry top layer of leaf-mould from the ground and it swarmed around him like black insects and the limbs of the ancient trees began to screech in protest as they were yanked to and fro by invisible hands.

'We will, we will.'

We will have victory once more and you will come to me and all that has been offered will be yours forever.

'Oh, yes.'

The trees groaned and shrieked as they danced madly around him. Close by there was a thunderous crash as one of their number lost its struggle to remain upright.

Rest now.

The fat man raised both of his hands to his mouth and kissed his finger-tips, then gently rubbed them against the horns on the skull, before wrapping it once more in the towel and carefully placing it back in the bag.

He slid down through the damp decay of the forest floor and cradled the bag against him. It would be a cold night, but the cold would not trouble him. He could feel the heat of his master.

As he slipped towards sleep, he smiled and rubbed at his crotch as he remembered the girl that he had stolen the airbike from and remembered what he had done to her.

From a safe distance, hardly visible in the dark branches, *they* watched him through the eyes of a tawny owl.

*

Sinclair blinked as his eyes strained to adjust to the dark. Night was a strange environment and one that was completely alien to him. He, like all the other inhabitants of the earth, had spent almost all of his waking hours between the setting and the rising of the sun without ever having been exposed to the warmth of the sun's rays but also having never spent any time real time in the dark.

He looked skyward and tried to imagine the huge vortex in the troposphere and the massive holes in the ozone that had been caused by the pollutants released during the centuries of human activity since the industrial revolution. Were those wounds healing? Would people be able to walk in the sun again in his lifetime?

He could see stars above as his eyes gradually found their night vision and thought that the constellation that he could see to the east might be the one that they called The Plough. Further north a three-quarter moon glowed pale blue. The world had been forced to live at night, away from the hostile rays of the sun, the naked rays unfiltered by the worn and tattered ozone layer which rapidly destroyed skin cells, caused melanoma and reduced the body's immune system. Yet through all his nocturnal life he had never really looked up at the night sky. Virtually every town and city and highway in the world was illuminated by the massive Daylites which recreated daylight perfectly. Even small out of the way villages and places like this battlefield were lit up by floodlights that recreated a safe imitation of day light and artificially provided the same health benefits that humans required from real sun light.

Now though, the lights had gone out. He was slightly amazed to find that his other senses began taking over from his lack of vision almost immediately. He suddenly found that he could smell the sweet perfume of the wild flowers and heather around him and could taste the tangy pine on the breeze and could feel the firmness and slope of the track under his feet. Around him in the trees and bushes and across the moor he could hear the rustle and scrape of nocturnal animals as they went about their business. The animals at least, had always lived that way. They had always found safety and refuge in the dark.

Beside him he could make out the black silhouettes of Namah and Cammie and wondered if the same thoughts were going through their minds. He listened to their careful breathing for a while and was about to ask what had made the lights go out when Namah reached out and tugged at his hand.

'Look,' she whispered. 'He's here.'

Sinclair looked down the track and held his breath when he caught sight of movement. There, for the first time since he'd left him the bonnet in his classroom, he saw the Highlander. He was about two hundred yards ahead at the corner of the track. He gave off a faint white light as if he still retained the luminosity of the floodlights that had just gone out. He remembered that it was the place where Namah had said that she'd first seen him.

They watched as he turned and began to move off around the bend.

The three of them began to walk along the track in the subtle blue light of the moon. Namah quickened her step as they lost sight of the highlander through the undergrowth and the two men fell in line behind her. They reached the corner and there she slowed. He waited up ahead, by the plaque marking the spot where the MacLachlans and MacLeans had formed up for battle.

Her pace quickened as he moved off the track again and then she began to run, fearing that she would lose him. Sinclair and Cammie followed, scanning the dark moor and catching glimpses of him now and then through the undergrowth.

Namah turned off the path and crashed through a thicket of whin. She felt a twinge of pain in her weakened ankle but continued onwards in the direction that she hoped the Highlander had taken. She stumbled over a rise coated in thick heather and came to an abrupt halt. The two men halted by her side. Sinclair gripped her arm to stop himself from tumbling down into the hollow.

There below them stood the Highlander with his face turned to the ground.

They stood for a moment, unsure what to do, and then Cammie stepped forward with the shovel.

Without looking up the Highlander raised his hand to stop him. Then he pointed his index finger at Sinclair. Sinclair took a deep breath, stepped down into the hollow and stood in front of the Highlander. The boy did not look up from the ground and Sinclair stood there feeling awkward. Then he felt the ground tremble through his feet and a swell of panic rose in his chest and he looked over his shoulder at the others for support.

'It's okay,' said Namah calmly, and he wished that it was her that was standing there. His thighs trembled. His feet threatened to pull away in long running strides and he had to concentrate to keep them planted firmly on the ground. He followed the Highlander's gaze, as Namah had in her vision, and saw the ground between them vibrate, faster and faster, churning up the turf and moss until there was only a patch of fine soil between them. It seemed to bubble and boil like a pot of rice. Sinclair waited for an almighty eruption, an explosion that he was sure would kill him, but instead a shape appeared. The fine soil was shaken from it and then an old and rusting flintlock pistol lay between them in the shadows of the moonlight. The pistol from Namah's vision.

Sinclair looked up to find that the Highlander was looking down at him, as if sizing him up. The moonlight had lost its blueness now and had become milky as it shone through the wispy edges of clouds.

The Highlander looked real now. He looked solid. He knelt on one knee and carefully picked up the pistol. Sinclair watched mesmerised as crackling blue light began to play around the hands of the Highlander. His nostrils were filled with the smell of hot metal and the blue light lit the hollow. The ancient pistol reformed in front of his eyes. The swollen rust fell from the barrel and the rotten wood of the grip strengthened and smoothed. His knees suddenly felt weak and he was afraid that he would pass out. Then the light dissipated and the Highlander looked up at him, holding out the pistol.

Sinclair looked back at Namah.

'Take it,' she said softly.

Sinclair turned back to the Highlander.

'What is it for?' he asked in a voice that he hoped had not quavered as much as he thought it had.

The boy only looked at him with eyes full of pleading.

'Just take it,' Namah said over his shoulder, this time with more conviction.

Sinclair tried to steady his shaking hand as he reached out and grasped the pistol. He inhaled sharply as the dead cold of it sucked the heat out of his hand and arm and he nearly dropped it. The Highlander smiled at him and he relaxed, cradling the pistol in both hands.

Then they were blinded as the floodlights came back on. They shielded their eyes with hands and forearms and winced as they tried to open them in the new brightness.

When Sinclair was finally able to see out of one half-open eye he looked around the hollow. The Highlander was gone.

As he looked up at the others on the rise he felt cold drizzle on his face.

'Now what?' he said.

Twelve

<u>Drumossie Moor, Scotland, April 16th 1746</u>

Seoras watched as the red soldiers halted. Only their huge standards continued to move, soaring into the air like great flames fanned by the wind.

The wait began.

The beast stirred in his veins, but now it seemed to be driven more by fear than the balance of emotions that he had felt at Falkirk. Across the moor he could see the *saighdearan dearg* wheeling their great guns into position. Along the red front-line they appeared with their barrels extended like the claws of a wild-cat. He could count ten of them thrust out between the the flapping colours of the standards.

He swayed on his feet, heel to toe this time, not foot to foot. Forward and back, not side to side. Faint, not pumped up. His head was heavy with fatigue and his gut empty and weak.

Tarlich turned to look at his sons. He reached inside his plaid and removed half a biscuit that he had stored from the day before. He broke it in two and handed a piece to each son.

'Eat.'

The boys bit into their piece of biscuit and chewed and handed the rest back to their father. 'Eat,' he said turning away. They turned to their cousins, Ailig and Euan and gave each a piece of biscuit.

'My belly thought my throat was cut,' said Euan.

The freezing cold sleet that dripped from Seoras' hair and bonnet was momentarily forgotten as he chewed the hard biscuit into a paste in his mouth. He carefully swallowed and his stomach began to growl and churn. His appetite was merely awakened by the food.

An explosion came from the front. He stopped his swaying and held his breath and waited for more. Only his tongue moved, as if independent of him, probing at his teeth and retrieving the last crumbs of biscuit.

It had begun.

He waited for another explosion and prepared for the thunderous shock waves. The sound of the pipes came to his ears, loud, snatched away by the swirling wind, then loud again. The rain and sleet splattered on his bonnet and targe. A pillar of smoke rose from the front where the Jacobite gun had fired and was caught by the wind and blown back down into the men behind. They spluttered and their eyes streamed.

Then the ground throbbed beneath their feet and moments later there was the whistle and thud of deadly incoming metal. Earth was kicked high into the air, along with limbs and parts of limbs. Entrails from burst bodies, splinters of bone. Sprays of blood.

Seoras dropped to his knees and heard with infinite clarity the squelch of the boggy ground beneath him. He felt dirt shower down with the rain in muddy splats.

'Close up! Close up!' the call came from the captains. 'Close up the ranks!'

Seoras was hauled to his feet and he stared in bewilderment. Where men had been tightly grouped around him there was now a large space. Broken bodies lay on the ground, some still screaming. To his left lay Ailig's torso, his wide eyes looking unblinking into the rain that washed biscuit crumbs from the corner of his mouth. Blood pumped from his body into the sodden ground in steaming jets. Seoras stepped over him as he was pulled forward and the gap in the ranks was closed. He looked across the moor and could not see the red soldiers or the steel claws or the vivid colours. Instead he saw a wall of smoke coming rapidly towards them on the wind.

The wildcat had lashed out at them.

Through the ranks of Highlanders, away to his left and to his right the agonised screaming went on. At the front, the men began to clash their weapons against their shields. They called out, taunting the enemy, trying to prise the wildcat from its lair.

But the red soldiers remained solid. The guns fired again and through the smoke came the lethal spheres of metal. The whistle and thud reached Seoras' ears and it came steady now. Some hitting close, others on the flanks or going over to the second line where the Prince sat on his grey gelding behind the French and the Irish, the small regiments of English Jacobites and deserters and the small cluster of cavalry.

The metal hit and the men were cut down and they cried in agony and rage. They clashed their swords and the pipes played on.

*

They halted in position, and behind him Jack could hear the wet cloth of the battalion colours cracking in the wind. He stood in the front rank and looked out across the moor at the dark clumps of Highlanders, unable to distinguish individual men. The cold sleet hit the back of his neck and shoulders and ran down his back. He heard the drone of the pipes and he shivered. To his right, in the gap between his battalion and the next, he heard the gunners moving forward. 'Move up, move up!' the bombardiers yelled and the gunners grunted and the wheels squealed as they heaved the artillery into position. There was three gunners to each gun and one bombardier commanding each of the guns. The bombardiers stood out front to make sure that they were aligned along the front rank, and then they stepped back behind their guns. The bombardiers fell silent and Jack waited and listened to the wind snapping the colours and the sleet that rapped steadily on his tri-corn.

Then he heard a thump and saw a cloud of smoke appear at the front of the rebels and he heard metal sing through the air above them. From behind there were cries and the panicked neighing of horses.

Then the bombardiers began to yell the drill. Trained for this moment. Professional.

'Powder . . . Ram!' Gunners moved without thought.

'Load . . . Ram!' The ball placed into the muzzle and pushed home with the rod in two sharp movements.

'Ready . . .' Flame poised at the powder channel. The bombardier looked along the line at the other nine, arms raised and then together they dropped.

'FIRE!'

Jacks shoulders hunched and his eyes closed tightly as the ten guns fired as one. He knew that it was coming but there was nothing he could do to stop himself from flinching. His ears rang. He opened his eyes and saw the swirling smoke and the gaps that had appeared in the dark clumps across the moor. Then, as the smoke rose and obscured them he watched the rebels converge and fill the gaps. Immediately, the bombardier was ordering the reload and then the fire. Now the guns were firing at will, not waiting for one another. Firing, reloading, firing. The gaps in the rebel ranks appeared and then closed again, as if they were firing into a lake.

Jack was sure that the dark huddled clumps were getting smaller. He tried to see as smoke and sleet was driven into the rebels along with the artillery fire. He could see dirt spraying up into the air as the shots struck. He could sense the suffering. But still the rebels stood.

'They're getting fucking massacred,' said an excited voice behind Jack.

'The artillery're blowing the shit out of them and they're just standing there taking it,' said another. An enthralled murmur spread through the ranks that had previously been silent. Each man had been concentrating on his drill, making sure that he would survive the battle. It seemed that their chances of doing that were increasing with every artillery shot that the rebels stood and took.

'Raise elevation!' the bombardier called to his gunners. They were firing at the rear of the Highlanders now.

The guns continued to fire and with each shot the morale of the infantrymen was raised. Jack watched the ball cut swathes through the rebels and he could hear yells and shouts and howls of agony across the moor. With each shot came the murmuring in the ranks around him as more rebels were cut down, 'Fucking, yes,' through clenched teeth. The fear was going out of the men as their spirits soared.

Higgins leaned over and hissed out of the side of his mouth: 'I 'ope they stand there all day . . . we won't even 'ave to fire a shot.'

'Too good to be true,' said Jack. Higgins returned his attention to the slaughter, not detecting the cynicism in Jack's reply.

Jack doubted that they would stand there all day. The pounding that they were taking certainly meant that the enemy was being severely weakened, but at the same time he wished that it would end. It had gone on for over ten minutes now and in that time hundreds must have died. He closed his eyes.

He knew that they would not stand there all day and he knew that the battle would not be won this easily. The rebels had stood there with their leaders under this awful punishment. Faithful, loyal. He doubted if the men that stood around him would be capable of such integrity. Soon, he thought, the rebels would break and it would not be in retreat.

*

Tarlich stood in front of his sons and next to his brother and nephew. Fear for his family, fear that he would lose more of them had gone now. The fear had been consumed by total, burning rage. Red rage came down like a thick mist and through it he saw the carnage continuing around him. He was ready to explode, his grasp on sanity slipping as his raging mind tried to get to grips with the lunatic situation that they were being forced to endure. Another Government shot came cutting through the nearby MacLeans. *'Close up, close up,'* came the call from the officers and Tarlich snapped.

'Close up? What the fuck for? So that we make a better target for their guns? You fuckin idiots, we should be chargin not fuckin standing here waiting for them to cut us all down.' He screamed his rant into the air, towards where there might be officers who would listen, venting his rage through his body and letting it shoot up through him like a geyser. 'Where's the order tae charge? Do ye want us all dead?

Other men around Tarlich began to shout towards the back, demanding the order, pushing forward, begging for the order and an end to the butchery. Those at the front bashed their targes and called out to the lines of red soldiers, taunting them, trying to make them break into their own advance so that they would have to go out to meet them. *'C'm on ye bastards, C'm o-o-o-n!'*

But the lines of red remained immobile, watching through the sleet and smoke.

Still the guns cut through them. They stood and they waited and they waited and still no order came.

Tarlich turned, shouting towards the back, towards the generals on horseback that he could not see. He shouted in the direction of The Prince, with whom ultimate responsibility for this indecision rested. The Prince who had chosen this awful field to fight a field where the Government should never have been able to mobilise their guns This awful moor where troops of red coated cavalry waited to cut them down when they should have been fighting on land that was useless for horse.

'Give us the order ye fuckin morons, can ye not see what's happenin?'

He could see a cluster of flags behind the second line, the place where the Prince must be and he ranted in that direction. His sons and the men around him ducked as metal came singing low over their heads and he was silenced as he watched it smash into the men standing twenty yards behind them. He saw a horse ripped in two and blood and steaming entrails splattered the white faces of men close by. His anger knew no words now and he roared at the sky like a caged lion.

The men shouted to the front and to the back. *'Just go, fuck the order, just go.'* And they began to push forward, ready to charge. On a hair trigger, ready to explode forward. One man running would set them all off.

Still the shots cut through them and still no order came. Still they stood fast waiting to get at the *saighdearan dearg*. Against the western and southern sky the mountains stood like giant ghosts, the line of their shoulders and peaks blunted by the grey cloud. They looked down on the children of their land and they wept.

Then like a raging bull, Tarlich pushed through the men in front of him.

*

Lieutenant John Sullivan looked worried, listened to the Prince, nodded, and scratched at the paper on his thigh with black ink. The horse beneath him would not stay steady and he was not surprised. He shouted for the boy and the boy came at once and stood waiting at his heel. Sullivan handed him the paper, told him the name.

The boy sprinted down the right of the second line, turned left and continued his run along behind the clans. A stitch burned in his side as he covered the boggy ground, leaping over waterlogged dips and channels, dodging foot-twisting hummocks. Thrust under his plaid he held the paper tightly in his fist, protecting it from the sleet, the paper for MacDonald of Keppoch, who waited on the far left flank.

Not far to go now, four hundred yards maybe. He could hear the cannon balls coming in, could hear them ploughing into the men, could hear their screams. The stitch in his side felt like a hand twisting his lung and he gulped in air that was laden with smoke and laced with earth and blood. He clutched the paper in his fist and despite the stitch he pumped his legs faster. He knew the paper was important. He knew that it must be the order to charge that he had heard the clansmen shouting for. He blanked the pain out of his mind and raced through the smoke. He passed the back of his clan, his own people. Two hundred yards to go now.

The smoke stung his throat bringing tears and the wind whipped freezing rain into his eyes, but through his watery vision he could make out the MacDonalds up ahead, the mighty clan of Keppoch, formed up in their hundreds. He heard the yells and screams of men, the frightened whinnying of ponies, the thump of Government guns from across the moor and the sing of metal cutting through the air. Louder than before, he was sure. Louder, clearer, so that all other sounds around him became muted and he could hear only the note that the metal ball was singing.

Lachlan's fist lay on the soaking ground, tightly clutching the edge of the paper. It flapped for a moment or two in the wind, like a dying bird, and then the sleet beat it flat against the moss. The rain pooled in its folds and the black ink ran and mixed with the blood and grey mess of Lachlan's smashed head. As the clans awaited the order to charge, the boy's legs twitched.

*

Seoras saw his father push through the men and disappear into the crowd. He tried to follow but all the men around him were pushing forward now and breaking into a run. The push forward rippled along the clans and then the Highlanders were charging forward like a wave.

The charge pushed on and the wave gathered slow momentum as men stumbled over the uneven ground and their feet sank into bogs. The charge was not going to hit the redcoats with its usual velocity but still the Highlanders pushed on and still the mass picked up speed. Seoras glanced around him and looked at the men of his clan as if taking one last look at them to remember them. Their bonnets were pulled low on their heads and their wet faces were solid and defiant. Their mouths were wide open and filling with rain as they yelled ancient battle cries. Hair was plastered to their faces and necks and heavy plaids sodden with the rain were pulled up high so that they could run faster. And in that glance Seoras saw them in detail, saw all of them, every part of them as they charged. The blue flowers tucked behind the white cockades in their bonnets, the rain and tears and mud and blood on their faces, the ornate brooches pinning the heavy tartan cloth to their shoulders - sometimes silver, sometimes steel, sometimes wooden, but always beautiful, always made by their own kin. And their faces showed no fear. He went forward with the mass of his clan, not swept along as he had been at Prestonpans. Not a boy, but a man, ready to fight for his clan and his people and in that glance the last drops of fear within him dissipated. The fury in his heart was gone. The beast in his blood was calm and focused. He charged forward with the men of his clan towards the lines of *saighdearan dearg,* towards their deadly muskets and bayonets.

*

The dark mass on the other side of the moor began to break forward. Jack's stomach twisted and his hands began to tremble.

To his right the bombardier called to his gunners: *'Switch to grape!'*

Slick, fast, well-drilled, the gunners acted. No powder charge to ram home this time. Just one cartridge, one paper cartridge about the size of a child's head, stuffed with musket-ball, nails, scrap metal. One lethal cartridge rammed home and pierced through the charge hole, power laid in the channel. Grape shot ready to fire.

Jack watched the dark mass grow into men, screaming, yelling men, flooding the land that lay between the armies. His knees felt weak and bile rose to the back of his throat.

'Shit,' said Higgins, and then the grape shot began to sing its dreadful song,

*

The churning black-grey sky began to lighten as it rolled eastward over the mountains. The hammering sleet began to ease and over the foothills skirting Daviot and Drummossie Moor to the south of the Moray Firth it faded to drizzle. On the hillside Anghas and Anndra gripped the boulder as they watched. They knelt in the soaking heather and huddled against each other and shivered in their sodden plaid.

They had arrived the previous afternoon from their home in Strath Bran, having left well before dawn that day. They had thought that they were going to miss the battle but had found that the Highland Army still waited with no enemy in sight. They had watched from this safe distance as the Jacobites had waited and then at night had followed them part of the way to Nairn before falling asleep in the heather. When the Jacobites returned they had awoken and returned to this vantage point on the hillside. Like the army below them they had spent the morning cold, wet, hungry and waiting. And when the wait was over, when the columns of red appeared in the east, beating their drums, their flags flapping high above them, the brothers had forgotten their fatigue and hunger. Ever since the first shot had been fired they had peered over the boulder with wide eyes and gaping mouths.

They watched the wave of Jacobite soldiers break forward from the clumps that they had been standing in. The Jacobites bulged forward from the centre left and the bulge rippled quickly along its length and the wave moved forward, slowly at first, but building up speed as it raced towards the Government red. The two armies were not lined up parallel and so the Highland charge was heading towards the right flank of the government troops at an angle. The wave picked up speed as it raced towards collision and from their safe place the brothers could hear the cries and shouts of the Highlanders. Then the government guns fired and the wave stopped dead, as if it had smashed into an invisible harbour wall. Anndra hid his face in his brother's shoulder and clapped his hands over his ears but he could not block out the screams.

'I want tae go, Anghas, I want tae go hame.'

Anghas didn't listen to his brother's plea. He continued to watch the battle with his eyes wide and his jaw slack. Quarter of a mile away the charge had recovered from the blast of the guns and, like a shoal of fish, had changed direction as one and now raced towards the left hand side of the red ranks.

Anndra tugged at his brother. 'Anghas, we have tae go back, Da'll belt us.'

Anghas glanced round. 'No, Anndra, he'll belt me. I'll tell him I made ye come. And I'm goin tae get belted whether I go now or stay a bit longer.'

'But ye'll get belted worse the longer ye stay. Are ye no scared.'

'Scared! No! I wish I was doon there, fightin wi the Jacobites.'

Anndra looked down at the battlefield and saw that most of the charge had been halted. Some were even turning back. On the far side the Highlanders had come within twenty yards of the enemy only to be halted again. The crackling thunder of scores of muskets being discharged in unison reached Anndra's ears. He watched the plumes of smoke rise into the sky.

'Ye'd be killed.'

'I'd be a hero.'

'C'mon, let's go. Please.'

'Soon, I just want tae watch them. Look! They're breakin through.'

On the moor below, the Highlanders had at last reached the redcoats on the far left and the boys could make out their great claymores arcing through the air as they hacked at the enemy.

'They're goin tae win, I know it.'

Anghas watched and Anndra buried his face in his shoulder. Neither boy was aware that they were shivering or that their stomachs growled. They clung to the boulder on the hillside and did not notice that the drizzle had stopped and that above them the dark sky had turned to light grey.

*

Seoras' leg sank knee deep into a ditch and he was struck from behind as men piled up and threatened to trample him into the water. As he struggled to pull himself out he heard the new song. In front of him and over his head he heard the hiss and zing of metal in the air and with agonised clarity he heard the dull thump of the musket balls that sounded like picks being driven into soil as they connected with men. The rip of flesh being torn away, the smash and splinter of bone.

Seoras struggled to his feet and around him the charge had halted. He could not see through the mass of men to the front, but he could hear. And then, sensing that if they remained where they were they would be massacred, the men began to charge again. They tripped and stumbled over the mound of dead and dying men who had been at the front when the first volley of grape shot had hit.

Seoras charged on and he made his way to the front and looked ahead for a glimpse of the *saighdearan dearg* but a thick curtain of white smoke swept into them and stung their eyes. Then, as he tried to see through blurred vision, the wind pulled the curtain of smoke up from the ground and he could see scores of legs, white and grey, one foot behind the other, and the muskets fired and all about him men dropped to the ground. He felt pain in his left arm and saw that his plaid was ripped and blood seeped into the torn cloth. Once more the charge was halted and the clansmen around him began to beat their targes and shout at the redcoats.

Then the smoke lifted away altogether and the redcoats could be seen clearly. They stood row upon row, hundreds and thousands. At the front they raised their muskets to fire another volley, single eyes looking out from under their black tricorns as they levelled and took aim. Their muskets cracked and bucked in their arms, fresh thick smoke obscured their upper bodies again.

The hiss of metal filled the air and more men were knocked viciously off their feet. They hit the ground and spilled their blood, dead or writhing in agony. Splinters of wood cut into Seoras' face as a chunk of his targe disintegrated. He held onto the remains and stood where he was.

'C'm on ye dirty bastards! We'll take all of ye! Come on and fight ye fuckin cowards!'

Less than a hundred clansmen had made it this far, and rather than charge into the wall of bayonets they tried again to taunt the redcoats into breaking ranks. Seoras clashed the remains of his targe and yelled. Each time he struck it sent fresh pain through his wounded arm. The *saighdearan dearg* of the second rank raised their muskets and fired.

Seoras shut his eyes and waited for the shot that was going to send him to the turf with the others, but the metal whizzed and thumped around him and he remained on his feet. When he opened his eyes again he saw that the first rank had reloaded and were preparing to fire.

The band that had made it this far was diminishing. They could not stay here. The redcoats were not going to break ranks when they could pick them off with their muskets as they had done earlier with their artillery.

No one gave an order. The muskets cracked at them as they sprinted forward in one last desperate and violent charge.

*

Jack watched the Rebels come across the moor and Sgt Pullman began the musket roll.

'Front rank, make ready!'

Jack dropped onto one knee and pointed his brown musket forward. He looked across the moor and he could see that the rebels were still about a hundred yards out and he let out a long slow breath. They seemed to be heading for the other side of the front-line. Then shards of metal ripped through the air from his right as the nearest artillery gun spat its deadly venom into the rebels. For a moment Jack thought that the charge had been halted but the murderous velocity of the grapeshot had only succeeded in deflecting the enemy. They turned sharply on the moor and were now heading directly towards Jack's Battalion.

'Present!'

Jack raised his Brown Bess to his shoulder and sighted along it from hammer to muzzle. A nerve in his closed eyelid twitched and fluttered and he drew breath in shallow shaking gasps. Through the smoke of the guns he could see the rebels coming at them. Their weapons were held high and their faces twisted into hideous masks of rage and their blood and mud streaked legs pounded the turf like stampeding horses. The howls that screamed out of their throats sent a current of ice water gurgling down Jack's spine and through his limbs. He clenched his left fist around the wet furniture of his musket to hold it steady, afraid that it would slip out of his shaking hand. Despite the weapon in his hands and the regiment around him he felt weak and defenceless. The rebels were thirty yards away now and the current of fear that had coursed through him centred in his chest and rose to the back of his eyes, freezing his brain. Suddenly he knew how it was going to feel to have cold steel driven through his fragile skull.

'Fire!'

His finger flinched back against the trigger more in startled fear of the order than in response to it. His open eye caught a glimpse of the rebels being thrown to the ground in sprays of blood before fresh white smoke whipped across them on the damp, cold wind. He had no time to watch for them re-emerging from the smoke.

'Reload! Second rank, make ready!'

He sprang up and stepped behind the second rank as they stepped forward and knelt on the soaking heather. He reached into his side-pouch for a cartridge and his numb and useless fingers seemed to take forever before he gripped the familiar shape in his fist. He pulled the cartridge out and tore off a corner of the thick brown paper with his teeth. His shaking hand spilled some gunpowder into the firing pan and then he detached his ramrod. He struggled to find the muzzle and his fingers fumbled as he drove the cartridge deep into the barrel.

Everything seemed to be taking too long and he was sure that the rest of the rank must have reloaded by now. But he could hear the rattle of ramrods being pulled free and re-attached as he re-attached his own. Glancing out of the corner of his eye he could see the long line of bayonets being lifted onto shoulders. Somehow they shone in the dull light, as if each possessed an aura. And now the cold behind his eyes was only a dull throb and the world gave the impression of having slowed down. Even the noise of the battle seemed to have muted, as if his senses were reluctant to send their messages to a brain that was becoming overloaded. The stuttering explosion of the second rank firing brought him back to real time.

'Reload! Front rank, make ready!'

His knee sank into the soft ground and the rebels burst through the smoke ten yards in front of them. There was no order to present or fire, only the shocked bursts of muskets being discharged along the line before the infantrymen sprang back to their feet, unable to believe that the rebels had broken through the volleys of fire that were supposed to keep them at bay. The howling rebels crashed into the front-line and Jack's mind scrambled for the drill. To his right a rebel brought his sword back ready to bring down on Higgins, who himself was dealing with the rebel to his right.

'Do 'im, Jack, fucking do 'im,' Higgins shrieked and Jack drove his bayonet upwards, stepping forward and putting the weight of his body behind it. His vision was blurred and he felt his lunge stab through the air. There was no resistance and for a horrifying moment he thought that he had missed his target. The terror forced him to focus and he saw that he had not missed. His long bayonet had driven into the throat of the rebel, upwards under his jaw and ripped out through the flesh of his cheek like a bloody finger. He saw the young eyes blinking up at the grey sky, the red wetness pulsing down his musket towards his hand. Suddenly the rebel looked a lot smaller.

A boy. Just a boy.

The boy's eyes rolled into the back of his head.

Pain ballooned in Jack's head and it swirled with blackness. He sank towards the ground with the young rebel still on the end of his musket. He was dimly aware that men were clambering over him, blotting out what little light the day had provided, making it dark. Men stood on him but it did not hurt. Instead he tried to tug his twisted bayonet free of the boy's jaw.

*

A bayonet thrust forward and embedded itself in the remains of his targe and Seoras hacked downwards with his claymore. He remembered Falkirk and once more he had become strangely detached. His life could end at any moment but he felt no fear.

Pain spurted through his side, but even this seemed numbed. He looked down and saw that a redcoat's bayonet had sliced into his right side, just below the rib cage. He swung his blade up and around cutting the redcoats face in half, before stumbling forward with the momentum of the rush.

The clansmen who had made it through the red line were spilling into an area of open ground only to be faced with another wall of red. They had no time to consider this and no time to feel disheartened and no option but to push on. They were now sandwiched in between two battalions of government troops. The band of thirty or so men who had broken through stumbled forward into the second battalion and the recoats closed in around them.

Seoras was acutely aware of the smells of grass and leather, spiced with polish and the smoulder of cordite. Men pressed around him, black tricorns of redcoats and blue bonnets of Jacobites, sweat and blood filled his head. These were not smells sensed through his nostrils but part of the air that he breathed. The aromas came not at once, mixed together, but shifting through the air as if in pockets. A strong smell of leather, then fading, then a faint smell of polish, getting stronger, sharp, overpowering. Then gone, replaced by fresh blood. Then the hot appalling stench of spilled entrails. He had no idea where he was going or who was around him. He was jostled around and pushed and pulled in the melee. He was aware of the dull clashing of metal around him, splintering wood and bone, the crack of pistol and musket fire. He heard calls and shouts in the English, men on horseback in his periphery bawled out orders that he did not understand. His own people were shouting to each other in despair and at the *saighdearan dearg* in rage. But below it all he could hear fainter voices, softer. Calling.

Another bolt of pain exploded in his side and he clenched his teeth and closed his eyes. He did not call out but sank slowly to his knees, lost in the forest of legs thronging around him. He dropped his claymore and went on all fours and the cold, sodden turf cooled his burning hands. He took no notice as a boot came down on his fingers. Slowly, he lowered his body and laid his burning side on the cold soft turf. The sounds drifted down to him as if from another plane and his eyes flickered open. Above the surging horde of fighting men he could see the grey sky and more clearly now he could hear the voices.

*

Men who had survived the charge were turning and Ailen turned with them. He turned with the tide of the clansmen and made his way back across the moor and the sight that awaited him made it seem like a miracle that any of them were still alive. He had been aware that men had fallen around him during the charge, but *this*. The moor that he had looked out across before the charge was gone. The world that he had been a part of was gone.

The icy fingers of the Moray Firth stroked the dead as Ailen stumbled over the carnage but the only cold that he felt was in his veins. Around him, the few remaining survivors of the charge made their way away from the redcoats, some quickly stooping around the piled bodies looking for brothers or sons.

As he made his bewildered way forward, he tripped over a leg. He fell with his hands held out in front of him to break his fall and splashed into a water-filled hollow. The muddy water was turning to red as the surrounding bodies drained their life into it. He knelt in the cold, red-brown water and shuddered.

He stared at the remains of a head lying at the edge of the pool, the jaw ripped off, a chunk of shrapnel embedded in one eye and the other staring back at him accusingly.

How did you survive?

The shivering wracked his body and his raw eyes began to sting under the bitter flow of tears. A hand reached out to grasp his forearm and Ailen pulled away instinctively and scrambled to the edge of the bloody pool. His red eyes looked over his shoulder to see the pale form of his brother reaching out to him.

'Ailen, we have tae get back . . . tae the glen.'

Tarlich's face was white and his eyes dark and hollow and at first Ailen recoiled, thinking that his brother was a demon. Then he reached out for Tarlich with a hand that trembled.

'Have tae get back.' Tarlich's voice rattled and sounded to Ailen like a plough breaking the thin stony ground of a hillside. He gripped his hand and pulled him out of the waterlogged hollow. Tarlich moaned through gritted teeth and Ailen stopped pulling.

Ailen looked his brother over as he lay on the lip of the hollow with his feet still in the water. He could see nothing wrong with him.

'Where are ye hurt?' He looked again, feeling his legs. Then he pulled his feet out of the water. 'Aw Jesus, Tarlich, yer *foot*.' Ailen's head span at the sight of his brother's ruined foot. It was a pulp of smashed bone and flesh barely recognisable as a foot. 'Jeeesus, oh Jesus.' Ailen turned and ripped the shirt from a corpse dimly aware that the body was still warm. He couldn't do much here but he would have to stop the bleeding or Tarlich would not make it off the moor.

'Back . . . tae the glen, Ailen.'

Ailen quickly tore the shirt into rough strips and wrapped them tightly around Tarlich's foot. 'Ye're foot, Tarlich, yer fuckin' foot.'

'Bad?'

It'll have to come off, he thought. 'Ye'll nae be fuckin' dancin' for a while. Fuckin' grape-shot. It's broke.' He tightened the makeshift tourniquet and hoisted Tarlich onto his shoulder with a grunt. He picked his way over the bodies and he continued his way back across the moor, his strength renewed now that he had purpose, now that he had his brother with him. He gripped Tarlich tightly around the thighs and the muddy water from Tarlich's sodden plaid ran over the back of his neck and down his arm.

He was almost back to the point where the charge had began and the tattered remnants of the clans were bunching together before making their way back in the direction of their respective homelands or towards areas of the country where they would be hidden and protected by the terrain; east into the Grampians Mountains, north into Sutherland, south to the forests of Argyll or west towards the Islands.

Behind him the government cavalry had taken off in pursuit of the retreating MacDonalds, but he could see the long lines of red soldiers stretching right across the moor were beginning to pace forward, sweeping the battlefield. He struggled on under the weight of Tarlich and his brother's bandaged foot swung in front of him and the bandage was already red with blood. He picked up speed as he crossed areas free from littered bodies and then, twenty yards in front he could see men on horseback. He recognised the Prince, his face thin and pale, speaking rapidly to half a dozen men that glanced around nervously. Then they split into two groups and galloped away, the Prince and his trio headed west.

Whisps of steam curled up from the backs of Ailen's hands as his temperature rose under the exertion and anger rose with it as he watched their leader flee without a backward glance at his loyal followers.

'Run ye cowardly fuckin Italian!' he shouted to the backs of the retreating horsemen. *'Run ye Bastards.'*
*

The cold wind that seemed to cut through his ribs carried the words: 'Rest your arms.'

Jack planted the butt of his musket into the spongy moss. He rubbed lightly at his swollen cheek, barely able to believe that he was still alive. He looked down at his buckled bayonet and the tacky blood coated the blade and muzzle of his musket. The touch of the musket seemed to burn his hands and he had to fight the urge to throw it away from him.

He looked out onto the moor and around him the others of the platoon stood silent. The wind lifted the last of the thick smoke away from the dips of the undulating moor and the sight was like nothing that even the oldest veterans amongst them had ever seen. Not even at Fontenoy after the fiercest of the fighting with the French.

Jack shut his eyes tightly and tried to blot out the field of death but the image would not go away. And he could still hear the fading cries of the dying.

His legs burned with the desire to run, to get away. But he waited for the order. Pullman was waiting for him to fuck up. He would wait for the order and then they would be away from this field. Their work was done here and the rebels were crushed, there was no doubt about that. So he waited for the order to form up in ranks and march away from the death. As soon as the opportunity to desert came, he would be gone.

Along the front line the sergeants and officers started to bark out instructions and with horror it dawned upon Jack that they would not be leaving the field yet.

Sgt Pullman's turn came and Jack could almost hear the glee in his voice as he called out: 'A Company, forward march. Bayonets at the ready.' And the government troops began to sweep the battlefield in long lines. They stabbed any surviving rebels with their bayonets or clubbed them with the butt end to finish them off.

Jack's companions laughed as they ended the lives of dying rebels and violated the corpses of those already dead. They splashed in pools of blood and threw limbs at each other and Jack stepped forward trying not to see.

And then came the massive shape of The Duke riding across the front of them on a large black stallion that laboured to remain upright. He waved at his men and they raised their hats in return. His horse tottered across the front of the advancing men and crushed the bones and skulls of rebels under its hooves.

In front of them the leg of a rebel kicked rhythmically and Higgins drove his bayonet ferociously into the body. 'Fucking 'eathen scum,' he said. He drove down his musket again and again, grunting with pleasure and sounding to Jack as if he was fucking the rebel instead of stabbing him.

Jack pulled him back by the collar. 'He's already dead, you fucking arsehole.'

Higgins looked at him stupidly with his face splattered with blood. Then he smiled and Jack could see blood on his teeth. 'Just making sure, mate.'

The Duke came along the line getting nearer and Jack could hear him calling out to the men. 'Well done, my brave men. And here are my brave Pultney's. Well done. Remember the order that was found this morning boys. . . the rebels would afford us no quarter had they won and so we will afford them the same compliment.' He passed by and Jack wondered if The Duke had ever felt hungry or cold in his life. Then the Duke pulled his horse up and turned and halted a few yards in front of Jack. He was shouting down at a figure that crawled along the ground. 'You, you there, to whom do you give allegiance?'

The man on the ground was badly injured and his shirt red with blood and he had no hat on his head. He stopped crawling at the shout of The Duke and seemed to realise for the first time that there were scores of soldiers bearing down on him. He tried to get to his feet but the effort was too much for him and he fell back to the ground and propped himself up with his elbows.

'Well, man,' demanded The Duke. 'State your allegiance.'

The injured man hawked and spat as hard as he could in the Duke's direction and then laid back smiling to himself and panting with the effort.

The Duke's face filled with red and he turned around in his saddle to face his men. He raised his arm and pointed to Jack.

'Private, shoot the insolent dog.'

Jack loaded up his musket with shaking hands. He stepped towards the injured rebel and pointed the muzzle down at his head. Suddenly he could hear no sounds and he felt alone with this rebel on the bleak moor. This man who he had been ordered to kill in cold blood.

He looked along the barrel and the rebel looked steadily back at him.

'Shoot him,' Cumberland called from the horse.

Jack's mouth dried up and he lowered his weapon. He turned and looked up at The Duke, his voice shaking. 'Your Grace, he's going to die anyway,' he pleaded.

Cumberland's face became purple. *'Shoot him!'*

Jack lowered his head. 'I can't,' he said quietly. 'I can't kill him, Your Grace.'

The Duke looked over Jack's head at the stunned men of his platoon and spotted Pullman. 'Sergeant, what' is the meaning of this? Is this one of your men?'

Pullman glanced at Jack ruefully. 'Yes, Your Grace.'

The Duke nodded and rode over to the rebel and pulled his pistol from his belt. 'We can't have this Sergeant, it's no good at all.' When he was directly over the rebel he pulled back the hammer and pointed it down at him. 'Have him arrested, Sergeant.'

He pulled the trigger and fired his pistol into Seamas McLachlan's head. The redness faded away from the Duke's face and he smiled and looked back at Pullman. 'And have him hung with the rest of the traitors in the morning . . . gross insubordination.'

He turned his horse and continued along the line, waving as he went. 'Well done my brave boys.' And the men cheered in return.

Pullman dashed over to Jack and grabbed his musket and smashed him in the face with the butt. Jack sank to his knees cupping his shattered nose. Pullman pointed to Higgins and another. 'Strip 'im down.'

*

They were moving away from the battlefield now and into the shallow mouth of a glen. Ailen struggled on with his brother on his back for about another mile, occasionally stopping to crouch in the bushes and gorse while Government troops galloped past in pursuit of the retreating clans.

The rain had completely stopped now and the sun managed to push some cold, blue early-evening light through the blanket of grey. The smoke was gone, but Ailen could still feel it burning at the back of his throat and stinging his eyes. Gently he laid Tarlich down and knelt by the side of a slow running burn. He scooped cold water over his face and dipped his head into the running water and drank. The pure water soothed his burning throat. He lifted some water out of the burn and carefully dribbled it onto Tarlich's lips and into his mouth.

Tarlich looked up at him with dark half-open eyes and swallowed and coughed. '*Tapath leat*,' he said.

'We have tae get on,' Ailen said preparing to lift him again. 'The red-coats'll be searching these glens.'

'Ailen,' whispered Tarlich, making his brother pause with his arm locked around his back, their faces an inch apart. 'I'm sorry I made ye come.'

'Ye didn't make me come . . . the Chief did.' He steadied his legs on the ground and heaved Tarlich onto his back. 'Anyway, we couldn't just let the cunts saunter into the Highlands without a fight.'

*

Seoras crawled away, clutching his stomach and feeling the heat of his wounds sear through him. Nobody seemed to notice as he dragged himself towards the copse of birch, to where he could hear his name being whispered on the wind. Behind him, he left a trail of glistening blood on the heather.

He came to a burn and the peaty water was swelled and quickened by the rain. He rolled in and lay on his back and the burn gurgled around his ears and over his face and shoulders and the water cooled his pain.

Seoras. Help us.

Seoras gathered his strength and turned onto his front and dragged himself against the flow of water. Behind him, ribbons of red swirled in the water. He went on until he was under the thin early spring canopy of the birch trees that stood around the banks of the burn and with the last of his energy he dragged himself onto the grassy bank. His head rested in the grass and his legs swayed in the current of the water. The heads of bluebells looked down at him nodded and whispered to each other in the wind.

Thirteen

<u>Culloden Battlefield, April 14th 2146</u>

'So we wait on the battlefield then,' said Sinclair.

'Aye,' Cammie took a sip of tea from the steaming mug.

'Hidden.'

'Aye. In an observation point.'

'Like in Namah's vision.'

'Aye.'

'And what do I do?' Namah asked.

The three of them sat in Cammie's work-shed drinking tea and wishing that they had something a bit stronger. They had retreated there after the Highlander had unearthed the pistol to pull themselves together and to decide what they were going to do.

Cammie put his mug on the bench and looked at her. 'Stay in the visitor centre.' If there's any action . . . if anything happens, we can stay in contact with our fones.'

'But nothing'll happen,' Sinclair said.

Cammie looked at his feet. 'No, probably not.'

Although Cammie hadn't had any previous encounters with the Highlander, maybe *because* he hadn't had any previous encounters, he had been the one to stay calm and take control of the situation. He had said that for whatever reason the Highlander was in desperate need of their help. They had to do something and what Namah had seen in her vision didn't seem like a bad idea. He'd said that he would probably have opted for that strategy anyway. He had plenty of experience of watching and waiting and gathering intelligence. So he'd decided on setting up an observation point and knowing the moor like he did, he said that the place where Namah had seen them concealed during her vision was actually the best place to locate it.

Namah shook her head. 'I don't know. What if we're setting the scene for . . . something bad?'

Cammie shrugged and swirled hot tea around in his mug. 'I personally think that something *is* going to happen and I don't know if it'll be good or bad but either way I don't think that anything *dangerous* is going to happen. Nothing that we need to worry about. It looks to me as if you two are just pawns in this.'

'Pawns are expendable,' she said.

'Pawns are used to entice your opponent,' Cammie replied.

'Bait, you mean.'

Cammie shrugged.

Sinclair sipped at the tea and tried to get some warmth into his body. The night had become a lot colder. He thought about what he had just heard and in particular the word 'dangerous'. Since this had begun it had never crossed his mind that it might involve danger and he didn't like the idea of it now. He was leaning against the worktop and had to twist round to see the pistol that lay on its surface. The metal and polished wood gleamed under the strip-lights. The others followed his gaze.

'So when?' Sinclair said without looking up.

Cammie picked the pistol up and turned it over in his hands and studied the mechanism. 'I'll stay out there during the day and then you can join me tomorrow night. Once you've had some sleep.' Gently, he pulled back the hammer and checked that the firing pan was free from powder. There were no scorch marks to be seen - it had never been fired before.

'Fine,' Sinclair said. 'But when are *you* going to sleep?'

'I'll catch a couple of hours after you join me.' He looked up from the pistol and saw Sinclair's doubtful glance. 'Don't worry, I'm used to it . . . it's sort of like a hobby.'

'What, staying up all day looking out for ghosts?'

'Not ghosts, no.' He eased the hammer forward again. 'I monitor wildlife in my spare time.'

Sinclair looked across at Namah.

She raised her eyebrows and nodded back. 'Aye, he does.'

Cammie, having finished inspecting the pistol, placed it back on the workbench. 'So that's settled then?'

'What if nothing happens?' Sinclair asked.

'Then we'll wait another day and night.'

'And what about visitors?' Asked Namah.

Cammie shrugged. 'We don't get that many.'

'Maybe not tomorrow night but the night after is the sixteenth.'

'The anniversary of the battle,' said Cammie.

'On the anniversary of the battle,' Namah explained to Sinclair, 'The Jacobite Society come and perform a ceremony at the Memorial Cairn. There's only about a dozen or so of them now, mostly old guys, but there used to be a lot more. They dress up like clansmen and march round the battlefield. We kind of roll out the carpet for them . . . apart from being one of the few groups of people who actually care about this place, they've raised a lot of money for us over the years.'

'Well, even if there are visitors, we'll be concealed,' said Cammie.

'And if someone spots the two of you under the bushes, what do you tell them?'

'We'll just tell them that we're-'

'Watching birds,' finished Sinclair, raising a hand to conceal the smile.

Cammie laughed. 'Aye, but that's if we're spotted, Namah. I doubt if we will be, though.' He pulled a backpack out from under the workbench. 'I've got all the gear, and I've had plenty practice at concealment over the years.'

Sinclair felt the chill in the air and cupped his hands around his mug. He wondered how cold it would be the following night, out on the moor. 'I hope you've got a heater in there.'

'Yer only heat'll be yer own body heat, but don't worry, there's plenty o warm clothin,' he said slapping the backpack.

Sinclair forced a smile. 'Great.'

'You two had better get back up to the centre. The time's wearin on and I want to get this OP set up before daybreak.'

Namah and Sinclair drank the last of their tea while Cammie shouldered his backpack. As they went out into the night, he handed Sinclair the pistol. 'Ye'd better hang onto this. He said it was for you.'

Sinclair took it from him and found that it felt comfortable in his grip. Almost as if it was made for him. He tucked it into his waistband.

After Cammie left them Namah and Sinclair made their way back up the path towards the centre. Although it was mid-April the tail end of winter had remained and a bitter wind had got up and it carried only the faintest trace of spring. They walked in silence with their minds locked on the night ahead.

'I think Cammie's enjoying this,' Sinclair said before they reached the centre.

'He's lovin it,' admitted Namah. 'I may be the manager of this place, but he's the one runnin it.'

'This stuff about setting up an observation point and keeping watch, it's almost military,' said Sinclair. 'Did he used to be in the army or something?'

'I think so,' answered Namah. 'But he never speaks about it and I never ask. My Dad has hinted to Cammie's past when he's had a dram or too. I think they might have had some connection in the past.'

When they got back to the centre they found Alex with his briefcase in hand about to leave,. 'That must have been some tour,' he said.

'There was a power failure for a while,' said Namah, pulling off her facemask. 'And then we got talkin to Cammie. He invited us for a cup o tea in his work shed. Ye know what he's like.'

'Yes, I do,' said Alex, his forehead creasing. 'A power failure you say, everything was okay here.'

'It was just one section of the floodlights,' she said rubbing her hands together. 'It's gettin cold out there.'

Alex turned his attention to Sinclair. 'I hope you enjoyed the tour, anyway.'

'Yeah, it was great thanks. Very interesting,' he said, trying to avoid Namah's eye.

'Good, I'm glad,' said Alex. He went over to Namah and kissed her cheek before making for the door. 'Maybe you could encourage a few more of your Antipodean colleagues to visit us.'

'It would be great if I could,' Sinclair said, unsure if Alex was being sarcastic or not. He added a smile just in case.

'Hmm.' Alex opened the door to leave, and said over his shoulder, 'I'll e-mail the power company when I get home, Namah. Those floodlights should be looked at.'

'No need, Dad. I'll message them now.'

*

Namah opened the wine.

~ 234 ~

When she discovered that Sinclair hadn't sorted himself out with a place to stay, she'd suggested that he should sleep on her sofa. He'd agreed and they had stopped off at the nearby supermarket to get a few things.

Sinclair had volunteered to cook and said that he would make the Florentine tomato sauce recipe that his grandfather had passed on to him. It had been many years since he had made it, in fact the last time that he had made it had probably been under his grandfather's guidance when he was still alive, but he wanted to give it a go. They scanned pasta, chicken and the sauce ingredients that Sinclar could remember into their bag and were about to leave when Namah spotted the wine. A *sauvignon blanc* from New Zealand. She took two bottles.

'I know it's not real *sauvignon blanc.* I mean, I know it comes from New Zealand but it won't have a unique taste characterised by New Zealand's climate or anything. Not like the old days.' She began pouring the light-coloured wine into the glasses. 'It's all made the same way now isn't it? All under the same roofs, all in the same controlled environments.'

'More or less I suppose,' said Sinclair around a mouthful of pasta. They had made plenty as they were both famished. Neither had eaten all night and neither had even noticed their hunger until food was mentioned.

'*Sauvignon blanc* from New Zealand is the same as *sauvignon blanc* from California, isn't it?' Namah dug into her large plateful without waiting for a reply.

'I suppose it is.' Sinclair washed down his mouthful with some of the wine. 'It's nice though,' he said raising his glass.

They chewed and swallowed quickly. Neither of them felt in the least apprehensive about eating with a stranger for the first time. If they could still be called strangers after the night that they had just spent together.

'I just thought it would make you feel more at home to have something from New Zealand.'

'It does. It was a nice thought. I'm touched, really.'

They continued to eat in silence until they had both finished off their meals. Namah cleared the plates away and took their glasses and the bottle through to the sitting room. Sinclair collapsed into a chair, patting his stomach. 'Do you think that the anniversary of the battle has something to do with the Highlander appearing?'

Namah sat across from him and refilled their glasses. 'Aye, I think it does. Definitely. It will be exactly four hundred years since the battle.'

'Is that figure significant?'

'It must be to someone.'

Sinclair took his glass and began to swirl the wine looking into the whirlpool that he was creating. 'You said earlier that you had some ideas as to what was going to happen but we never got around to discussing them.'

She thought for a moment. 'Something got me thinking, after the Highlander took me out onto the moor, and that . . . that man was there. And the dogs.' Namah put down her glass and cleared her throat. 'I don't think you'll like what I'm going to tell you but I'll tell you anyway. It's not as if I'm right, anyway, but after that experience I had with the vision on the moor . . . that underlined what I had already thought.'

'Which was what?' Sinclair finished off his wine in one gulp and reached for the bottle.

'It's all to do with the battle, or more accurately, the aftermath. When it was over the British Army went on a killing spree that was more or less ordered by the Duke of Cumberland. He used a document that was found on the battlefield as an excuse, a set of orders written by the Jacobite command stating that if they were to win that day, they would afford the enemy no quarter.'

'Meaning that there would be no mercy for the prisoners or the wounded. I read about that, but it was a fake.'

'That's right. The order was forged and the Duke himself must have ordered the forgery. His men were fired up by this and set about murdering all the Highlanders they could, starting with the wounded on the battlefield. They also made false charges against civilians who had nothing to do with the rebellion and hanged them after mass trials. In the Highlands, the Duke was known as The Butcher of Cumberland but elsewhere in Britain they called him Sweet William. After months of killing, which can only be described as genocide, he returned to London and to his father, the King, in a blaze of glory. The people paraded him wherever he went. In their eyes he had saved the country from the rebels. The fate of the Highlanders didn't matter to them. Although the atrocities were reported in the London press, if only briefly, the Highlanders were perceived to be dangerous savages that deserved everything that they got.' Namah paused to take a drink. Her mouth was beginning to feel dry.

'I still don't see what you are getting at,' said Sinclair.

His glass was empty again and Namah went to get the other bottle from the fridge.

'I think he was *evil,*' she said, returning with the fresh bottle and a corkscrew.

'Well maybe not quite evil,' said Sinclair. 'I guess he was highly ambitious and had a general disregard for human life, as was the norm in those days. He certainly wasn't the first or the last Brit to slaughter and enslave weaker peoples, from what I've recently read.'

'No, that's true. He wasn't.' Namah uncorked the wine and refilled their glasses. 'They certainly weren't finished with the Highlanders by any means and none of what followed was down to Cumberland. Tens of thousands were deported to North America, The Caribbean or South Africa, Australia and New Zealand. Westminster outlawed the wearing of tartan and the playing of bagpipes. Young men were forced into the very army that had destroyed them so that they could fight for the British Army against the rebelling Americans and against Napoleon's French. Power was taken away from the clan chiefs and the land was sold to Lowlanders and English. They decided that there was a lot more money to be made from wool. Prices were high due to the industrial revolution in England. The clans were brutally evicted from their ancient ancestral homes during the Highland Clearances so that the land could be used for rearing sheep.

'When the soldiers serving the British Army were no longer required they returned home to find that their families were gone and their homes had been burned down. They were left to wander, destitute and starving.' Namah felt her stomach tighten. She shook her head. 'That's just what they did to the Highlanders. They did worse things to people all over the world under their Union flag in the name of their great Empire. Their wealth was built on slavery and the theft of land and resources.' Her head felt hot and she slammed her glass down on the coffee table, spilling some wine. 'Did you know that during the Boer War the British kept Boer women and children in concentration camps long before the Nazis came up with the idea?'

'No, I didn't,' Sinclair admitted. 'But if what you are saying had nothing to do with The Duke of Cumberland, then what makes him so evil compared to the others who ordered stuff like that?'

'Sorry, I was strayin a bit. I just got wound up talkin about it.' She took a deep breath. 'The point I'm tryin to make is that while other military leaders and politicians and monarchs and whoever else ordered and instigated all these crimes against humanity, they were in it for greed, or out of misguided loyalty to their country or whoever was on the throne at the time, or just to cover themselves with glory.'

'So what was Cumberland in it for?'

'I don't think that he directed the murder of all those innocent people because they were a threat to the security of the country or to keep others in their place or even to show how powerful he was. Sure they were all reasons, but I think that he wanted them murdered for personal reasons. When I say evil I mean just that. I think that he was into some kind of devil worship.' She picked up her glass and took a gulp. 'I think that he wanted their souls.'

Sinclair was in mid-gulp and spluttered wine into his glass. 'You think that he was crazy, like Hitler-type-crazy,' he said wiping his mouth.

'No, not crazy . . . or mad. I think that he was *evil*. I think that he was in league with the devil.'

What Namah had just said hung heavy in the air like a dark and thunderous cloud. She was glad that she had finally said what had been within her since she'd had her first inkling years before at university.

'I know that what he did was . . . bad' Sinclair put down his glass. He was aware that the conversation had taken an interesting turn and he wanted to concentrate. 'Cruel, unforgivable,' he continued. 'And of course it's more than just history to you, that it's more personal because the atrocities were perpetrated on your ancestors, but what you're saying . . .'

'It's not the first time that it's crossed my mind. Why do you think Cumberland isn't famous in British history or that there are no great monuments or buildings dedicated to him?'

'I don't know.'

'That's what I wondered when I first read about the history and when I studied it at university. In the eyes of the British he saved the country and the monarchy from dangerous rebels. He was a hero, if only for a short while. He should have had the same treatment as Nelson or Wellington or Churchill. Instead he doesn't even get a statue. He was the son of a *King*. No streets or squares named after him. Nothing. Why?'

Sinclair rubbed his forehead. 'He must have done something to disgrace himself.'

'Exactly. That's another question I asked myself. Times were changing and less than twenty years after the rebellion the first legal objections to slavery were made and maybe they decided that Cumberland's overzealous ethnic cleansing in Scotland wasn't something to be proud of. I could see how they might not want to shout about that from the roof tops in a world that was modernising and revolutionising. But if he disgraced himself why don't we know anything about it. Of all the history books about the 1745 rebellion few of them tell us what became of Cumberland after returning to London and the cheering crowds. Plenty of them tell us that Charles Stuart was a fugitive in the Highlands and Islands before eventually escaping to France. It's been well romanticised in story and verse. We even know that he went from there to Florence where he lived a life of womanising and drinking before he eventually died penniless. He deserved nothing - he used the loyalty of the Highlanders for his own selfish means before betraying and abandoning them - yet he has been immortalised in songs and poetry as some kind of hero. He even has a monument in Florence where he died a broken-down drunk.'

'But you must have found something about Cumberland that points to devil worship,' said Sinclair. 'You can't just make a statement like that without some way of backing it up.' Sinclair scolded himself for sounding like a teacher.

'You're right. And I did do some research of my own. I didn't even have to look very far. He has an entry in *The British National Biography*. William Augustus. There are parts that stick in my head.'

'And those parts point to devil worship?' Sinclair raised his eyebrows.

'Not exactly, but if you read between the lines.'

'So what do the lines say?'

Namah looked to the ceiling and recalled the print in the old volume. 'The biography tells you that he's the third son of George II, I think that the second son died in infancy. It says that he had a couple of victories in Flanders against the French and was shot through the calf in one battle but carried on and earned the respect of his men. Then there's his involvement in the quelling of the '45 rebellion and his victory at Culloden, which was actually fought on Drumossie Moor but the battle was named after the nearby Culloden House. After returning to London he was sent back to Flanders where he wasn't quite as successful and he returned to London. There are a couple of accounts of the King mocking him and disgracing him at state functions. It tells you a bit about his life, saying that he was grossly overweight, that he never married even though the King tried to marry him off to a physically disabled European princess.'

'Okay,' said Sinclair. 'So he was fat and ugly and not the favourite son of the King.' Sinclair sat back in his chair cradling his glass. There was nothing to read between the lines that troubled him. 'That hardly makes him a devil worshipper.'

Namah sighed. 'There's more, if you want to listen.'

Sinclair wasn't sure if he wanted to hear more, but he nodded.

'He lived in some big house in London,' Namah continued. 'A recluse, save for a few servants - a son of a king and no hangers-on - highly unusual in my opinion, no matter how detestable he might have been. And then there was his cause of death.'

'Which was?'

'In the biography it said that he suffered a brain haemorrhage caused by two preternatural bones growing in his skull.'

'What does that mean?'

'I wasn't sure myself so I looked it up in a medical encyclopaedia. It said that it was a very rare occurrence, an unnatural build up of bone that rarely causes a risk to health. Cumberland had *two* . . . and it killed him.

'So . . .'

Namah cut Sinclair short before he started rationalising. 'So I think that he had horns.'

Sinclair froze, unsure whether to laugh or get out of there right now and work his passage back to New Zealand. 'You're not serious?' He managed to squeeze the words out of his numb mouth.

'I am.'

Sinclair shook himself out of his trance and poured some more wine, drank and refilled. He sat back to study Namah. 'That's some amount of reading between the lines,' he said.

'I know it sounds far-fetched, like I've got an over active imagination, but it all makes sense now. It's made sense ever since the Highlander came.'

'Well,' said Sinclair putting down his glass and standing. 'That's the wine gone. Look, about the moor tomorrow night, maybe it's better if I don't . . .'

'Do you believe in the visions?'

Sinclair's smile faded. Something in Namah's voice made him sit back down again. 'Well . . . yeah. Of course I do.'

'The bonnet in your bag is real, isn't it, and the pistol the Highlander gave you tonight?'

'Yes, they're real. He gave them both to me, you know that.'

'So if they're real, then what the Highlander showed me on the moor and what 1 saw in my vision must also be real.' Tears appeared at the corners of her eyes. 'Do you believe that?'

'I . . . Yeah. I do, I have no choice.' He stood looking at her, dazed, his voice drifting from him.

'Then I believe that there's more to this. I believe that there is evil involved in this.' She wiped moisture from her cheek with the heel of her hand. 'No, I don't believe it. I know it.'

'You mean that the ghost of The Duke is out there somewhere too?'

'Something like that. Maybe he's come back as someone else.' More tears rolled down her cheeks, glittering under the light. 'Four Hundred years is not a coincidence, it means something. I know that The Duke has their souls and now there is a chance for them to be free, and I think that he's going to try to stop that.'

'Now you *are* scaring me.' Sinclair went and sat by her. He watched liquid swell in her eyes then spill over onto her cheeks. Feeling awkward, he reached out for her.

'So much blood spilt here.' The words fell softly over her trembling lower lip. 'So much violent, sudden death.'

He looked into her eyes and felt that he was being enticed into a clear, sparkling lagoon, the water warm and cleansing. He clasped his hands over hers, touching her and feeling the warmth of her seeping into him.

'He's used them, used their souls for his own sick reasons. Maybe someone has granted him immortality, someone powerful and maybe after four centuries his power is fading. I don't know for sure, we may never know, but what we do know is that we can help those souls. *You* can help those souls.' She began to shudder and Sinclair grasped her by the shoulders. 'The souls of defenceless women and children, the souls of innocents. The souls of soldiers conned into dying for a cause that was not theirs.'

Sinclair pulled her to him and held her tightly and she buried her wet face in his neck. 'I don't know what to do. I don't know how to help them,' he said.

'You'll know when the time comes. You'll know what to do.' She reached up under his arm and wiped her face. 'You've come this far already, not knowing what to do, or even why you're doing it.'

Sinclair nodded and her hair felt like satin against his cheek. 'That's what scares me.'

Namah squeezed him. 'I'm afraid too. Neither of us has asked for any part in this. But we have to help them.'

Sinclair nodded.

'Promise you'll go through with it,' she whispered.

Sinclair nodded. He pulled back and looked into her eyes. Their lips brushed.

'Stay,' she said.

*

The first light of dawn seeped into the sky and Cammie stood back to inspect his work. If he didn't already know that it was there he would never be able to spot it, even at this short distance.

It had been a long time since he had constructed an observation point as meticulously as this. Not since the occupation.

He used two old green army groundsheets, one on the ground and the other as cover. The roof was two feet off the ground at the front, sloping towards the back and held in place by bungees threaded through the eyelets of the groundsheet and hooked to the branches of the surrounding bushes. The shape of the shelter was rigged in such a way to be deliberately uneven, leaving as little unnatural lines as possible. During his basic training, one of the first things that Cammie had learned was that the trick of camouflage was blending - there are few straight lines in nature, so edges and shapes familiar to man have to be broken up. When searching an area of countryside, the eye of the hunter will always fall upon familiar shapes: Fences, gates, posts, the human form. To further break up the shape he'd draped branches over the sides, bending them and manipulating them, never breaking them off. Finally, he'd scattered some of the debris from the surrounding ground, using only the top layer so as not to expose dark patches of earth.

He'd worked in darkness, and now, like the people themselves, the darkness was retreating from the light. Cammie stood amongst the last of the pools of night and could see that the sun would be breaking over the horizon in a few minutes. Cold drizzle fell softly against his face and he longed to stand and welcome the dawn of a new day as he had done as a child and young man.

He crawled into the shelter and arranged his equipment. He took out a large flask of water that would be kept hot through its connection to a small portable solar panel that was rolled out to where it would gather the light of the sun. It was capable of drawing power even if there was cloud cover, as there was today. By his side he had his backpack that contained camouflaged coveralls and a sleeping bag for Sinclair. There was also quilted clothing in case it got colder. From a side pouch he withdrew binoculars that were capable of night vision and detecting heat sources. Once everything was in place he took out a map.

Looking out across the moor he could see that the patches of darkness had receded and were now no more than grey shadows, the last remnants of night. The trees and scrub were silhouettes against the lightening sky. Above him drizzle pattered softly on the ground sheet like the hooves of tiny galloping horses. Every now and then a larger drop of rain fell from where it had collected in the trees above, and tapped above his head like a ghostly finger, reminding him to stay alert.

He spread the map of the local area out before him and studied it for the most probable route that someone might use to approach the battlefield on foot or otherwise. As he did so he could feel the hackles rise on the back of his neck and was aware of the blood pulsing faster in his ears. That old feeling from long ago that he remembered so well. He almost welcomed it.

From his top pocket he removed a stunted pencil and began to circle the three areas on the map that he had noted as the most likely approach routes. The soft tip of his pencil then glided over the waterproof surface, connecting the three zones with the observation point. He had planned a patrol route of about half a mile in length. He folded the map so that the area he had marked was outer-most for easy reference and he tucked it into the top pocket of his coveralls.

He put his binoculars to his eyes and scanned the battlefield, pinpointing the areas that he had marked on the map using dominant trees and features as landmarks so that he could locate them quickly. Mentally noting these areas, he reached again for his backpack and removed a cereal bar. Then as an afterthought he removed something else and tucked it into his waistband.

He thought about it and realised that physically his pistol was older than the one that they had seen unearthed the previous night. He'd had the 9mm automatic since the early seventies. Seventy odd years now. He felt numb thinking about those years. The change. The *time*. He pulled the pistol out of his waistband and laid it by his right hand, keeping it in his periphery. Apart from target practice all those years ago, like the pistol that Sinclair was now in possession of, it had never been fired in anger.

Cammie peeled open his cereal bar and slowly began to chew. The grey had faded as much as it was going to on this miserable mid-April day and he was sure, even though night had gone, that it wasn't getting any warmer. He poured some tea and settled to watch, knowing that someone was coming. He had no need of second sight or visions to know that much.

His senses were at their peak and he was aware of the wet scent of moss and pine . . . and the approach of danger.

Fourteen

<u>Drumossie Moor, Scotland, April 16th 1746</u>

Anghas clung to the rock, watching. He was unaware of the cold and his fingers were numb. He was also unaware of his brother hanging on to him. He focused on the battle and the battle alone. His eyes darted around the field and devoured the action below, seeking out the details. At the beginning, he had been enthralled but that had changed to dread and horror. Instead of turning his head away as his younger brother had done, the horror only served to hook him more.

They weren't going to win. He knew that now. The highlanders had broken though and driven into the heart of the redcoat lines and he had hoped he would see a great rush of men flowing into the enemy troops. Instead he saw another large group of men moving up the side of the battlefield, behind a dyke. The men were highlanders dressed in plaid with the bonnets of the Campbells and the red coats of the Government troops. They were armed with muskets that they poked out over the top of the dyke. The swirling wind carried the sound up the mountainside mixed with the smoke and he could hear their weapons being discharged into the flank of the attacking Jacobites and could hear the Jacobites cries of pain and fear and rage.

He could see dozens of highlanders falling to the ground. Their charge was being halted from the front and from the side. The men who had broken through the front line were now on their own, a diminishing group barely visible through the churning smoke. The redcoats had turned in on them and snuffed out any hope that remained in Anghas' young and optimistic heart.

Then the highlanders had begun to scatter. The group on horses at the back had stayed until the men had reached them and then they too had turned and bolted in the opposite direction.

Anghas could see some small pockets of men and single riders on horseback that were not taking flight. They were still charging at the enemy and he cheered them on. Very few of them made it to the redcoat lines and those who did could inflict little damage before sinking to the ground. And then these final flurries were over and the highlanders scattered and were off the moor and were running and riding in all directions away from the redcoats and Anghas could see that some were coming up the hillside in his direction. As the field emptied of able men, Anghas was stunned at what they left behind.

The bodies were strewn all over the ground.

In places there was only a scattering but where the clans had originally stood and where the charge had been halted in front of the redcoat lines the ground was covered. In places, he could see that the bodies were piled up on top of each other.

The redcoats had regrouped into straight lines again and most of the surviving highlanders had left. A wave of cheering rose from the redcoat lines and the sound of joy amongst so much carnage made Anghas arch his back against the strange sensation that was spilling down it. Through the cheering came the steady beat of drums and like a broom being pushed slowly across a floor, the *saighdearan dearg* began to advance.

Anndra became aware that the noise of the battle was dying down and he pulled his head out from where he had buried it in Anghas' shoulder. Anghas had forgotten that he was there. He had forgotten everything. He felt bizarrely conscious of coming back into his own body having left it for an indeterminate period. He had been so immersed in watching the battle that he hadn't even heard Anndra's continued pleas to go home. He had no idea how much time had passed.

He shook his head and looked at Anndra. His face was pale and there was a faint blueness around his lips. His eyes were wet and red and his face imploring. He dared a glance at the moor out of the corner of his eye and then looked back at Anghas. A weak voice whispered through his lips. '*Please . . . can we go home now?*'

Anghas became aware of the aching throb in his fingers and feet. He looked down at battlefield again, meaning to take a final glance before leaving but instead his eyes snapped wide. Anndra had started to get up and Anghas pulled him back down behind the boulder omitting a squawk as he crashed against the stone. Anghas clamped a hand over his brother's mouth and saw in his eyes that he would not be able to stand up to much more without bursting into a fit of hysterical tears.

Then Anndra heard what Anghas had seen and his eyes opened wide. The thudding of feet was coming up the hillside. Tears spilled down his pale cheeks and over the fingers of his elder brother's hand.

The thumping of feet grew louder and was joined by the panting of heavily exerted lungs. Seconds later a highlander crashed down behind the boulder. He seemed surprised to see them there but only gave then a quick glance. He peeked up over the boulder and then ducked back down. 'Fuck.'

He now took a closer look at the boys.

'We're on your side.' Anghas held his voice steady but clung tighter to Anndra in spite of himself. The clansman held a dirk in his fist and a wild look in his eyes. He smelt of blood and smoke and rage. His hair was knotted and his face was gaunt and smeared with brown and black and glistening red. Great spouts of steam pumped out of his mouth in thick jets and spiralled from his hands and legs. Anghas could feel the heat from his body.

The highlander reached out and clapped Anghas on the shoulder and Anghas could not stop himself from recoiling. 'Well thank fuck for that,' he said.

'We're just goin home now,' Anndra managed to whisper.

'Me too,' The Highlander winked. He peered over the top of the boulder again and Anghas followed his gaze. The highlander pushed him back down but not before he saw two more clansmen running up the hill. Behind them had been three redcoats on horseback, gaining on them. This low down, the slope was still shallow enough for horse.

The highlander sank back down and clutched the dirk to his breastbone.

The two clansmen pounded up the hill about twenty yards to their right and were unaware of them behind the boulder as they concentrated on where they were putting their feet. The thud of hooves was very close as well but they couldn't look now. They sat, pressed against the boulder and held their breath. Then came the cracking of a volley of pistol fire. Anghas and Anndra pressed their hands to the sides of their heads, too late to block the noise but in time to muffle the cries of the two fleeing men. The hooves had slowed to a trot now and they could hear the redcoats talking and laughing. Anghas could see the two of them move over to the felled men and one of them unsheathed his sword and leaned out of his saddle and stabbed at the groaning man and the man quivered and became silent.

The third redcoat pulled up directly beside the boulder. He could not fail to see them from this angle. For a moment he looked into Anghas' eyes and then he reached for the pistol in his belt.

*

A crowd had formed to watch the battle. They stood along the road to Drumossie Moor, as close as they dared go. They jostled for position but they could not see much. There were trees and a low ridge between them and the rear of the government troops. After the battle was over, some of them planned go onto the battlefield to look for family. Some wanted go on to look for anything of value.

And the battle was nearly over now. The noise had died down and the guns and muskets had stopped firing. The smoke was being blown away into the hills. They stood for a while waiting and whispering amongst each other as the turmoil of the battle subsided. Nervous speculation swept through them.

Elspeth clutched her blanketed baby to her chest and listened to them, young and old. Her Malcolm was out there somewhere, maybe. She had not seen nor heard from him for many months, not since he had joined the Government Army. The news had spread that there would be a battle at Drumossie and like a sheep she had followed the flock, not knowing what else to do. The cries of the wounded and dying were weakening. Was Malcolm among them? Did he make it this far?

They were behind the government lines and the government troops were not retreating. They had surely won.

The whispering grew to a murmuring. She heard the voices float around her.

'What'll happen now?' A young girl.

'The redcoats'll go tae Inverness.' An old man.

'Should we go and look at the field now?' A boy.

'No, wait 'til they've gone.' His mother.

A great cheer whipped over their heads from the moor and the murmuring grew to talking.

'D'ye think we should stay here?' An old woman pulling her shawl tightly around her shoulders.

'What·d'ye mean?' Her husband.

'D'ye think we should go hame, like?' Her neighbour, squinting eyes saying *don't be ridiculous*.

Then, from the direction of the field came the muffled thunder of hooves, becoming an audible thudding as they hit the road.

'They're coming up the road.'

The talking became shouting.

*

He brought the axe down and the split wood tumbled off the sides of the wide tree stump that served as a chopping block.

The noise being carried on the wind from Drumossie was dying down.

He freed the axe from the chopping block with a slight shake of the shaft and raised it onto his shoulder. His young son picked up one of the pieces and put it back on the block and stood back. He looked intently at his father, wondering what he was thinking. Mary stood over by the door, also watching her father. She'd filled the big wicker basket with chopped up wood but she was too small to lift it.

He glanced up at the sky and saw that the smoke was clearing. It had risen from the south in great plumes earlier, not the steady rise of smoke from a fire, but the ghostly, disjointed clouds of gun smoke. The children had been afraid when they'd heard the dull thumping in the distance and the boy had asked. His father had replied: big guns.

He returned his attention to his work and swung the axe again and the split wood flew off the block almost hitting his son on the shin. Taking no notice, the boy put a large piece back on the block while Mary ran out and collected the small pieces. Having done so she skipped over to the overflowing basket and tried to balance them on the top. They tumbled off and joined the other sticks lying around it. She picked them up and tried again with no success.

'Go inside, Mary,' her father said without taking his eyes from the chopping block

'No want.'

He brought down the axe, then swung round and glowered at his daughter. Mary stuck out her bottom lip and ran inside where she peeped out from the crack in the door. Her father felt the familiar ache in his chest and wished for the tenth time that day, as he had every day of Mary's three years, that her mother had made it through the birth.

In the sky the white gun smoke had almost disappeared.

He continued to swing the axe and his son continued to line up the wood for him and Mary watched them through the crack in the door.

*

The highlander had looked dead on his feet and incapable of running another yard or even raising his dirk. When the redcoat had seen them and reached for his pistol though, he had leapt off the ground and rammed his dirk into the redcoat's chest before he'd even withdrawn the pistol from his belt. But the redcoat had time to let out a yelp before sliding from his mount and his companions were alerted. They turned from where they had slain the others and their smiles dissolved.

The boys watched the highlander move rapidly towards the second and third redcoats, using the dismounted horse as a shield. He reached the second before he had time to reload. He reached around the horse's neck and shielded himself from the third and he yanked the second from his horse. The redcoat was much smaller next to the highlander now that he had been dismounted and he could not get his balance and he slipped on the ground. He raised his arms and whimpered and dropped the pistol as a lost cause. The dirk drew back slightly and jabbed forward, this time into the throat.

The third redcoat was still unsighted but had had time to complete the reloading of his pistol. Now he jostled with his horse and tried to get a clear shot at the highlander. The highlander had retained a grip on the horse while dealing with the second redcoat and was trying to keep on the blind side of the third.

Anghas' eyes widened when he saw the red soldier level his pistol with the highlander's feet. He called out to warn him, not even able to select a word before the alerting noise burst from his mouth. 'WHAAAA!'

The highlander, maybe because of the warning, or maybe because he had anticipated the shot, leapt onto the horse as a clod of earth was thrown up from where he had been standing. He was now less than an arm's reach from the remaining redcoat, who scrabbled in vain for his sword. His face had gone white and his eyes were like ice melting from his skull.

The dirk sang through the air and the redcoat was knocked from his horse and landed on his dead companion. He gurgled, clutching his throat and stamping his feet. The highlander retrieved his dirk and wiped the flat of his blade across the horse's mane in two strokes and then returned it to his belt. Anghas and Anndra were standing looking down at the redcoat who was still clutching at his gurgling throat. Then he ceased drumming his feet and his body slackened. Anghas looked up at the highlander as Anndra once more buried his head under his brother's arm.

The highlander took no notice of them. He looked down the hill where he saw more redcoats coming in their direction on foot. He turned his horse northwest and dug in his heels. The horse took off and Anghas reached out to his retreating back. He glanced down the hillside and saw the advancing men and he wrapped his arms around Anndra. He looked longingly at the retreating highlander.

Then the rider stopped.

He looked back over his shoulder and then down at the advancing *saighdearan dearg*. He turned the horse around and thundered back towards them. Anghas cringed and screwed his eyes shut and the horse pulled up just short. He snatched Anndra from his arms and set him down in front of him in one swift movement. Then he reached down to Anghas.

'They'll kill ye if ah leave ye here.'

Anghas gripped his forearm and was hoisted up behind the highlander. He reached around him and gripped his brother and his head was filled with the salty sweat and heat of man and horse.

Again the highlander dug in his heels and they galloped away.

*

They thundered around the corner and Elspeth could feel the trembling earth beneath her feet. They galloped forward, not in the regimental manner in which they had approached the battlefield, but as a marauding army.

The soldiers all seemed to be wearing the same expression, as if they wore masks. She had expected the solemn face of duty, maybe even joy. She saw only delightful menace.

The rest of the crowd had seen it too and the sensation of impending danger spread through them like a blast of wind driven sleet. They cringed against the dykes at the sides of the road and those that could scrambled to get over to the other side.

And then the redcoats were upon them. The crack of pistol fire filled the air again, punctuated by the thud and chunk of blades hacking into flesh and bone.

Elspeth crouched against the dyke shielding her crying baby. High-pitched screaming filled her head.

Then a stink filled her nose and she looked up into the flared and huffing nostrils of a horse. The hot, expelled air from its lungs was pumped into her face. The rider had already dismounted and he reached for her.

'No,' she cried, cowering further into the cold sharp stone of the dyke.

He grabbed her shoulder and spun her around, exposing the baby. He grabbed the bundle under her arm and yanked, but she resisted.

'No,' she pleaded, and he yanked again, harder. She felt a snap. Her baby was screeching. She let go, thinking, *he just wants the baby out of the way – it's me he wants*.

The redcoat pulled the baby from her grasp and the blanket floated to the road as he did so. He stared down at Elspeth with the child hanging by his side, gripped by a leg. His eyes burned with hate. He bared his teeth in an evil grin and he raised the baby over his head and swung him around and then released him, sending him over the dyke and into the field beyond.

For a moment Elspeth could not move for shock. Her brow arched as her mind struggled to comprehend. '*No, no, no, no, no . . .* '

This seemed to amuse the redcoat and he began to laugh. Not an evil laugh, but in the circumstances far worse. A deep, wholehearted laugh. He clutched his sides and doubled over.

Elspeth snatched the blanket from the road and turned and began to clamber over the dyke in search of her baby. But she did not make it. Pain reverberated through her body as the booted heel of the redcoat struck the base of her spine. Paralysed by the agony, she crumpled back onto the road.

Further along the dyke, through her dimming vision, she could see the twisted body of an old woman, smoke rising from her blackened chest and blood seeping onto the road beneath her. Beyond that a girl fought to shield herself as three redcoats laid into her with their musket butts.

Then Elspeth was kicked again and her skull cracked on the jagged dyke.

*

Ailen splashed across the water of the burn and continued southward until the light began to fade. It was still only early afternoon but greyness had filled the day. Out of the gloom he could make out the shape of an old barn. He stumbled towards it and squeezed in through the gap in the door. In the darkness around him he saw the faint glitter of the eyes of other fugitives. Metal flashed as weapons were laid back down. He laid Tarlich on the damp straw.

Outside the darkness came down thick and Ailen's eyes drooped as he listened to an owl hoot in the trees. He lay down in the straw with his brother and covered him as best he could with his plaid to keep him warm. He listened to his shallow breaths and thought about his sons and hoped that they would be halfway back to Argyll by now and then exhaustion took its toll and he fell into a deep sleep.

*

Mary watched her father swing the axe down and turn the wood into kindling. She watched her brother as he piled up the sticks and put fresh wood on the block. Then her father paused and rested the head of the axe on the ground by his foot. He tilted his head and as young as Mary was, she knew that he was listening.

Her father looked over at the boy. 'Get inside,' he said.

The boy put the sticks he'd been holding in the pile by the basket and looked back at his father began to walk towards the door.

'Quickly,' his father said as he turned towards the road that passed their croft.

As the boy approached the door to their small home, Mary pushed it open for him. With the door ajar she could now faintly hear the thunderous sound coming up the road. She had recognised the sound and knew that it was soldier horses. She stood with her brother in the open doorway as the sound of hooves became louder. Then the horses and their red-coated riders rounded the bend and came into view a hundred or so yards down the road.

They were going at speed with mens' coat tails and horses' tails flying and weapons and equipment rattling and clattering. There were much more than she could count. Now she could feel the beat of the hooves through her feet as the fore runners galloped past and up the road towards Inverness, the riders with their heads down as if in a great race. She felt strange and dizzy as she watched them pass with her eyes wide and her mouth opening in a big smile. Subconsciously, she drew closer in to her brother's side. Then an important looking horseman with a different coloured hat passed and he pulled on his reigns and turned his horse around to look in the direction of their father. He stayed at the side of the road and kept some distance. Mary could see anger in his look and her smile began to fade. Then the important horseman returned his attention to the passing riders on the road and he raised his hand. Two more of the horsemen pulled hard on their reigns and their horses came to halt by the side of the road and the horses blasted jets of steam into the cold afternoon air as they whinnied and scraped at the dirt.

The important horseman with the golden thread in his hat pointed at their father.

'He's armed,' he said to the other two. 'Deal with him'. Then he pulled on his reigns and twisted the head of his horse and kicked in his heels and the horse took off again and joined the last of the riders as they rode towards Inverness.

The vivid red of the riders began to fade off into the distance and the trembling in the ground beneath Mary's feet began to die down. Only the two riders remained. They sat on their stirring horses and looked at Mary's father. They looked across at each other and then Mary saw one of them gently nudge his heel into the side of his horse. The animal slowly moved forward a few paces and as it did so, the rider reached across himself and pulled a pistol from his belt.

Then her father turned with his face red and his eyes wide. 'Get inside, children,' he yelled at them in a voice that Mary had never heard before. Her father turned back to face the red coated horsemen and laid his axe on the ground and raised his hands. Mary was rooted to the spot and watched to see what would happen but her brother dragged her off her feet and back inside. He dragged her through the kitchen to the back of the house as they heard an explosion from the front. He lifted her and he pushed her out of the back window. She scraped her knees and flailed at the air as she fell to the ground on the other side. The wind was knocked out of her and she lay face down on the hard earth. She felt pain in her hand as her brother stood on her getting out of the window himself. From nowhere she found the ability to scream but it hitched in her throat as her brother grabbed her around the waist yanked her up. He began running away from the back of the house in the direction of the woods and Mary's feet dangled above the ground.

From the front of the house they heard another bang reverberate through the air and Mary began to wail. They were getting close to the trees now and Mary looked back towards the house to see if her father was following. Instead she saw the two horsemen gallop around the building and she wailed harder. This spurred her brother on and he reached the line of the trees and headed for where the trees were thickest and darkest and he skipped deadfall and hollows and prayed under his breath.

Behind them the cavalry men reached the edge of the wood where they pulled up their horses. They pointed their pistols into the trees and leaned from side to side trying to get a good shot at the boy before he disappeared. They discharged their weapons at the fleeing children.

Mary felt her brother lunge forward as if an invisible hand had shoved him. They crashed into the undergrowth and again Mary felt the wind being knocked from her. Mary lay whimpering in her brother's arms and she looked into his face. Blood trickled from the corner of his mouth.

'Shh,' he said quietly. 'Shhh.'

She kept quiet and watched her brother's face as it drained of colour. Then he closed his eyes. Still she kept quiet and lay clutching him on the floor of the wood. After some time she heard the snap and crackle of flames coming from the direction of the house. Through the trees and bushes she could see smoke rise into the darkening sky. And she could hear the sound of hooves fading into the distance.

*

Ailen emerged shivering and aching from a fitful sleep and pain pounded from his head down through his shoulders and into his back. He tried to open his eyes but found that the effort only increased the pain in his head. Then he became aware of a hand pushing at his shoulder.

'Wake up,' a voice whispered close by his ear.

With effort he managed to turn his head and open his eyes. The barn was small, probably only used to shelter cattle in severe weather. Through cracks in the wooden walls a weak dawn penetrated into the gloom in thin shafts. He raised his head slightly and craned his throbbing neck and looked around and could make out the occupants that had only been shadows when he arrived. There were about a dozen of them propped against the walls or scattered around in the straw. One crouched at the door that stood slightly ajar and looked out through the opening. Beside Ailen knelt the man who had awoken him and he helped Ailen into a sitting position.

'There's redcoats out there,' he said.

Ailen reached out for Tarlich and he felt cold and he turned him onto his back to get a look at him. His body moved stiffly and his arms were crossed over his chest and his fingers gripped the cloth. His face was white. Ailen looked up at the man who had woken him.

'I think there's only the three of us able to fight,' he said.

Ailen covered his brother's face and then struggled to his feet. He stooped over to the door where the other man looked out. He could see about two dozen redcoats marching across the field in two neat files and to their right an officer on horseback. About fifty yards short of the barn the officer halted them and formed them into ranks where they promptly set about preparing their muskets. Ailen turned back to the others.

'We can't fight them,' he said.

Then from outside the officer shouted towards the barn.

'Anyone know what he said?' Ailen asked.

He heard a weak voice from the floor croaking an answer and he knelt by the highlander on the ground that had spoken. Blood glistened on the crude bandage around his stomach. 'He wants you to throw out your weapons,' he said weakly.

Ailen went around the barn and stooped to collect swords and dirks, including his dead brothers. He opened the door about a foot wider and began throwing them out into the field.

'Throw out everything you can find,' Ailen said. 'We can't give them an excuse.' They threw all they had out the door and the weapons clattered and jangled in a heap in the grass.

Again the redcoat officer called out to them and again the injured highlander gave them a translation.

'He says to stay back,' he wheezed. 'Away from the door.'

The three able men backed up against the far wall and then two of the redcoats ran forward and slammed the door shut and swung down the iron bar that secured it from the outside. Ailen went forward again and peered out through a crack in the door. The *saighdearan dearg* fanned out and surrounded the barn in a wide circle while the officer barked out orders from his mount. Two of the redcoats laid down their muskets and lit torches. They ran towards the barn and threw them onto the thatched heather roof.

'Fuck,' Ailen yelled and began kicking the door as above them the roof began to crackle. The other two joined him and they kicked as hard as they could till the door began to screech and give a little. Then a volley of musket fire thudded against the wood sending splinters flying and driving them back. The injured translator cried out as a large shard cut into his face. The heat from the roof was upon them now and burning debris began to fall to the floor. The three of them returned to kicking and booting the door. Screaming came from behind them as burning heather fell onto one of the injured men. The straw was beginning to dry out and ignite in the heat. Ailen could feel his exposed skin tightening as the heat increased and he kicked harder at the door. The hinges creaked and started to give way but still the door held. He lunged forward and began yanking at the wood and then felt the immense bolt of pain in his arm and knee as another volley of musket ball thudded into the barn and ruined his hand and leg. He collapsed backwards onto the floor of the barn and began to weep. The barn was filled with smoke and he had no choice but to suck it into his lungs. He felt himself begin to lose consciousness and tried to get back towards the door but the roof had collapsed there now and the flames were blistering the skin on his arms. He began to fade into darkness as the smoke filled him and he began to see shapes reaching out to him. He could smell burning hair and flesh and he could hear agonised screaming. He sucked in the smoke but the agony kept him conscious and he roared into the flames.

*

Jack felt the throbbing coming from his teeth first. Then the pulsing began to swirl around his head and shoot like forks of lightning down his spine and into his ribs and stomach. He slid his tongue round the inside of his gums and explored the unfamiliar and broken landscape littered with splinters of teeth. He tried to spit and managed to spray some clotted blood and saliva over his split and swollen lower lip.

'Here,' a voice said from above. 'Drink this.'

He tried to open his eyes but found the right had swollen shut. He could make out the shape of a hip flask being held out to him.

He winced as he heaved himself up against the cold, damp wall and his bare feet slipped on a layer of sludge that covered the earthen floor. Needing air, he sucked in the foul stench of human waste and coughed it out again.

'You're lucky you can't smell anything through that mess of a nose.'

Jack could see a vague shape in the gloom and reached out. Gently, the flask was placed against his hand but he found that he could only curl one finger and was unable to grasp it. His other arm was at his side, supporting him, and he knew that there was no way he would be able to shift his weight. The flask was lifted to his mouth and he sipped. The liquid burned his lips and gums, but it was good.

'Thanks,' he said.

'You can pay me back on the other side,' said the voice.

'Other side?'

'Next life, whatever you want to call it.' The flask was lifted to Jack's lips again but he raised his injured hand. 'We're all going there tomorrow.'

Jack absorbed the news and found that it dulled his pain. 'But there has to be a court martial, I haven't defended myself.'

'Trial's over, mate . . . you were found guilty. We all were. All it took was an officer to sign against your name.' He screwed the lid back onto his flask. I helped hold you up while they read out your charges. Cowardice in the face of the enemy and,' he paused, '. . . gross insubordination.'

Jack swallowed down a lump in his throat. 'That's not, true,' he said, feeling his body begin to shake.

'True for us all,' said the voice. 'We're being 'anged at dawn.'

Jack pulled himself up the wall and his hand slipped on the slime and his hip flared as he collided with rough granite. As he lurched past the other prisoners to the front of the cell he stumbled on a foot and cried out as he fell against the bars. He could see the purple-blackness of his hand in the light that leaked through the door at the end of the corridor. Outside a guard stood with his back to the bars with a musket slung over his shoulder.

'Guard,' croaked Jack.

The soldier turned and looked Jack up and down. 'What d'you want?'

'I need to write a letter.'

'Not much point in that is there?' the guard smirked. 'Unless you've a fortune to leave behind.'

'I need to write to my fiancé.'

The guard shook his head and his smile faded.

'Please.' Jack gripped a bar with his good hand and straightening himself up. 'I need to explain things to her.'

The guard looked at the ground and then turned his back again.

'I'm not a coward,' Jack said softly. 'I fought the French.'

The private looked over his shoulder at Jack again and then went through the door at the end of the corridor. He returned with a scrap of paper and a stub of pencil.

'Only 'cause you were in Flanders,' he said. 'You've five minutes and then I need the pencil back.'

'Thank you,' said Jack. He sank to the ground by the bars. He spread the paper on his thigh and held it steady as best he could with his injured hand while he began to write.

*

In the privacy of his room and with his most trusted servant at the door, the Duke knelt in front of his pentagram and his candles on his portable altar. Through the window, out in the darkness, cries and moans could still be heard from the battlefield. Shouts and laughter from drunken troops punctuated the night.

'*Now they are mine*,' the Duke whispered into his fists. Glee rippled through his fat belly and he raised his face and hands to the roof. Glaring eyes and teeth glowed in the dark and he laughed.

He wrapped his arms around himself.

He laughed uncontrollably.

But then his smile faded and his eyes widened. He groaned and gripped his head and fell to his knees. He pulled off his wig and rubbed at the lumps above his forehead.

'They are mine, not yours.' He gritted his teeth and pressed his palms over the stretched, burning skin on his head. 'I am a prince, damn you. I . . . am . . . *immortal.*'

The candles blew out and the servant knocked on the door.

'Your grace, do you require assistance.'

'Leave me,' the Duke roared into the darkness.

*

'Up and out, all of you,' the sergeant's lamp was brilliantly bright at the bars of the cell.

Jack hadn't slept, but his mind had been drifting far away from the cell all night. In the darkness he had found his way home to the boy he had once been and to parents that he loved and missed. The darkness turned to light and he was playing in the lanes and in the fields with his childhood friends. Then he had seen the young man he had become, full of enthusiasm and craving adventure and a young man that had lost his innocence in the violence of war. Still young, he had found himself trapped in a brutal system he longed to be free from so that he could live in peace and be with the girl he loved. But he had made mistakes and he had made enemies and so darkness now engulfed him. He had made enemies simply by trying to help others. He had been stupid, not looking out for himself and not biding his time. Now, still young, he was going to die.

The lamp pierced into his darkness and illuminated the cell. Jack blinked in the harsh light. Iron shrieked and the bars were pulled open. Soldiers reached into the cell and grabbed prisoners and hauled them out. They gripped Jack's arms on either side and he was yanked abruptly to his feet. They dragged him and he tried to walk and he tried to stop his swollen ankles from striking against the walls and bars. The soldiers moved too quickly for him though and his feet slipped and floundered on the filth covered floor.

The soldiers stopped by the door of the guardroom and Jack hung between them with his head slumped. He drew in breath through raw lips and tried to focus. The guards' boots were caked in mud and their gators were splattered in blood up to the knees. Jack's face was lifted up by a handful of hair

'Stop your struggling.' Jack was dragged up to full height and he tried to place his feet on the floor.

'There'll be no getting away from the gallows for you, you fucking traitor.' Jack was shocked by the sheer hate that filled the eyes of the soldier. Then a shockwave swept through his genitals and lower abdomen as a knee was hammered up into his groin. A thunderous tremor shook through his pelvis and hips and erupted up his spine. His body twisted and bucked and he fell free of the grasp of the soldiers and out through the guardroom door where his forehead smacked the cobbles. He rolled onto his back and sucked cold fresh air into his aching chest and fought to stay conscious. He fumbled in his waistband and felt the paper.

Above him daylight filtered into the dark sky and he tried to force his swollen eye open so that he could see his last morning with both eyes. He saw only grey before an officer stooped over him. The officer was young, no more than the boy that Jack had been such a short while ago. His eyes were wide and fearful. He sighed and shook his head before looking up at the guardroom entrance.

'I have a letter,' Jack's voice was little more than a whisper.

'Get him up, please.'

The soldiers lifted him up and Jack was able to find his feet on the cobbles and managed to take some of his own weight. The officer stood in front of him with an open ledger held across his forearm and a pen poised above it.

'Name?'

'I have a letter, sir.' Jack's head spun and he swallowed back the bile that rose in his throat.

'Pardon?' the officer tilted his head.

'Answer the lieutenant's question.' Jack's head flopped on his limp neck as he was shaken.

'Easton. Private Easton, sir.'

The lieutenant's pen searched the list of names on the page in front of him and then made a scratch. He looked up. 'Private Easton, in accordance with martial law you are to be taken from this place to a place of execution where you will be hanged by the ne-'

'I have a letter, sir.' Jack reached inside his waistband and pulled out the folded paper. Written across it, as neatly as Jack had been able to manage in the gloom, was Lucy's name and address. His hand shook as he held it out to the lieutenant.

He looked at it in surprise for a few moments and then sighed and reached out his hand. Jack saw his fingers begin to close on the corner of the envelope, and then, at a time when nothing should frighten him anymore, he heard a voice that chilled him.

'It's probably best if I take care of that, sir,' said Pullman. 'I'm his platoon Sergeant.'

Without waiting for a reply, Pullman took the letter and slid it into his jacket. He turned and smiled at Jack. 'Don't worry, Easton. I'll make sure this goes where it's supposed to.'

The young officer flicked his head and gestured towards the cart where the first prisoners had already been bundled. Jack's hands and feet were bound and he was thrown onto the cart with the others.

Jack tried to keep his head up off the floor while the cart bumped along the road. A short distance from the barracks it came to a halt under a wooden beam. Nooses hung from the beam like the foliage of a weeping willow. Two soldiers climbed into the back of the cart and one by one got the prisoners to their feet. They slipped the nooses around their necks and tightened the rope with a sharp jerk. The rope burned into Jack's skin and he fought to keep his balance,. He gasped hot breath into the cold morning air.

Through wet eyes he looked out on the square where he had been brought to die. Soldiers and officials dribbled from grey buildings across the wet cobblestones and the thin crowd congregated in front of the cart where they turned their morbid faces up to the makeshift gallows. At the back of the crowd was the smiling face of Sergeant Pullman.

Jack watched as Pullman reached into his jacket. He took out the letter and waved it like a punter with a winning betting slip. Jack shook his head. Pullman snorted and flamboyantly tore the letter in two like a magician performing a trick. He put the two pieces together with his free fingers outstretched like skeletal wings and tore again. Together, and tore again. And again and again. A whip cracked and the paper exploded from Pullman's fingers like confetti and swirled and floated in Jack's watery vision.

Jack's toes scrabbled as the cart slid from beneath him and then he swung out into the abyss.

*

Mairi threw her brooch into the blanket along with the bread. Her mind screamed and she couldn't think.

'C'mon, woman,' Donald McLachlan shouted. 'There's nae time.'

'I'm comin.' Feverishly, her eyes scanned the room. Then she balled up the blanket and stuffed it into a pot. On the way out of the door she snatched up a ladle.

'Get movin, Mairi.'

'You as well, Granda.'

'I need tae hold them up a bit.' Donald hefted a shovel in his hands. The proper weapons had all gone with the younger men.

'I don't think so.' Mairi tugged at his arm. 'They'll kill ye.'

'They won't hurt an old man.' He nodded towards the forest. 'Go, catch up wi the others. Catriona's carryin my great-grandchild an you need to make sure she's a'right.'

Mairi looked over her shoulder. Anna and Catriona were almost at the ford. Her head turned and she looked past Donald towards the mouth of the glen. Smoke rose into the sky. The *saighdearan dearg* were getting closer. She thought she could hear the crunch of quick marching boots and the thud of hooves. They couldn't be far away now. They had to get to safety and they had to get to the secret place in the forest and wait until the redcoats had gone.

'Ye won't have time to get into the forest unless I hold them up.'

'Be careful,' she said, and hurried after the others.

She was catching up on them when she got to the ford and she could see them at the base of the slope. On the other side of the water she looked back and the redcoats were riding up to the croft house. Torches burned in their hands and flew through the air and onto the thatch. The old man raised his shovel and he was small and fragile against the oncoming horsemen. Cracks echoed from the slopes of the glen and the redcoats came on and Donald disappeared under them.

Mairi flung the pot to the ground and lifted her dress and turned towards the forest and her legs pounded the earth.

'Run,' she screamed.

Anna stopped and turned with her arms around Catriona.

'Run, Get off the track.'

They looked back and saw the burning croft and the oncoming redcoats. They remained where they were with their faces drained and their eyes wide.

'RUUUUUN.' Mairi emptied her lungs in an effort to get them moving again. They turned and made their way off the track and into the soaking grass and heather. Catriona stumbled and floundered and Anna struggled to keep her moving up the slope.

Mairi was still on the track but gaining on them. She looked behind her and the *saighdearan dearg* were crossing the ford. Her blood thudded in her ears and she ran into the heather. The horsemen pulled up on the track behind her and something whistled over her shoulder and thudded into the heather. The bang in her ears made her dizzy and her breath was suddenly loud and furious in her head. Yards behind her she heard the redcoats calling to one another. Their laughter sounded like gurgling water in her ringing ears. She turned to face them. One had dismounted and the others rode on.

He strode towards her over the heather and unsheathed his sword. Mairi stayed on her feet and when he was close enough she spat at him. He lunged forward and the blade went into her stomach and out through her back. It burned through her but she couldn't scream. She couldn't utter a sound and couldn't move. She remained there, impaled on his blade until he pulled it out of her. She sank to her knees and watched him return to his horse. She began to feel a cold numbness quickly course through her, and watched bright red blood drip from her chin and onto her hands. She looked at the the blooming scarlet on her stomach.

From higher up the slope she heard Catriona - *'my baby, not my baby'*. But she couldn't turn to see. She felt tired and she lay down with her head on a tussock of cold wet grass. She slipped away to another world where she began running again.
*

Slowly, his blood seeped into the earth at their roots and they came closer. The bluebells crowded around Seoras as he began to slip away. He looked up through the trees to the sky and the pain was gone, replaced by peaceful calm. High above, a bead of water dropped from a bright spring green bud and fell into his unblinking eye.

His people rushed to him then and in this terrible place they knew what he was. He was not the demon here and they would not drive him away.

Fifteen

Culloden Moor, Scotland, April 15th – 16th 2146

'Behind you, to the left.'
Sinclair didn't look around. 'As I walked up here I was struck by a thought,' he said out of the side of his mouth.

'You're wondering if he's watching us.' Cammie's voice came out of the undergrowth.

'Yeah, I don't want to blow your cover.'

'It's ok. There's no one out there.'

Sinclair crawled into the hide beside Cammie.

'Do I have to put that shit on my face?'

'The form of the human face is the most instantly recognisable shape known to man. It's the first thing you ever see when you come into this world and it's usually the last thing you see before you leave it. It's the shape you see most throughout your life.' Cammie passed Sinclair a thick, make-up stick, one half green, the other brown. 'You need to break up the outline of your cheekbones and the bridge of your nose. Your forehead can catch the light. And if you've watched old twentieth century war movies, forget about the fancy shapes you've seen them paint on their faces. It defeats the purpose. Nature is random.'

Sinclair began to dab at his face with the stick and he saw Cammie's teeth glint in the dark.

'Here, let me,' he said.

Cammie began to draw the stick across Sinclair's face in short sharp strokes. 'Did ye bring the pistol?'

'I did, but I don't know why,' Sinclair patted his hip.

'And the bonnet?' Cammie pushed Sinclair's head back and began marking his jaw line like he was a barber using a cutthroat razor.

Sinclair patted the paper bag.

'Good,' said Cammie.

When he'd finished he put the cam stick away and pushed the coveralls into Sinclair's arms. He took out the map and flattened it out on the ground in front of them and began to point out the main approach zones. It was dark now so he had to give Sinclair reference points that fell within the illumination of the floodlights. Sinclair did his best to pay attention while wrestling himself into the drab green coveralls.

'These binoculars can be switched onto night vision mode with this button,' Cammie was saying, 'use this button to focus-' He waited till Sinclair had pulled the coveralls up to his waist and had time to look up and then he tapped the buttons on the top. 'They can also detect heat from quite a distance.' He laid the goggles on top of the map as Sinclair buttoned up the coveralls and stuffed the paper bag containing the bonnet into them.

'If you start to get cold there's a quilted jacket and a pair of gloves in the backpack and if you're hungry, there's food in here,' he said patting a side pouch.

Sinclair nodded.

Cammie rolled out a sleeping bag and zipped himself into it in a few smooth movements.

'I'm going to have a couple of hours sleep now. If you see or hear anything wake me up,' he said covering up his head with the padded hood.

'Don't worry, I will.'

Instantly Cammie was still and Sinclair lay propped on his elbows looking at his shape for a while before remembering that he was meant to be watching the moor. He turned his attention to the map and looked up from it to the moor and tried to remember what Cammie had just told him about approach routes. He picked up the goggles and turned them over in his hands to find the button that had been pointed out to him. Finding it, he put the goggles to his eyes and found that by nudging it to the left and right he could pull and zoom focus. He spent a few minutes getting used to this and then he scoured the illuminated areas of the moor to get himself acquainted with the terrain. He flicked the night vision switch and the viewfinder display told him that NV mode was ON. The floodlights glared in the viewfinder like tiny white suns, but in the darkness between he could clearly see the battlefield and the heather and bracken in ghostly shades of green.

He shivered and reached into the backpack and took out the jacket and gloves. He pushed his arms into the jacket and immediately felt the benefit of it. He reached inside his coveralls and pulled out the paper bag and took out the bonnet and looked at it for a moment before pulling it onto his head. It fitted perfectly.

He managed to remember which side-pouch the food had been stored in and before putting the gloves on he had a look inside. He found it full of cereal bars and sighed but took one out anyway. He unwrapped it and took a bite before laying it on top of the map and pulling on the gloves.

Chewing slowly, he picked up the binoculars and began to scour the moor again.

*

Night slid over the moor and an airbike glided silently to a halt by the side of the road.

He was close now.

He had travelled during the broad daylight and he had been free from prying eyes and safe to travel the roads without being disturbed but eventually the sun had hurt him. It had begun to burn and blister and peel off his skin in watery patches. The burning had kept him awake and made him feel alive. He missed it and began to shiver.

His hand went to his pocket and he pulled out a soiled handkerchief. He dabbed at his forehead and soaked moisture from the weeping raw flesh at the top of his head and above his ears and across his cheekbones. He patted his lips and stuffed the cloth back into his pocket. He put the bike into gear and eased it slowly along the road, keeping perfect balance despite his weight.

He pushed the throttle gently forward and could make out lights in the distance. His destination. The place where he would do battle and defeat his master's enemies.

And win his prize.

The first of the lights grew closer and he could see the heather and trees illuminated in the lights to his right. Over to the far right he could make out the visitor centre. He scanned as much of the lighted area as he could from the road. He cast his eyes along the paths and through the bushes and trees. He saw a group of men in a row at the far side and instinctively his fingers folded over the brakes before he realised that they were statues. He smiled, satisfied that the place was deserted. Further along the road the lights crossed over to the left and this was where he headed. He gave the airbike a bit more throttle and he swept off the road and came to a halt at the base of Cumberland's Stone.

He leaned the bike against the stone and released the holdall from the rack. Gently, he pushed it up onto the wide flat top of the rock above his head. Without pause, he stepped up onto the seat of the bike and the framework protested under his weight. Once there he pushed the holdall closer to the centre of the stone and into a safer position. Then he got his elbows onto the flat and in one movement hauled his great bulk over the rounded lip and onto the top. He got onto one knee and pushed himself to his feet. He looked around and he could see that he had plenty of room to move around on top of the oblong rock and then surveyed the moor from his new vantage point.

Further to the left of the road there was only darkness but turning back towards the direction of his approach, he found that the whole of the floodlit battlefield was clearly visible to him. To his left a red flag fluttered on a twenty-foot pole and at the opposite end of the moor there was a blue flag raised on a flagpole. He could see a memorial of some kind and picnic areas and he licked his red lips as he noticed the stones marking the mass graves.

Finding nothing else that interested him for the time being he turned his attention to the holdall. He unzipped it and he carefully exposed the skull. The red eye sockets glowed brighter as he pulled back the towel.

'We have arrived.' He cradled the ancient skull in both hands and lifted it level with his face. 'Your stone. The place from which you commanded your finest triumph.'

Your work has been excellent. Soon your reward will be great. The souls will be yours to devour forever.

The fat man turned the skull around to face the battlefield and he raised it above his head as if he was presenting a trophy to a cheering crowd.

*

Sinclair was sure he saw a faint white blur in the viewfinder. He panned back to his left, slower this time and saw it again travelling northward along the road. It seemed too fast to be someone on foot and too slow to be a vehicle. If it was heat the binoculars were detecting, then it was also quite large. He turned off the heat sensor and relied only on the infrared. He lost the shape and quickly scanned the area again. He focused and refocused and tried to zoom in on the road. He had to train the binoculars further north where the road was actually illuminated by the floodlights. He found the road again and began panning southward and adjusted his focus as the road travelled south to keep it in focus as it led into the darkness. Beyond the white pools of the lights the road itself became a dark strip that was flanked on either side by the eerie greens of the scrub.

Then movement caught his eye again and he saw something progressing along the road. With the heat sensor off the transparent white shape had become more solid. He could see hard edges defined by bright green lines and depth and shadow filled by darkening shades of green and eventually black. He glanced at the sleeping bag beside him and wondered if he should wake Cammie. Instead he adjusted his elbows slightly and tried to get rid of the shake that was detracting from his vision. He carefully zoomed and panned, not wanting to lose the subject. He held his breath as it travelled closer to the floodlit section of the road and watched it grow more distinct.

He let go of his breath. It was a rider on an airbike.

Sinclair lowered the binoculars as the bike moved into the pool of the first floodlight. While he had been out on the battlefield with Namah, Sinclair had been aware of infrequent traffic whooshing along that back road, but as this bike was moving a lot slower he presumed that it wasn't local. As if to confirm his suspicion, the rider raised himself up on his heels and craned his neck to study the moor.

Sinclair glanced at Cammie. He reached out to shake his shoulder, but let his hand drop.

He tapped the NV button on the binoculars and brought them up to his face again. Quickly, he located the rider and got a good, clear focus on him.

'Jesus,' he breathed, seeing his inflamed, red face. The dome of his head had lost the skin and raw flesh glistened in the lights.

The rider was big, far too big for the bike Sinclair reckoned, but at the speed he was going he needed to have exceptional balance to keep it from seesawing all over the road. The bike braked slightly and Sinclair thought he saw a flash of teeth before it sped up again.

He put the binoculars down and was glad that the rider was on his way. Then he saw the bike pull off the road by the base of the Cumberland Stone, and he quickly picked the binoculars up again.

'What is he doing?' Sinclair whispered to himself.

The rider dismounted quite gracefully, Sinclair noticed with a certain amount of surprise. He detached a bag from the rack at the rear of the bike and reached up and slid it on top of the Cumberland Stone.

'Must be a camera.'

Then Sinclair was surprised again as the rider stepped up onto the saddle of the bike and got himself up onto the top of the rock. The guy was very fat and didn't look like he would be able to tie his own shoe-laces and Sinclair felt as if his eyes were being deceived by some kind of illusion. But in no time at all and with very little effort there he was, on top of the huge flat-topped boulder, beginning to walk around with his holdall.

Sinclair decided that this guy would have to be moved along, or at least directed into the visitor centre to pay the admission fee and be kept out of the way. He glanced at Cammie one more time before taking the decision himself. He hung the binoculars around his neck and used his elbows to drag himself quietly out of the hide. He pulled the blue bonnet tighter onto his head and swung his legs over the wooden railing at the front of the viewpoint. He jogged down she short, steep incline and found himself on the floor of the moor about halfway between the Jacobite and Government lines.

The smell of heather was much stronger here and instantly filled his head. Underneath it lay the moist smell of damp grass and earth. He cut across the field in a diagonal and headed in the direction of the Cumberland Stone. He found the going difficult and when he looked up towards his destination he noticed that he couldn't see the top of the stone from this lower ground. He craned to see the rider and almost went over his ankle. He moved on and took greater care over where he laid his feet. As he walked he tapped his wristfone to let Namah know that they had a visitor.

'There's a guy out here.'

'What?' She sounded alarmed.

'It's okay, he's just a tourist I think. He's climbed on top of the Cumberland Stone. I don't know how though, he's pretty big. Looks like he's been out in the sun as well – his face is burned.'

As he walked, he noticed that the smell of the moor around him was changing. There was still the strong aroma of heather but now he could smell something else that he couldn't identify. It smelt like smoke, but with a metallic tang to it. A wind had picked up, bringing with it some moisture, the coldness of which stung as it hit his face.

When he had covered about a third of the distance to the stone, he could see movement on top again. He stopped and could hear sighing sounds around him. He thought it could be singing. And there was music; pipes definitely, and maybe drums. He wiped the cold rain from his face and lifted the binoculars to his eyes.

'I don't like it, Sinclair. That's where Cumberland commanded the battle from,' Namah's voice was coming from the wrist-fone, 'And just how big *is* this guy? That's too much of a coincidence.'

Sinclair focused the binoculars on the head and shoulders that were visible above the lip of the boulder. He could see the rider raising something above his head.

'Go wake up Cammie. He should know about this.'

Sinclair didn't hear her. His senses had been distracted away from conversation. On the wind he could make out other smells that he could identify. Like sweat and polish. He looked around and across the moor he saw faint white shapes moving in clusters, like when he had watched the rider using the binoculars in heat sensitive mode. But he wasn't using the binoculars now. He could hear shouting, as if from far away, and the clank of metal.

'Sinclair?'

He turned back to the Cumberland Stone and saw what the fat rider held aloft, and he saw the sockets of the skull glare red. The red reached out to him in beams and he realised that it was not singing that he heard on the moor. It was wailing, and the percussion was charged with gunpowder.

'Sinclair?!'

On top of the rock, the rider pulled the skull down towards his head. The air crackled crimson around him and blinded Sinclair. When he could see again, the man on the boulder had changed.

*

The air thumped and shook the cover of the hide. Cammie burst out of the top of his sleeping bag and instantly grabbed his pistol and adopted a prone defensive position. The dull thudding came up through the earth and sent shock waves through the air that could visibly be seen crashing against the trees and rippling through the branches. To Cammie the sound of artillery fire was unmistakable. Seeing that Sinclair had gone from beside him he looked around for the binoculars. Unable to find them, he rolled out of the hide. He halted in a crouch behind the information board at the viewpoint and quickly scanned the area.

His eyes widened and he tightened his grip on the pistol. He crouched further behind the board. There was so much smoke that at first he thought the heather was alight. But there were no flames. He tried to locate its source and it seemed to be coming from the government lines to his right where there were frequent flashes followed by the earth-shaking thumps. In the gloom he could make out the faint silver-grey of artillery guns, illusory and translucent. And as he looked closer he could see faint rows of red-coated soldiers standing perfectly in rank.

'*Saighdearan dearg*,' he whispered. 'They've come back.'

The wind from the north strengthened and filled the standards and colours that flapped above the spectral ranks. The wind drove through the decorative cloth and southward over the moor and brought with it the shouted orders and yells of the redcoats.

Sleet filled Cammie's eyes and he turned to face the south. There, on the other side of the moor, he could make out the groups of the gathered clans. They too were faint and ghostlike. In the dips of the wind the echoic skirl of pipes came to his ears.

He looked back across the moor and scanned it for Sinclair. With all that was happening on the moor he must have missed him, but he had no idea how. Sinclair stood out, solid amongst the ghostly shapes and forms that now populated the field. On his head he wore the Jacobite bonnet, brilliant blue under the floodlights. He had his back to the viewpoint and Cammie followed his line of vision to the far corner of the field where the Cumberland Stone was situated. Cammie's fingers dug into the wood of the information board as he saw the glowing red eyes.

There was no mistaking who they belonged to. He had seen his picture so many times in books and paintings. The Duke of Cumberland was dressed in his splendorous red and gold coat and immaculate white breeches and shining black boots. He stood with legs apart on top of the rock. A white plume flowed from the gold edged tri-corn sitting on top of his powdered wig. Over his shoulder a Sam Browne was slung that secured the jewel encrusted hilt of a sword to his left hip. Cammie had always been amazed at the way his obesity actually added to his regal appearance. At the base of the rock a huge stallion snorted and reared and its muscular flanks shone black and sleek in the lights.

'The Butcher.' Cammie wiped his mouth and considered his next move.

*

'Sinclair!,' Namah shouted again into the wristfone. He didn't answer but he didn't disconnect either. Something was wrong. Namah grabbed her coat and burst out of the door. An icy blast snatched at her and took her breath away as she emerged into the night. The weather was wilder than she had anticipated and she fought to pull on her coat. She began to sprint down the path to the field and as she ran a high-speed mental debate began in her head. The thoughts raced along the paths of decision faster than she herself could run. Soon she would reach a fork, one route heading west and the other south. The last she knew Sinclair and Cammie were at the main viewpoint, but Sinclair had mentioned the Cumberland Stone. She came to the decision that she should head there, along the westbound path. And then, as she came within yards of the fork, she called out to Sinclair again.

Then another thought occurred to her.

What if I'm giving their position away?

She was at the fork now and hadn't reached a decision. She halted and her feet nearly slipping out from under her on the thin layer of slick mud and sleet that had formed on the surface of the path. Now that her feet had stopped beating the ground, she heard someone shouting above the wind.

She looked around, unsure where it was coming from.

*

Cammie's head turned to the see Namah racing down the path from the visitor centre.

'Over here,' he waved towards her. He didn't want her going onto the battlefield after Sinclair. Her pace didn't slow, so he cupped his hands and yelled into the wind: 'Namah!'

This time she came to a halt and looked around and when Cammie called her name again she turned to face him. 'Come to the viewpoint', he waved his arm to beckon her.

She started off in his direction but then she paused again. He could see her staring at the battlefield – transfixed by the ghostly battle scene.

'COME ON!' he bellowed, burning his throat. Shaken from the trance, she signalled to him and hurried along the path again.

The path went around behind the Memorial Cairn and a grove of silver birch and hawthorn and within seconds she was out of sight. Cammie expected her to be coming up behind him in a couple of minutes. He returned his attention to Sinclair and The Duke. Crackling red light caught his eye about two hundred yards to his immediate right. The statues of the redcoats were moving and on the Cumberland Stone the glow from The Butcher's eyes brightened intensely and two beams shot out like searchlights towards Sinclair. They struck him square in the chest and the beams broke up and radiated away as if it were a jet of high-powered water. Sinclair was knocked off his feet and landed on his back in the heather.

Cammie sprang to his feet and scrambled down the bank onto the battlefield. He ran through the heather towards Sinclair and was suddenly aware of new movement to his right. He glanced in that direction and stumbled on the uneven ground. A band of about twenty wraith-like creatures, kilted and red-coated, raced from the government lines and cut off his path to Sinclair. He turned to face them with his pistol held out in front of him.

The wraiths came to a halt, wielding their bayoneted muskets.

'Campbells,' hissed Cammie, trying to hold the gun steady. Behind them he could see Sinclair struggling to his feet.

Hideous growls and snarls echoed through the driving wind from the rotting jaws of the Wraith-Campbells. They advanced on Cammie and lunged and thrust their bayonets at him.

He fired into the nearest, hitting it in the skeletal head. Fragments of ancient brown bone and dead hair burst apart and swarmed like wasps around a bin. The wraiths paused briefly and then continued to advance, quicker and louder. Cammie fired another shot into them and this time they halted.

Their heads turned as one towards the south of the moor.

*

'Come on!' Cammie's voice reached Namah and the urgency in it got her feet moving again. She dragged herself away from the spectacle on the battlefield and took the path that would lead her southward to the viewpoint. She ran behind the silver birch grove and as she approached the well of the dead she ran into an obstacle that knocked the breath from her and sent her sprawling onto the path. Her hands went out in front of her and slid along the gravel. Sharp stones ripped her skin and embedded themselves in her flesh. Her arms and face plunged into the open well itself before she finally came to a stop.

She rolled quickly away from the well and coughed out a mouthful of water and pain was already biting into her hands. She knelt on the grass verge and looked wildly around for whatever she had run into. She saw nothing. Then she realised that the water from the well wasn't cold as it should have been. It should have been freezing, but her arms and face felt warm. Slowly, she held her hands out in front of her. The red glistened. She tried to wipe the blood from her hands on the grass and tried to wipe the blood from her face with her sleeve. Then she became still and looked up from the blood filled well.

Around the well she could see dim white shapes. They were indistinct but as she watched they took form and she could see that there was a group of men that crouched and knelt by the well. As they solidified she could see some wearing the uniform of the government troops, others the redcoat and kilt of the Argyle militia. One wore the blue bonnet of the Jacobites.

They jostled and pushed at each other around the well and scooped the blood into their mouths with their skeletal hands and the blood dripped down their mandibles and the more they drank the stronger and more distinct they became. Above her, the floodlights crackled and died, but she could still see them clearly in the darkness. The hollow eye sockets of the wraiths turned their red glare towards her.

Slowly, Namah got to her feet.

From their hunched and kneeling positions the wraiths also raised themselves up. One that was wearing the epaulettes of a captain drew a pistol from his belt and cocked it. Namah listened to the click of the hammer as it echoed into the night and then she burst into a sprint along the green verge and back onto the path.

Within seconds she felt sharp fingers digging into her shoulder and her heel was clipped. She sprawled face first onto the gravel with her hands once more taking the force of the fall. The wraiths were on her as soon as she hit the path and they pinned her to the ground before she even had a chance to struggle. She was flipped onto her back and skeletal hands held her fast to the cold ground.

The wraith wearing the blue bonnet stepped to her feet. Bile rose to her mouth as she watched the ancient skin and sinew stretch on his skull and it dawned on her that this was a smile. A deep rattling came from his throat and sounded at first like a low growl and then syllables and words were formed. She realised that he was speaking to her in Gaelic. The words he spoke were difficult to decipher, but she heard them.

'Gillies McGilchrist, soldier of fortune,' rumbled from his throat.

Around her the wraiths began to rip and tear at her clothes and McGilchrist stepped forward, between her legs.

'At your service,' he said, pulling up the tattered remnants of his kilt.

Namah's skin crawled with revulsion and her body shuddered with rage. She shot her foot upwards between McGilchrist's legs and heard the sound of snapping and tearing deadwood. Her foot drove downwards again while her back arched, freeing her from the tight grasp of the wraiths around her. She rolled onto her feet and kicked McGilchrist in the head as he bent double and his skull smashed apart like a sandcastle. She turned, wanting to get to Cammie, and as she did so the butt of a musket hit her between the eyes. Bright yellow sparks exploded in Namah's head and she went down heavily on her knees and all the strength was sapped from her. She felt herself falling towards the turf.
*

Cammie heard the cries over the whipping wind and followed the gaze of the Wraith-Campbells. Sleet drove down onto the moor in piercing shards that made visibility poor but the floodlights managed to penetrate into the middle of the battlefield. Through the driving sleet Cammie could see that the mass hoards of the clans were advancing over the field. The sound of their howls built like the thundering of an incoming tsunami as they rushed towards their enemy. As he watched they gathered speed until he could pick out individual men brandishing weapons from the mass silhouette. On they came until he could feel the rumble of them through the earth and until their thunderous war cries became ear splitting. Then the ground shook with a thump that was more violent than the charging clansmen. From behind him, the artillery had started up again. The air was filled with whining and buzzing and Cammie ducked as he felt the air around him being cut and slashed by flying ballistics. The highlanders halted and the manner of their cries abruptly changed. The cold-blooded howls were silenced and replaced with screams of pain and agony and fear.

Searing pain exploded in Cammie's arm as if a hammer had suddenly shattered his wrist. He cradled his arm against his stomach and stared down at his injured limb expecting to see some horrific injury. But there was no physical evidence of his pain.

He sank to his knees, and as he did so, the Wraith-Campbells returned their attention to him. As one, they raised their muskets.

Beyond them Cammie could see Sinclair and the Jacobites as the grape-shot continued to fire into them. The wailing and screaming continued but they neither advanced nor fled. Sinclair was staggering around, lunging in one direction, then wheeling around and going in the other. He looked up at the Cumberland stone and the Duke loosed a bolt of red lightning and he saw Sinclair scream in agony as a red bolt pierced through his stomach like a javelin. And then Sinclair fell to the ground.

Cammie gritted his teeth and got to his feet. The wraiths were only yards from him now and he raised his gun and fired into them. The pistol bucked in his hand until the hammer clicked on an empty chamber. He knocked the nearest of the bayonets aside and swung the butt of the pistol at their heads as he charged into them. He beat madly at their snarling jaws and tried to forge a path through them to Sinclair. Above their growls he could hear the highlanders and he glanced in their direction. Blue light crackled as volleys of shrapnel rained into them and gaps were beginning to appear in their ranks. Amongst the screaming he could make out shouts of anger and frustration. The Jacobites were trapped in the storm of grapeshot not willing to retreat and not able to advance.

A flash of pain sparked in Cammie's head as a wraith drove a musket butt into his temple. He swayed and fell again to his knees and through gaps in the legs of the Wraith-Campbells he could see Sinclair struggling back to his feet.

Pain speared into him from all around as bayonets were driven into him and he yelled in agony and dropped his gun onto the heather. A boot swung into his face and he could feel the cold, rain soaked leather and the taste of blood filled his mouth. His head swam and his vision blurred, but for an instant he saw Sinclair. He stood in the driving sleet with his face turned up to the sky and his arms outstretched. In his right hand he clutched the ancient flintlock pistol. The soaked blue bonnet was pulled down on his head.

The mass of Jacobites screamed and beat their targes and strained at their leash but they seemed held back by an invisible force and Cammie could see a boy crawling through their legs and his head was a mess of blood and broken skull. The boy crawled out from the thumping feet that pounded the turf and he dragged his broken body along the turf on his elbows and he clutched at the turf with the fingers of one hand and held something to his chest in the other hand.. He crawled out from the Jacobites and made his way slowly and painfully towards Sinclair. The Wraith-Campbells saw him and turned away from Cammie and fell upon the boy with their bayonets and musket butts. The boy writhed in agony on the turf and he turned his remaining eye towards Cammie and he stretched out his hand towards Cammie's and in his fingers he held a sodden scrap of paper that was smeared with blood and ink.

And then Cammie understood what held the Jacobites back.

He gripped a musket barrel and pulled himself to his feet. He grunted through clenched teeth as he wrenched the weapon from the wraith and ripped the hands from the creature in the process. He swung the musket around him and bellowed with rage and beat them away from the boy on the ground and he took the piece of paper from the boy's outstretched fingers. He cut a swath through the wraiths and made his way towards Sinclair. But then another squad of wraiths cut in between them and cut him off from Sinclair and Cammie was surrounded and overwhelmed. Suddenly the pain of the attacking Wraith-Campbells became too much and he crashed to his knees once more as the bayonets pierced him and the musket butts beat him..

He screamed out to Sinclair and Sinclair turned to face him.

'Give them the order!', Cammie held the piece of paper out towards him and a wraith officer tried to snatch it from him with his skeletal fingers.

Sinclair lowered his arms.

'Lead them!' Cammie yelled. 'LEAD THEM!'

Then another musket butt connected with the back of Cammie's skull and his face sank into the drenched and freezing turf.

*

Sinclair lay on his back and freezing rain cascaded down onto his upturned face and washed away his fear and pain and confusion. The fat man on the rock had become a creature that attacked him had sent pain bursting through his body and had smashed him into the ground where he now lay. The spirits of the highlanders had filled his head with pleading. He had felt everything being focused on him. He'd tried to block it out and tried to get away but the creature on the rock was intent on destroying him and the voices of the highlanders drilled into his head.

And as he lay on the sodden turf something was happening. A part of him felt that he was dying, but also that he had been transformed. He felt the weariness and stress flow from his body to be replaced by a warm calmness. He knew that in a way he had died, and that he was not Sinclair any more. He felt reborn.

He knew now why the highlander had come to him and why the phantom clansmen filled his head with desperate pleading and why the fat man wanted to destroy him. And he understood what he had to do.

He rose to his feet and raised his hands to the sky and turned his head skyward and opened his mouth to catch the sleet and the coldness filled his mouth and spilled down his throat. He felt cleansed and ready. He lowered his arms and felt the flintlock at his hip. He heard his name being called and turned in the direction that the cry had come from. He saw that Cammie was surrounded by the wraiths and that he was being overpowered. Cammie shouted towards him to give them the order and Sinclair nodded and smiled.

He knew.

Then Cammie was knocked into the ground from behind and the smile vanished. The change was complete and the calmness was replaced by urgency.

Sinclair pulled the flintlock from the bandolier that now crossed his chest and pushed back the hammer with the heel of his hand and cocked it. He levelled it at the wraiths around Cammie and pulled the trigger. Blue light pulsed from the flintlock and smashed half a dozen of the wraiths and their yellowed bones shattered into oblivion.

He lowered the flintlock to re-cock it and the pleading of the Jacobites filled his ears. He started towards the Jacobites and as he went he fired another destructive shot over his shoulder into the band of wraiths. The rest of the band that had been attacking Cammie begin to slink back towards the government troops and Sinclair ran towards the Jacobites.

He felt the heat of the Jacobites in the air as he reached the front of their lines and he could see steam rising from their ghostly flesh. A clansman strode out and thrust the reigns of a grey horse into his hand. He had never been on a horse in his life but he looked into the shining black eyes of the gelding for a moment and then swung himself up onto the saddle as if it was second nature to him. The muscular horse immediately fell under his full control and he steered left and right to take in the hordes of the Jacobite Army. In their faces he saw a host of emotion and he felt them channelling it all towards him: anticipation and anger; determination and hope.

He wrapped the reins around one hand and raised his pistol into the air and fired into the sky and as he lowered it again he dug his heels into the flanks of the horse and the horse bolted forward and the clans cheered and rushed on behind him with their weapons held aloft. Wind blew into his eyes and forced his head low by the neck of the horse. He could feel the heat from the shining grey hide and the vessels and sinew pulsed below him and the moor flashed by. The horse slowed and veered and he found himself at the front of the government lines. The redcoat muskets swung up in unison and Sinclair cocked back the hammer of his flintlock with the heel of his hand and fired into those directly in front of him. The pistol bucked and blue sparks showered from the firing pan as the hammer hit and a blue beam fired into the demon army of redcoats and the redcoats shattered like fine porcelain and left a gaping hole in the ranks. The remaining men discharged their muskets and the balls seared past Sinclair but both he and his horse were unharmed by the deadly volley. He slammed back the hammer of his pistol again and fired into the redcoats, not even taking the time to aim. More wraiths disintegrated under the blue beam and weakened their ranks further.

Then a huge roaring filled his ears and he felt his horse lifted below him as if by some massive wave. Around him the Jacobite army had caught up with him and they charged out of the darkness and were crashing into the government lines and their tartan soared and their pipes skirled and the keen edges of their weapons glinted blue in the night and their swords and axes swung as they hacked into the *saigdearan dearg*. The disciplined redcoats raised their bayonets and carried out their defensive drill and many Jacobites were pierced and slashed on the redcoat's blades, but the sheer force of the charge carried them forward and they smashed through the redcoats and Sinclair went forward with them. Suddenly he found himself between the first and second lines with two long ranks of redcoats on either side. He cocked and fired the flintlock again and again and pain jarred into his hand and up his forearm. Scores of redcoats were obliterated as he rode between the lines. The Jacobites took full advantage of the breaks in the ranks to swarm through and in behind and were immediately hacking into the second line. He watched as the ordered drill of the government troops descended into panic and left them even more exposed to the slashing metal of the highlanders.

Sinclair reigned in his horse and turned to take account of the attack. Around him the red lines were collapsing and groups of redcoats were backed into small pockets. This battle scene had played out repeatedly over the centuries. The defeat of the highlanders had been replayed over and over beginning where it ended and the terrorisation and torture of the souls had been constant. Now, the demon that had captured their souls and devoured their fear and agony was on the verge of defeat.

Sinclair looked beyond the second line and there he could see awful shapes bolting through the darkness at speed and bearing down on the leading Jacobites. A troop of wraiths were mounted on sleek black horses in perfect formation and they were armed with glittering lances and sabres and they thundered into the front of the Jacobite charge and they instantly halted it. They steamed forward skewering highlanders and their own infantrymen alike on their lances. The wraith-lancers worked quickly and savagely, riding out and driving back into the Jacobites in disciplined and deadly waves and hacking the highlanders with their sabres at close range. Now that the Jacobite charge had stalled, the red infantry in the second line began to reform.

Sinclair feared that they were losing the advantage, and that his men were going to be trapped between the red lancers and infantry. He feared that they faced defeat again. He pulled his reigns sharply and turned his horse away and galloped westward between the lines. Redcoats thrust their bayonets at him and stray musket ball flashed by him as he went. Fifty yards in front he could make out the end of the lines and as he raced toward it a squad of Wraith-Campbells veered out of the darkness and blocked his route. He retightened the reigns in his fist and lowered his head by the neck of his gelding and spurred on. The horse lowered its head and Sinclair raised the flintlock on an outstretched arm. Through the rain and steam from the horse he sighted along the short barrel and when they were within yards of the wraith cavalry he squeezed the trigger. The horse leapt as the wraiths exploded in the night air. He felt shards of bone and smouldering ancient skin fly past his face, stinging his cheek. He shut his eyes and mouth tightly and when he felt the horse's hooves hit the turf he pulled him up and turned him in a tight arc to his left.

He opened his eyes again and found himself facing the left flank of the red lancers. Another wave was going in with lances low and driving into the head of the Jacobite charge. He flicked his heels and his horse bolted forward.

Now, with no barrier, he could fire into them at will. He rode forward, firing again. Those cavalry on the unprotected flank spun around, getting in the way of a new attack wave. Horses collided and riders were thrown and red cavalrymen disintegrated before the blasts from the flintlock. In front of them, the Jacobites stole back the advantage and strode in amongst the chaos. The astonished redcoats were pulled from their horses and disappeared under the arcing blades of the claymores.

Sinclair watched as the rest of the cavalry at the rear turned and retreated away into the dark and to the flanks the red infantry were running and melting into the blackness. Some pockets of troops on both sides were still unaware of their respective turns in fortune and continued to fight savagely, but even these remnants were beginning to get new orders from their captains and sergeants. Quickly, the battle had turned, and he knew that it would soon be over.

He rode around the remains of the government troops and halted by an abandoned artillery gun. Ahead of him, in the darkness he could make out the Duke sliding down from the stone like a slug. He mounted the shining black stallion tethered there. His stallion reared up and its forelegs clawed at the air and dragon-like steam flared from its nostrils. The Duke's hat and wig tumbled from his head and fully revealed the skull and horns and the bone shone dully under the floodlights. The Duke reined in the stallion and when he had it steady he slid his glimmering sabre from its scabbard. He raised it into the air and the blade threw red beams around him. Then he lowered the sabre and pointed it at Sinclair. The Duke's eyes glared red and Sinclair could feel the pure hate and malevolence projected towards him, and then the Duke spurred his stallion and charged forward.

Sinclair twisted his feet in the stirrups and gripped the grey gelding's flanks with his knees and steadied himself and onward came The Duke on his thundering reptilian stallion. Then, The Duke was there in front of him and The Duke's sabre swung through the air towards Sinclair's throat. In instant reflex, Sinclair arched back in his saddle and the razor tip of the blade sang past his exposed neck.

The Duke thundered past on the stallion and the reek of burning and rotting meat filled Sinclair's senses. Sinclair felt his neck stinging and pressed the back of his hand against it. He took it away and glanced down to see a thin line of red across his skin. He turned his horse to face the Duke and he watched him steer around for a second charge. This time he could see flame dancing at the nostrils of the black stallion.

The Duke dipped the horns on his head like a bull preparing to charge and the red burning eye sockets glared at Sinclair. Sinclair gritted his teeth and raised his flintlock as the Duke raised his sabre.

Then they charged.

*

Her head hung limply from her shoulders and she felt herself falling face first towards the turf. Then a cold hard hand was in her hair gripping tightly and wrenching her head backwards. Her vision was blurred and swimming with the red coated wraiths around her and she felt a cold sharp blade being pressed against her throat. Her arms hung limply by her sides and she could not find the will to lift them to try and defend herself. The wraiths cackled around her and she could not open her mouth to speak or protest and she waited for the blade to move across her throat and end her life so that she would no longer have to listen to the vile sounds they made.

But then the malicious cackling halted abruptly and there were cries of surprise and fear and Namah felt the blade at her throat waver and she found the strength to seize the skeletal hand that held the knife and push it away. The wraith had given little resistance and was struggling to get away from her. Swathes of blue filled Namah's blurred vision and she clenched her eyes and tried to clear her head. When she opened her eyes she could see a band of Jacobites had attacked the wraiths and the wraiths were trying to flee from the blue arcing blades. An arm went around Namah's shoulders and gently lifted her onto her feet and she felt the familiar presence of the young highlander from her visions. She looked into his face and all the misery and despair had been replaced with hope and determination. A smile lifted at the corner of his mouth and he turned from her and joined his comrades as they chased the wraiths towards the burn and the copse of trees.

Namah turned and ran in the opposite direction. She went around the cairn and ran towards the viewpoint. She heard the sounds of battle from through the trees and the gunfire shook the leaves. She ran down towards the viewpoint and she was not prepared for the scene that had unfolded across the battlefield. She leaned on the plaque to steady herself. The clans of highlanders were on the moor and they were translucent and ghostly and the red coated government troops were skeletal and menacing. The battle was in full swing but this was not the battle that she had studied at university. This was not the battle that she had retold scores of times to visitors. The clans had gone forward in numbers and they had breached the front line of the government defences and had overrun the artillery and they were in full attack against the second line. She could see sparks flying from their blades. And in amongst it all, leading the clans, she could see what looked like the prince. He was mounted on a grey horse and the tails of his sky blue coat flapped behind him and his silver buttons glinted as he led the charge into the second line. He wore the same blue bonnet of the clansmen and he was armed with a flintlock pistol and as she watched he levelled it at the skeletal red coats and fired a bolt of brilliant blue that smashed dozens of them.

On the moor, between where the main fighting was taking place, movement caught Namah's eye. There seemed to be piles of rags and bones on the turf that smouldered and dissipated as she watched. The movement had not come from a ghostly highlander or a wraith-like red coat though. She could see Cammie struggling to raise himself up from the ground.

Immediately she sprinted down to him and as she reached him he fell back to the turf. She cupped his face in her hands and his forehead was split and bleeding. She wiped the blood from his eyes and he groaned and his eyes flickered open. He looked around bewildered.

'Come on', she said.

She pulled him forward and he struggled to his feet and with her support they managed to get back up to the viewpoint. Cammie groaned and pointed to the hide-out in the trees that he and Sinclair had shared and

Namah left him holding onto the hand rail while she went and rifled through his backpack and returned with the first-aid kit and the binoculars. She tended him all the while keeping an eye on the battle that was unfolding on the moor. With some sterile wipes she cleaned the blood from his face and eyes as best she could and then she ripped a field dressing from its pouch and wound it around Cammie's head and taped it to hold it in place. While she worked shots zinged through the air and they instinctively ducked. Once the bandage was in place they held each other and watched the battle.

The highlanders had the advantage and the government troops seemed to be on the verge of defeat but then the redcoats had been reinforced by a troop of cavalry that appeared form nowhere. They rode into the highlanders with their lances and forced them away from the second line while the infantry regrouped. But then the prince had rounded on them and had fired brilliant blue bolts from his flintlock.

'We have to find Sinclair', Namah said as she scoured the moor.

'We don't', Cammie pointed towards the prince. 'He's there on the horse'.

The wraith cavalry had been defeated and beaten back and once more the highland charge drove into the government second line and this time the recoats were completely over-run and beaten backwards into small pockets.

They watched the Prince patrol and survey the last of the fighting and he fired the flintlock into the last of the larger groups of redcoats that were giving the most resistance. Then he backed up away from the fighting and he looked towards the Cumberland Stone. Namah and Cammie followed his gaze and there Namah noticed the Duke for the first time. He was climbing down from the Cumberland stone onto a large black horse that shimmered in the darkness. They saw the red fire flare from the nostrils of the stallion as it reared and they saw the horns on the Duke's head as his hat and wig fell away and they gripped each other. Namah made to run down onto the moor but Cammie held her.

'No', he said. 'You can't interfere. It has to come to this.'

They held each other tightly as the Duke's eyes blazed red and he charged at Sinclair and swung his blade at Sinclair's neck and for a moment they were frozen in horror as Sinclair raised his hand to his throat. Then the Prince and the Duke raised their weapons and charged at each other.

*

They thundered towards one other and Sinclair levelled his flintlock once again. The thunder of their hooves shook the ground and sent shockwaves through the air. The blue bolt exploded from the muzzle of the flintlock and blasted into the Duke's skull, knocking it spinning into the air. The Prince had no time to see where it came down as the headless remainder of the Duke's body came on with the sabre still pointing from the right arm and the reins still gripped in the gloved left fist. Before he had time to think, the blade had pierced him, pushed on by the Duke's huge frame and driven into his chest.

He instinctively lashed out at the headless body with the butt of the pistol, while simultaneously wheeling away.

Then he took a breath and searing agony gripped his chest and held his sides like a vice.

He looked down and he could see the golden hilt of the Duke's sabre protruding from centre of his chest. None of the blade was visible; every inch had gone into him. He reached his arm up behind him and curled his fingers around the blade. He tried to cry out, but the only sound to come from him was a faint gurgling at the back of his throat. He could taste steel.

Around him the battle was over and not a redcoat remained and the Jacobites were making their way towards the road and the hills in groups. As they left the battlefield, they faded into the darkness.

Looking up, he watched the Duke's body slide from its saddle. The stallion, dull and leathery now, knelt down on its forelegs and toppled over on to the turf. Both the body of the Duke and that of the stallion became powdery in the wind and blew away into the heather. And then the wind began to drop and there was no more sleet in the air.

He suddenly felt tired and his eyelids were heavy, but he forced his horse around and went to look for the Dukes skull. He found it quickly, lying face up against a rock. It grimaced into the sky; red eyes still faintly alight.

With an immense effort, the Prince leaned forward in his saddle and swung his leg over the back of the horse and lowered himself to the ground. He removed his other foot from the stirrup and held on to the horse for support with his head against the warmth of its neck. When he felt he had sufficient strength, he turned to look down at the skull. Then he lifted his leg and pressed the sole of his foot against it and applied more and more pressure until it cracked against the side of the rock. The horns folded in on one another and the bone crunched like an eggshell. He took his foot away and looked down at the mess. The red light had been extinguished. The evil was gone.

He took hold of the reins again and led the grey horse off the battlefield, going slowly and carefully and stopping now and then to find more strength and to rest his sweating forehead against the against the neck of the horse. When he reached the memorial cairn he stopped and let go of the horse. He slapped the horse's flank and it cantered off into the darkness.

He gripped the hilt of the Duke's sword in both hands and took in as much breath as he could. Then with all his might, he yanked it forward. Half the blade came out of him, scraping against his breastbone. Quickly he moved his hands down and wrapped them around the exposed blade and yanked again. The sword came free of him and he threw it from his lacerated hands and sank to his knees. He felt warmth filling his insides and watched blood spill from his chest. He bent down and placed his hands on the ground and with a groan he gently lowered himself onto his back. The warmth filled his body and his breathing slowed and the hot liquid trickled down his cheeks. He felt the wind and sensed the souls and he heard the singing and the music.

He smiled and sighed and then his eyelids fluttered and closed.

*

Namah screamed when she saw the sabre slam into Sinclair's chest and she dropped the binoculars and began to run down towards the Cumberland Stone, but Cammie held her. She struggled to free herself but he had her held tight and he pulled her against him.

'Wait', he said.

She kicked and writhed and tried to punch but Cammie held her and they watched as Sinclair trotted the horse over to where the Duke's skull had landed. They were also aware that the remaining redcoats on the field were disintegrating and that the Jacobite army was fading away into the darkness.

The Prince led his horse off the battlefield and they lost sight of him behind the trees as he headed towards the Memorial Cairn. Cammie let Namah go.

She ran down the path towards the cairn to meet what she hoped would be Sinclair and as she ran she could hear laughing, singing and fast swirling music on the air. Sounds that she had never associated with the moor. She was about a hundred yards down the path from the memorial cairn when she saw the stones begin to glow a brilliant sky blue. The singing and the music became louder. Fiddle music rang in her ears and an angelic voice cut through the night. The glowing cairn became brighter until the intensity of the light hurt her eyes and she had to look way. From the direction of the viewpoint. Cammie hobbled along the path behind. As he reached her, they held each other and tried to look at the cairn, shielding their eyes with their hands.

As the cairn became brighter so the volume of the music increased. Then, from within the light, bright flashes appeared and broke away from the stones. They floated upwards, a few at first, then they increased in number until scores of flashes lit the trees around the memorial and floated skyward in a stream. They soared upwards in a spiral and then sprayed out in all directions, flying away east and west towards the mountains and south down the great glen and north to the coast of the Moray Firth.

Namah and Cammie watched the lights disappear into the night and then realised that the glow from the cairn had begun to diminish and as it did so the number of flashes decreased and the steady stream of lights ascending into the sky receded to a trickle. Then the music and the singing began to fade away.

Cautiously, they moved along the path towards the cairn, still holding each other. The flashes only came every five or ten seconds now and the blue light around the cairn had dimmed to a faint glow. As they neared, one final flash appeared, and then floated upwards, fading with the laughter of a small child. When they reached the cairn the light was gone and they stood in silence.

Then Namah crouched to the ground and picked up the blue bonnet and flintlock pistol that lay at her feet.

Sixteen

<u>Culloden Moor, Scotland 16th April 2146</u>

The master of the ceremony finished speaking and raised his claymore and kissed the blade. As he stepped aside the first of the clan representatives paced forward bearing a wreath of vibrant bluebells and halted in front of the tablet which was inlaid at the base of the memorial cairn.

> The battle of Culloden was fought on this moor
> 16 April 1746
> The graves of the gallant highlanders
> who fought for
> Scotland and Prince Charlie
> are marked by the names of their clans

At the rear of the gathering, Namah looked at Cammie and smiled.

She had read the inscription a hundred times before, as a small girl with a sense of awe at these wild men led by a romantic prince who could only have existed in a storybook world. Then as she had begun to learn the history the words filled her with the pride and passion of youth. Her learning developed though, and as she came to understand the whole story of the Jacobite Rebellion and of the Highlands, these feelings were replaced with an overwhelming sense of sadness. But now, standing here amongst these people who had come to remember the fallen, the words carved into the stone brought new meaning to her. For the first time, they brought peace to her, as if reading the epitaph of an elderly relative who had brought a warm glow to dimly remembered childhood days. She remembered also the words of Coinneach Odhar, The Brahan Seer. *The shadow over Culloden will rise and the sun will shine brighter.* This prophesy had been fulfilled, at least metaphorically, and she wished that one day it would be as literally true for Culloden as it would be for the entire planet.

The Jacobite knelt and laid the wreath. He paused there for a moment and then returned to the group. The next paced forward bearing a wreath of purple heather.

Cammie took her arm and led her along the path, away from the service. The evening breeze was cold on their faces, but it had shed the winter harshness. They stopped by the information board and looked out over the battlefield.

The cold breeze carried the melody of a lone piper's lament from the memorial cairn. As she looked out across the moor, she felt that it had changed, that the atmosphere had changed, as the words inscribed on the memorial cairn had changed their meaning to her. She knew that a burden had been lifted from the land and that the very air felt lighter and easier to breathe.

'Do you feel it?' she said.

'Aye,' Cammie answered. 'They've gone.'

She wiped her eyes on the heels of her thumbs and watched as a dozen or so starlings drifted across the field and over their heads. They settled in the silver birch above them. She looked down at the ground where a carpet of shoots was spearing up through the turf beneath the trees.

She turned to Cammie and put her arms around his neck and he held her tight.

'I hope he's gone with them,' she said.

*

Sinclair felt the heat on his face and could see the brightness glowing through his eyelids. Carefully, he opened his eyes. Above him the dazzling sun was shining down through the opening in the treetops and bathing the clearing in warmth. In the periphery of his sight he could see shapes moving, and he turned his head. He could smell the fresh green stalks of the bluebells as they nodded down at him.

He sat up gingerly, but found that there was no pain. He gazed in wonder for a moment at the lush blue carpet around him and he let the shapes and colours flit around in his head. The beauty and vividness seemed to sharpen his vision and heighten his senses. At last he looked beyond the bluebells and into the trees at the edge of the clearing. There he saw the forest floor, softly lit and dappled with bright gold from the sun. A few yards into the trees, he watched a young roe buck chewing the leaves of an alder.

Feeling refreshed and full of energy, he got to his feet, ready to further explore his surroundings.

He turned around, and at the edge of the clearing a figure stood in the shade.

Seoras stepped forward into the light.

'You're awake,' he said.

Sinclair nodded and stretched.

'Are ye ready?' Seoras asked.

Sinclair smiled and went forward to meet him.

They strode along the forest track and Seoras pointed out the animals and birds as they went. Before long they came to halt at the edge of the clearing. They stood in the shade of an ancient Scots pine that towered above them.

Below them, in the floor of the glen they could see the croft. The rigs were green and lush and the river sparkled. Around the buildings and the fields, people were busy tending the crops, fishing, weaving. Singing drifted up to where they stood and they knew that winter was a long, long way away.

'I am come home', Sinclair said.

Together, they walked out into the sunlight and down into the glen.

Please leave feedback
visit @iainmac.author on facebook
you can also rate/review this book on amazon

THANK YOU *to all those who have supported me during the writing and rewriting of this book. Thanks for all the feedback, criticism and encouragement. Special thanks to my wife, Cherry. Also to family and friends especially those who read the early version of this book and gave feedback including: Ann, Allan, Julie, Jimmy, Steve, Caitlin, Pete, Raymond, Gordon, Terry & Janette.*